R obin Hull was a general practitioner near Stratford-upon-Avon in Warwickshire before becoming a peripatetic academic teaching General Practice to medical students visiting all the continents and teaching on five of them. He has published several medical books and many articles in the medical press. He founded the General Practitioners Writers Association and for some years was its President. In addition he visited many of the islands of the West Coast of Scotland, sometimes teaching on courses, doing locums or just holidaying with a fishing rod, climbing boots and binoculars. He retired from medicine in 1991 to fish, to garden, to watch, and to write, about birds. He is the author of the novel *The Healing Island*, and his nonfiction titles include *Scottish Birds: Culture and Tradition*.

He lives in Perthshire and is married to Gillian, a tourist guide, who also writes articles in *The Scots Magazine*, *The Lady* and other periodicals. He has three daughters and seven g

SILVER SEA

ROBIN HULL

Steve Savage
LONDON AND EDINBURGH

Steve Savage Publishers Ltd
The Old Truman Brewery
91 Brick Lane
LONDON
E1 6QL

www.savagepublishers.com

Published in Great Britain by Steve Savage Publishers Ltd 2007

ISBN 978-1-904246-27-5

Cover illustration and map: Stephen Strong

Typeset by Steve Savage Publishers Ltd
Printed and bound by The Cromwell Press Ltd

For my
Seven Grandchildren

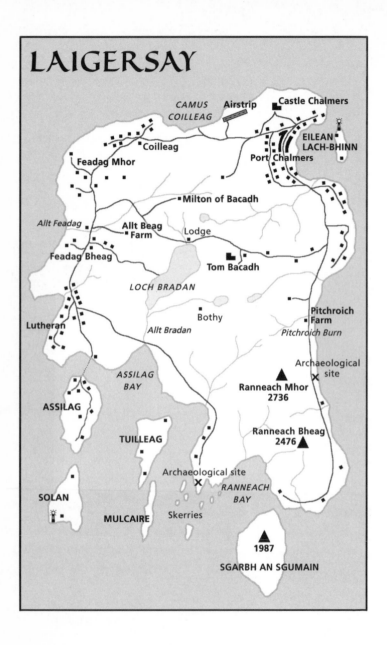

LAIGERSAY

CAMUS COILLEAG · Airstrip · Castle Chalmers

Coilleag

Feadag Mhor

EILEAN LACH-BHINN

Port Chalmers

Milton of Bacadh

Allt Feadag · Allt Beag Farm · Lodge

Feadag Bheag

Tom Bacadh

LOCH BRADAN

Bothy

Pitchroich Farm

Pitchroich Burn

Lutheran · Allt Bradan

Archaeological site

ASSILAG BAY

Ranneach Mhor 2736

ASSILAG

TUILLEAG

Ranneach Bheag 2476

Archaeological site

RANNEACH BAY

SOLAN

MULCAIRE · Skerries

1987

SGARBH AN SGUMAIN

CHAPTER I

A Cure for Stress

When I moved to the remote Scottish island of Laigersay, I expected to find peace and quiet, but the move involved me in high adventure. I became embroiled in a drug cartel, and in the process Fiona, my wife, and I had both nearly drowned. Since then the island had regained its usual peace, though life had not been uneventful. In the spring of my second year there, Fiona gave birth to our twin sons. Two years after our marriage Fiona's father, the Admiral, died and I inherited the lairdship of Laigersay, and with it, the crumbling Castle Chalmers, so fulfilling a prophecy of the aged 'witch' Maggie McPhee.

I was deeply in love with both my beautiful wife and the lovely place where I was struggling to make my way as the island's new doctor. Country doctors tend to live in the privacy of a goldfish bowl. Their lives, their behaviour and habits form the marrow of public scrutiny and gossip. In my own case, not only was I new—medically speaking—but I was married to the laird's daughter and, as rumour quickly had it, was laird-elect myself. All this in a man who, though Scottish by blood, was an incomer from what the islanders always referred to disparagingly as 'the South'!

The problem of being an incomer obtruded itself most often in language. I learnt a great deal from my partner, Hamish Robertson (also known as Old Squarebottle), and my factor, Erchie Thomson, with frequent recourse to Fiona for translation of some of the latter's curious phrases. Thus being 'fordweblit by jallisie', or feeling 'wambled with the molligrups', meant being very weak, or enfeebled, from illness or nauseated with colic. 'Waumish' was to be faint and sick while 'a kirkyard deserter' was one so ill he should be in the grave. 'Peelie-wally' I remembered from my mother meant to be pale and wan, but I did not understand its derivation until I admired a pair of Staffordshire dogs at a croft and heard them called 'wally-dugs', or china dogs.

The penny dropped: 'wally' meant china and 'peelie-wally' translated as looking like pearl or china, very descriptive of the white and drawn appearance of a sick child.

I worked hard at understanding the islanders and began to lose my feeling of being an outsider. But, despite my attention to the practice and my deepening relationship with the island folk, I could not entirely shut out the sense of doom that pervaded the late 1960s and early 70s, with the horrors of Vietnam and nearer to home the festering sore of Northern Ireland. East and West still snarled at each other, and the threat of nuclear attack from foreign powers seemed ever with us. This sense of doom was heightened now that I had family responsibilities. It made me tremble for my dependents. Once I confessed this anxiety to my dour senior partner Hamish Robertson.

'Aye laddie,' he replied, stroking his black beard in a reflective manner, 'ye may well be right an' afore long we'll all be turned into little piles o' radioactive dust. It doesnae bear thinking on, so I dinnae. Ye best dae the same an' get on wi' your job here in Laigersay.'

Perhaps Hamish was right, for there was plenty to do. I threw myself into work in an attempt to forget the outside world. Becoming laird had done little to alter the lives of Fiona and me, other than burdening us with added responsibility. Castle Chalmers was slowly mouldering back into the rock from which it was built. The roof was leaky and some of the timbers in the attic were suspect. We felt a duty to the old place, but the finance of restoration was beyond the capability of a young island general practitioner. My meagre earnings from the practice were boosted by an additional, but insufficient, income from rents and sporting lets from the estate.

Perhaps Fiona's life had changed more than mine. As the mother of six-year-old twin boys she was always busy. Nevertheless she had managed to find time to survey the natural history of the island and to write a little book on the flora and fauna of the island, which was selling quite well. In consequence she was much in demand as a lecturer on the island's natural history and, in summertime especially, was always being consulted by visiting naturalists.

And the practice was doing well. Changes following the Doctor's Charter of the mid-sixties were beginning to improve living standards for rural practitioners and at last we could consider moving the surgery out of what had been the old Port Chalmers primary school. By 1970, when the twins were nearly four, we had secured the promise of a government interest-free loan to adapt the cottage hospital and add a new wing as a modern surgery. At last, it seemed, twentieth-century medicine was coming to Laigersay. Dr Hamish Robertson, whose way of medical practice predated the development of penicillin, had announced his intention of going part-time so as to devote himself to researching and writing about the island's flowers. However, with his usual *laissez faire* attitude, my senior partner had not yet got round to it.

Planning the new surgery, and the frightening finances involved, had taken its toll on me. As the plans progressed, the costs escalated. I found difficulty in sleeping, and in consequence was given a blast from Fiona.

'Listen!' she commanded one Friday evening. 'You are getting difficult to live with, you're working too hard and very short tempered. You need a break.'

'How can I take a break? The builders haven't finished, the bank is being tiresome and of all things we have a great big opening party, which we can't really afford.'

'That's why you need a break. There's nothing you can do but worry. You should go away, even if only for a weekend. I'm sure your problems will resolve without you. It would certainly make life a great deal more pleasant for me!'

'I'm sorry if I've been a bore...'

'No, not a bore, just bloody insufferable!'

'Oh, thanks!'

'Listen, Rob, you know perfectly well I love you dearly but you've been a bear with a sore head lately. I've fixed a weekend's fishing in Assilag with Alex Farquharson—he's the most calming influence I know. Hamish is going to cover the practice, and neither the builders nor the bank manager will know where you are. Just go and do it.'

At times of crisis my adorable wife adopts some of her late father's autocratic, almost Nelsonian, behaviour. Feeling like a junior officer facing an admiral's wrath, I went to pack my bags. Even as I did so, a load lifted from me. Old Alex Farquharson had spent his life on the sea, first as a merchant seaman sailing the world's oceans, then having a rather too exciting war, which he seldom spoke about, and finally, in retirement, fishing the sometimes treacherous waters around Laigersay. Now over eighty, he was as active as ever. Alex was a devout member of the Wee Frees and, as such, intensely pious. I enjoyed fishing with this marvellous old man, to whom Fiona and I owed our lives. (If it had not been for Alex we would both have drowned in the savage tidal rip which made the southern islands off Laigersay so hazardous for small vessels.)

Just as Fiona had said, she had fixed everything. When I drove the aging estate van down to Assilag the following morning, I found Alex expecting me. He was sitting outside his cottage on an upturned wooden bucket, mending creels and smoking his pipe.

He laughed when he saw me. 'I doot ye've had yer marching orders,' he said. 'When that lass o' yours takes an idea into her heid there's no two ways, ye chust hae to dae as she says. But sit ye doon while I hae a smoke, for we'll not be going anywheres till a change o' the tide. It's chust a gran' day that's intil it.'

With that the old fisherman took his pipe from his mouth, spat at the sand by his feet, and remarked conversationally: 'Whit d'ye mak o' all this nonsense at Iceland? They tell me ye were there yersel' the last time the fishing dispute came up.'

'Yes, that's quite right. It was back in 1959. Iceland proclaimed a twelve-mile limit, and wouldn't allow foreign trawlers to fish inside it.'

'Aye, I had friends oot o' Buckie, they were fair affrontit!'

'I bet! Anyway, the British trawlers ignored the limit and the gunboats boarded a Grimsby trawler, but a Royal Navy boarding party swung on board the trawler with grappling irons and reclaimed her—along with the Icelandic seamen trying to take her into port.

'That led to an international crisis. Iceland protested to our ambassador in Reykjavik over the Navy's action in "removing" his coastguards from the Grimsby boat. There was a big demonstration outside the British Embassy.'

'Aye, feelings would run high; they're phleegmatic folk up there until they get cross,' chuckled Alex.

'That's right; well, by the summer of 1959 things had got pretty bad, and three Battle Class destroyers, *Dunkirk*, *Trafalgar* and *Jutland*, were sent up to keep the peace, and also to provide engineering and medical support in case of mechanical breakdown or illness in the trawler fleet.'

'Aye, I wondered aboot that at the time—three muckle great destroyers did seem overreaction to the peedie Icelandic navy.'

'I joined HMS *Trafalgar* on a beautiful calm June evening just under the Forth Bridge. I was in Rosyth the day after I got the order—I travelled up by train. Most of them were ashore when I got on board, but I met up with the doctors from the other two destroyers and learned that between us we had to look after about fifteen hundred men. Each destroyer has about two hundred men and there were about nine hundred in the trawler fleet. The forecast was dire, and we had to be prepared to cope with anything from meningitis to major surgery or severe injury. It sounded as though it was going to be either rather too exciting or intensely boring. However gin cost only a penny a nip, so there were consolations.'

'Aye, that was a great benefit we never had in the merchant service,' remarked Alex. 'I often wondered how the Navy kept sober.'

'Ah, to be honest, there was very little drinking at sea. Anyway, we sailed next day in rapidly deteriorating weather. I'm not too bad a sailor but that trip was hell. *Trafalgar* was in a hurry and we were in a force ten gale gusting to severe gale, eleven. The Admiralty wanted us on station north of Iceland as quickly as possible, and we were butting into the gale in very high seas. I have been at sea in a hurricane, but this was much worse. Destroyers in a hurry are not comfortable in rough weather. I had nothing to do until we arrived, and so I just lay in my bunk and puked.'

Alex chuckled as he contemplated his repair of the lobster pot, and commented, 'Aye, the North Sea can be nasty and ye probably went through the Pentland Firth an' that can be gey choppy.'

'We did and it was. Well, after a while, things were a bit better and I enjoyed meals again. HMS *Trafalgar* was patrolling the northerly fishing area, north of the Arctic Circle. We recognised the Icelanders' increased limit only as far as four miles and continued to fish between four and twelve miles. The Icelanders said this was illegal and tried to arrest the trawlers. As I say, our job was to prevent that, and provide assistance when necessary.'

'And did ye have much medical work to do?'

'In the first week I had two sick fishermen. One had a broken forearm. I had to take him back to *Trafalgar* and reduce the fracture under local anaesthetic. The second man I treated in the trawler.'

'How exactly did ye get over to the trawlers? In a bad sea surely that would be verra deeficult.'

'It was dramatic when seas were high. The destroyer fired a line to the trawler with a Costen gun. The fishermen hauled over a cable, which was attached to a rubber dinghy. With watertight thermal suits on, two of us, myself and an Able Seaman as escort, were lowered over the side in the dinghy and the trawlermen hauled us over. After I had dealt with my patient, we'd be cast loose, and just drifted waiting for the destroyer to pick us up.'

'That sounds alarming!'

'Oh, yes. When the little dinghy was down in a trough, the destroyer was out of sight—even when barely a hundred yards away. I gained a new respect for the captain, who was expert at picking us up even when the sea was really rough. I don't mind telling you I was scared. Have you ever been really frightened for your life, Alex?'

For a moment the old man stopped work on his creel and stared at the distant horizon as though searching his memory. His eyes narrowed.

'Aye, chust the once. Do ye ken I've never told a soul aboot it. I was juist a lad, eighteen or thereabouts, an' we were up in the Yukon. My ship was laid up for a wee whilie an' I got permission to land, for I was unco keen to see the land: it was famous for gold, ye ken. Well, I went walking in the mountains near the coast. Lovely country, but cold, mind. It put me in mind o' Skye.'

'I'd love to see the Yukon. I bet it has some good birds.'

'Aye, an' beasts too: elk and lots o' beavers. The whole country fascinated me.'

'So what was so frightening?' I prompted him.

'I'd got up on a narrow mountain path wi' a great precipice beside me, when I smelt honey. It was only when I turned a corner I realised why. There was a wild bee's nest in a crack in the rock. But that wasn't all. Standing on his hind legs was a huge grizzly bear. He was taking the honey, see. He was only a few feet from me, and when he heard me he stared right at me and growled. I was scared oot ma wits.'

'I should think so! What did you do?'

'There was naething I could do. The bear was so close he could hae killt me wi' a single blow o' his great paw. I've never been so feart. Then suddenly I remembered my dad teaching me that if ever I was in mortal peril and didna ken whit tae dae I should stand stock still and pray to God. So I froze, an' I asked God to help me. I stood absolutely still while bees buzzed about me and stung my face and neck. The bear drew his paw from the bee's nest and licked it clean of honey. Then he turned and, wi' that funny shuffling walk bears have, he ambled away—and left me thanking God for saving me. D'ye ken, it's a funny thing but I can't abide the smell o' honey to this day!'

'Good Lord, you were lucky!'

'Ye're right aboot the guid Lord, but it wasnae luck. God didna want me that day, an' he heard my prayer. Do ye ken, I've never ever been frightened since. If things look really bad, I stay quite still and ask for God's help. If ye are the wise man I take ye for, ye'll always do the same.'

'Thanks, Alex, I'll remember that. I rather hope I shan't ever have to put your advice to the test.'

'Och, ye never know. But go on telling me aboot the adventures ye had off Iceland.'

'Well, most of the time up there it was pretty quiet. Every now and then an Icelandic gunboat came pottering past. Mostly we just ignored each other, but once *Thor*, the Icelandic gunboat, made aggressive moves as though to ram *Trafalgar*. It was very rough and as *Thor* made a sharp turn to avoid us a huge wave washed one of her seaman overboard. A man does not survive long in Arctic waters. There was an immediate order over the tannoy from my captain: 'Medical Officer to the dinghy.' In no time the sailors had me into a lifejacket and over the side. It was easy enough to pick up the lad, who was swimming hard between the two ships. He was very cold but none the worse when I got him aboard *Trafalgar*. He didn't speak English but seemed grateful to be alive. I gave him a large tot and made him comfortable in the sickbay. Next day we returned him to *Thor*.'

'So even though ye were not the best o' friends ye respected the law o' the sea. That's the way it should be.'

'After that, there were no more dramatic transfers for me, just routine sick parade. When it was fine, it really was gloriously beautiful, particularly at night. The sun did not set at all—there was the pinkish light of sunset most of the night, which looks wonderful on Iceland's icy mountains in the distance. I was able to watch birds and whales; I suppose they were minke.'

'Aye,' said Alex, still patiently checking and mending his nets, 'most likely minke up there. I bet ye had a lot o' fush. Trawlermen are often very generous wi' their catch.'

'I should say. We ate fish twice a day, mostly cod. Once a trawler gave us a huge halibut—delicious, and so big it fed the ship's company for two days. My admiration for those who provided fish and chips for their landlubber fellow Britons was profound—living in squalid, wet, freezing discomfort, and working in impossible cold and danger. They all had chapped skin, and a curious thing they called salt-water burns which produced horrid sores on their hands. The nauseating smell from boiling up cod livers for oil pervaded everything.'

'Aye, but ma friends frae Buckie tellt me the oil brought them more money than the cod sold as fush.'

'My last trip in the dinghy was in dense fog to pick up an old trawlerman whom I suspected had lung cancer. Heaven alone knows why he went off in a fishing vessel. I did that trip in dense fog. *Trafalgar's* captain told me jovially afterwards he thought I might get lost—not very amusing. We got back eventually, after sitting in the dinghy for a long time with the destroyer nowhere to be seen. In the end Britain and Iceland began talks, which settled the matter in Iceland's favour. Now it seems to have all started up again. Iceland wants her exclusive fishing zone to come out fifty miles from the coast. They sank two British trawlers last September, and it's anyone's guess how things will go now. Anyway I'm out of the Andrew now, so it won't involve me.'

Alex knocked his pipe out on the side of the bucket he was sitting on. 'Aye, we maun wait an' see, but the tide's coming nicely the noo, time to get fishing.'

CHAPTER 2

Mulcaire and Solan

The old man stood up, stretched, passed some creels to me, shouldered the rest and led the way to the 'Ornithologist'. Pointing to the newly-painted name of his boat, he said, 'I finished cleanin' her up for the new season chust last week. She's a braw sight, eh?'

Before long we were chugging out into Assilag Bay, so calm the cliffs were reflected perfectly in the water.

'Rather different from the ither time I took ye oot into the bay,' Alex mused. 'D'ye mind that day when ye thocht ye'd lost yer bonnie new wife?'

'I am not likely ever to forget it, Alex. When the "Howling Hottentot" sank, we were all lucky to survive.'

'Och, it wasnae chust luck, for the Good Lord didnae mean us to dee that day.'

Alex carried on across the bay. 'I'm takin' ye to try a place for fush the day, that ye've no bin to afore,' he said. 'There's a deep hole ower towards Mulcaire that's often guid at the start o' the season. Not that I want to go too close, mind.'

'Isn't there some sort of mystery about Mulcaire?' I asked. 'I remember that Mulcaire was excluded from the estate I inherited, but there was so much to deal with that I never asked why. Do you have any idea, Alex?'

The old man shook his head. 'Och, nobody likes the place. I remember it way back afore the war. It was inhabited then—there was a family called McTavish, an old couple wi' a couple o' grown sons and a wee half-wit girl, who scratched a living on a croft there. Nobody liked them, they were a godless lot and they used to shoot at people who tried to land. Then both the boys were lost at sea in the war. Nobody went there much afore the war. The place had a reputation for witches an' ghosts an' all sorts o' nonsense and people took a scunner to it. Aye, an' that was afore the crash.'

'The crash?'

'Aye, in the war. I was at sea when it happened but I heard aboot it frae Archie McPhee. It was aboot 1944. Archie was on Home Guard duty at Solan lighthouse that night. A big American aeroplane supposedly on its way to New York crashed there in a storm. A terrible storm it was, they say, wi' thunder and lightning that went raging on for a week. They say it upset the plane's navigational instruments. Nobody could get a boat oot to help. By the time it was fit to do so all sorts of officials, dressed in fancy suits like moon-men, came up frae the south. All the McTavish family were killt and they do say a lot o' the selkies too—I mind they used to be gey common on Mulcaire afore the war—well, a lot o' them were killt as well. The selkies never go there now, nor do any folks unless they're oot o' their minds.'

Alex took his pipe from his mouth and spat in the calm sea to emphasise his point.

'Sounds bad. Did they ever discover exactly what happened?'

'If they did, they never let on.' Alex stared at the distant horizon and I guessed he was remembering the past. 'Aye. I was always puzzled aboot it masel', a big aircraft crashing like that. I did try to find out what happened, when I got home from sea. Apart frae Archie McPhee there was another Home Guard man, a fella called Jock Tomlinson—he's deid long since—I askit him aboot the accident. He was on watch, chust like Archie, but at the lighthouse on Sgarbh an Sgumain. It was a foul night wi' a wild storm; he thought the plane came over Laigersay from the northeast. It was somewhere over Ranneach Bay when there was this flash o' lightning, and a moment later the aircraft seemed to be on fire. At the time he thought it must have been struck by lightning, but afterwards he said he wondered if there had been an explosion in the plane.'

'What would cause that?'

Alex shrugged, 'Dear knows, but it's all so long ago, I doot we'll ever ken the rights o' it. Apparently the plane chust burst into flames, an' cam down in a fireball, an' crashed into Mulcaire, aboot fifty yards frae the McTavish hoose. All the crew were killed, and so were the couple at the farm. Their bodies were supposedly found between the hoose an' the crash, but nobody knows exactly what happened. When I started asking around I got a ticking off frae the polis. The place has been wired off ever since, with War Office or MoD notices every few yards sayin', "Danger, unexploded ammunition. Keep out". But ye ken up here we're a God-fearing lot and it's the association wi' the de'il that makes us tak a scunner at the place rather than Sassenach notices. Och, it's ancient history now, an' best forgotten, I'd say.'

Alex lowered his anchor, indicating that the subject was now closed. 'An' this is as near as I'm goin' the day. But it's chust aboot here I'm told there are good haddies.'

We settled down to serious fishing and soon had a creel full of sizable haddock. The business of hauling and re-baiting kept us busy till lunchtime.

We soon had plenty of fish, so after a sandwich lunch we started the outboard and pottered slowly northwards along the more hospitable east coast of Tuilleag to turn and pass below the cliffs fringing the northern part of Assilag Bay. Alex was streaming a line with a darrow, a concoction of feathered lures, in the hope of picking up a good pollack or, as he called them, lythe. These were his favourite eating but I who lacked his ability to detect their reputed flavour of almonds, found them tasteless. I lay back in the stern of the 'Ornithologist' enjoying the sunshine and scenery. From below, I could see the myriads of breeding birds thronging the ledges of the cliffs. Most were auks of one kind or another: guillemots and razorbills, with some black guillemots and a few early puffins. The cliffs were whitened with their guano, and raucous with their calls.

Suddenly Alex was hauling in his line. 'Aye, this'll be a good lythe,' he said and sure enough a pollack of about half a stone was added to the creel. 'That'll keep me busy tonight, making a pie for tomorrow, so I needna labour on the Sabbath,' he said. 'Talking o' which, ye are most welcome to stay in my cottage the night as Mistress Fiona suggested, but I'll be awa' to the kirk early the morn an' I know ye for a godless chiel who'll no want to gang wi' me. Ye might like a walk doon the shore, and I've asked a pal o' mine to tak ye ower to Solan. But mind and be back on Assilag well afore the back o' four when the rip starts, I doot ye dinna want to get into that kinna stramash again!'

'Indeed no, but that does sound a good idea. I hear Solan is very good for birds.'

'Aye, it's named for the solan geese that breed there. There's a big gannetry on a stack chust by the lighthouse.'

We supped on fresh haddies, which Alex fried along with some tatties from what he called his planticru. Never having heard the word I asked for explanation.

'Well, though I'm a Uist man myself, I spent some time in Orkney. That's where I met my wife, God rest her, and I learnt some o' their ways. They built stone enclosures, like sheep fanks here. Planticrus are to keep sheep oot rather than in, and they grow vegetables, mostly kail and tatties, inside the walls. There's one beside every croft in Orkney, along wi' a peat stack. It's a braw way o' growing tatties, it protects them frae wind an' salt spray an' keeps the rabbits oot forbye. We're fair plagued wi' rabbits in Assilag. Noo, if ye've had yer fill o' haddies I'll mak a brew o' tea. Then I'll get ma chores done and when I hae made the fish pie for the morn I widnae say no to a wee taste frae yon flask ye brought wi' ye.'

So it was that I sat listening to Alex reminisce over a dram or two until precisely 23:59. Then he finished his whisky, and left to make his orisons for the next day.

When I awoke, the croft was silent. Alex had left early to walk to the causeway to reach his kirk at Lutheran. The population of Assilag was too small to support a kirk of its own. At Lutheran the times of divine service fluctuated with the tides, to allow the godly folk to cross the causeway safely. In the kitchen I found bread and butter on the table and two eggs by a pan of water. The big black kettle simmered on a chain over a fire of peat. Beside the fire was a pile of tinder-dry driftwood ready to make an instant blaze to bring the hot kettle to the boil. Alex might lead a simple life, but he knew how to make himself and his guests comfortable.

I enjoyed my breakfast in the sun on a table outside the front of the cottage watching the sea. A passing herring gull landed beside me, looking expectantly for handouts. On the shingle shore, pairs of ringed plover flirted at the water margin, and a heron flew slowly by on a beautifully still Hebridean spring morning.

Once I had washed the few dishes, I set out to walk southwards along the shore. Assilag has a scattering of crofts, mostly owned by fishermen-crofters who kept a few sheep on the machair and boats for the lobsters in the bay. On this Sabbath morn there was little sound of life except for the odd collie that challenged me at some of the cottages. It seemed that everyone but me was at the kirk. However, at the last but-and-ben, I was hailed by a man I did not know.

'Is't yourself?' he asked. I pondered answering 'who else?' which seemed the most appropriate answer, but he forestalled me: 'I'm Josh Macrae,' he said. 'Alex said ye might be wanting to go across to Solan.'

He extended a huge horny hand. 'It's guid tae meet ye, Doctor, I hear much aboot ye. But I hope I never need yer services! The tide's still on the ebb the noo: if I tak ye ower to Solan soon, ye'll have time to walk on tae the lighthouse an tak a piece wi' Jack Fordyce the keeper. I gave him a ring an' said ye might be coming.'

As he spoke Josh was walking with me along the shore. 'Here's ma wee boat.' he pointed to a half-decked rowing boat with a mast up for'ard. 'Ah'm afraid she's no so grand as Alex's "Ornithologist" but it'll get ye across to Solan. Now you maun be sure to be back at the jetty by four or the tide rip'll no let ye away the day at a'.'

Josh settled me at the stern of his boat, pushed off and rapidly rowed the few hundred yards to Solan. Exhorting me again to be back before four o'clock he dropped me on the Solan jetty and returned across the water to Assilag.

Small islands have their own character; Solan was no exception. Basking in the spring sunshine, it seemed utterly peaceful. The air was sweet, faintly perfumed by the countless primroses that shone like stars from the close-cropped fescue grass of the machair. Alex might grumble at the rabbits, but they certainly made effective lawnmowers. There was a small croft near the jetty, and the map showed it to be the only inhabited house on the island apart from the lighthouse itself. Someone was walking down the path from it—an old woman dressed completely in black.

'Good day to you, Laird, I'm Meg Murchison. It's no' often we hae visitors and on the Lord's Day too. Come ben and hae a cup o milk; Nanny's being generous just now.'

Realising it would give offence to decline the goat's milk—something I had never tasted—I followed the old crone. Her cottage was tiny but spotless and I was amazed to learn that she lived here alone. Sipping at the surprisingly good milk, I recalled the fierce independence of blind Maggie McPhee who, until recently, had lived in a black house near Lutheran. We chatted, and Old Meg told me she had been born in the box-bed let into the wall of her kitchen, and had lived here all her life, except when boarding at the hostel in Laigersay while at school in Port Chalmers.

'I wed one o' the lighthoose keepers,' she went on, 'and we had three boys. They were all at sea and we lost them in the war. The Lord made the Germans torpedo them, such was His will, but it was great sadness to Murchison an' me. Then Murchison hissel' was called away an' noo I stay on ma lone. That's why it is so good to see ye. I maunna keep ye, for Mr Fordyce at the light is expecting ye for lunch. Ye'll look in again afore ye leave wi' young Josh? I was baking yesterday—and after walking back frae the light ye'll need yer tea.'

So I left Old Meg, and sauntered through the spring morning with skylarks singing above me. Peesieweeps danced in the air, calling their 'pee-wits' and diving recklessly to impress their mates on the machair below. The path along the east side of Solan was in full sun. At my feet were carpets of primroses, wood anemones and the first spring squills, whose immaculate little blue flowers I had not known till I came to Laigersay. I was especially fond of them—they had been used in medicines for coughs and heart complaints since Culpepper's day. Fiona would have loved these flowers, but perhaps it was as well for us to be apart for a while. I felt her cure was working. Though I did not share the simple, almost fatalistic faith of so many of my friends in the islands, something of their calm acceptance of what life brought to them was rubbing off on me.

I went down to the shore and skittered flat stones across the calm sea. 'There,' I said as the ducks and drakes bounced over the water, 'that's for the bloody bank manager, and *that's* for the builders who never come when they say.' As the stones made their sixth and seventh leaps across the water, a great weight shifted off my shoulders. I tore my clothes off, and rushed naked into the sea. Gulf Stream or no, the sea was cold and I was soon running along the machair in my birthday suit trying to get unfrozen.

Warm again after a few moments, I stopped, threw myself on the fine grasses of the machair—mowed by sheep and rabbits to resemble a manicured lawn—and roared with laughter. Where else in the world, I wondered, could a man cavort mother-naked in spring Sabbath sunshine. Then, reminding myself that as laird I should perhaps behave with more decorum, I dressed and walked on to the lighthouse.

Jack Fordyce saw me coming up the path and was at the door of the lighthouse to meet me. His black labrador came bounding to greet me, grinning widely, also clearly pleased at new company. My senior by perhaps a decade or so, Jack was a big, heavily bearded man, bronzed with the deep permanent tan of an old seaman. He clasped my hand, shaking it violently in his great paw.

'I'm right glad to meet ye, Doctor, or should I say Laird. Och, whichever, its good tae see ye. We dinna get many docs, no, nor lairds neither, oot here. Come an' I'll show ye my kingdom.' He glanced up at the stubby tower above him. 'At least it's no sic a climb as the Bell Rock light. Come awa' up an' I'll show ye'.

Jack led the way up the spiral climb to the lamp, and kept talking, growing slightly breathless as he went higher.

'This was one o' the Stevensons' later lighthouses, built in 1874, just after Dhu Heartach near Mull. It was built by David and Tom Stevenson, with a little help from Robert Louis.'

'Was that the man who wrote *Kidnapped*?'

'Aye, he didna follow the family tradition o' building lighthouses. He preferred using his pen an' ended up better known than the rest o' the family. And they had saved countless lives with their lights.'

I paused, breathless at the spiral climb. 'I always liked the RLS yarns.'

'Aye, they're guid stories. Well, this light here must hae been one o' the easier tasks for the Stevensons. By the time they got round to building it, they had a hundred years o' experience behind them. Solan's only forty feet high and it's perched on the cliff wi' handy rock in a quarry nearby. They didna hae to carry stone oot to sea, like at Bell Rock. It was built in less than a year.'

'Did I not read somewhere that the family were building lighthouses as late as 1940?'

'Aye, right enough; that was Alan Stevenson, great-grandson o' the great Robert who built the Bell Rock back around 1810.'

Jack paused, waiting as I came up a curve or two behind him. 'Even though it's no' very big it takes a lot o' puff to get up, but, man, it's worth it for the view.'

As I joined him beside the great reflectors, I could see what he meant. He opened a door on the leeward side of the balcony and I felt I could see forever. Behind us lay the low mound of Solan Island with Assilag beyond. Further still were the volcanic peaks of Laigersay and way over to the northern and eastern horizon were the white snow-capped mountains of mainland Scotland. Below, I could see the path where I had walked from Old Meg's cottage.

Jack chuckled quietly and said, 'I can spy a lot from up here. Did ye enjoy your skinny dip this morning?'

Laughing, I said: 'I can see nothing misses the eagle eye from this eyrie.'

'Aye, that's true, but it's the western view I love most.' He pointed. 'There is nothing that way until you reach Labrador, where my auld dog hails from. I say there is nothing, but that's no true, there is aye something to watch from up here. Like that sailing yacht away to the northwest. We get no end o' whales; minke mostly but an occasional humpback. And there are dolphins an' selkies in abundance.'

'What about birds?'

'Aye, I was coming to them, for I hear tell you are interested in siclike critturs. There's a pair o' white-tailed sea eagles that breed on the east point, and we get every sort o' seabird. Just look at Stac Dhu, there. There must hae bin a time when it was as black as its name, but it should be Stac Bhan the noo, for it's white wi' breeding gannets, and what's not birds is centuries o' their shite!'

'Does the light bring any of the landbirds here?'

'Aye, and it's the little birds that I love. On migration they're drawn to the light at night and many rest on this balcony, sometimes by the hundred, perching wherever they can.'

'What sort of things do you get?'

'Warblers of all sorts; the rarest here being icterines and an occasional Arctic, then there are lots of the commoner warblers. Strangest, I think, are the tiny goldcrests that we sometimes see in flocks of a score or more at a time.'

Jack led me back to the great light, which in its daylit room seemed quite an insignificant glim. 'This is an occluding light,' he explained. 'The beam is off more than it's on. All lights have a different frequency of flash to make identification easier. Solan flashes for two seconds, twice, each flash two seconds apart, and then is dark for twelve seconds. The sequence repeats endlessly.'

'It seems a surprisingly weak light.'

'In here it does, but the huge prisms focus it to produce a beam visible from the distant horizon. The control is all mechanical; it's much easier since they brought the electric. Afore that, it was oil.'

'With electricity on Solan isle, I'm surprised old Mrs Murchison doesn't have it.'

'I've tried to persuade auld Meg to have the electric but she says what she's used tae's best. So now everything here works automatically, and if anything goes wrong I am alerted immediately. Fortunately that seldom happens. If it does, there are all sorts o' procedures I have to go through to re-establish the beam. The system is so foolproof I dinna think it'll be long before I, and people like me, lose our jobs to full automation.'

'Don't you go mad with boredom all by yourself?' I asked.

'They say you have to be an unusual sort o' person to make a lighthouse keeper. Perhaps so, but I never get bored. There is a lot of routine work maintaining the light and the foghorn, and regular log-keeping. I bring plenty o' books when I come to Solan for my three-week tour o' duty. Nowadays we have the television too, though I rarely watch it. I keep in touch by radio with other lights in the neighbourhood. For example, I play chess with a chum who keeps Muckle Flugga away up north o' Shetland, we radio our moves every day at 5pm.'

'That must make for a long game!'

Jack laughed. 'We usually get through a game in a single tour o' duty.'

'Your dog must be great company.'

'That's Boozer. I call him that because that's the first place the pair o' us go when our tour o' duty's over. We have a strict rule about no alcohol on duty.' He grinned at me apologetically, 'That means a dry lunch, I am afraid, though I do use a little wine in my cooking—speakin' o' which we should descend to my living quarters, where I do have a few things to attend to in the galley.'

Lunch was excellent: delicious scallops, followed by lobster salad and carragheen. 'I love cooking,' said Jack, 'especially seafood. I collect recipes and I'm always experimenting. The Assilag fishermen keep me well supplied. Sometimes when my experiments don't work out too well, Boozer gets the benefit. That's why he's so fat.'

'Did you ever know a labrador who refused anything?'

'He's a wise auld dog, he always knows when it's Tuesday. That's one o' the days Meg gets her messages wi Josh Macrae an' she has a bone sent over wi' her butcher meat just for him. He knows when to go for it.'

As he spoke an alarm clock shrilled 'Ah!' he said, 'Twelve forty-eight, that's to remind me of the shipping forecast. Forgive me while I just listen for a few minutes.'

Jack left me sitting at the table where Boozer, perhaps sensing I was not over fond of seaweed puddings, laid his great head on my knee and turned on the 'nobody ever feeds me look' which all labradors have perfected. He helped me with the carragheen.

When Jack came back I was startled by a loudspeaker crackling above me. 'Hallo Solan Light, this is Sail Yacht "Narwhal" out of Reykjavik. Do you read me?'

'Hallo "Narwhal". Aye, I hear ye loud an' clear, and I've seen ye since early morning,' Jack replied into a microphone.

'Good day, Solan Light,' came the Nordic accent again, 'I am making for Port Chalmers, but there's very little wind. I was planning to go north along the west coast of Laigersay; what do you think?'

'Hallo "Narwhal". Ye'd be better to get round the south o' the island. Ye'll pick up a sou-westerly breeze on the east side; it's due to freshen in the afternoon. That way ye'll be in Port Chalmers by opening time.'

'Thank you Solan—sounds good advice. I'll do that. Over and out.'

By then it was time to leave, for I had my date with Old Meg before meeting Josh Macrae for the trip back to Assilag. As I reached the spot where an hour or two before I had had my swim, I turned and waved back at the light. Up on the balcony I saw Jack's arm go up as he returned my salute.

Meg was waiting for me with a beautifully laid tea table, groaning with scones of many varieties, a fresh honeycomb, home-made jams and, as a *pièce-de-résistance*, a huge Dundee cake. This was island hospitality at its best. When first I had been treated to the carbohydrate excellence of such a meal, I worried that so much trouble had gone into its preparation. But I came to learn that an island housewife's greatest pride was her table, and that she knew no greater pleasure than loading it with goodies for her guests. All I had to do was to eat as much of it as I could, so that forever afterwards she could boast that 'the laird couldna resist' her baking.

Having done justice to the spread, I gently questioned the wisdom of a lady—who I privately calculated must be well over seventy, maybe even eighty—living alone, with only the busy lighthouse keeper two miles along the shore as neighbour. She was clearly astonished.

'Och, Doctor dear, I've aye lived here, and the last twenty years by mysel'. Haven't I my pussycats for company, and that rascal Josh Macrae coming over wi' the post an' my messages twice a week. Then I have to keep an eye on the keepers at the light, an' I aye bide there a wee for a crack and a dish o' tea. Man, I sometimes dinna ken how I fit everything in, I'm that busy. And the Lord is always with me, as He has aye bin and will be, till He wants me for Himself. Mind, I wouldna be fashed if He kept the rheumatism to Hissel', it bothers me times.'

She busied herself in the kitchen for a moment and came out with a parcel. 'There, I've packed up a good piece o' Dundee cake. I ken Alex Farquharson, thrawn soul that he is, likes a bit o' cake. Take that back wi' you for his supper. The man doesna tak nourishment enough since his Martha was called to her Maker.'

So, laden and thoughtful, I went to meet Josh Macrae. Fiona's cure had worked. I had spent time with simple, honest God-fearing folk who had no complaint at the position in which their God had chosen to place them. As a landowner and physician, living in a most idyllic place with a beautiful, adoring (if occasionally critical) wife, what on earth did *I* have to grumble at?

CHAPTER 3

The New Surgery

By late May 1972, after years of fund-raising and planning, the surgery was finished. The party to open it was in the tradition of most island ceilidhs and was held in the new waiting room. Hamish's comment was: 'You and Fiona host it: after all, it's all your folly'. Despite his lack of enthusiasm, the party was a great success. Fiona was at her most beautiful. Now in her late twenties, she had matured into the gracious and lovely lady of Laigersay, enhancing any social occasion. I knew most of what little success I had achieved in the island was due to her. She stood beside me now as we welcomed our guests.

The ceilidh began slowly at 5pm with a few pensioner patients viewing the suites of consulting and examination rooms for Hamish and myself. Each examination room had a built-in couch with a good light source; gone were the days of sending patients needing an examination home to sagging double beds in dimly-lit crofts! My pride and joy was the small minor operating theatre where we could attend to the many lacerations, cysts, warts, wens, burns, blisters and boils that a never-ending stream of sufferers brought to us.

That evening the first to arrive was an old crone, whose multiple pathology caused frequent attendance for support and a pharmacopoeia of pills. Aggie Henderson combined wisdom with simplicity. Once, looking at the many tablets that she swallowed every morning, she regarded me quizzically and asked: 'Will they all know where to go?' Today she took me by the hand and dashed my pride by saying: 'Congratulations, Dr Chalmers, it is all wonderfully modern, but will *you* still be the same?'

That was a salutary lesson; when I passed her comment on to Hamish, he frowned and grunted: 'Remember that, laddie. Dinna swell your heid to grow oot yer boots.'

The party really started at six when Angus Andersen made the official opening with a pretty speech and a little blessing, before apologising that he must slip away briefly to collect another guest.

Jennie Churches, who had served us as receptionist into her late seventies, had chosen this time to retire. She made a little speech about the old school that had been her workplace nearly all her life, first as pupil, then teacher for years, before becoming headmistress. When the school had eventually closed and became Hamish Robertson's surgery, she stayed on as his receptionist, and her knowledge of the island and its people had compensated for many a medical oversight. Now she was being replaced by several part-timers with differing skills—receptionist, dispenser, secretary and a practice nurse. These ladies were present with their husbands. Jennie, with typical grace, wished them all well.

There were many old friends. Of course, Mhairi Chalmers was there. Though she no longer ran the Charmer Inn and now lived in Port Chalmers, she was renowned for her prowess on the grouse moor and the excellence of her home-brewed ale. Fortunately she had passed that skill, and other secret recipes, on to her daughter who had taken over the inn. The whole island speculated on her relationship with the much-loved minister Angus Andersen. Erchie, master of the soubriquet, had named the couple 'The Publican and the Sinner'. Angus is said to have laughed aloud on hearing of their nickname. Greeting Mhairi, I asked where Angus was.

'He'll be along in a wee while. I think he's planning a surprise for you.'

'That sounds intriguing: can't you give me a clue?'

'Och, ye'll just have tae bide on tenterhooks.'

The enigmatic Sikh, Tetrabal Singh, who for years had acted as housekeeper to Hamish, had recently retired from the employment of my gruff senior partner. Rumour had it that at last he had grown tired of Old Squarebottle's sardonic silences punctuated with caustic humour. Of course Tet, the soul of immaculate manners, would never say so, but having suffered the rough side of the old doctor's tongue myself, I could sympathise with the quiet Sikh. Tet had become a bestselling author of cookery books and had recently launched out into establishing a restaurant overlooking Port Chalmers Bay with a superb view of Island Lach-bhinn. His cuisine was attracting epicures to visit Laigersay, wishing to experience the gastronomic treat of 'dining at Tet's'. He had marked the occasion of the opening ceilidh at the new surgery by making a great basin of his renowned smoked trout pâté, one of his most mouthwatering specialities. In his usual self-effacing way, Tet greeted us by making *namaste* and then quietly withdrew to the sidelines.

It was good to see Tom and Helen Chalmers from Pitcroich farm. They came with Thomasina, my very first Laigersay patient. On a stormbound night when no aircraft could fly her to the mainland, I had removed her appendix in the same building whose extension we were celebrating. Since then, the Chalmers family had been among my closest friends. Thomasina, the awkward schoolgirl, had blossomed into a gifted beauty whose ambition was to read veterinary medicine. To my delight, her father marked the occasion of the opening of our new surgery by bringing a present of a splendid five-pound sea trout.

'I took him from the tidal pool by the farm,' said Tom, 'the one where you nearly drowned. Perhaps this was the very fish you lost that time.'

'Och no! it wasnae,' growled another voice behind me. 'The laird's fush was a muckle brute, that's just a minnow.'

I turned to find the vast bulk of Erchie Thomson, poacher, illicit whisky distiller, champion caber-tosser, leading piper of the island and now my factor, grinning at me. 'But,' he went on, 'it puts me in mind o' a time when a few ribs cracked,' and with that he slapped me on the back, nearly cracking them all over again.

Hamish led the blind Jack Gillespie over to me. I had not seen him for a year or more but remembered him as one of the heroes at the coming of Fuileach Mick, when, along with Erchie, my Fiona and others, he took part in the emergency blood-donors' session that saved the life of Maureen, long-suffering wife of the Irishman Patrick O'Flynn after a major post-partum haemorrhage.

'Where's Galla?' I asked. The blind man beamed with pleasure at the mention of his guide dog.

'I wasn't sure if I should bring her in here,' he said, 'and I have to say I don't think she was too keen either. I believe she thinks it smells like the vets.'

'Now don't you go calling my surgery smelly,' another voice cut in and Douglas White, the island veterinary surgeon, shook me by the hand, adding: 'I think Galla should be welcome anywhere. She is the most intelligent bitch I have ever met. She even rivals Cuhlan for wisdom.'

I laughed at the reference to the old laird's Irish wolfhound, who now lived with us at the castle, and Jack Gillespie beamed at praise of his beloved Galla. Douglas was another friend with whom I had tramped Laigersay's many hills and fished its burns and lochs. We shared a love of the natural history of the island—and of its many dogs. We also exchanged notes on some of the diseases our patients shared. As a man of about my own age the vet provided professional company when Old Squarebottle's heavily conservative hand felt too oppressive.

Wullie Stewart was the coastguard who had come to the rescue of Alex Farquharson, Fiona and me when Alex's boat the 'Howling Hottentot' foundered in Assilag Bay. Wullie had since been promoted and was the senior coastguard responsible for all the inshore waters of Laigersay and much of the surrounding Atlantic as well. I was glad Wullie was there, for he often called me out when he needed medical assistance in maritime or coastal emergency. Indeed Wullie had helped to obtain grants for the extension of the surgery and, as a result, we now had a helipad beside the new extension. On several occasions I had been collected from the surgery to be landed on another island or winched on to the deck of a ship with a sick or injured man aboard. The helipad was one of the most conspicuous signs of medical progress in Laigersay.

Then my recent host, the shy quiet fisherman, Alex Farquharson, handed me one of the largest lobsters I have ever seen. He explained in his soft Hebridean accent, 'I found him in one o' my creels last week an' I chust thought you and your lady might enchoy him.'

Then, when nearly all the guests were assembled, there was a commotion outside and a strange, bearded skeleton of a young man burst in with a placard announcing:

Is there no balm in Gilead; is there no physician there?
(Jeremiah 8:22)

Hamish growled, 'Och, why d'ye let that fella in here? The man's a fair disgrace.'

'No, Hamish, Nutty Jakes is quite harmless so long as he takes his medication,' and, turning to the tall text-bearer I added, 'Welcome to the new surgery, Jakes, I expect we'll see you here quite often.'

'Reckon so, Doctor Laird, I need my balm in the Gilead o' this benighted isle o' sinners. But ye must repent, or Doctor, the de'il hissel' will get ye.' Then Jakes changed perceptibly and added conversationally, in a polished Oxford accent, 'Actually I just dropped in for a second to wish you luck with your new enterprise. I'm away to a bible study group at Feadag Mhor. They're a terrible heathen lot of fornicating blasphemers up there and I must save them from their hochmagandie.' With that, the strange, schizophrenic, religious maniac abruptly shook my hand and hurried from the building.

'Poor soul,' muttered Alex Farquharson.

'Do you know, Alex,' added Angus the minister, who had arrived with an unfamiliar, tall, fair-haired man just after Jakes' noisy entrance into the hall, 'I sometimes envy him. He has a faith that's stronger than mine, even if he's as mad as a hatter much of the time.'

Hamish growled again 'He should be certified and shut away. As I say, he's a disgrace.'

'Laigersay, like Prospero's island, "is full of strange noises",' I quoted. 'Nutty does no harm and so long as he takes his medication, society tolerates him ... speaking of odd characters, do you see who has just come in?'

Hamish turned, and said with some humour, 'Now she is a different matter. She's not mad, just wildly eccentric and probably a witch. I'm all for a bit o' eccentricity.'

I winked at him, saying, 'I've noticed that once or twice,' and my senior partner had the grace to laugh.

But he added: 'Though, ye know, there may be a lesion in one of the temporal lobes o' the auld carline's brain.'

We turned to observe the old couple, who had just entered the waiting room. Maggie McPhee was led by her brother Archie for, like Jack Gillespie, she was quite blind, but unlike him she was very deaf as well. Maggie McPhee is the strangest woman I have met. Until recently she had lived alone at the southern end of the island near Lutheran in a black house, where her parents and grandparents (and dear knows how many previous generations of McPhees) had lived before her. The house was a throwback to an earlier Scotland when most people had shared such shacks with their cattle. There were no windows, and smoke from a central peat fire drifted out through an upturned and bottomless bucket in the roof. Everything within, including its human and animal inhabitants, ended up black. Maggie had always lived like that and, as was so typical of many islanders, refused to change her ways. She never changed her habits, never changed where she bought her 'messages', and lived by a precise daily routine even to the exact time that she let her cow out of the house she and the animal shared. Her brother watched for the cow; if it did not amble past his house at a quarter to eleven every morning he knew his sister required his help.

Maggie must have been quite a personality in her early life, for she was well read and widely travelled. Had she been born into a different century, she would certainly have gone to university and could have succeeded in a number of professions. She had lost her sight in middle life, but this had not deterred her from living in splendid independence with minimal help from her brother, who had lived nearby. Maggie had finally decided a few months previously that it was time to accept what her friends and doctors had been advising for years; she moved with her brother into sheltered accommodation in Port Chalmers. Now, watching her being led towards me, I found myself thinking of old Meg on Solan and hoping she would do the same.

Maggie was blessed, or possibly cursed, with the gift of second sight. When I had first met her she reminded me of the witches in *Macbeth* when she predicted that I would become laird of Laigersay. At the time that seemed quite impossible, but within a few years it had come about. Now that she had accepted the comfort of a bed-sitter in the home in Port Chalmers, complete with all modern conveniences, including television, she seemed to have lost much of her eccentricity, but she was still given to making Delphic pronouncements about the future of the island.

Archie, her ancient brother, who looked older but was, at a mere eighty-five, much her junior, led Maggie to me. Maggie must, by now, have been well into her nineties, but for all her years she was erect and walked with a grace that a woman half her age could have been proud of. As she crossed the room she paused by the tall blonde man who had come in with Angus.

'A stranger?' she asked, 'but I doot ye'll no be that for long.' Then, turning to me, she said: 'Good evening, Doctor and Laird, I like the looks o' your new palace. You will have years o' work in this place for the good o' the people o' the island. Your work will be hard but in time you will bring prosperity and worldwide fame to the little isle o' Laigersay.'

'Och, dinna fash yersel, Dr Rob, she's just haverin' again.'

'Wheesht! And I'd be most grateful, young Archibald, if you'd haud yer tongue an' no speak aboot things ye dinna ken,' snapped his sister before adding, to me, 'I'm glad you're kind to poor Nutty Jakes, he's only mad when the wind's nor-east; he knows his hawks and handsaws all right. But now that I've said my piece to welcome ye to the new surgery, I'll take young Archie home. There's his favourite programme on the telly tonight, and I suppose I maun watch it wi' him.'

So the pair of them departed, leaving me to wonder, as I always did, at the way she, who could not see, used words like 'look' and 'watch'. She professed to hate the television installed in their joint sitting room, but the staff at the home told me she 'watched' it most of the day. Maggie assured me it was 'just for Archie's sake'!

In fact the television had become a *cause célèbre* in the home in Port Chalmers. Maggie turned the volume control to maximum, much to the annoyance of other residents who were blasted by the noise. I was summoned urgently to prevent a pensioner's riot at the decibels of Maggie's telly. I managed to solve the problem by equipping the old lady with earphones which, when plugged into her set, let her hear without deafening the other inhabitants.

After the two McPhees departed, the party speeded up. First Angus apologised for his late arrival and introduced the young man with him. 'This is Thorfinn Theodorsson, a young Icelander here in Laigersay with a yacht in Port Chalmers harbour. I met him by chance this afternoon and took the liberty of bringing him to your party for the surgery... I hope you don't mind.'

I turned to the young man and welcomed him. He really was extraordinarily good-looking, tall, tanned and with straw-coloured hair, the sort of good looks that one sees in Hollywood idols. I fancied that a number of island lassies might be very impressed.

The newcomer bowed and said in faultless English: 'It is good of you to accept a complete outsider to your celebration, but when Mr Andersen told me about it I particularly asked if I might attend. I do hope you forgive what I believe you call a "gate crasher"?'

'Of course. We are never very formal at a Laigersay ceilidh, but you may have to sing for your supper.'

'Mr Andersen has already explained that; I shall have to see what I can do.'

'Angus,' I asked, 'will you see that your friend is at home and gets to know everyone?'

Whisky and Mhairi's ale circulated, accompanied by Tet's delicious smoked trout pâté and other canapés. Chatting to my guests I noticed the young Icelander. He was not only attracting glances from around the room but was conversing easily and eagerly with everyone Angus introduced him to. Though he spoke perfect English he had that slightly sing-song intonation one often hears with cultured Scandinavians.

But it was not long before Angus took out his fiddle and started playing the music of Niel Gow. That set feet tapping; even the toes of Alex Farquharson, who held that dancing was 'the work o' the de'il', were seen to twitch. Soon partners were taken for the first eightsome reel of the evening. I took Fiona on to the floor, Hamish danced with Mhairi and Erchie lifted Jeannie Brown, the new receptionist, off her feet on to the floor. The eight was completed by Jack Gillespie and Jennie Churches. At first I wondered how a blind man would cope but, with little help from Jennie, Jack proved himself an excellent dancer. The weakest member of the team was Jeannie. Erchie occasionally compensated for her confusion by lifting her in his huge arms and carrying her through her steps.

With the reel done, we stopped for breath and an embarrassed Jeannie was carried back to her husband Gordon by Erchie who was already, as he commented himself, 'as fou' as a puggie'. However he was not so drunk that he could not take over from Angus and was soon piping an energetic Strathspey. Angus relieved Hamish of his Mhairi and I was again dancing with Fiona. Thorfinn the beautiful delighted Jennie Churches by partnering her and I heard him tell her: 'I need the tuition of an experienced woman to learn your Scottish ways,' and was delighted to hear Jennie's peal of laughter. There was much life in that old lady yet!

So the musicians alternated fiddle and pipes for Strip the Willow, Gay Gordons and more sedate waltzes to restore breath. Then there followed individual contributions, which Angus led by singing 'The Braes o' Killiecrankie'. First he gave an explanation for the benefit of people, such as Thorfinn, who might have difficulty with the Lallans of Burns' verse.

'The singer of this song,' began Angus, 'was probably a southern Scot in the pay of the English army under General Hugh McKay. This army was marching northwards through the Pass of Killiecrankie in Perthshire. The Highlanders were led by Viscount John Graham of Claverhouse, better known as Bonnie Dundee. He was killed when he received a "clankie" in the battle. But the day was a great victory for the Covenanters over the redcoats. Pitcur, who fell in a furrow or grave, was James Hallyburton of Pitcur. He was a man of great stature, and is described as being "like a moving castle in the shape of a man". The singer himself was lucky to escape being food for a gled, as scavenging buzzards were called, from nearby Blair Athol. Perhaps it was he who made the famous soldier's leap across the Garry and established a visiting place for generations of tourists. Anyway here's the song, which, apart from one or two contrived rhymes, is one of Rabbie's best.'

Then in his fine tenor voice Angus sang:

> Whare hae ye been sae braw, lad?
> Whare hae ye been sae brankie, O
> Whare hae ye been sae braw, lad
> Cam ye by Killiecrankie, O?
>
> I faught at land, I faught at sea,
> At hame I faught my auntie, O;
> But met the Devil an' Dundee,
> On the braes o' Killiecrankie, O
>
> The bauld Pitcur fell in a furr,
> An' Clavers gat a clankie, O;
> Or I had fed an Athole gled,
> On the braes o' Killiecrankie, O

As this was one of Angus's party pieces, we all knew the chorus and joined in after each of the verses:

> An ye had been whare I hae been,
> Ye wad na been sae cantie, O;
> An ye had seen what I hae seen,
> On the Braes o' Killiecrankie, O.

When applause for the minister had died down, Fiona sang one of my favourite Scottish love songs, the Eriskay Love Lilt. I am sure one reason we had gained popularity in the island was our transparent love for each other and, as she sang, she kept her eyes on me. The words of the song, 'When I'm lonely dear white heart, Dark the night or rough the sea, 'Tis then my heart finds, The old pathway to thee', brought a spontaneous burst of applause.

Then I, remembering Maggie's reference to the island fortress, recited John of Gaunt's speech from *Richard II*. These marvellous lines, though they referred to England, summed up all I felt about my island of Laigersay. Especially dear to me was: 'This happy breed of men, this little world, this precious stone set in the silver sea.'

So the evening wore on with songs, recitations and stories until all had contributed their party pieces except the Icelandic visitor. Suddenly he got to his feet, and his height and good looks commanded immediate attention.

'I see,' he began, 'that everyone has to contribute to the entertainment, so I have a story for you. As some of you have already discovered, I come of Danish forbears but my family have lived in Reykjavik in Iceland for several generations. That makes two reasons why it is strange for me to be here tonight. In the past my forbears as Vikings came to your country, especially these islands of the west, bent on rape and pillage. And today there is disagreement between your government and mine over the vexed question of fishing. But I want to tell you an Icelandic saga, which is even stranger than the presence of a potentially dangerous alien in your midst. The sequel to this saga I only learned myself this afternoon. Now for the saga.

'A long time ago there was a ship called after the Norse god Thor. Like many Icelandic ships she was built for fighting. One day in an Arctic storm she met up with what she considered to be a pirate ship in her national waters. Despite the ferocity of the storm and the fact that the other ship was so very much larger she immediately challenged the pirate. Guns were aimed but, perhaps fortunately, the sea was tossing the two ships so violently that gunners on both sides were unable to score hits. The opposing captains broke off the engagement for the sake of saving their ships. As *Thor* turned for home a great wave broke over her and a young boy seaman was swept into the icy Arctic Ocean. There appeared to be no hope of saving him. Then an odd thing happened. The larger ship manoeuvred beside him and lowered a man in a little boat like an old-fashioned coracle. This frail vessel floated over the tumult of the sea and the man was able to grab the body of the boy. Then the little boat was hauled back to the pirate ship and the boy's life was saved.'

The speaker paused and looked round the room. 'Perhaps you find my saga interesting but not remarkable,' he added 'but I guess that at least one memory in this room is stirring. For my tale is not finished. You see the episode I have described was not that long ago. In fact only fourteen years ago. *Thor* is still serving in the Icelandic navy. The pirate ship was a British destroyer called HMS *Trafalgar*. I was the drowning boy and the man who saved my life was your laird, then Surgeon Lieutenant Robert Chalmers.'

There was silence for a moment, followed by a cheer. The surprise predicted by Mhairi had completely astonished me. Thorfinn walked across the room and embraced me.

'It is due to Angus Andersen that I have found you again and have the opportunity for thanking you for what you did.' He hugged me again and turning back to his audience explained that after the rescue he had been returned to *Thor* and had never seen me again until this very day.

As a buzz of chatter spread round the room, it was Erchie's turn. The big man seemed unsteady on his feet and his voice was a trifle slurred. He handed his pipes to Angus, also an accomplished piper, and abruptly left the room.

'Is he all right?' I asked the minister.

Angus laughed. 'Aye, he'll be fine. He minds me of my fiddling hero Niel Gow, also a great whisky drinker. In the eighteenth century he was in demand in the ballrooms of the great houses. He would walk the dozen miles from Dunkeld to Perth, play all night, and walk back in the wee small hours. To the remark that it was a long way, he replied that it wasnae the length o' the road so much as its breadth that worried him.'

Then Erchie came back, bearing two claymores. He laid the two huge swords on the floor in a cross and nodded to

Angus. We watched the big man dance a furiously intricate but faultless sword dance. Faster skirled the pipes and faster and faster twinkled Archie's feet, while his kilt spun almost horizontally to the shocked amusement of some of the ladies present, and making Alex Farquharson tut. As Angus blew the final chord of the dance Erchie swept up the two great swords, brandished them before me and lay them at my feet in the time-honoured gesture of a Highlander to his chief. With a deep bow, he passed out in front of me. We put him to bed in my examination room—the first patient to use it.

CHAPTER 4

A Cure for Hangovers

I have to confess I woke on the morning after the party with a headache. However, hangover or no, I had to conduct my first consulting session in the new premises. At the surgery I found Jeannie Brown brewing strong black coffee.

'Wasn't he awful last night?' she giggled. 'Och, I was fair affrontit when he picked me up and carried me in the eightsome reel!'

She gave me the distinct impression that she would not mind it if Erchie Thomson manhandled her again. He seemed to have that effect on all the lassies, but I suspected Erchie might soon be eclipsed by Thorfinn the beautiful.

'He's still dead to the world on the couch in your examining room. Away in an' gie him a jag in the bum wi' a needle. That'll wake him up, an' then I'll resuscitate him wi' strong coffee. Mind, ye look as though you could use some yersel'.'

But as Jeannie spoke, the door of the examination room opened and Erchie, shielding his eyes from the light of day, emerged with a groan.

'I hope the laird'll no open a new surgery often, it's gey debilitatin',' he grumbled as he sipped the coffee Jeannie thrust into his hand.

We bundled Erchie out of the back door, away from the gaze of curious early patients, and I settled behind my new desk. Jeannie had a list of appointments and I saw a number of well-known names. Some filled me with gloom, for it seemed as though the first surgery in the new building was to be celebrated by all the chronic attendees whose names on the appointment list always made my heart sink. With an effort I got to my feet, walked to the waiting room, now tidied up from the night before, and called Hector Morrison. Hector was a fussy, retired incomer who consulted almost weekly and whose multiplicity of symptoms had never been explained by anything other than an obsessionally hypochondriacal personality.

'Good morning, Doctor,' he said, laying a suspicious-looking parcel on my desk. 'I have brought a specimen which I would be glad if you would test. I wanted to be the first to see you here, to thank you most sincerely for looking after a silly old man so kindly. The specimen, incidentally, is of the water of life from the island of Islay. I hope you will drink to my health with it. Now I will take no more of your precious time, for you have a crowded waiting room. All the best in your new palace.'

With this speech, delivered while my mouth was open in astonishment, Hector bowed, and left my consulting room before I had time to recover my wits and thank him. He was out of the building before I could say my 'thank you'.

I turned to the waiting patients, and called Betsy Smith, another incomer, this time from Glasgow. Betsy was a chain-smoking, immensely obese soul who seemed to live entirely on sweeties, beer and chips. Four years of attempting to modify her habits had exhausted my patience. She too bore a package.

'I'm no ill, ye ken, Doc,' she wheezed, 'but I wantit to be one o' the first to welcome ye in yer new place. I made ye a bag o' my favourite taiblet, for I ken fine that yer wee wifie has a sweet tooth.' Betsy laid her package on my desk, adding, 'I jalouse the whole island's grateful tae ye. You make a change from someone else I could name.' And with that she too was gone, leaving behind her a palpable criticism of Hamish.

So surgery progressed; everyone brought a gift and for once nobody was ill, demanding, tiresome or dependent. It was a spontaneous expression of gratitude such as I had never experienced. However, these lovely people with their simple expressions of thanks were the same people I had sometimes denigrated as wasting my time with their incessant trivial demands. Instead of being uplifted I was curiously sad. I felt rather a heel.

When I went into the common room, where we held our practice meetings, even Jeannie Brown was moved. On her first day at work she had been presented with more boxes of chocolates than she had ever seen.

Surgery over, I started to drive round the island. In those days, half or more of a general practitioner's work was carried out in the patient's home. The very old and the very young were frequently seen at home, the former often on a monthly basis. Though we did not tell them this, one reason was that when it came to filling out a death certificate the signing doctor had to have seen the patient alive fairly recently. If the doctor could not state that he had attended the dead person a week or two before death the Procurator Fiscal had to be notified. Such a referral to authority increased the anxiety and grief that followed a sudden death. It was much better to visit regularly anyone who might be nearing the end.

That day there was a list of a dozen or so visits. This was the part of each day that I loved most. In the first place I was driving round my beautiful island at a time when, except if I was very busy, there was a chance to watch the progression of the seasons, marked by migratory birds and new wildflowers each month. In winter, masses of geese, mostly pink-foot and greylag, grazed on the haughs by the larger burns. Along the shore there would be purple sandpiper and huge flocks of knot and dunlin. Then as spring was heralded in mid-February the oystercatchers would leave the shore to pair in the meadows, among the newly growing grasses, in celebration of St Valentine's Day. This day, traditionally the day of pairing of birds, has come to have special significance for human lovers. The fieldfares, that had visited us briefly the previous autumn to strip the berries from the rowans on their way south from Iceland, came in March for a longer visit on their way north again. A few weeks later the first willow warblers sang their soft cadences. Next, other warblers heralded the swallows, the wagtails and the flycatchers of summer. Then, when it was their turn to leave, the first of the geese returned.

But the pleasure of visiting was not just ornithological. There was the warmth and friendliness of the people who revelled in the ancient hospitality of the Highlands and Islands. 'Come in Doctor, cup of tea Doctor?' was the usual greeting. There might be a dram, or a large slice of a cake baked specially. Everything turned on what was beginning to be written about in journals under the pompous title of 'the doctor–patient relationship'. This was a very special affinity between the physician and his people. It turned on trust on both sides. For the patient, it rested on an awareness that if need be the doctor would be there at any hour of day or night. But there were changes in the air: many doctors argued, perhaps with good reason, that they were trained as physicians, not as taxi drivers, and that time spent travelling could be spent more usefully seeing patients in the surgery.

However, I was loath to reduce my visiting. A much older bond between people, especially in the Highlands, was that of hospitality. No matter how poor a household, there was always shelter and a share of such provisions as were available for travellers and visitors. On my rounds I was both traveller and visitor. When someone sought my advice in the surgery he or she was the visitor and I the host. In their homes this relationship was reversed, and as guest in the house of my patients I came to know them more closely. Hamish said his phenomenal diagnostic ability depended upon his intimate knowledge of the island and its people. When I complimented him on making a brilliant diagnosis, his reply was: 'Och, it just comes o' knowing the patient better than he knows himself—as well, of course, as knowing one's medicine.'

I learned from the difficult, sometimes off-putting man who was my senior partner to ask myself, when confronted with a difficult diagnostic problem, 'What do *these* symptoms mean in *this* person at *this* time?' This paid off with some unusual diagnoses, like that of Luigi, a Sicilian who had married an island girl.

Luigi had never fully mastered English despite having been a prisoner of war in Orkney, where he had helped to build the famous Italian chapel on Lamb Holm. But he was a cheerful man and a great singer, who always had a wave for the '*dottore*'. Luigi was a near neighbour of ours, in charge of cattle at the mains farm near Castle Chalmers. Luigi's wife became worried in case he lost his job, for there had been problems with calving and the farmer was reducing his splendid Ayrshire dairy herd. I had to wait less for the herd to cross the road in front of my impatient bonnet when driving past the farm. Some of the best pasture was being put under plough, there seemed to be something less cheery about Luigi's wave and he sang less often. Odd, and I did remember that my father, a teacher and a great naturalist in his way, had taught me that if things looked odd they needed investigation, for that was often when something really interesting cropped up. But I was too busy to spend time worrying about a cowman's employment prospects.

One hot August day Luigi asked for a call. I found him lying in the same bed in which I had delivered his sons. He was drenched in sweat and greeted me with, 'I gotta da flu.' Instantly the picture jumped into focus. There was no influenza at that time of year. The calves, the dwindling herd, the ploughed pasture—all now made sense.

I said, 'No, Luigi, you've not got flu: you've got acute brucellosis.'

Blood sent urgently to the mainland for serology confirmed my diagnosis. It took time, but eventually the bacterium *Brucella abortus* was eradicated from Luigi's blood.

Such exotic diagnostic rarities were not uncommon in so rural a practice, for even then many of my patients had worked overseas. On another occasion a particularly obnoxious English incomer called Parker had come to the surgery and presented a card—with the aim of acquainting me with Her Majesty's bestowal of a CBE (for work in the Colonial Service in Africa). He seemed to expect that the CBE on his card would win him special privilege at the surgery. It didn't. He was clearly put out at having waited for half an hour. What's more he made it plain he had expected to see a more senior doctor. Dutifully I enquired about the CBE. 'Oh, water engineering in East Africa,' he replied with an assumed casualness, before requesting referral to a specialist. I drily enquired if he had medicine or surgery in mind, and his pomposity eased a little. 'I just don't feel well and I seem to run a fever at night, at least I have profuse sweats.' There was little else: despite several years service in Uganda, he had never been ill there and had been scrupulous in taking antimalarials. Indignantly he denied overuse of alcohol and said he had never had any external blood loss. Examination was normal, apart from a large and tender liver. Fortunately I had seen just such a case before when I was in the Royal Navy.

'Yes,' I said, 'I will refer you. I have a colleague who is particularly good on amoebic hepatitis.'

It was a gamble, of course, but a blood count revealed the typical white-cell picture of a parasitic problem and the diagnosis was confirmed by biopsy. My hospital colleague congratulated Parker on his choice of GP. The pompous little man's attitude towards island medicine changed as a result, and after that he used to bring me a bottle of whisky at Christmas.

There was no doubt I had gained more wisdom in my few years in Laigersay than I had acquired in medical school. I sometimes found myself feeling for some of my more dependent patients the same sort of emotion that I had for my sons. I especially enjoyed the sayings and mistakes the twins made. Recently they had had their first day at school. Hamie complained that it was all right but hard work; Jamie quite liked it but remarked that he didn't think he would bother to go again!

Paternalism is a dirty word for doctors, yet it describes how many view their patients. Doctors and fathers alike boast about triumphs and success. When kids do well or patients recover, even when the achievement is unlikely to be down to parental or medical influence, who does not bathe in reflected glory? More than anything, doctors and dads like to recount the funny things said to them.

My mind went back to when, as a student in Paddington, my first patient was a delightful Londoner whose philosophy had been toughened by enduring the blitz. Now she was sick, her heart valves narrowed by old rheumatic fever. She had had seven children and on my enquiring about her husband she interrupted to say he was not her husband, as the one thing her old doctor had told her as a child was that she should never marry... 'not wiv *my* 'eart'. This was an early lesson to me that one should always say what one meant!

The Paddington accident and emergency department, then always known as 'casualty', produced many strange encounters among the postwar rubble of human disease and disaster. A colleague whose father had died when he was a child was treating a New Zealand visitor in his late fifties for a lacerated hand. The visitor eyeing the doctor's name-tag commented on his unusual surname. As he stitched, the doctor told the patient about his long-dead father. A week later, returning to have his sutures removed, the New Zealander surprised the doctor by asking his date of birth. The doctor gave the date and his patient astounded him by saying, 'Doctor, I think you may be my son.' So it turned out. (The doctor's mother had found death easier than desertion to explain to her son, and had reverted to her maiden name.)

Casualty kept one busy with minor—and sometimes major—crime. As Casualty Officers, we were often in court, even at the Old Bailey. Once I was made to feel ten feet tall by a barrister saying to me in court, 'How nice to see you here again, Doctor.' But not all counsel were so gracious. Another barrister tried to discredit a colleague of mine by asking his qualifications, which, as for most London graduates, were MB BS. The barrister asked for explanation and on being told the letters stood for Bachelor of Medicine and of Surgery said disparagingly: 'Oh! So you're not a doctor at all'. The doctor thought briefly, and replied, 'That is technically correct, but my profession refer to me as "doctor" much as yours refer to you as their "learned friend".'

Game, set and match to medicine!

So it was, on this fine May day, that I drove round the practice, which increasingly I thought of as 'my island' and gloried in the burgeoning of spring. Visiting was routine and swiftly accomplished, so I planned to be returning by one o'clock for lunch at home. My last call was at the home of the Simpson sisters in Lutheran. I smiled to myself as I remembered my first visit to their house. I had been met at the door by a terrible mongrel that I had taken as belonging to the patients. It caused a commotion in the house and the two fussy elderly sisters, thinking the dog was mine, did not demur as it routed their cats and cocked its leg against the furniture. Hettie and Hermione Simpson were what Hamish called the valetudinarian sisters of Lutheran, and they cherished their imaginary illnesses. I had taken to doing a routine visit on them because that saved unnecessary requests for visits. Besides I liked Hettie's Dundee cake.

As usual there was nothing much the matter, but I took a cup of tea and a slice of cake while listening to their woes. The phone rang—Jeannie from the surgery.

'We've just had an urgent call in from Ali Frazer of Allt Beag Farm. Dr Robertson says as you're out that way will you see to them?'

'Sure, but I'm not sure where Allt Beag is.'

'Wait an' I'll ask Dr Robertson...'

There was a pause and then I heard Hamish's familiar growl: 'It's Cold Comfort Farm, laddie, leastways, that's what I always call it. Real name is Allt Beag Farm. It's a dour place. Auld Norrie, the tenant farmer, is all right but I canna abide the son Alastair. The farm's way up on the moors above Feadag Beag. The road crosses the Allt Beag burn at the northern end o' Feadag Beag an' then you go up a track beside the burn for nearly a mile. It always seems dreich up there, that's why I call it Cold Comfort. Good luck tae ye, laddie.' With that, the line went dead.

I excused myself from the Simpson sisters, who tutted when I said I'd had an urgent call to the Frazers. It seemed from their expression that they, like Hamish, did not care for the people at Allt Beag Farm. Hermione, stroking her cat, observed to it, 'He doesna like pussies, but dinna fret. I'll no let him near you!'

It was not too difficult to find the farm track and I was soon bouncing over its rough, potholed surface. I suspected the farm must be pretty run-down from the state of the road. Eventually I arrived at a group of buildings arranged round a square yard. A gate into the yard was marked 'PRIVATE—Trespassers will be prosecuted'. For a moment I smiled, remembering the sign in *Winnie the Pooh* reading 'Trespassers Will', which Piglet thought referred to his uncle Trespassers William. That was the only smile I could raise on that visit and I soon realised why Hamish had called the place Cold Comfort Farm.

There was a large midden by the gate where I parked the car. I noticed the mangled body of a freshly dead ginger cat among the manure. As I contemplated it, a voice startled me.

'We have far too many cats here. Are you the doctor?'

I turned and found myself looking at an ugly, cross-eyed runt of a man. 'Yes,' I replied, 'are you Mr Frazer?'

The man, nodded 'It's for my Da, he's taken a shock,' he said. 'This way.'

I followed him across an untidy yard piled high with the slowly disintegrating bric-à-brac of many years of chaotic subsistence farming, and was taken into the farm kitchen where a woman was kneading bread. She looked unsmilingly at me and went on pummelling the dough. Without speaking, Frazer led the way upstairs.

Glancing behind me I saw the woman wipe her hands on her apron and leave the kitchen. I could have sworn she was weeping. On a table on the landing there was a shotgun. Its barrels looked very short.

'He didna come down to his breakfast,' explained Frazer as he led the way into a bleak, chilly bedroom, 'so I came to look for him. He was like this when I found him. I thought I'd best call you out... In case anything happened, like.'

I knelt by the unconscious old man on the floor. He was partly covered by a blanket but was breathing stertorously and had obviously suffered a severe stroke. He had been incontinent of urine and his pyjamas were soaking wet. I glanced round the spartan room and guessed he would get no tender loving care here.

As if reading my mind, Frazer said 'Poor ol' bugger's had it; you should get him into hospital.'

'Can't you manage him here?' I asked without much hope, but I did not like the man's attitude.

'No chance.' Then he added, as if by explanation, 'My wife's very delicate, ye see.'

Together we got the old man's wet pyjamas off and put him back to bed.

Then I said, 'There may be a bed in the cottage hospital but I'll have to ring and check. Have you got a phone?'

Without wasting words Frazer led me back to the kitchen. As we crossed the landing, I indicated the foreshortened gun.

'That looks a nasty weapon,' I commented.

'Aye, it's always there, loaded ready wi' buckshot, in case anyone breaks in at night.'

The woman had disappeared from the kitchen. I dialled the hospital and fixed old Frazer's admission and for the ambulance to collect him. The son led me back to my car without a word. Nodding in the direction of the midden, I asked, 'What happened to the cat?'

'It got caught in the grass cutter. We've ower many o' them.' With no word of thanks Frazer turned and walked back to the farmhouse, leaving me with an uneasy feeling that the cat's demise had not been accidental.

When I got back to the surgery the mail from the evening ferry had arrived bringing a letter in an unknown hand. It was addressed from Nith View Community Home, Near Friar's Carse, Dumfriesshire and dated a day or two before.

Dear Dr Chalmers, (it read)

Every year we plan a camping holiday for a number of our residents all of whom live and work in our community. They all suffer from some form of mental incapacity but tend, on the whole, to be physically pretty healthy.

This year we are negotiating a campsite at Pitchroich farm in Laigersay in early June. It is an obvious requirement that there should be medical care available in case of accident or sudden illness. I am writing to you to ask if you would be prepared to provide medical cover for us in the unlikely event of our needing it. To reassure you perhaps I should add that over the last four summers we have only had to ask for medical help once, and that was for one of our volunteer staff with an acute tummy upset.

If you want to know more about us and our camping arrangements, you could ask Mrs Helen Chalmers at Pitchroich Farm or, if you would like further information from me, please telephone me.

I do hope you will be able to provide medical cover for us.

Yours sincerely,

Patricia Tomlinson

I rang Helen and she confirmed the booking for the camp but had little to add other than that Mrs Tomlinson sounded very pleasant and extremely efficient. I phoned the home to say that I would be delighted to provide cover and explaining about the regulations for accepting temporary residents as patients.

CHAPTER 5

The Orraman

'How are you feeling?' asked Fiona when I returned home to the castle.

'Much better after a heart-warming surgery and round, but I still have a headache.'

'Well you did rather deserve one, but I must say the party was an immense success. Angus was round this morning to say how much he and Mhairi had enjoyed themselves. He said again that he hoped you didn't mind him bringing Thorfinn. I said of course not and that I enjoyed the story of my husband's life-saving heroism.'

I snorted. 'It was nothing of the kind—purely routine. But it was extraordinary the man turning up out of the blue like that,' and I told Fiona about hearing the Icelander on the radio at Solan Lighthouse.

'He'll break a few Laigersay hearts I don't doubt. He really is astonishingly dishy! Anyway Angus brought a little note for you.'

So saying, she gave me a letter: 'Thank you again for an excellent party and more particularly for my life. I hope one day I can do something for you in return, sincerely. Thorfinn Theodorsson.'

'Thorfinn seems very grateful. Angus said he met him over lunch at Port Chalmers hotel—Thorfinn invited him and Mhairi to the "Narwhal" for a drink. Apparently it's absolutely beautiful. Thorfinn seems to have made pots of money growing tomatoes...'

'Tomatoes? In Iceland? Hard to believe, we have enough trouble trying to grow them here.'

'Well, that's what *I* said. Angus told me they have more sunshine in the summer than we do, and as for heat, they have plenty of that for free, from geothermal activity.

'Anyway they were talking about the cod war, and that's when Thorfinn told the story about you. Apparently he had no idea that the man who saved him back then was the Laird of Laigersay. So Angus asked him to the surgery opening. I'm glad he did, it made a splendid climax to the ceilidh.'

'Yes, I was quite astonished... And it was good to see old Maggie McPhee looking so well. She was in good form. What did you think of her soothsaying?'

Fiona smiled. 'I have started noting her pronouncements. It's easy to forget what she says: then when her prophecies seem to come right we re-invent what she said originally to explain things. So as soon as I could get a pencil and paper, I copied down what she said last night. It was: "Your work will be hard but in time you will bring prosperity and worldwide fame to the little isle o' Laigersay".'

'Gosh, I wonder what that means ... I must admit I regard her sayings with some foreboding. I'm still mystified about how she managed to predict me inheriting from your father... What's for lunch? I'm hungry.'

'Finishing up, I'm afraid. There's still some of Tet's pâté, and Tom's fish, and lots of bits and pieces...'

'"Funeral baked meats did coldly furnish forth the marriage table"!'

'Get away: they're nice funeral meats, so come and get it. The boys are still out with their friends the Nicholsons, they stayed there last night and went back there after school, so we've got a little peace.'

As I ate, I told Fiona about Allt Beag Farm. She listened and said, 'I think I heard Daddy speak of that family; they always kept themselves to themselves, but there were rather strange rumours about them. I used to know young Frazer's wife, Catriona, a bit. She was a big girl when I first went to school in Port Chalmers. She was a bit of a recluse even then. She must have a lonely life out at that remote farm. I've heard he gives her a bad time.'

'That doesn't surprise me. It is quite clear that Hamish doesn't like them. I must ask him about Frazer. He certainly did not seem to be worried about his father—he'd left him lying on the floor in soaking wet pyjamas. Anyway he'll be in the cottage hospital by now. They'll look after him, but I doubt if he'll be with us very long.'

Fiona looked at what was left on the table. 'The funeral baked meats seem to have met with your approval after all. Can't you manage that last little bit of Tet's pâté?'

'Oh, very well, I'll be a martyr.'

Fiona burst out laughing. 'I forgot to tell you what Jamie said the other day. "Why," he asked, "does Daddy always say *I'll be a tomato* when he finishes up the last goody from a dish?"'

'Good for him,' I smiled, as I piled the last morsels of smoked trout on to a wafer, 'and here's to tomatodom!'

Setting out on my afternoon visits, I thought about my family. The twins, Hamish and James, named after Dr Robertson and the Admiral, Fiona's father, were thriving and growing fast. They were now nearly six and extremely active. Hamish was the elder by a few minutes, about as far as H is ahead of J in the alphabet. School, after their first distaste, was a huge success and they spent all their spare time with friends out on the moors, or in the woods, guddling in the burns for little fish, or on the shore. In some ways I was envious of them, for they had been born into an idyllic boyhood in superb country. They were rarely in the castle but during storms, when lashing rain kept them indoors, there was the rambling old building to play 'hide and seek' in, armour and weaponry (strongly forbidden) for dreams of adventure and the Admiral's museum of souvenirs from foreign parts and his collection of semi-precious stones to explore under Fiona's supervision. They certainly had what most would say was an ideal childhood.

My own boyhood was spent in the Sussex Weald. That was nice enough country but the meandering, muddy River

Arun was no match for the lively burns of Laigersay; the south coast beaches were too far away (and, for the most part, out of bounds during the war). Already the twins were learning to use their eyes and to observe the natural history of Laigersay. There were frequent sorties to the beach where they built castles and searched for 'treasure' on the shore.

The boys' greatest joy was one I shared. The burns teemed with minnows, little trout and salmon parr, which were occasionally caught in their shrimping nets. These catches they called by the names their school friends taught them, such as banstickles or spriklybags for stickleback. Gatties were minnows and beeran were the tiny fingerling trout which teemed in every burn. I remembered the first wriggling bar of silver in my own boyhood's net and the spell it cast over me, making me a devoted angler from that moment on. My first catches had been gudgeons and miller's thumbs from the River Arun; my lucky twins started out with game fish even if they were tiddlers. I looked forward to the time I could teach them to cast a fly.

Already there was a difference between these identical twins whom we had christened with linguistic versions of the same name. Angus had said when he baptised them that it was a good thing they were not triplets or we might have been tempted to call the third Seumas! Hamish, or Hamie as he called himself, was the more fascinated by beachcombing while brother James was the keener fisherman. Their identical physical appearance was modified when three-year-old Jamie scarred his nose falling out of a tree; before that only their mother could tell them apart.

On a fine morning a few days later, as I was coming back from a visit to a croft under the shoulder of Ranneach Bheag, I pulled off the road and strolled to the cliff edge. I remembered my first visit here when Hamish had lent me his car on my second day in the island. Then the late autumn storm had been at its highest and the great Atlantic rollers crashed on to the rocks at the base of the cliffs. Spume from the breakers was blown high up on to the road, a hundred feet above the level of today's calm sea.

What a difference! Today there was only the slightest zephyr of wind, perfumed subtly by the countless primroses that blossomed wherever the plants could find crevices in the rocks. Nearly past their best, they were soon to be overtaken by the pink and white of thrift and sea-campion. Fulmars circled stiff-winged on the up-current of breeze at the cliff edge, and a pair of terns swore their ugly curses at me.

As I watched the sea swallows, I became aware that I too was being watched. An old man, working on a dry-stane dyke by the roadside where a small burn tumbled down from Ranneach Bheag, had straightened his back and was staring at me. I walked over to see the beautiful work he was doing. To some people, stone walls are just piles of rock, but I was learning that constructing a dyke properly was a matter of great artistry and enormous skill. Here I was looking at the work of a master. I noticed that he was left-handed.

'Good morning,' I said. 'A fine day for a job like that.'

'Aye.' He looked me in the face. I was looking at a tall, skeletally thin man who appeared to have been battered by nearly a century of harsh life on the Atlantic margin. He was lined and deeply tanned and his clothes looked as though he had owned them for years. He regarded me with a level gaze. He might be a menial worker but there was nothing subservient about this fine old islander.

'You are making a great job of that dyke.'

'Aye, 'tis coming well.' The old man was clearly no great conversationalist.

'You've been dyking for a good few years, I can see.'

'Aye, man an' lad, three score year an' more.' He pushed back a battered tammy and wiped sweat off his forehead. 'I saw ye keekin' at the picatarries. Ye like thae cattle?'

I must have looked my bewilderment for he added, 'The terns ye may call them—they're mostly arctic but there are a few common there too. If ye want to be posh, they're *Sterna paradisaea* and *Sterna hirundo*.'

I stared in astonishment. That the man should know the birds by common names was one thing, but I had not expected him to reel off their scientific names.

'Did ye see any rosies?'

Again I was puzzled.

'*Dougalli*,' he explained.

'Ah! you mean roseate terns. Are they here too?'

'Aye, they bred here last year. You'd be the doctor laird, wad ye no? Then ye should know yon crittur, 'twas named for a medical man like yersel'.'

Again I was astonished. 'Yes, you're absolutely right. The bird's scientific name was given after a Glasgow GP called Peter McDougall. Where did you learn that?'

'I read about birds. Hereabout is the northern limit for rosy terns. I see a nest most summers.'

'I've never seen one in my life.'

'Then I'll send word if I see them.' With that, my extraordinary teacher went back to his work.'

Later I met Erchie and told him about the master dyker.

'That'll be Charlie Kerr, the orraman...'

'The what?'

'Orraman. An orraman is an odd-job man, who works from farm to farm about the island. He's gey skilled in ancient trades that we're in danger o' losing. He's not only a great dry-stane dyker, but he can lay a beautiful hedge, make ditches, better than any I know, as well as turn his hand to any skilled farm work such as shearing and ploughing. Aye, that's Charlie Kerr. He's lived in the island all his life, working as a skilled itinerant labourer. He is something of a recluse—with a reputation for strange knowledge and abilities. He has an old dog fox that comes to his call and people say he talks to the seals and the dolphins by the shore. He has a deep understanding of nature and he's a mine of what he calls "knowledge o' the auld days".'

'I was amazed when he trotted out scientific bird names.'

'Aye, I heard he was up on that. He has bird-watching friends from the continent and he says the only way he can tell them what he is seeing is with the Latin names. He's a character, is Charlie Kerr. He comes from an ancient family. It's a funny thing they all tend to be cack-handed an' if ye go to a Kerr castle you'll find all the spiral staircases have a reversed spiral to make it safer for left-handed swordsmen.'

Chapter 6

Letter from Stanley Johnson

Not long after the Admiral died, I had my first challenge as new laird. We had a small but serious outbreak of poaching. One of the chief assets of the estate was the salmon fishing, which with the grouse moors brought in the small annual income that we desperately needed to keep the property going. Fish were reported being sold openly in mainland markets as Laigersay salmon. As in medical matters, when in doubt, I consulted Hamish. Old Squarebottle listened to my problem and my theory as to who was responsible.

'Och,' he said 'I doot ye're wrong. I've known Erchie Thomson for a guid few years. There's nae doot he's a rascal, but his loyalty is beyond question. He'll certainly take a fush or two for hissel' but I canna see him indulging in wholesale pilfering o' his laird's property. But there's an old saying "set a thief to catch a thief". If ye ask Erchie to be yer factor I'm sure ye couldnae have a more loyal servant.'

So I approached Erchie. When he was appointed as factor in charge of the estate and its staff, the other keepers were having difficulty controlling poachers. When I asked Erchie if the poachers were giving him any trouble, he replied that they were 'nae bother.' At first Erchie's appointment was not well received by the other keepers, who told me: 'If Erchie did his job properly he'd see the poachers often enough.'

I was far from happy at this, and decided to investigate for myself. I went out one night with a gun and fired a shot near Erchie's house. Hearing the shot the big man came out with a stick and chased the 'poacher' down to the river, caught him and so belaboured him with his stick he nearly killed him before realising who his victim was. I was in bed for a day or two nursing horrendous bruises, and when I was recovering I sent for Erchie, who was covered with confusion and very apologetic. I had to admit that it was my own fault and that, if he treated the poachers as he had treated me, then it was not surprising he had no trouble from them.

One of the first things to disturb the peace of that early summer in Laigersay was a missive from Stanley Johnson. I opened his letter at breakfast but propped it against the marmalade jar. I did not read it for several minutes but slowly ate the finnan haddie that Fiona had set before me. I like finnan haddie and, as I savoured it, I thought back over Stanley's previous involvement with the island. Before I came to Laigersay he had spent some time here, ostensibly for the fishing, and had rented a cottage on the Tom Bacadh estate. It was through Johnson that I had become embroiled in the scandalous affair at Tom Bacadh when Fiona and I both nearly lost our lives. There was thus good reason to view a letter from Stanley with some caution. I unfolded the sheet of paper and read:

Dear Rob,

I am coming to your lovely island next week to do a spot of fishing and will be staying at the Port Chalmers Hotel. I hope I may be able to meet up with you as I have a proposition to put to you. If you should see my old friend Tet do tell him I'm coming and that I hope to test his culinary skill.

Yours sincerely,

Stanley.

On the face of it, the letter seemed innocuous enough but where Stanley was concerned I was on my guard. Always a secretive person, he had in the past held all sorts of strange governmental jobs which involved counter-espionage and drugs. It was wise to use a long spoon, I felt, when supping with Stanley Johnson.

There was no sense in worrying about the letter, so I finished my breakfast and went to the surgery. My first patient was Nutty Jakes, disturbed and confused as usual. Poor Nutty suffered the delusion that he had swallowed a pair of scissors and that they were lodged in his gullet. On bad days he used to demand that I forced a magnet down his throat to retrieve them and on better days he commented that they were 'going down nicely'. I reflected on what I knew of the strange person seated in front of me. His medical record showed that he had been a university undergraduate until struck by the dreadful condition of schizophrenia in his early twenties. He had spent months in a mental hospital, until an enlightened psychiatrist had stabilised him on a drug called Largactil and pronounced him fit to live in society. Hearing from friends about the alleged healing quality of Laigersay, Jakes had moved here a year or so before I came.

At first the community had been horrified at having a 'loony' in their midst, and people were worried at the evangelising piety expressed through his placards prophesying imminent doom. After a bit he was seen for what he was, a completely harmless individual, with strange ways and a habit of wandering all over Laigersay. In an island where eccentricity was almost the norm, he came to be tolerated, treated as something of a joke and even loved by some. He was particularly good to children and had an endless supply of sweeties for them.

Today Jakes was less nutty than usual, the scissors were 'nearly down' and all he wanted was a repeat prescription of his Largactil. 'You will keep taking them regularly won't you, Jakes?' I asked.

'Yes, Doctor, I take them by the clock. Look and see when I was last here.'

I glanced at his notes and saw my last entry was exactly four weeks before.

'You gave me a hundred and twelve tablets then... two to be taken twice a day. I have taken a hundred and ten of them and have two for tonight. That shows how strictly I've been taking them.'

'All right, Jakes, so long as you take the pills you'll be fine.'

'That's right, Doctor. I don't want ever to go back to hospital.'

As Nutty left, I spent a moment looking back over his notes and thinking of Hamish's comment at the surgery party. Occasionally I had to sign a section of the Mental Health Act depriving some unfortunate disturbed patient of their liberty. I always found this a heavy responsibility, for to incarcerate a patient in an asylum seemed a terrible thing to do to a fellow human being. Sometimes there was no doubt that an individual was a danger to himself or others, more often things were not black and white, but shades of grey. In poor Nutty's case I felt it right to support his claim to be a free individual.

I got up and walked to the waiting room and called Martin Gray to see me. He was fit and well with a healthy outdoor tan, but it had not always been thus. Martin was a quiet, unassuming, but obsessional fellow, who kept the sports ground of the Port Chalmers secondary school in immaculate order. He used never to come to the surgery but I knew of him because his vegetables won so many prizes at horticultural shows. Then, late last summer, he had presented with a most unusual problem. He appeared in an evening surgery clearly ill, with beaded sweat across his forehead on a cool evening. He said he had been feeling ill for some days with what he took to be flu but had now started getting severe upper abdominal pain and a feeling of nausea. His abdomen was slightly distended with marked tenderness over his liver. I was perplexed; the appearance was one of an acute abdominal problem but with no localising signs. Wondering about a fulminating inflammation of his gall bladder I phoned the surgical registrar on the mainland who advised putting him on the evening flight for immediate admission. By the time that was organised I was way behind, and surgery did not finish until after 9pm.

Later that night the registrar phoned me at home. 'That chap Gray you sent in... he's interesting. I agree that he looked like an acute abdomen, and we were just about to take him to theatre when we got his blood count back. He's got a very high white cell count with forty percent of eosinophils. I've asked the physicians to see him but we don't have a diagnosis yet. Can you help?'

'Only by suggesting that the blood picture indicates some sort of parasitic infestation, but, tell you what, I'll go and see his wife and see if I can get any more information.'

Gray's wife, having seen him off at the airport, had gone home to await the outcome of his expected surgery. She was alarmed to see me on the doorstep; unexpected doctor's visits, like those of the police, often cause concern, especially late at night. However this time I could be reassuring. Together we explored all she knew about Martin's work and anything that might have brought him into contact with some parasite. We drew a complete blank, but she was glad of my visit and, in the way of country people, wanted to give me something as I left.

'Do you like watercress?' she asked. 'Martin has found some marvellous cress in a little burn at work and we've been having quite a lot of it; he likes it in his sandwiches.' I accepted a large dripping bundle and looked forward to the morrow's salad.

It was only on the way home that the penny dropped, but they were ahead of me at the hospital, where a clever physician had already diagnosed acute hepatitis caused by *Fasciola hepatica*. The common name of this parasite, the 'sheep liver fluke', is misleading, since it is found in many animals other than sheep, including humans. Parasite eggs are passed in the host's faeces. Some find their way into water courses where they enter their first intermediate host, a small freshwater snail, and later form cysts on vegetation, particularly watercress. Eating contaminated cress then infects the human host. Once inside the small intestine, the immature worm penetrates the gut, and then munches its way through the liver to reach the bile ducts. No wonder Martin Gray felt so ill.

Three days later Mrs Gray was in hospital with hepatitis too. Dr Francis Noble, the consultant physician, was so intrigued he flew to Laigersay and he and I, armed with shrimping nets, visited the stream bordering a sheep pasture on the edge of the school playing fields where we caught specimens of the snails that formed the intermediary host for the flukes. After that we spent a few hours on Loch Bradan and I was able to send Dr Noble home with a salmon.

Both the Grays did well, but came to see me for a routine follow-up every three months. There is no better way of acquiring grateful patients than by solving their difficult diagnostic problems. Martin always came bearing a good bottle of whisky and produce from his garden... but the Grays had given up eating watercress and, I am glad to say, never offered it to me again.

After Gray had left, morning surgery went on with its usual routine of minor summer ailments: sunburn, hay fever and tourists with blisters from hill walking or tennis elbow from unskilful fly-fishing. Sometimes as I dealt with these medical minutiae I wondered if I was needed at all; probably my staff could have dealt with these problems by themselves. Then I remembered the Grays; I might not be needed very often but, when the need for me did arise, it was often great.

As usual Hamish and I met for coffee after we had seen our last patients of the morning. In the old days Jennie Churches had spoiled us with freshly made coffee and her excellent shortbread. Now we had a drink made with powder from a tin optimistically marked 'coffee' and the biscuits came from a packet. Usually Hamish grumbled that things were not what they had been. But today he had other things on his mind.

'I had Kitty Tibbles in this morning ... about her nerves as usual. She was even more upset than usual and said it was my fault. I'd forgotten but when she was in before, in her usual fraught state, I suggested that perhaps she might try and find a gentleman friend... What she really needs is a good...'

'Quite, Hamish, I get the drift.'

'Well, I'd quite forgotten, but she took it to heart and d'ye ken what she did? She wrote to a dating agency. Look, she even gave me the address.' He showed me a card which read 'MacMaster Agency for Lonely People'.

'She got a form to fill in. She sent that back, then she'd a phone call from a man calling himself Captain MacMaster asking to come and see her. That really put her in a state! She said no, she was just leaving Laigersay and didn't know if or when she'd be back. Och, ye ken I've no great patience wi' ineffectual people like Kitty Tibbles but I've even less wi' those who batten on their gullibility. I bet this MacMaster fella was out to get whatever money she had.'

At that moment the practice nurse and midwife, Alison Goodbody, came in with the morning's messages and requests for visits. Hamish liked chatting to our very attractive nurse, and launched into the tale of Kitty and her Captain. She listened, and then said, 'Those people are dreadful. My sister once got involved with some sort of dating agency as a joke. She had a terrible time getting rid of a most unpleasant bloke who said he wanted to marry her. They should be taught a lesson.'

Hamish was delighted. 'Good idea, Alison; let's do that. Now, here's what we'll do. You write to this MacMaster fella and say you're looking for a man, and we'll run him a dance. Don't worry, I'll back you up and see nothing happens to you. Och, I can't abide the way people like that prey on the likes o' Kitty Tibbles.'

By now time was running on, and I left to do my round of visits—on a fine summer morning when Laigersay was looking at its very best. We had opened a little branch surgery in the south of the island, at Lutheran. This was largely for the convenience of the patients in Assilag and the tiny communities round the south of the island. In those days few of the fisher folk and crofters had cars and I had argued that a branch surgery there would take some of the pressure off visiting. The branch surgery and its little dispensary soon became extremely popular. We took it in turns to consult there every other day either in the morning or late afternoon. After an afternoon at the branch we hurried back to Port Chalmers for the evening surgery which ran from half past five until the last patient was seen, sometimes as late as eight o'clock.

One morning, two or three days later, when I knew that Hamish would be having his post-surgery coffee, I phoned as usual from the branch surgery to see if there were any nearby calls before returning to Port Chalmers. When Alison answered, I assumed a very English voice, announced myself as Major MacMaster and asked to speak to Miss Alison Goodbody. A gasp was followed by a rather breathless: 'I am afraid she's not here at present.'

'When will she be in?' I asked, adding, 'It's a business matter and confidential.'

'Um, I don't know. Hold on and I'll make enquiries...'

Then Hamish came on the phone. 'I am afraid Miss Goodbody is not here at present. This is her employer— can I help?'

By now I was convulsed with laughter, and said, 'Morning, Hamish, this is just Rob from the branch surgery asking if there's any work for me down here?'

There was a long pause, then my partner said: 'You *bugger*! Don't you ever do that again!'

Hamish was very cross. When a letter did come a few days later from the marriage agency, he crumpled it up and threw it out. Nothing further was heard of the matter. Nothing, that is, except that sometimes, when the phone rang, I would say, 'Perhaps *that's* MacMaster.' Hamish was never amused.

My receptionist Jeannie Brown told me that the campsite at Pitchroich was now occupied. Patricia Tomlinson and her team of four helpers had moved in with eight handicapped young adults. Mrs Tomlinson looked in to the surgery one morning just as I was leaving on my visiting round, and I stopped the car for a word. She seemed a pleasant, capable woman in her mid-thirties. I wished her a good holiday and promised that I was about if needed.

'I hope we will not need to disturb you, Doctor, but we do have to make sure that medical help is available in case of need.' As we were speaking, Nutty Jakes came by on his little motor scooter.

'Message for you, Doctor,' he said as he waved a paper.

Not sure what to expect, I took the paper from Jakes.

'Charlie gave it me, and asked me to put it in your hand,' he explained, smiling cheerfully but rather inanely at Pat Tomlinson.

I unfolded the paper and glanced at four words written in a surprisingly well formed hand: 'The rosies are back.'

Thanking Jakes, I let in the clutch, noticing in the rear view mirror that he had stopped to chat to Mrs Tomlinson. Nutty liked to talk to visitors, usually in an effort to save them from eternal damnation. I suspected that Pat Tomlinson would soon guess his problem.

My round that morning took me across the island to Feadag and Lutheran and it was not until early afternoon that I drove back to the east coast past Tom Bacadh to Pitchroich. From the road I could see the campsite just south of Pitchroich Farm. There was a circle of bell tents round a central small marquee. It was all very efficiently laid out. I was amused to see that Nutty Jakes' scooter was parked in the centre of the camp. He had obviously lost no time following up his chance meeting with the camp leader.

I stopped the car by the dry-stane dyke Charlie Kerr had been building. It was now neatly topped off with upright coping-stones. Charlie's tools were lying beside it and his bicycle was propped against it, but of the old man himself there was no sign. A path led down beside the burn, which chattered its way down the steep hillside to fall vertically, in a spraying iridescence of rainbow colours, to the cove below.

Having been to this site many times, I knew the zigzag path that led between near vertical cliffs down to the cove, where there was a large cave undermining the cliff. At some remote time in history part of the cave roof had collapsed, bringing thousands of tons of rock down into the cove below. This was a favourite place for seal watching, as the fallen rocks had left good sunbathing places for them with easy access to safe deep water.

At each bend of the path there was a grassy knoll where one could sit in comfort and observe the cove below. I settled into one of them with my back against smooth rock and enjoyed the sunshine and spectacular view across to the distant, and still snow-capped, mountains of the mainland.

After a while, I lay flat on my belly and peered over the edge. On the sand of the cove below me two people were walking. One was a rather untidy, shapeless-looking woman. She was moving very slowly towards the rocks in the sea. I could see a party of grey seals basking there. The animals clearly knew she was there because they had all turned their heads towards her.

Behind the woman, stalking her as she stalked the seals, was a man. Even at a distance he was immediately recognisable as Nutty Jakes. For a moment I felt alarm. Though I was certain that Nutty was as harmless a young man as one could find anywhere, it occurred to me that the woman could not know that and might be frightened.

I was not the only person watching, for below me on another knoll by the path, yet still thirty feet above the cove, was the unmistakable figure of Charlie Kerr. He was studying the scene below intently through binoculars.

The woman crept nearer and nearer to the seals. An eddy of the breeze brought a high-pitched keening sound to my ears and it seemed to be coming from her. She was now only a dozen yards from the seals, partly hidden from them by the rocks. Slowly she stood up. As she did so a seal slipped silently into the deep water round the old rock-fall. One by one, the others slid into the water. Instead of diving as I had expected, they formed a circle round the woman, their great dog-like heads above the water watching, listening. Then slowly they swam towards her, circling within a foot or two of the rock she stood on. One ponderously heaved itself on to the rock where the woman stood and she leaned forward and stroked the beast's head. All the time she kept up her strange lamenting song.

I could not take my eyes off the astonishing sight. I had heard stories about seal women who could talk to the selkies but had always discounted these as old wives' tales.

But I had forgotten the other watchers. Nutty Jakes appeared beside the woman and the seal, scared by his sudden movement, dived into the water. In its panic, it knocked into the woman. She fell with a scream. I could see her foot slip into a crevice and then she fell sideways.

I was down the path in an instant but ahead of me was the spare, running figure of old Charlie Kerr. The woman was crying with pain and I could see the deformity of a fracture dislocation of her right ankle. Distraught, Nutty was not much help, so I sent him to the camp to get something to use as a stretcher. I knelt beside the woman and told her I was a doctor. She turned uncomprehending, almost seal-like, deep brown eyes on me and I noticed her abnormally large head. I realised I was dealing with one of Mrs Tomlinson's charges.

Charlie Kerr held the woman's hand and to my amazement started making the same keening noise that the woman had been singing to the seals.

She seemed to hear and she turned to him, smiled, and then, to my astonishment, laid her head on his breast.

'I ken the lassie,' was all he said.

Then Nutty was back with a couple of strong young men. They had brought a hard upright chair, which, angled backwards, was excellent for carrying the woman over the rocks to the campsite. I walked beside them explaining that I was worried about the blood supply to her foot. The fracture dislocation was jeopardising the arterial supply.

'I need to reduce that fracture as soon as possible, then she'll have to go to the mainland, because she'll probably need surgery to pin the bone fragments adequately.'

Pat Tomlinson came running up. 'I didn't think we would be calling you so soon, Doctor.'

'I actually saw it happen,' I told her. 'Now I am going up to get my car. I'll get her over to the surgery straight away. I could use your help, Mrs Tomlinson, and I suggest one of your helpers comes up to the surgery too.'

'May I come?' a soft voice asked. I turned to find Charlie Kerr looking at me. He repeated, 'Ye see, I ken the lassie.'

This was not the moment to explore exactly what the old man meant by this. I ran off up to the road to get my Land Rover, while Mrs Tomlinson soothed her charge.

As soon as we reached the surgery, I gave the woman morphia and asked about eating.

'No, she missed lunch, because she went off by herself to see the seals,' Mrs Tomlinson informed me.

That was fortunate. As soon as the morphia began to work, I was able to give her gas and air from my midwifery gear and soon had the dislocated joint approximately the right shape. Then, with the blood supply to the foot no longer in jeopardy, there was less hurry. I splinted the foot, and put in a request for the air ambulance to take the patient to the mainland for definitive orthopaedic surgery.

Charlie Kerr must have followed on his bicycle for, by the time I had finished fixing admission, he was talking with Mrs Tomlinson. Over a cup of coffee Mrs Tomlinson told me Nutty Jakes had pestered her and followed her to the campsite. It was only after he had disappeared that she noticed Mandy had gone too.

'Mandy?' I queried

'That's the name of your patient. Mandy McTavish, though she calls herself Maantie. She is remarkable. She was born with a severe brain deformity—I gather she was not too bad at first—I am afraid I don't understand the details but she had water on the brain and grew a hugely swollen head. They did not think she would live. I believe she had some form of experimental surgery, long before I knew her, of course; she's thirty-eight now. She can't talk or hear much, but she seems to have invented her own form of communication, and several others in the community can understand some of the grunts and signs she makes.

'I can tell you the seals understand her,' I said,

A voice said, 'Aye, they can that.' We had forgotten Charlie Kerr, and now Pat Tomlinson turned to him.

'Did you say you knew her?' she asked.

'Aye, and I taught her to treesh the selkies, but I haena set eyes on her these thirty years. Indeed, I thocht she was deid, I haena heard o' her for sae lang.'

'How did you know her?' I asked.

'My kizzen Caitriona, she bided on the croft on Mulcaire afore the war. Mandy, or Maantie as she callit herself, was her bairn.'

'You were a cousin of her mother's?'

'Aye, imphm, so I believe. A kizzen o' some kind.'

'Can you tell us what happened.'

'She was aye a brosie-heidit wean but no sic a glundie as she seemed. Caitriona aye made a dossach wi her but I took a skeel to the puir bairn.' The old man spoke very slowly in what seemed to me almost to be a foreign language. 'Aye,' he continued, 'I took a fair goo to her. Her faither hadna time for Maantie an' her mither would mak sic a fuss ower her, between them they made Maantie waur than she really was. But I could mak her onnerstaund me an' I could onnerstaund her. It was me as learnt her to sing to the selkies.'

The old man nodded and took a deep breath. I got the impression he had not made so long a speech for years.

'Aye,' he went on, 'She aye looed the selkies. Then the war came and the mither an' faither were kilt. Maantie was awa' wi' her mither's sister awa doon in Bute when it happened. I never saw her mair till the day's morn.'

I looked at Pat Tomlinson. 'Can you take up the story?' I asked.

'Only vaguely. She was referred to us by social services who found her living in squalor in the Gorbals at the end of the war. They established that she had lived in Arran on a farm but had run away. By that time she had had surgery and her head was no longer growing but of course she was outwardly imbecile. Despite that she has some ability to look after herself; she always keeps herself clean. She's very friendly, too friendly for her own good I think. We have to watch her with men.'

Pat turned to me and said: 'We had a battle with the medical authorities at the home. I feared that some man would take advantage of her and get her pregnant. I tried to get them to sterilise her, but the doctors got all ethical and refused. One of them saw my point, however, and he inserted a coil. I don't know if she ever has had a man but she certainly flirts, so I think it's likely.'

'Difficult, but I rather agree it would be unethical to sterilise her.'

Pat raised her eyebrows. 'But can you think what sort of life a child would have?'

I shook my head, not wanting to be drawn, but I saw Charlie Kerr looking distressed. 'It could be quite normal; hydrocephalus is not inherited,' I said.

Then the ambulance came and took the still sleeping Maantie to the airport. Charlie Kerr hesitated a moment, and asked, 'Did ye see the rosie terns?'

I shrugged. 'Not yet.'

'They're nestin' an' they'll bide a wee. Tak a keek when ye're by.' With that he jumped on his bicycle and was away.

Nutty Jakes came to see me in evening surgery later in the day. He was in a strange state. His mind was clear enough, for he made no mention of the scissors he was so sure were lodged in his gullet. His eyes were shining, and he was tearfully remorseful at having caused the accident.

'Will she be all right?' he demanded, and when I told him that I had checked with the hospital, that she had had her operation and would be returning to my care in the cottage hospital in a day or two he was so relieved he left the surgery singing.

CHAPTER 7

On Dogs and Bees

After the following day's morning surgery Hamish was rather non-committal about my new patient. For one so experienced in neurology he had little patience with the mentally handicapped. However he was able to shed some light on what may have happened surgically to Maantie.

'She must have had one o' the early Spitz-Holter valves, they came in during the early fifties.'

'I seem to remember the name: wasn't the idea to redirect excess cerebro-spinal fluid through a one-way valve into the pleural or peritoneal cavities?'

'Aye, it was quite a story. This American engineer fella called Holter had a son who had hydrocephalus. Nobody would operate on him, there just wasn't the technology then. Anyway Holter invented a one-way valve and then persuaded a neurosurgeon called Spitz to operate on his son and drain the excess fluid into his chest cavity. Apparently the result was almost miraculous.'

'But by the fifties Maantie would have been twelve or thirteen. How could she have survived till then?'

'Well some o' these big heads do live a few years and I think you said she was not too bad at first and then had some sort o' experimental surgery. Presumably that tided her over till the Spitz-Holter valve became available.'

Though at least some of Maantie's early history was becoming plausible if not much clearer, there was no chance for further discussion. Alison Goodbody came in and said, 'The coastguard's on the phone for you, Dr Chalmers.' She picked up the phone, asked for the call to be put through and handed the receiver to me.

'Morning, Doc.' It was the familiar voice of Wullie Stewart. 'I'm afraid I've got business for you. I've just had Jack Fordyce from Solan on the radio. He says Josh Macrae has come running to say old Meg Murchison has had a fall and can't move. I've scrambled the chopper and

Peter May is already doing his pre-flight checks—he'll be with you in a few minutes. Once you're in the helicopter you'll be able to speak with Solan Light directly.'

'Okay, Wullie,' I replied, 'I'll get my emergency gear and will be ready as soon as Peter gets here. Bye now.'

Replacing the receiver, I turned to Alison. 'Looks like I'm flying to Solan, Alison. Please check on everything that is scheduled for today and if there's anything urgent ask Dr Robertson to do it; and less urgent things contact the patients by phone and say I'm delayed.'

Collecting the emergency bag from my car, I ran to the store and found the Neil-Robertson stretcher, thanking my naval emergency training that had taught me how to use it. Already I could hear the throb of the coastguard helicopter on its way from Wullie's headquarters just north of Port Chalmers.

Peter May landed neatly on the pad, just as I would expect with such an experienced pilot. I ducked low and ran to the machine. George, his crewman, was already trying to raise Solan Light.

'Come on Jack, you're not usually so slow to answer,' he was saying to himself, then he repeated: 'Hallo, Solan Light, this is Port Chalmers coastguard helicopter, do you read me?'

There was a crackle, then the breathless voice of Jack Fordyce was audible. 'Solan Light here, wait while I get ma breath... I was out milking the goat... I had to run all the way up the steps... There, I'm getting better noo... Are ye coming for poor auld Meg?'

'Solan Light, what the hell are ye doin' wi' goats? I've got Dr Chalmers here and he wants a word wi' you.'

George passed the headset to me and I spoke directly to the lighthouse keeper many miles to the south: 'Hallo Jack, can you tell me all you know about Meg? Over.'

'Hallo, Doctor. I don't have much information. Josh Macrae came running over this morning wi' Meg's nanny goat. She hadna been milked for at least a day. Josh doesnae onnerstaund animals. Anyway he found Meg when he delivered her weekly messages. She was on the floor o' her kitchen barely conscious—just able to say she couldnae stand up.'

'Did Josh say anything else?'

'Och... something about her right leg being twisted outwards. I sent him straight back to be with Meg and to make sure she was warm.'

'Thanks, Jack, we'll be on our way. I'll be in touch again when we see what we find. Thanks again for your help, over and out.'

Turning to Peter, I added, 'Sounds like a fractured neck of femur. If Meg's right leg is rotated outwards, that's the provisional diagnosis. Let's get there.'

'Okay, but there is a slight problem. There's a stiffish westerly at the moment. We'd be best to fly down the east o' Laigersay and then when we get opposite Solan to turn into the wind for the crossing of Assilag Bay.'

'You're the boss, Peter. Just get me there as soon as possible. It sounds from the state of the goat as though poor old Meg has been in trouble for a day at least.'

The chopper rose with a whirr and soon we were crossing the coast not far from Pitchroich. Below me I could see Pitchroich Farm and the campsite where Pat Tomlinson and her people were holidaying.

We flew down the steep cliffs of southeast Laigersay and were soon over the sea south of Ranneach Bheag. The visibility was superb but as we left the shelter of the mountains the westerly wind caught us, bouncing the helicopter about quite violently. Peter turned the aircraft so that we were head-on to the wind and it steadied a bit. On the port side, the vast bulk of Sgarbh an Sgumain, the most southerly of our three ancient volcanoes, passed below the tiny machine. Then we were over the sea with the skerries to starboard. Seconds later we were directly over Mulcaire and I was seeing the island as I had never seen it before. I could see the old farmhouse at its northern end, with its derelict steadings around it. From what Charlie Kerr had said, this was the former home of the McTavish family, of whom the half-wit Maantie might be the sole survivor. More than ever I wanted to solve the mystery of Mulcaire and what had happened to the people who crofted there.

But we were now crossing the turbulent passage between Mulcaire and Solan itself. I could see that the fierce currents of the rip, made angrier still by the westerly wind, which was whipping the sea below me into a white-capped frenzy.

The helicopter landed on the machair close to Meg Murchison's cottage. Josh Macrae came running out to us. 'She's bad, Doctor. She canna speak clearly, I doot she's been lying there for an awfu' long time and she's all wet.'

Meg was lying in front of her fire, long since burnt out, but which had perhaps helped to keep her warm to begin with. As Josh had said, her right foot was externally rotated, a sure sign of a fracture of the femur near the hip joint. I knelt beside her, holding her hand and explaining who I was, and was encouraged to see a glint of recognition in her face. I explained that she had broken her thigh and that we needed to get her into hospital.

She seemed to understand and started to protest: 'Ma pussies an' Nanny...' she said.

'Don't worry about them, Meg. Jack at the light has already seen to Nanny and Josh here will take the cats in until you're home again.' I looked at him and he nodded. 'Now I'm going to give you an injection to ease pain while I put you so that we can move you, and then we will fly you in the helicopter to hospital on the mainland.'

'Never bin to the mainland in ma life,' the old woman murmured as I slipped a small dose of morphine into her arm. Waiting for the drug to take effect, I unpacked the lightweight stretcher. Neil-Robertson's special stretcher was designed for lifting injured seamen from awkward spaces in a ship and was ideal for getting people with fractures into a helicopter. We soon had Meg strapped firmly in.

'Now,' I said, 'I'll take her head. Peter, you go aft and take her feet, George and Josh take a handle port and starboard, and when I say *lift*, ease her up nice and steady and carry her over to the chopper.' At the helicopter,

George put me on to Wullie at the coastguard station and I reported what had happened.

'Wullie, will you get on to the surgery and ask them to contact the hospital and tell them I'm sending in Meg with a fracture of the neck of her right femur. She's been lying here for at least twenty-four hours so she'll almost certainly have developed pneumonia. I've given her as much morphine as I dare.'

'Okay, Doctor, I've got all that and will get onto the surgery directly. Over.'

'Right, Peter can drop me at the surgery before taking Meg to the mainland. I'll send the practice nurse as escort, warn her to stand by for the trip. Out.'

'Okay Doctor. Over and out.'

Turning to Peter, I said: 'Best to wait a bit till she's sedated, then between us we'll get her into your aircraft. Meanwhile, since we've a spare moment, let's put Jack Fordyce in the picture.

Peter called up Solan Light and Jack was keen to hear the news. I explained what was happening and he was relieved that Meg stood a good chance of recovery. 'I was worried,' he continued, 'when Josh came here this morning—the man's no verra bright and he didna ken what tae dae. The puir goat was near demented wi' her udder fit tae burst.'

I told him I had said to Meg that he would look after the goat.

'I'll be delighted,' he said, 'Boozer an' Nanny are well acquent and will be company for each ither. I'll get news o' Wullie which ward they send Meg to an' I'll send a postcard to her to tell her that Nanny's all right.'

It was time to get our patient aboard for her journey to hospital. The trip to the surgery was uneventful; the wind had eased, allowing a more direct route across the island, to drop me off in about twenty minutes. Alison, pleased at the prospect of flying to the mainland, was ready and waiting by the helipad. I could see from her large bag she meant to take full advantage of a surprise trip. Soon Peter had the chopper *en route* for the mainland.

I was then able to resume my normal work, not that there was much to do since either Hamish had seen to it or the practice staff had rescheduled it. There was one task for me however. A consignment of drugs was on the ferry, and I would have to sign for them personally. Meeting the ferry is a twice-daily celebration at Port Chalmers and there is always a crowd of islanders waiting to greet disembarking relatives and friends. I walked down to the harbour that evening with our dog beside me.

When my father-in-law Admiral Chalmers died, an odd thing happened with his dog, Cuhlan. The rather mystical Irish wolfhound who lived with the family at Castle Chalmers disappeared for three days and it was feared that he had come to a sticky end on one of the island roads. Then we had a message from Archie McPhee that the dog had returned to Maggie in her black house near Lutheran apparently none the worse for living three days on the moors. The dog and Maggie McPhee were old friends; she had bred him and raised him from a pup. The wolfhound had changed his allegiance back to Maggie when the Admiral died. Fiona and I debated what to do and decided that Cuhlan would do exactly what he wanted and that he should remain with Maggie.

The Admiral's funeral had been a sombre, stately affair. The Royal Navy was represented by a contingent of very senior officers, many in uniform and much bemedalled. Almost the whole island had attended, to show respect for the much loved laird. I found myself moved by the sacramental removal of the plaid from the old man's coffin. Angus, who presided at the service, folded the plaid and handed it to me as the successor to the lairdship. I took it in the knowledge that it would probably not be used again until my own obsequies. About a week after the funeral Cuhlan reappeared at Castle Chalmers as if nothing had happened. He must have accepted me as the new incumbent and from then on accompanied me whenever possible.

The ferry gave its pathetic little toot and berthed at the jetty. Then suddenly, among the passengers, I saw someone I knew—Stanley Johnson hailed me.

'Rob,' he said, 'how kind of you to meet me, and with Cuhlan too. How did you know I was on this ferry?'

Before I could explain why I was there, I was roughly elbowed aside.

'Repent ye! Repent ye! The day o' the Lord is nigh!' shouted Nutty Jakes, shaking a religious placard in Johnson's face and almost knocking him over.

'Steady on, Jakes,' I rebuked him. 'The man is a friend of mine.'

'Sorry, Doc,' said Nutty, 'but friend or no, he's a mortal sinner and needs to fend against the wrath o' Almighty God!'

I grinned at Stanley. 'He's all right really, just a touch evangelical.' To my schizophrenic patient I said, 'Leave him to me, Jakes, I promise to remind him to repent but he needs to get on to the island first.'

'OK, Doc, and thanks for sending word the other day that Maantie is going on all right.' The text-bearer ambled off good-humouredly to badger other sinners among the tourists.

'Good heavens, is this place peopled with madmen?' asked Johnson. 'There was a most extraordinary man on the boat with a beard and long hair. He seemed to be clad in a dressing gown and sandals and he was covered in jewellery. He strummed a guitar all the way across.'

'Well, from that description I guess he must be the silversmith fellow Erchie Thomson tells me has taken a place in Lutheran. Sounds like yet another eccentric settling in this isle of odd people. Listen Stanley, I have business with the ferry skipper, go and get yourself settled in and then give me a ring and we'll get together.'

During morning surgery the day after Stanley Johnson arrived, he phoned to make an appointment to see me. 'I'm not ill, you understand: I would like to sound you out about a business proposition.' He would not be drawn further, and I had to abate my curiosity until the afternoon, when he came to the estate office at the castle.

Even then he was remarkably circumlocutory and took a long time to come to the point. Eventually it became clear that he wished to take a long lease on Tom Bacadh Castle for a client. Dealing with Stanley generally seemed to involve a long-winded discussion when the matter in hand was really quite simple. I told him that Tom Bacadh was currently empty and that we were looking for a tenant. Discussing terms in broad principles, I learned that his client was interested in acquiring the grouse shooting over the southern part of the island and shared fishing rights in Loch Bradan.

'My client,' he said, 'will probably not be here very much, but has asked me to administer the estate for him. I would be grateful if your solicitor could draw up a provisional agreement and let me have it. I shall need to take that to London for my client's agreement but I can assure you that he will require a long lease and is relatively easy about rent. He may wish to carry out some minor alterations, decorating and so on. If you are not happy about that, I am asked to assure you that the castle will eventually be returned to you in the state in which he found it and that any alterations would be restored unless, of course, you wished them to remain.'

Mentally I rubbed my hands with glee, for this was just the sort of offer that Erchie, in his capacity as estate factor, and I had dreamed of. I agreed to instruct Mr McFadden, the Writer to the Signet who looked after estate affairs, to prepare the required document. As I shook hands with Johnson, he remarked that he was due back in London in a fortnight but would like a little fishing while he was here. I told him that would be fine, and to liaise with Erchie.

As Stanley Johnson walked slowly away from the office towards his car I noticed his limp, and my mind went back to the time in Tom Bacadh when Oleg Karkovski, the pretended gamekeeper there, had shot him in the thigh. But Oleg was not a keeper at all; he was a member of the drug trafficking syndicate that had leased Tom Bacadh from my father-in-law, Admiral Chalmers. Stanley had been lucky to get away with only mild neurological damage to the femoral nerve, but it had left him with partial paralysis of the muscles of his right thigh and he walked with a limp. I wondered that he should want to return to Tom Bacadh where he had so nearly have lost his life.

Hamish, for all his deficiencies, was an immensely wise man who taught me a great deal, not only about medicine but also about human nature. There was a time as a young GP when I loved nothing better than to diagnose an acute lobar pneumonia or a pernicious anaemia. Then I could exhibit the magic effects of penicillin or vitamin B_{12} and feel eight feet tall because I had cured a patient and probably saved a life. Such occasions come rarely and if one is to rely on them for job satisfaction there will be huge deserts of disappointment. The truth is, one rarely if ever saves life.

The nearest I may have come to saving a life was with Hamish himself. As one of his many interests, Old Squarebottle kept bees. One off-duty afternoon I was pottering about the garden of Castle Chalmers when the phone rang and a voice I barely recognised said: 'Bee stings ... surgery.'

At the surgery, I found Hamish slumped unconscious on the floor of the office, by the phone that he must have used to call for help. He had been badly stung while working with his bees and had developed acute anaphylaxis.

My first thought was that he was dead. He was cold and sweaty, looking as if he had suffered a major heart attack and was in cardiogenic shock. Round his neck was a weal of red in which I could see a number of bee stings held in the skin by their minute barbs. Then I managed just to detect the weakest of pulses. Although my relationship with Hamish had swung between extremes of love and hate, now, while his life hung in balance, I suddenly felt a deep affection for the dying man and was desperate to save him. For what seemed an age, I laboured with adrenaline, hydrocortisone and a great deal of prayer. As soon as I could, I telephoned the hospital for help. He was not fit to move but more than anything else I wanted support. It is very frightening being alone with a friend and colleague who is desperately ill and knocking on the gates of heaven.

In no time I had the support of a senior nurse. Slowly Hamish's condition improved, but it was half an hour before I could measure a recordable blood pressure.

Despite all that had happened, Old Squarebottle steadfastly refused to give up his bees.

Nowadays my pleasure in working in general practice usually came from a less dramatic source. Sometimes, after a rather vague, discursive consultation with a familiar patient whose distress was not quantifiable by any medically recognised diagnosis, the patient would turn at the door and say: 'Thank you, Doctor, I can *talk* to you.' I never clearly understood what had happened, but I do know that I experienced the same warm glow of satisfaction that I used to get on revisiting a case of lobar pneumonia, so miraculously better after antibiotics that it was hard to believe that the patient had been so sick just the day before.

Just after my partner's encounter with his bees, I made a routine visit to the cottage hospital. Maantie, now back from the mainland with her leg in plaster, was making progress and there was a letter saying that Meg Murchison had a new hip, was recovering well from the pneumonia she had contracted while lying on the floor and that she too would soon be returning to my care at the cottage hospital.

To my surprise, old Mr Frazer was considerably better. He was warm and clean and had recovered consciousness but was still confused and could not speak. A severe stroke had left him with no movement on his left side. I was none too hopeful about much recovery, but at least he was not going to die as soon as I had predicted. Nobody had been to see him since his admission, though the staff said Mrs Frazer, his daughter-in-law, had phoned twice. His son, seemingly, could not care less about the old man.

Leaving the hospital, and pondering on man's ingratitude to man, I drove south towards Lutheran. Walking along the road towards the village I saw Galla leading the blind Jack Gillespie. I pulled up to have a crack with him.

'Not swimming today, Jack?' I asked.

'Oh, we're just coming back from the beach, aren't we, Galla?' he replied. 'And how is the laird today?'

'Actually, Jack, I'm a bit fed up. Sometimes I find the attitude of a few of my patients a bit tiresome. They seem to expect everything to be done for them, especially when it comes to looking after their elderly relatives. I sometimes wonder what ever happened to filial duty.'

'Aye, things have changed a lot. When I was a lad, one's main responsibility was to the old folks. But that was before the welfare state took over from the individual. Mind you, Doctor, I'm grateful to the welfare people, they bring me the talking book and help with my pension. I don't need anyone to look after me, thank God, except Galla here. Right now she's taking me to the post office for my messages.'

'I vaguely remember someone saying, "The more I see of men the better I like dogs"!'

Jack chuckled, 'Aye, that was Madame Roland. She was guillotined in the French Revolution. She was right about the dogs, for they wouldnae hae cut her heid aff!'

'Gosh, Jack, how *do* you know all these things?'

'You know, doctor, being blind has compensations. I can read braille very easily and I spend a huge amount of my time with my books. The library people are very good at getting me almost anything I want. Galla always gets excited when I put the talking books on. I believe she thinks they just want to talk to her, don't you, girl?'

The labrador gazed up at her master and wagged her tail. I noticed she was greying at the muzzle. Galla was aging, and I wondered what would happen when her life came to an end. Jack would be bereft.

Wishing him good-day, I continued on my round thinking about dogs. There were many labradors in the island; several were kept as working gundogs, or like Galla had special duties; many were just pets. I never ceased to be surprised at the innumerable sheepdogs whose incredible skills at rounding flocks into enclosures were to be seen most days. Locally the farmers called this 'dogging their yows into a fank'. Then there were border, aberdeen and fox terriers and a few bizarre little creatures like papillon, pugs and pekingese kept by people who wanted canine company without too much obligation. But of all the breeds in the island the strangest creature was Cuhlan, the great, austerely mystical creature that seemed to have embodied some of the character of Maggie McPhee, the old *cailleach* who had bred him.

Dogs are important to many a lonely man or woman; in the isolated crofts of the island they provided company for old people. I thought of Hamish; when I first arrived he had two labradors; the black one was called Florin and the yellow one, who had been almost white as a pup, was Siller. For some reason he named his dogs after currency. Florin had died, full of years and wisdom, three years after I joined Old Squarebottle's practice. Siller was still active and constant company for my partner on his rounds. As Hamish sat in front of the fire in the evening, puffing his pipe with a glass of whisky beside him, Siller would leap up without invitation and sit bolt upright on his knee with one paw resting on his shoulder. From there she would look at anyone else in the room as if saying, 'Mine.'

This strange, lonely man had such a love affair with his elderly labrador that I dreaded bereavement when, as was inevitable, it came. The trouble about man's relationship with his best friend is the disparity in their lifespans. I trembled to think of what would happen to their owners when Galla and Siller died.

When Maantie had returned to the island she was all smiles. Her leg was in plaster after the operation to fix the fibula with a steel plate. She was in no pain, and clearly enjoyed being nursed and pampered. Though the staff could not communicate with her by word of mouth, she had a seraphic smile with which she thanked all around her. I took advantage of her being in bed to undertake a formal examination. Her head was huge with a bulging forehead that had the effect of rotating her orbits downwards so that she had to lift her head in order to look one in the eye. But her eyes, like those of the seals she loved, were dark, moist and knowing. What they knew there was no telling. Apart from the big head, she was a normal young woman, and had a not unattractive virginal body. Physical examination, from the head down, showed no abnormality apart from the palpable catheter, which ran subcutaneously down through her neck, under her right breast and disappeared into her abdomen. I wished I knew more about her medical history, but it seemed that all her documentation had been lost.

Suddenly, as I was examining her, Maantie caught my hand and pressed it to her heart, and her face lit up with her smile. I was not entirely sure if this was in thanks or out of pleasure at a man handling her body. I hoped it was the former but began to see why Pat Tomlinson had been so anxious about Maantie.

She made an attempt at speech. 'Maaa...ntie,' she said and her right hand came up and touched her nose. 'Maaa...ntie nose,' she mouthed. With her left hand she squeezed my hand which she still held over her heart.

I smiled, withdrew my hand and left to write my examination notes.

Sitting in the waiting room, Nutty Jakes was holding a huge bouquet of thrift, sea campion, primroses and rather wilting bluebells. He also had a card with a picture of some seals.

Schizophrenic or no, he certainly knew what Maantie would like.

I was delighted to welcome old Meg Murchison back from the District Hospital, where she had been in the same ward as Maantie, to my care at the Cottage Hospital. The two had formed quite a friendship, though Meg like everyone else found it difficult to understand the younger woman. They seemed to enjoy doing their physiotherapy together and always seemed to be laughing. On my way back from the hospital I waved to Stanley Johnson, who was driving into Port Chalmers. He had rather slipped from my mind but I had heard from Erchie that he had installed himself in Tom Bacadh. It was good to know the castle was tenanted again; the estate needed the rent.

We kept Maantie in hospital for a month after Pat took her charges back to the home in Dumfriesshire. I had agreed that we should wait until Maantie was walking well with a stick and progressing with her exercises before she went home. She became the star patient of the cottage hospital, everyone spoiled her, as it was easy to do—she was as appreciative as a pet dog. Nobody could understand the noises and gestures she made, except for her repetition of her name, which she always pronounced 'Maantie'. There were two exceptions: Charlie Kerr and Nutty Jakes. The former visited her often (and one day honoured his promise to show me the pair of breeding roseate terns near where Maantie had her fall). Charlie would sit by her bed and sing in the same keening whine which Maantie had used herself with the seals. She became excited when he did this and soon they were singing a duet together.

After one of his visits he said to me, 'She says she's as seily here than she ever kens.' For once I could understand: 'seily' was a word I had heard Erchie use and I knew it meant happy.

The other person who understood her was Nutty Jakes. He came every day, sometimes more than once. He spent his time talking softly to her, always using his hands to amplify what he said. She was sitting up in an armchair with her foot raised and her head back so that it was easy for her to maintain eye contact and she watched his mouth intently and copied his hand movements.

One day he saw me in the hospital corridor.

'Mandy's much better,' he said. 'I am beginning to understand her. She says the accident was not my fault and she wants to see the seals again. Can I take her?'

I remembered Pat Tomlinson's concern and I could see that the friendship between Nutty Jakes and Maantie was developing fast, perhaps too fast.

'I don't see why not, but I think you should take one of the nursing staff along. We don't want any more accidents...'

'And Charlie?' asked Jakes. 'She wants her cousin Charlie there too.'

I said I'd think about it when the ankle was better. When I told Morag Finlayson, one of the nurses, she offered to take them in her car—she would be fascinated to see Maantie with the seals. So it was arranged.

Later when Morag Finlayson brought a very happy Maantie back she was herself bubbling with excitement and bursting to tell everyone about the excursion.

'Maantie is fantastic,' she began. 'There is an awful lot more going on in that big head o' hers than anyone would ever guess. And Charlie Kerr is something o' a wizard too. We went down to the place where they all camped, way down beyond Pitchroich. Then Charlie told Jakes an' me to keep well behind and then he followed Maantie over the rockfall towards where the seals were lying in the sun. Then Maantie started singing, sometimes a low sustained note, like you hear from a cello, sometimes a higher-pitched whine. The seals turned to look at where the sound was coming from. Charlie kept out o' their sight and Jakes an' me, we were couried doon among the rocks where we could watch. Then Maantie stood up where the seals could see her and went on singing. One by one the seals slid off their rocks and swam to only a few feet from where she stood on a big rock. Then Charlie started singing too and he came to stand with Maantie, and the seals were all up-ended in the water watching them. Then Charlie pulled some mackerel from his bag and fed them one by one, an' he singing all the time.'

Morag's eye glistened: even as an islander and quite used to wild creatures, she was amazed to see them so fearless of humans. 'But it didna last; Jakes was so excited he moved and all the creatures disappeared into the sea, and we never saw them again. But I learnt a new respect for Maantie this afternoon. She adores Charlie and they seem to understand each other quite well. Jakes says he's beginning to pick up some o' the things she wants to tell us. He says when she says her name and touches her nose it means "Maantie knows".'

CHAPTER 8

A Misplaced Fly

By late summer there was obviously going to be no further improvement in old Frazer. Still unable to speak, he could get around with a walking aid. He was fully continent and could get to the lavatory by himself. He had had no visit from his son, so I rang the farm to tell them we were sending the old man home. I spoke to Mrs Frazer, who listened and said she'd tell her husband. An hour later Ali Frazer himself rang up and said they could not have the old man home. By that time I had left the hospital and the message was relayed to me later at the surgery.

When I eventually managed to raise Frazer at the farm he was adamant that his father could not return home. We were at an impasse and there was nothing I could do but agree to keep the old man at the cottage hospital for a bit longer. I commented that it was surprising that he had had no visitors during his stay in hospital.

'That's as may be,' was Frazer's reply. 'But it's been gey busy on the farm.' He rang off leaving me with a feeling of frustration. We needed the bed at the cottage hospital and I was seething at Frazer's seeming disregard for his father.

A few days later we held a case conference at the hospital and Flora Jamieson, the island's new social worker, was despatched to talk to young Frazer. When she came back, she too was livid with the man. She had spent an hour haranguing Frazer who had eventually consented to have his father back to the farm. However he had added darkly, 'But I won't be held responsible for what may happen.' So the poor old man returned to the farm and I, for my sins, promised to call on him routinely to see that he was getting on all right.

The next major problem began simply enough. A Mr Porteus, who was a guest at the Port Chalmers Hotel, rang one evening to ask if it was possible to have a day on Loch Bradan with the hope of a salmon or, better still, some good sea trout. I explained the usual terms and said I thought I could arrange a ghillie for him.

Erchie was in the office and he checked his diary. 'Aye, I'm free all day tomorrow, not the next day—I've promised that to Mr Johnson frae Tom Bacadh—but the day after I could manage. I could gie him a day, either o' those. What sort o' a man is he, d'ye ken?'

'He sounded pleasant enough on the phone, a very English accent but he didn't say much about himself.'

'Mebbe if I return his call, I could sus him oot a bit. I like to learn something aboot a body I'm gaunnae spend a day on the loch wi'.'

'OK, Erchie.' He rang the hotel and asked for Mr Porteus. Soon I could hear the man's deep voice on the line.

'Is that Mr Porteus?' asked Erchie. 'This is Erchie Thompson here, Dr Chalmers' factor frae the castle. I believe ye were asking aboot a day on Loch Bradan?'

There was a pause while Erchie listened. 'There's a vacancy tomorrow or in a couple o' days' time. Would either o' those suit ye?'

Again there was a pause while the voice from the other end spoke. I saw Erchie smile and nod.

'Och, if its sea troot ye're wantin' ye should be in luck, for they're running well the noo. I had a gentleman there at the back o' last week and he had six, an' the best was nearly five pounds. Have ye fished for them much afore?'

Erchie listened again 'That's guid... and at this time o' year I think I can guarantee a good day. They tend to take smallish flies, mallard and claret's always guid and so's a teal, blue and silver. There are guid grilse as well, an' in Loch Bradan they'll often take the same fly... So I'll see ye the morn's morn, at the back o' nine; best come up to the castle and I'll run ye over to the loch in the Land Rover. Mind, wi' the weather as it is, it'll be chilly on the loch, so wrap up well.'

After explaining about the usual estate charges, Erchie rang off and turned to me: 'Terribly English, dontcher know,' he mimicked. 'But for a' that he sounds a decent sort o' chap. Seems quite an experienced fisherman, so I shouldn't have too boring a day.'

I went back to my office chores smiling at Erchie. Normally the most tolerant of mortals, when ghillying he became an arch snob. This seems to run in the blood of many a ghillie. They have to put up with all sorts of mankind on the moor or loch. Some clients consider themselves very important people; a few of them really are. Some are experienced with rod or gun, some so new to the game as to be positively dangerous. Erchie distrusted unknown clients, and with good reason. A few seasons back he had taken a Frenchman out shooting pheasants. The man was a novice and seeing something move in the bracken he fired, killing Erchie's spaniel. It was just as well I was there, for I may have prevented a homicide, as my big factor went for my guest with his fists. I told the Frenchman to leave, as I could not vouch for his safety.

The next morning it was clear that Erchie and Porteus would hit it off. When Erchie brought him over to me as I was leaving for my morning surgery, I saw a cheerful looking man in his late fifties, sensibly clad in tweeds with an old Barbour jacket as protection against forecast showers. Unlike myself he wore a tie, and I smiled because I knew Erchie considered a tie to be the mark of a gentleman. Though he was as loyal to me as ever a Highlander was to his Laird, he despaired of my ungentlemanly tielessness when fishing.

Porteus came over to me to shake my hand, asking, 'Dr Chalmers? They tell me you are a really expert fisherman.'

'I doubt if that is true, but almost all I do know I've learnt from my factor. If anyone can fill your creel today, it'll be Erchie Thomson. But have you got enough warm clothes? The wind can be pretty cold out on the loch.'

'I think so, I meant to bring a scarf, but I must have left it behind.'

'No problem, we've got all sorts of gear here if you don't mind borrowing.' I went into the gunroom and inspected the rack of spare warm clothing. Most of the scarves were old woolly things; amongst them was a light but warm garment of fancy texture. I had worn it myself when fishing on cold days and knew it was much better than the heavier woollen scarves.

'Try this, it's rather a dramatic colour, but it's very warm. I believe someone gave it to my wife, but she didn't like it. One of our guests won't go on the loch without it ... says it always brings him luck!'

Porteus laughed and said 'With Erchie and the lucky neckwear I should do well. I'm really looking forward to this. I haven't had a day after sea trout since I fished Loch Coruisk in Skye with a lawyer friend of mine who had a lodge up there. He used to catch enormous fish by dapping? Do you do that here?'

'I don't dap myself but I know there are one or two folk who enjoy that style of fishing. What do think, Erchie?'

'Oh aye, a few fush are taken on the dap right eneuch. I prefer a small wet fly fairly near the top myself. The fush'll sometimes take that wi' a great bang. But I'll put a dapping rod wi' a floss line in the boat an' we can gie it a try.'

So, dressed in his glamorous scarf and Barbour jacket, Porteus clambered into the Land Rover and that was the last I saw of him until the evening.

I was busy that day with a morning surgery, rounds at the cottage hospital, and then visiting folk way down to Lutheran and right on to the tiny hamlet above Ranneach Bay. There I had to call in at a fisherman's little but-and-ben by the harbour, where a wee boy had a fever. It did not take long to find the cause, as Geordie Farquharson's tonsils were reddened and oozing pus. I was able to reassure his mother, Morag Farquharson, that penicillin would soon put the lad right. She had the kettle boiling and soon I was sipping scalding tea and having scones thrust on my plate. This was one of the joys of visiting— I loved the easy relationship I had with the islanders, particularly when I visited them at home. Morag, a bold-featured redhead, told me that her husband Dugald had brought in a good catch of haddock the evening before. Would I like some to take home?

'Yes, indeed I would,' I replied. 'My wife and I are very fond of fresh haddies, Where did he take them?'

'Och he likes fishing just south o' the tip o' Mulcaire. He's there the noo; ye can see his boat from the windae.'

The young mother pointed across the calm expanse of Ranneach Bay where I could just make out a small fishing boat. 'He likes it there and has marks for a spot where he gets good haddies, but I wish he wouldnae fish near Mulcaire. Its an unlucky island, they say it's haunted and it's been out o' bounds since the war.'

'Yes, I have heard something about that. Alex Farquharson, from Lutheran—he must be a relation of your husband's—anyway, he told me about it. When I took over the estate, I found that Mulcaire had been requisitioned by the War Department—way back in the 1940s—so it's not my property.'

'Aye, Alex is a great-uncle o' wee Geordie's. He comes ower here sometimes in that boat o' his wi' the queer name; he likes a good crack. Och, I don't think there is anything to worry aboot wi' Mulcaire now; but for all that none o' the locals will go there. It's a' wired off and there are lots o' keep-oot notices. That doesn't stop some folks; there was a big sailing yacht in there only last week wi' a lot o' visitors frae Port Chalmers.'

'Well, Morag, thank you for tea, but I must get along. I am sure Geordie will soon settle. If he complains of pain, give him a soluble aspirin, get him to gargle it and then swallow it. He should be fine but if he's still running a fever in the morning, give me a ring. When your husband can take time away from his boat, get him to run Geordie over to the surgery. He's had rather a lot of tonsillitis, maybe we ought to think about them coming out.'

'He'll not like that!'

I pulled a face but said, 'He's a bright lad, it doesn't do for him to be missing school, but we'll not decide in a hurry.'

As I pottered off back towards Lutheran, my mind went back to what Alex Farquharson had told me about Mulcaire. If people were visiting the island I thought I might go over there myself one day. The mystery still intrigued me and, anyway, it used to belong to the estate.

I noticed Hamish's car parked outside a croft near Ardranneach Point, where I knew he had a young patient called Campbell Patterson, who had recently had a leg amputated because of a malignant melanoma under his big toenail. Hamish was visiting him frequently, checking the healing of the stump and giving support to both Campbell and Isobel Patterson. The couple had a wee boy, and there was much fear for their future. They needed a lot of support.

From the Patterson croft I took a track down on the left of the road from where I could see across the skerries off Ardranneach, the point that lay between the islands of Tuilleag and Sgarbh an Sgumain just north of Mulcaire, the island that Morag had spoken about. I parked the car and walked to the huge standing stone which towered beside an ancient burial chamber on a small cliff beside the shore. The superb view extended over the rocky coastlines of Sgarbh an Sgumain and way south-westwards out to the Atlantic.

It was one of my favourite spots, especially of a summer evening where I could watch the sunset over the ocean. Today the sea was so mirror calm that I could see fish breaking the surface, like rising trout, a hundred yards from shore. In the reddening, crepuscular light, the low-lying islands of Assilag, Solan, Tuilleag and Mulcaire showed like purple-backed whales above the darkening Hebridean Sea. The westering sun of early evening shone over the olive, sage and ochre of the moorland grasses and sedges and the hills were splashed with the purple paint of the heather.

I lowered myself into the burial chamber and, as I stooped to examine its stonework, a curlew flew over me uttering its eerie, evocative cry. A cold shiver ran down my back as I straightened up to look at the bird, and an intense feeling of *déjà vu* linked me with the man who built the burial chamber and who must have heard that self-same call when, millennia before, a curlew flew over his bent back.

Climbing out of the chamber, I looked further west to the island of Mulcaire. It was a long stretch of low land two miles or so long by only about 500 yards at its greatest width. It lay like a beached cetacean nearly three miles off the coast, south of the larger and still inhabited island of Tuilleag. Hoping to see white-tailed sea eagles, I slipped my binoculars round my neck as I walked towards the cliffs. I could see Dugald Farquharson's boat across the still waters of the bay. He was working along the southern end of Mulcaire. There was a mass of gulls round the boat so I guessed he was cleaning his catch before going home to see how wee Geordie was.

After searching the sky fruitlessly for eagles I found myself scanning Mulcaire and wondering about the rumours I had heard about mysterious wartime experiments. I still had only a hazy concept of what had happened on that night about a quarter century before when the plane crashed, killing not only all on board but the two inhabitants of the island, as well as many seals. From my recent helicopter flight over Mulcaire I knew that the farmhouse was reasonably intact—the plane had not smashed into it. The crash had been late at night when presumably the crofter and his wife would have been asleep in bed. But if it was not the impact of the crash that killed Mr and Mrs McTavish, then what had? And what would cause the death of the seals? I began to feel that, proscription or no, sooner or later I should have to explore Mulcaire for myself.

It was getting towards evening and there was not a breath of wind; yet here, where tranquillity and the memory of past violence coexisted, I felt a premonition of terror yet to come, world unrest culminating in another, still more terrible war. Recently there had been more trouble in the Middle East when Israeli aircraft shot down Syrian planes. I shuddered for my sons and thanked God I lived in Laigersay. Here at any rate we should be safe from the nuclear holocaust that loomed. Then I remembered that even here, less than a hundred miles from the Polaris submarines in Holy Loch, we were less safe than the peaceful Hebridean sea in front of me suggested. Even now, there could be fissile material down deep below the surface, where the haddies lay.

There were no eagles and as the sun began to drop it grew chilly. I shook off morbid thoughts and got back in the car to drive home through the early autumn gloaming. At the castle Erchie and his client were unloading their gear by the castle gunroom.

'Have you had a good day?' I queried as I got out of the car beside them.

Porteus turned to me with a wide grin. 'Great,' he said, 'just great! And Erchie has been a wonderful ghillie and most entertaining company. And just see what we have here—and after returning most of them.'

Porteus stood back, to reveal several large fish in a basket in the back of the Land Rover. 'I had the best sea trout fishing I have ever had—better even than that day on Coruisk. The best fish must be six pounds if it's an ounce. This one is not quite so big, but it was incredibly exciting. I tried a dapped fluffy fly that Erchie suggested and it erupted from the depths like a mini-Polaris and seized the fly in the air. It was a real battle to net that one, I can tell you. Then there were several grilse. Erchie said with a catch like that it was the done thing to give you the best salmon so here it is, with my thanks for the best day's fishing of my life.'

Porteus' simile brought back a twinge of anxiety; by referring to Polaris, he had echoed my thoughts at Ranneach Bay. But the man was as pleased as if he were a boy and this his first day's fishing. Enjoying his enthusiasm, I glanced at Erchie who also looked pleased.

'He's no sae bad at the fushin',' said Erchie, in what, from him, was praise indeed, 'But he's gey haphazard wi' his cast.'

Porteus roared with laughter, showing that ghillie and client had enough respect for each other to exchange banter. 'Yes, that's fair comment, Erchie.' Then turning to me he said: 'I landed a fly in my neck. Erchie had to stop being ghillie and take on a surgical role while he got it out, which he did very efficiently. I was very worried I can tell you: it was the teal, blue and silver that had taken most of the fish. I thought he'd ruin it but it took several more fish afterwards.'

'You're not hurt?' I asked with some anxiety, though I knew of Erchie's expertise at extracting guests' flies from either themselves or from his own skin. Once a disgruntled and fishless nincompoop had threatened to sue, but his protest subsided as Erchie muttered, 'Och, I doot ye wadnae want everyone to know how useless a fisherman ye are.'

'Come in and take a dram,' I said, 'You both deserve it after that catch.'

Porteous was delighted and was soon nursing a generous measure of Old Scapa. 'This has been a remarkable holiday,' he told me. 'You see, I have been under your profession a bit lately and I was determined to have a good time here. I have major surgery waiting for me at home, so I wanted to fit in as much as possible.'

Duty bound, I asked about the surgery. 'They tell me my circulation is dodgy. I had a heart attack last year, and they say that without surgery I am a candidate for another.'

I made professional noises of sympathy, which he shrugged away. 'Don't worry. I have had a great life and intend to go on having it as long as possible. That's why I have been living it to the full up here. Last week I had three days in an ocean-going yacht exploring the islands off the south of Laigersay. Absolutely beautiful.'

I pricked up my ears. 'You didn't by any chance go to Mulcaire?'

'Yes, funny you should ask, we landed there for lunch, but one or two local crewmen were upset that we did so. There seems to be some superstition about the place; it looked as though nobody had been there for years; we had quite a struggle with a mass of rusty barbed wire.'

We chatted for a few more minutes and then Porteus got up, protesting that he had to get back to the hotel for a bath before dinner. He shook Erchie warmly by the hand and I saw some notes slip into the ghillie's willing paw. Then he turned and shook my hand. 'I cannot tell you what a pleasure it has been to meet you and to get to know your island.'

At the door he paused. 'Thanks again, Erchie, you have given me a day I'll never forget.' With that he pulled a rueful face and rubbed his neck. 'Oh,' he said, 'I nearly forgot to give you the scarf back. I was glad of it on the loch.'

When he was gone I returned the scarf to its peg in the gunroom. Erchie cleared his throat: 'Och I dinna mind how often ye have the likes o' him. A proper gentleman and a great fisher; it was a pleasure to be wi' that yin.'

CHAPTER 9

Misdiagnosis

The following day I was free from the practice and Fiona had a guided tour with a party of naturalists. When the boys came home from school I fulfilled my promise of taking them on our annual expedition to collect rowan berries. Rowan jelly is a delicious accompaniment to venison and other game and I am very fond of its combination of acid, bitter and sweet flavours. There was a particularly good clump of trees just inland from the estuary of the Allt Feadag burn. The twins liked me to take them there because there were always some small sea trout, or finnock as they were called locally, at the mouth of the burn. These small fish would sometimes take a worm mounted on the three-hooked Stewart tackle which made things a bit easier for the twins. The fishing was especially good on the incoming tide when there was a bit of a spate on. The boys were not up to casting a fly yet, but could manage to catch fish of up to half or three-quarters of a pound on a worm. Even if they did not catch fish, I knew this would keep them busy for the hour or so that I needed to fill my basket with rowans.

Having set them up and baited the hooks by carefully threading on a worm to hide the irons, I showed them the sort of places where the fish might be lying, just behind a rock or under an alder where the current had undercut the bank. I assured them that I would be within hailing distance and left them to it.

That year the berries were unusually prolific. I had just filled my basket when shouts from the river made me run back to the twins, expecting to find one or other fallen in. However a different picture met my eye. Jamie, always the better fisherman, was struggling with a fiercely bent rod. This was no half-pounder, and he was tremendously excited. I got beside him and told him to keep calm and hold his rod tip well up to absorb most of the strain of the fighting fish. The trout made a dash for the sea and Jamie's little reel sang out the noise that gladdens every fisherman's heart.

'Let him run, Jamie, and keep your rod tip up,' I shouted, but the boy seemed to know instinctively what to do and the fish was still on. That run exhausted it, and it was soon lying on its side. Unfortunately, not expecting anything but small fish, I had not brought a landing net.

'You'll have to beach him, Jamie. Wait while I have a look round.' A wee bit upstream I spotted a shingle beach that might do.

'Listen, Jamie,' I said, 'you'll have to walk him up till you get to that shingly bit. Go slowly and try to keep an even tension on him.'

The boy never took his eyes off the fish and slowly worked his way upstream to the exposed shingle.

'That's great … now gradually pull the fish on to the shingle but keep him on the surface as you work him in.' Again Jamie seemed to know just how to manage and in a trice I was on the fish with a finger in its gills. The fine two-pound sea trout was ours. Jamie was ecstatic and I tried my hardest to reassure Hamie that there were as good fish in the burn as ever came out of it. Five minutes later, to my considerable relief, it was Hamie's rod that curved to a fighting fish. Though it was nothing like as good as Jamie's, it satisfied honour and all three of us carried trophies home.

Fiona and I spent an hour taking the twigs and leaves from my basket of berries. Then she stewed the fruit and strained it through a muslin bag, before adding sugar and a little apple to help it set. We had enough delicious rowan jelly to last until next year's rowan season.

I saw Adrian Porteus sooner than either of us expected, for he came to the surgery two days later.

'I wonder if you'd mind looking at my neck. I think the fly I managed to lodge there the other day has introduced some infection. I hardly had any sleep last night. I was sweating a lot and it's very itchy.'

The small puncture wound was indurated and red, and there was a little swelling below it.

'Hmm,' I said shaking down the thermometer, which was registering 99° Fahrenheit. 'It does look a little infected. I think you may have a staphylococcus up to no good in there. I'll put you on some penicillin.'

'Unfortunately I'm allergic to penicillin—and I'm not very keen on antibiotics. I've had rather a lot recently and I'm scared of getting any more allergies in view of the surgery I told you about. If it's all the same to you I think I'd rather let it settle by itself, but can you give me something to help me sleep? I'm due to travel south in three days' time.'

Although I wrote a prescription, I was a bit unhappy about it. The lesion on his neck was very small, but he did not seem to be the sort of man to fuss, and I was surprised at the slight fever he was running.

'Very well,' I said, signing the script. 'Let's see what it looks like tomorrow; if it's no better then I think you ought to go on to antibiotics.'

In his usual courteous way the man thanked me and said he'd look in the next day. I rang for the next patient and forgot about the pleasant fisherman.

When Porteus came the next day I did not like the look of him at all. Hamish was away on one of his mysterious jaunts to the mainland. He seemed to have an unhappy knack of being away when I really needed his experience and wisdom. Looking anxious, Porteus was pale and sweating and held his neck stiffly as though the slightest movement was uncomfortable. He had a higher fever and a fast thready pulse. When I looked at his neck I saw that the tiny wound where the fly had struck him was swollen and had darkened in colour. Below the wound a red track of swollen tissue ran downwards over his collar bone to produce an inflamed flare on the upper part of his chest.

'Is it very painful?' I asked

'It's sore and itchy rather than painful, but I feel *dreadfully* ill,' he said through gritted teeth. 'I'd never have thought so small an injury could cause such dreadful malaise. I must have run quite a temperature in the night. I was shivering so violently I was shaking with it and then I was sweating like a pig. Perhaps it's the flu.'

By now I was regretting allowing him to persuade me not to start him on antibiotics the day before, for the man was obviously quite ill. Whatever caused this illness, it had come on very rapidly. Perhaps the neck wound was a bit of a red herring. I thought back over what he had told me the night before. He had had cardiac problems: it was just possible that infection introduced through the wound had reached previous damage inside his heart, a potentially serious condition known as subacute bacterial endocarditis. I went over him very carefully but found nothing abnormal.

'I tell you what we'll do,' I said. 'You've obviously got a nasty infection in there and I don't like the way it's spreading down on to your chest. That's cellulitis, or possibly erysipelas. Neither is very serious and they are quite treatable, but we need to get you into the cottage hospital because I want to get a bacteriological diagnosis and then have you on antibiotics as soon as we can.'

Porteus spoke softly, as though raising his voice caused him pain. 'OK,' he whispered, 'but remember I am due to go south the day after tomorrow.'

Warning him that we would have to see about that, I phoned the ward to arrange his admission and told them to start the patient on a large dose of tetracycline. I took samples of blood and swabs from the side of the skin lesion where some small vesicles had appeared. I felt fairly confident that I should be able to get the answer I was looking for by examining a stained slide from the swabs. Thinking of endocarditis I also asked for a blood culture. Then I phoned the airport and asked them to hold the morning flight to the mainland until the specimens could be got to them. Alison, the practice nurse, drove the package for the path lab over to the airstrip at Camus Coilleag.

A friend from the hotel had brought Porteus to the surgery. I had a quick word with him, asking him to collect anything from the hotel that the patient might need. I went into the little lab in the surgery and on a glass slide started making what is known as a Gram stain of a smear from the swabs. This technique had been a problem to me in the bacteriological labs of my student days. Gram stain helps to differentiate various species of bacteria by sorting them into those that take up either a blue or red dye. Being severely colour blind, I had had to modify the staining technique when I was a student. Instead of red dye I found that a stain called Bismarck Brown turned Gram-negative organisms yellow while the Gram-positive bacteria were a contrasting blue. Between patients I stained the slide with blue, washed it with alcohol and counterstained it with Bismark Brown.

At the first gap between patients I got the microscope out of its cupboard and focussed down on to the slide I had prepared. I expected to see a mass of Gram-positive bacteria, either grape-like clusters of staphylococci or chains of slightly smaller streptococci. To my surprise there seemed to be no bacteria present at all.

As soon as surgery was over I went through to the cottage hospital ward. Porteus was looking a bit better and decidedly more cheerful and he said he was glad to be in hospital. 'The Port Chalmers hotel is nice enough, but it's not a good place to be ill in,' he commented.

His brighter spirits did nothing to reassure me; I could see that the man was seriously but mysteriously ill. I examined him again carefully. The lesion on his neck was if anything slightly bigger and more angry looking. The swelling and redness had spread further across his chest and he said he felt a slight constriction in his throat as if swallowing was difficult. I paid special attention to his cardio-vascular system; his blood pressure was slightly raised but otherwise there were no physical signs. There seemed to be no evidence of cardiac involvement. I reassured Porteus with greater confidence than I felt and went to write up his case notes.

Glancing at my watch I guessed there might be some news from the mainland and I phoned the laboratory.

'Hello, Rob, how are you?' I heard a friendly voice say when I gave my name. Dr Innes Ross, the bacteriologist, was an old friend who sometimes came over to Laigersay for a day's hill-walking and he liked a chat. With some difficulty I steered him away from mountains to bacteriology.

'Oh yes, we got your swabs and things, but it's too early to say anything. We've set up the blood culture and plated the swabs. The case description you sent with your specimens sounds like an acute staphylococcal or streptococcal infection.'

'That's what I thought. I did a Gram stain in the surgery but I couldn't see any cocci.'

'Well we'll repeat that here and see if we can find anything for you that you may have missed.'

I felt a little frisson of anger. Hospital doctors have a way of implying that we general practitioners are somehow incompetent. Brushing this aside I asked, 'Was there anything in the blood count? You may have been able to do that by now.'

'Don't know, I'll put you through to haematology.'

There was a click and a technician answered.

'What's the patient's name?'

'Porteus, Adrian Porteus.'

'Hold on, I'll have a look.' There was another pause, then: 'Looks pretty normal—there's perhaps a slight rise in the white blood-cell count, but it's only just above the upper limit of normal; otherwise nothing, I'm afraid.'

Here was another surprise. Given the obvious infection and constitutional disturbance, I had expected that Porteus' white blood cells, the body's first defence against infection, would have responded with increasing numbers. I was racking my brain trying to think of a condition that would produce such a profound systemic upset, but with no obvious bacterial presence and little, if any, increase in white count. As I stared out at the sea through the little window of the ward sister's office, a nurse erupted into the room.

'You'd best come, Doctor, he's taken a nasty turn.'

I jumped up and followed her into the ward. Porteus was pale, gasping, drenched in sweat, and clutching his chest as though in agony. I checked his blood pressure and found I could not record it. Remembering his previous history I suspected a catastrophic coronary thrombosis.

'Get some morphine,' I ordered, but, as I spoke, the man died.

I stared at the dead man in disbelief. I have seen countless people die, but have never got over the extraordinary feeling, in the presence of sudden death, of something leaving. I remembered the custom, widespread in Scotland, of opening a window to allow the dead person's spirit to escape. As if echoing my thoughts the nurse went to the window and opened it, crossed herself and said, 'God be wi ye!'

Then the feeling of awe left me, to be replaced by a feeling of rage—and impotence. Here was another patient I had let down as a result of misdiagnosis. Miserably I turned back to the office and reached for the drawer which held the book of death certificates.

It is always bad when a patient dies as suddenly as that. Here was a man who only about sixty hours before had been laughing and joking over a dram. Though I had known him for so short a time I had come to like him and now, abruptly, he was dead. I could not help recalling his wish to fit in as much as possible before the coming ordeal of cardiac surgery. Reflection on the fragility of life was compounded by doubt about the cause of the illness. The end was typical of a major overwhelming myocardial infarction. I supposed that might have been precipitated by the stress of his infection and the obvious anxiety it caused him. But there were still a number of unanswered questions in my mind. I wrote out the death certificate, giving the cause of death as Myocardial Infarction secondary to acute cellulitis of the neck for, at the time, that seemed the most likely diagnosis.

It was three days before I changed my mind. Innes Ross rang from the path lab.

'You know your man Porteus, how is he?' he asked.

'Dead. He had a massive MI.'

'Did he, by Jove! Well, I've got news for you. The blood culture has turned up *Bacillus anthracis*. Your patient had anthrax.'

'Good God, I wonder if that was what killed him.'

'Could be, tell me what happened.'

I described the events leading to Adrian Porteus' death. Innes Ross listened attentively.

'Yes,' he said, 'it fits. Anthrax bacilli are often hard to find, they tend to lie deep in the lesion. When you took your swabs, which incidentally we also found negative for anything but normal skin bacteria, you probably didn't probe deep enough into the lesion. You said the wound was dark. Anthrax typically produces a black malignant pustule—the name anthrax comes from the Greek for coal. The characteristic of fulminating fatal cases is that the patient finally suffers a form of overwhelming toxicity, which can look just like cardiogenic shock. The early toxaemia causes fever and intense malaise. I suspect that was indeed what killed him and not a heart attack at all.'

'I never even thought about anthrax; it's so rare.'

'That's true. I've only seen it in the Middle East, never in Scotland, though I believe there were one or two human cases earlier in the century. I seem to remember hearing of a few animal cases; it might be worthwhile speaking to your local vet. The important thing now is to trace the source. We don't want an epidemic on our hands. You'd better get on to the public health folk. I'll have to put in a formal report to Barry McEwen, the medical officer of health. He'll want to get his medical detectives to work. One thing, you should try to keep this under wraps for the time being. The press could start a major panic, and we don't want that.'

'I agree, especially as I have a hunch,' I told my colleague. 'I'll make some enquiries before McEwen gets in touch with me.'

'Good man. Oh, and Rob—I know you must be feeling pretty bad about all this. Don't. You are a particularly good GP. There is absolutely nothing you could have done to save this chap's life.'

'Thanks,' I said, but his words were of little comfort as I considered the 'what ifs'. Perhaps if I had thought harder, remembered more from my reading or, most importantly, had insisted on broad spectrum antibiotics whatever Porteus had said, then he might still be alive.

CHAPTER 10

Medical Detection

Even after pouring out my soul to Fiona and being comforted by her loving reassurance, I still felt guilty and suffered a sleepless night. Sometimes it is difficult in the face of a medical disaster like that of Adrian Porteus, to remember the routine work of general practice and that among the thousands of patient contacts I probably did more good than harm. Just as it is easy to rejoice too much when one is successful so it is easy to be cast down and depressed by adverse cases. As an antidote I threw myself into trying to find where Adrian had contracted this unusual disease. If there was a source of infection it could obviously lead to more cases, and I did not want any more deaths on my conscience. First I read all I could find on anthrax. However, this disease, so well known since antiquity, took up little space in my textbooks. Most of my reading simply confirmed what the bacteriologist, Innes Ross, had told me over the phone.

One thing that Innes had suggested was to talk to my vet. Douglas White, the local veterinary surgeon, was a great friend with whom I had before discussed cases of diseases that could be transmitted to man from wild or domestic animals. I knew he would be helpful and keep matters confidential. I rang him and suggested a pint at the Charmer Inn, where he regularly stopped on his rounds for lunch.

Fortunately the inn was empty, and we could sit in the sun at the tables outside overlooking Cockle Bay, where I had gathered shellfish with Jennie Churches soon after coming to Laigersay. There Douglas and I could talk in private over a plate of crab sandwiches and a glass of the inn's special ale. I asked Douglas if he had any experience of anthrax. He looked surprised and thought for a moment.

'Little personally. I believe anthrax used to be common enough in veterinary practice in the early part of the century. I seem to remember that there were several hundred cases reported in Britain prior to the First World War, but it's very rare now. Outbreaks have been reported in several animal species after eating feedstuffs containing meat or bone meal from carcasses contaminated with anthrax spores. You get apparently fit animals dying within a few days, often without showing signs of illness, though sometimes there may be bloody discharges from the mouth and anus. Because of the risk of cross-infection, there are stringent rules concerning the disposal of dead beasts infected with anthrax.'

Douglas sipped his ale and went on: 'I was involved in a case in the Midlands once. It caused quite a stir at the time. A Herefordshire farmer found a dead cow in a field. He suspected that it had swallowed a foreign body and he felt in the beast's mouth. You know what farmers are like; later he used the same hand—*unwashed*—to cut bread for his family at lunch. The implications of this were alarming when we discovered that the cow had died of anthrax, and I phoned the family doctor. But as it happened the beast was incinerated where it lay, and there were no more cases. That doctor was very concerned for the family for several days, but in the end nothing happened!'

'Wasn't there some problem about an island in Wester Ross? Do you know anything about that?'

'Hmm. I am not really supposed to talk about that.' Douglas paused and then continued: 'Although the presence of anthrax spores on Gruinard is no longer secret, the details are still classified. So you mustn't repeat what I tell you. A friend who was at Porton Down during the war swore me to secrecy when he told me about that island. So please treat what I say as confidential.' He glanced at me and I nodded.

'In 1942 it was feared that the Germans might attack the UK with biological weapons. So experiments on sheep were started at Gruinard Island—that's halfway between Ullapool and Gairloch in Wester Ross. Sheep were taken to an open field, secured in wooden frames, and exposed to spores scattered by a bomb. The sheep started dying almost immediately. Three days later the disease had wiped out the entire flock.'

'Gosh, it sounds like pretty nasty stuff!'

'Well, it is, in aerosol form. That way it is inhaled and can be rapidly fatal. I suppose, with the way things are at the moment, there is probably some boffin somewhere in the world trying to perfect a way of wiping us all out with an aerosol-delivered suspension of anthrax spores.'

I shuddered, thinking of Fiona and the twins. 'They say something was going on here on the island of Mulcaire. Do you know anything about that?'

'No. I've heard the rumours of course, but I don't know what happened there. Whatever it was I shouldn't think that had anything to do with anthrax.'

'The reason I ask is that a patient of mine was on Mulcaire a few days before he died—of anthrax.'

'Hmm, no wonder you're so interested. I wondered why.' He paused, thinking deeply. 'It's interesting, but anthrax experiments on Mulcaire don't seem very likely. Why would they have had two sites for the same experiment? But it's certainly an odd coincidence. Have you ever been on Mulcaire?'

'No. I've never had any reason to go there ... but I think I do now.'

We finished our drinks and Douglas said he had to get on, leaving me with much to ponder on. He promised to phone if anything occurred to him, and agreed that the matter should if possible be kept from the press.

As he was leaving, I called after him. 'Douglas, do you happen to know if seals get anthrax?'

'Haven't the slightest idea. I suppose in theory they could get infected. If they did, I would expect a high fatality rate.' He waved and drove off.

My next visit was to Maggie McPhee. Maggie was renowned for seeing the future but this time I was more interested in her knowledge of the past. The old lady was now in her mid-nineties but during the war she would have been a sprightly young thing of sixty-odd.

She received me in her room in the Port Chalmers sheltered accommodation. After the usual greetings and enquiries after her rheumatism I came to the matter in hand.

'Tell me,' I began, 'do you remember anything about Mulcaire, way back in the war?'

'Och yes. They stopped us going there. There's great beaches on Mulcaire and we used to swim there. But round about 1943 they put it oot o' bounds to everyone.'

'Why was that?' I asked.

'I'm not sure I ever knew the answer to that. There was so much secrecy during the war what with "Careless talk costs lives" and "The walls have ears" and "Even radishes repeat". They made us believe there was a German spy behind every bush. It got even worse after Hess flew to Scotland in 1941. They put Mulcaire oot o' bounds, I dinna ken why. I jalouse it was something to do wi' secret trials o' a new weapon o' some sort, or it may have been due to experiments wi' a new sort o' mine. We didn't ask.'

For once Maggie had not been of much help, though her speculation about a new weapon did not exclude some sort of bacterial investigation. As I was about to leave she said: 'Ye might ask Archie. He was aye busy wi' his wee boat fishing in the bay there. Food was gey short then, we needed all the fush we could get to survive. He's just watching the box, but I expect he'll leave it for the laird.' She banged on the wall and her brother came in rather irritably.

'What are ye wantin the noo?' he demanded and then, seeing me, added 'Oh hello, Doctor. I didnae ken youse were here.'

'Archie,' said his sister, 'the laird wants to know about Mulcaire in the war. You were often over that way in your wee boat. D'ye ken why it was put oot o' bounds?'

Archie pondered searching his memory. 'It wasnae till—let me see—the back o' 1942 or it might hae been early '43. There was that aircraft crashed on Mulcaire.'

The old man sat down, scratching his head. 'I was a corporal in the Home Guard in them days. One o' my duties was to be on watch at Solan Light. I dinna ken why, perhaps the army thought Hitler might invade via Solan, but nothing ever happened, it was awfy boring. But once, I misremember just when it was, there was a huge storm that lasted about a week. I do remember that, for we ran out o' grub at the lighthouse, it was too rough to get supplies to us. One night in the middle o' the storm I was watching high up in the lighthouse when we heard an aircraft overhead. The light was still working even in the war and I thought the plane was lost and trying to fix its position from the light. The plane suddenly altered course and flew straight over to Mulcaire. There was a huge flash o' lightning an' the next thing I saw was a ball o' fire over by Mulcaire. I really didna ken what had happened but I phoned my sergeant in Port Chalmers, and that's all I ever knew aboot it. When my shift at Solan was over I speired aboot what had happened but by then everything was top secret an' nobody would say a thing.'

'Alex Farquharson told me something about officials dressed in what he called moon-suits coming and investigating. Did you hear anything about that?'

'Aye I mind something o' the sort, but as I say everything seemed to become very secret. I mind being up before the CO o' the Home Guard an' him speirin' what I knew and telling me to say naethin' to naebody.'

Despite further questions, Archie's memory seemed to have nothing further that could help solve my problem. All he could add was that the War Ministry took the island over and it became very secret, with some sort of experimental work. 'I didna ken what it was all aboot but I did hear some men died ower there. There were all sorts o' rumours aboot special mines an' a new kind o' secret weapon, some said it was germs, but nobody knew for sure. The place has had an evil reputation ever since and nobody goes there now. What way d'ye want to know?'

I was prepared to be quizzed about my curiosity and had an answer ready.

'Oh, it used to be part of my estate and as I have never been there I wanted to find out something about it.'

'I shouldnae bother if I were you. They say people get ill who go there. The place is best left alone.'

I thanked Archie and his sister and went on my way. A picture was forming of the isle of Mulcaire of thirty years before. After Archie's reference to 'germs' I was becoming more and more suspicious that Adrian Porteus might have picked up his anthrax in Mulcaire. My reading about *Bacillus anthracis* had told me that its spores could persist in soil for fifty or more years and I knew Adrian had been in Mulcaire a few days before he was taken ill.

I went back to the castle and tried to piece together the scant information I had gleaned. The plane that crashed must have been carrying something very important to Allied security. Alex's description of people in 'moon-suits' suggested some sort of biohazard, such as poison, or biological or even nuclear weaponry. I tried to remember what stage research on the atom bomb had reached by 1943 and decided that radioactivity was the least likely. The fact that the people living on the island, as well as the seals, died so quickly indicated that whatever the hazard was it was extremely dangerous. Then I recalled Douglas saying that at Gruinard the sheep started dying soon after the release of the aerosol of anthrax spores and that the disease wiped out the entire flock. My hunch was that the plane had been carrying an aerosol of anthrax spores.

This convinced me that I had to get to Mulcaire. I rang Alex Farquharson in Lutheran and asked him if he would take me to the island.

'What d'ye want wi' that place?' he queried, 'It's no a very safe place by all accounts.'

I parried his question as I had Archie McPhee's, and hinted at an ornithological reason for wanting to go there.

After some considerable prevarication Alex agreed to take me on condition we did not stay for long. 'It's chust not a safe place to be. I tell ye the isle is fair steeped in evil, but if go ye must ye'll be safest wi' me.'

So it was that the following morning I joined Alex by his mooring on Assilag. It was a cold day with little wind and bright sunshine as the 'Ornithologist' puttered its way across the bay. Alex was out of humour and I guessed he was unhappy at visiting this island clouded by so much myth and superstition.

We arrived at a beautiful beach in the strait between Tuilleag and the northern end of Mulcaire.

'Dinna be long, Doctor. I'll chust bide in the boat till ye're back.' With that the old fisherman filled his pipe and settled sulkily in the stern of the 'Ornithologist' where his back spoke eloquently of disapproval.

I waded ashore, negotiated a tangle of rusty barbed wire and ran up the beach feeling like a schoolboy breaking rules. Apart from ancient War Office notices saying GOVERNMENT PROPERTY KEEP OUT there was nothing outwardly sinister about the island; the beach led to a sandy dune covered in marram grass.

First I walked to the northern end of Mulcaire, where the old house stood near the edge of a small cliff. The door was firmly padlocked, but to my surprise the padlock looked fairly new. For a house that had been uninhabited for so long it was not in bad condition. Nearby was an old well. I began to have ideas about renovating the wreck if ever I could regain possession of Mulcaire. But there was no clue to the mystery here, so I turned to the central part of the island. I could see the shambles of a rotting Nissen hut away to my right and walked over to it. There was nothing here either. The corrugated iron of the curved roof was slowly degenerating back into the soil. I entered the old building, which must have served as a cookhouse, for there was a rusting iron range, over which a wooden shelf was crumbling with rot interspersed with patches of peeling paint. There were still two or three cup hooks screwed into its rotting edge. A series of marks caught my eye and I wondered if someone had been counting days till the end of his stay in the island—it had to be a man; surely no woman would tolerate living in such a primitive place, even in wartime. There was another graffito in fading pencil. Peering in the half-light I was able to make out the words. 'Only another week in this bloody awful place,' it read.

There was nothing else to see and I left the derelict hut. A stone's throw away was a concrete structure partly hidden by rank grass. It was rectangular, about twenty yards square. I guessed that it had been the base of another hut, possibly living quarters for the men working here in the 1940s. I scouted around the concrete and my foot found a hole, tripping me full-length in the grass. Cursing and rubbing my lower leg I picked myself up and found that I had barked my shin on a crude metal cross lying in the coarse grasses. I felt the absolute certainty that I had stumbled over a grave. The cross had no mark on it and, to judge by its pitted rustiness, it had been here a long time. Questions filled my head. Whose grave was it? Could it have dated from the war? Most cogently, how had its occupant met his end?

I sat down and examined my grazed shin and my arm, where ugly bruises were forming. I heard a sudden noise behind me and, on turning, was aware of a fleeting shadow.

'Hallo!' I called, but there was only the slight rustle of the breeze in the marram grass. Perhaps it was just the shadow of a gull. Speculation was brought to an end by an impatient blast from the horn of the 'Ornithologist'. Alex was growing restive, which, bearing in mind his normal attitude of 'tomorrow will do,' was surprising. I left the grave and limped back to the beach.

As soon as Alex saw me I could read relief on the old man's face. 'Losh, I was feart something had happened to ye. And why are ye limping?' he demanded.

Without waiting for an answer he hauled me into the boat and immediately pushed off with an oar, 'Och, I dinna like it here at a'. I canna think why ye wanted to come to this godless place at a', at a'.'

It was clear that I was in the old man's bad books, so I shrugged, and sat nursing my hurts and thinking. I was puzzled by what I had found. If I was right and I had found a grave, why had a man been buried on Mulcaire? Surely his body would have been brought back to the mainland for Christian burial. Could the work have been so secret that his death was hushed up? And what had caused that death? The more I thought about it the more I began to add together all the twos and guessed that anthrax was at the bottom of it all. Then it occurred to me that, if my suspicions were correct, my barked shin was an ideal port of entry for anthrax.

I made my peace with Alex and said I was sorry to have worried him. The more so, I added, since I had not seen the bird I was searching for. Then I drove home full of intensely personal speculation about anthrax.

At the surgery there was a message from Dr McEwen, the area Medical Officer of Health. In those days all matters relating to the possible spread of infectious disease were overseen by the MOH. We had to notify all cases of measles, scarlet fever and other epidemic diseases to him. In most cases, that was pure routine reporting for statistical reasons. Anthrax was a different kettle of fish; Dr McEwen had the responsibility of tracing the source of infection and ensuring that it was contained. As I dialled his number I thought back to the famous 1964 typhoid outbreak in Aberdeen, about a year before I had come to Laigersay. The

Aberdeen MOH was then on almost every news bulletin. Though there were over 130 cases of typhoid, there were no fatalities. The infection was finally tracked down to a contaminated tin of corned beef from Argentina. That was bad enough, but anthrax was potentially much worse.

The MOH office answered and I was soon put through to Dr McEwen.

'Thank you for ringing back. As I expect you have guessed I want to speak to you about the case of anthrax in Laigersay. Have you any ideas about how your patient may have contracted the infection?'

'Nothing certain yet; I'm following up a hunch. As a matter of fact I have just got back from Mulcaire...'

'Mulcaire? Where's that?'

'It's a tiny island off the south of Laigersay. It has a bad reputation here. I had put that down to local superstition but it seems the War Department carried out work there in the 1940s and then declared it dangerous to visit...'

'I think I see what you're getting at: it sounds a bit like Gruinard.'

'Well, I'm not sure, but what I do know is that, although the island may be off-limits, my patient landed there from a boat and ate a picnic lunch on one of its beaches. That was just about six days before he died.'

'You say that you have been to Mulcaire?'

'Yes, I was there this morning. There's not much to see, just a few traces of derelict buildings, but I did find what I think may have been a grave.'

'Well, we ought to follow that up. I think I'd better come over. It is vital that we track down the source of the infection. We don't want any more cases of anthrax. I'll see about flights tomorrow and ring you back. Can you arrange transport to this wee island of yours?'

'I'll try,' I said, 'but there's another thing. I had a fall on Mulcaire and I cut my leg slightly. If the island is still contaminated with spores, I might be at risk.'

'Hmm, yes, I suppose you could be, but I think the risk would be minimal. However, you should have antibiotic cover right away. The organism is sensitive to penicillin—get someone to give you an injection of a million units right away, and to be on the safe side take tetracycline as well.'

Before McEwen rang back, I had another and more surprising call. This was from Stanley Johnson, the current tenant of Tom Bacadh Castle.

'Good afternoon,' he introduced himself. 'I am glad to have caught you. I have a matter of some importance to discuss with you. Would it be convenient for me to look round and see you?'

'Of course, but I am very busy this afternoon. Couldn't it wait until this evening?'

'Not really, I'd like to see you as soon as possible. In fact I would like to see you straight away. I am just about to leave Tom Bacadh. Please stay where you are till I get to you.' There was a click as he replaced his receiver.

I had mixed feelings about Stanley Johnson, but I had seen little of him since he had taken Tom Bacadh on a long lease several months before. I knew that he had held some mysterious governmental position, which had led to the goings-on with the drug cartel that had rented Tom Bacadh before him. His investigation had led to three deaths, his own wounding and grave danger to my wife and me. His curt and peremptory tone on the phone irritated me, but I did not have to wait long to discover why he was so abrupt.

A mere ten minutes after putting the phone down on me, he arrived. He was his usual urbane self and thanked me for allowing him to come so quickly.

'The fact of the matter is that I believe we have a rather sensitive matter on our hands. I understand that you visited Mulcaire this morning.'

'How on earth do you know that?'

'That doesn't matter, but I do know that you were there. I am afraid that island is strictly controlled by the Ministry of Defence and is a restricted area. Nobody is allowed there.'

I found myself growing very angry, 'Listen to me, Mr Johnson, I am responsible for the health of the people in the island and I have reason to suspect that Mulcaire may be a source of serious infection. I am acting to ensure that we do not have an epidemic.'

'I am fully aware of the problem, Doctor. However I must reiterate that Mulcaire is absolutely out of bounds to everyone, and that includes you.' The man spoke quietly enough, but there was no mistaking his order.

'I am afraid I cannot accept that. The matter is already in the hands of the Medical Officer of Health, who has powers allowing him access anywhere in the prevention and containment of infectious disease.'

'No, Doctor, you are mistaken. I have already spoken to Dr McEwen and under the terms of the Official Secrets Act, have forbidden both him and you access to Mulcaire. I fully appreciate the medical urgency and the belief that Mulcaire was a site of bacterial experimentation during the war. However I am in a position to assure you that no such research on anthrax, or indeed any other potentially communicable disease, was ever undertaken on Mulcaire. I must ask you for your reassurance that you will never again set foot on Mulcaire.'

'You can't do that—I am responsible for health here.'

'I assure you that I can and that your failure to comply will lead to your arrest under the Official Secrets Act.'

'I simply can't believe what I am hearing.'

Johnson sat down and took out a pipe. 'Do you mind?' He asked indicating his pipe. I nodded ungraciously.

'Listen, Rob, this is difficult for both of us. I am under strict orders from Whitehall to ensure you do not go anywhere near Mulcaire. Somehow they got to hear that Porteus had been there and they have been breathing down my neck ever since. Believe me, I realise the urgent need to trace the source of Porteus's infection but I am instructed to say to you categorically that there is no reason whatsoever to believe that he picked it up in Mulcaire. You will simply have to look elsewhere for the origin of the anthrax spores.'

Stanley lit his pipe and stared at me through the bluish smoke. 'I hope you understand. Now I must go. I am sorry to be heavy-handed but the matter is extremely sensitive. On no account should any of this reach the press.'

He got up and offered his hand: 'I do hope we can remain friends?'

Suddenly I remembered the occasion when Stanley Johnson had been shot in the thigh by one of the drug cartel. He had nearly bled to death then. I could not refuse his hand however reluctant I felt.

When Johnson had gone I was still feeling aggrieved and Jeannie Brown, my receptionist, must have sensed this, for she brought me in a cup of coffee.

'Bad day?' she asked.

'Mmm, don't think it could get much worse.'

'Well, have your coffee. I always find that helps.'

She left me cradling the cup in my hands, ruminating. I thought of ringing McEwen to see if he had had any further thoughts, but then the phone rang. It was Fiona wanting to know that I was back from Mulcaire.

'I just wanted to know you were all right,' she explained. 'I never liked that place. I think Daddy knew something about what went on there during the war, and he forbade Murdo and me sailing anywhere near Mulcaire. Any progress with your detective work?'

'Not really, but I've just had a visit from Stanley Johnson. He swears Mulcaire could not be the source of the anthrax. He got all pompous about the Official Secrets Act but insisted that whatever happened there, it was not like Gruinard Island.'

'Well, if that was not the source of the germ, I suggest you concentrate on everything that happened to Porteus except his visit to Mulcaire. That incident got you fixated on it, but now it sounds like a snare and a delusion. Anyway, don't be late home. I've got some lovely scallops for dinner. Love you. Bye.'

I put the phone down feeling better. Perhaps she was right: I had been fixated on Mulcaire. I went back over everything I knew about Adrian Porteus. It occurred to me that if the site of his infection had been the tiny pinprick caused by the sea trout fly then that should be the starting place for enquiry. Could the fly itself be the origin of the spore? Birds, I knew, were rarely infected with anthrax, so it was unlikely that feathers were to blame. But animal products were used in fly-tying. I used a lot of wool for imitations of insects. I used squirrel tail and deer hair in some of the larger flies. Perhaps this was the source. I knew almost all herbivorous animals were susceptible to anthrax, so deer and sheep could certainly be implicated. I was not sure about squirrels and I made a mental note to ask Douglas. The fly had come from Erchie's box and he might have used other mammalian hair when making his flies.

That led me to think about animals known to be carriers of the disease. Somewhere I had read about goats being the commonest carriers, but there had never, so far as I was aware, been any goats on Laigersay or its outliers, other than old Meg's Nanny. For a moment I considered the possibility of Nanny being responsible, but could not imagine how there could have been contact between Nanny and Porteus.

Then suddenly I had a moment of Archimedean insight. I did not actually cry, 'Eureka!' Instead I telephoned Fiona and asked a few questions.

Then I phoned McEwen. He sounded wary when he answered. 'Ah, Dr Chalmers,' he said, 'I was on the point of ringing you. I am afraid something has come up and I shall not be able to meet you tomorrow.'

Smiling to myself at his obvious reluctance to tell me why he had changed his mind, I asked: 'Tell me, can you trace anthrax spores in textiles?'

'Yes, but it's a complex business, involving washing the spores from fabric, concentrating them by centrifuging and then killing off any other contaminating organisms by heating, but only to a temperature that won't destroy the anthrax. Then you culture the residue on blood agar and, if you're lucky, you'll grow a culture of *B. anthracis*.'

'Fine. I've just time to send you something on the evening flight to the mainland. I may have the answer.'

Three days later I had another call from McEwen. 'Bingo!' he shouted down the phone. 'We have a pure culture of *B. anthracis*. How did you do it?'

'I can't claim credit, I'm afraid,' I answered. 'It was Fiona, my wife, who first put me on to it and then supplied the missing clue. Years ago a friend gave Fiona a scarf that she bought in the *suq* in the main square of Marrakesh. Fiona wore it for a bit, but didn't like it. It then found its way into the gunroom where we keep extra clothing for guests. Many of them must have worn that scarf, indeed I have used it myself. Adrian Porteus was wearing it when he lodged a fly in his neck. It was when I remembered Fiona telling me it was made of goat hair that everything slotted into place.

Whatever went on in Mulcaire during the war, Stanley Johnson was right: it was not the source of the anthrax.

When the day came for Maantie to return to the home in Dumfriesshire, I anticipated a tearful parting. So I asked Nutty Jakes and Charlie Kerr, the people with whom she communicated best, to be present to say goodbye. When she saw Pat Tomlinson, Maantie ran to her and hugged her, happy to see an old friend. As she realised she was leaving Laigersay she sobbed like a little child. Then she ran to me and kissed me and rubbing her foot said her name and pointed to her nose. This seemed to mean that she knew that it was I who mended her ankle.

Charlie said, 'She's thankrife tae ye for hailin' her cloot.'

Seeing my bafflement, Morag Finlayson explained: 'She's grateful to you for healing her foot.' I smiled at Maantie and gave her an avuncular peck on the cheek.

She turned to Charlie and sang a bar or two of her seal song. I was surprised to see the old man turn away to hide tears in his eyes. Then she looked at Jakes, took his hand and, as she had once done with me, laid it on her heart.

Nutty Jakes looked at her very intently and she fixed her eyes on his lips. To my surprise these two mentally impaired humans seemed closely attuned to each other.

Then I realised Jakes was singing too: 'Better loo'ed ye canna be, will ye no come back again?'

Then Maantie was in the car being driven off to the ferry.

CHAPTER 11

Practice Meeting

One evening about six months after the opening of the surgery Hamish rang me at home. 'Laddie,' he began in his usual irritating fashion, 'I think we need a practice meeting. There's things to discuss. Can you come round here tomorrow after supper? I'll provide the whisky.'

I dreaded these summonses from Hamish. Fortunately they were rare, but every now and then he got some bee in his bonnet. It never seemed to occur to him that for the two of us a formal practice meeting was rather ridiculous. But he was the boss and I agreed. At the two previous meetings he had harangued me over trivial misdemeanours. On one occasion he had grumbled that I had failed to empty the numerous 'specimens' that his own waiting-room notice had requested patients to bring with them to consultations. These did tend to accumulate, waiting to be boiled with Fehling's solution to test for diabetes. I had to confess I sometimes forgot to do the routine test, which so rarely revealed any abnormality. However I knew for a fact that while my omissions were occasional, Hamish's were almost regular. Jennie Churches once told me that before I came she got fed up with smelly specimens, which Hamish would often leave until fermentation made some of the bottles blow their corks. Jennie went on to tell me of an antenatal patient who had filled an empty whisky bottle with her specimen. 'When she got here she found the bottle had been stolen from her basket on the bus!'

I could not think of anything with which Hamish might reproach me this time but it was with some anxiety that I left home after supper the next evening, with Fiona's 'Don't get too drunk' ringing in my ears. Drinking whisky with Hamish was often quite a challenge.

When I knocked on his door, I could see Hamish wearing a dressing-gown over his working clothes, smoking an old briar and sitting by the fire with Siller, his pale yellow labrador, asleep at his feet.

'Come awa' in, laddie.' He puffed smoke all over me as he greeted me at the door. As he settled his tall, heavily-built frame deep in his winged armchair, the old dog looked up, wagged twice at me, and snored again. Hamish put his slippered feet on a stool and looked at me quizzically over his spectacles.

'Dram?' he asked.

'Thank you, a small one,' I replied, watching Hamish half fill a tumbler with neat whisky from a decanter.

'You know,' he said, 'I was just wonderin'—how long you have been here now?'

'It's nearly eight years.'

'An' ye like it here?'

'Yes, it's great. Perhaps a little busier than I'd like, since the estate gives me a lot of work too.'

'Aye, I ken that.' My partner paused, relighting his pipe. 'Imphm! I also ken the island likes you. Ye're guid for Laigersay and Laigersay is guid for you.'

Then he glanced at me and seemed about to speak again. However he hesitated, made a guttural Scottish noise into his grey-flecked beard and seemed to think better of whatever it was that he had wanted to say.

'I was glad ye took my advice and asked Erchie to help,' he said at last, 'and I don't see ye can be *that* busy. After all, afore ye came I used to run the whole shootin' match by mysel'. Just thinking back to afore the war... man, I was that busy. Did nothing but work.' Hamish drew on his pipe and exhaled a cloud of pungent smoke. 'But *I* didn't grumble. I don't know what the young are coming to these days.'

Sighing, I settled back into my chair and sipped the whisky. It was a good one, not his usual from the square bottle, but with a distinctive nose hinting of the salt and seaweed of the Western Isles; more subtle than Laphroaig, I thought, and with a hint of heathery sweetness. At least here was compensation for what sounded as though it was going to be a lecture.

Hamish got up and poked the fire into greater activity and settled again in his chair. I guessed this was one of those times when he would let his hair down and talk; I was in for a long session.

'Did I ever tell you about my chief at the Royal Infirmary?' he asked rhetorically. 'I was interested in neurology as a student and I impressed the Prof. So I got his house physician's post when I qualified. Now that *really* was a busy job. The Prof was in such demand that I had to work most of the night to keep up wi' him. His wards had all sorts o' queer cases. Syphilis was rife then, and many people had the nervous forms. Aye, the wily spirochaete got into a lot o' brains in those days. We used to call it all sorts o' names, because it didna do to let on that some titled bigwig had syphilis. Mostly we used the auld name o' lues, but my chief had a big steam yacht, bought on the proceeds from his neurosyphilitic practice. He called her "Phyllis" and always referred to syphilis as "Steam Yacht Phyllis". He was quite a wag in his way!'

Dutifully I smiled, wondering vaguely how many times Hamish had told me that.

'Alcohol pickled a good few brains,' he continued, 'besides there were industrial toxins like mercury and lead. Then there were tumours and head injuries ... aye, it was always busy, but then *I* enjoyed that.'

Hamish rekindled his pipe, adding the spent match to the pile in the ashtray. There were seven there already and I wondered how many there would be before I escaped.

'Anyway when the war came I was off to the RAMC and before I knew where I was I was in France with the BEF— British Expeditionary Force to you. Man, we were lucky to get out o' that. I was one o' the last oot o' Dunkirk—quite exciting. Then the tedium o' general duties in barracks up and doon the country till they sent me to North Africa.'

I sipped my whisky and listened with only half an ear.

'Jings, I was busy then too. I was in a military hospital in Alexandria dealing with casualties from Rommel's African campaign. My neurological experience stood me in good stead. I was soon in charge o' all the head injuries wi' a major's crown on my shoulder. It amazed me how much damage thick-skulled Thomas Atkins' heid would stand even with considerable quantities of brain tissue shot away.' He chuckled. 'Sometimes I think it improved them, especially whenever the temporal lobe was involved. Ye probably ken that's how they discovered the benefit of leucotomy in some mental cases.'

I nodded, counting the matches, and wondering where all this was leading.

'Most o' the casualties were patched up at field surgical units: by the time they got to me the really bad ones were a' deid, so most o' the ones that reached me survived. I remember one fella, an Egyptian civilian, who'd got in the way of a shell. Took the top off his cranium, just like the top off a boiled egg. He managed to get to town somehow an' I found him sitting on the hospital steps wi' his hat on. He took it off and I was looking straight at his brain, pulsating away under the layers o' meninges. He was conscious and seemed unconcerned.'

'Good lord!' I interjected, 'What did you do?'

'Och, there was nothin' I could do. I gave him a couple of hundred cigarettes—told him to keep his hat on. He was still there two days later; he asked me for more fags!'

'Later on in the war, after D-day, I looked after a number of people you know, like Peter Kidd, Stanley Johnson and, of course old Tetrabal Singh. They were some o' my successes but they all were lucky to survive quite severe head injuries.'

Hamish paused, topped up his glass and waved the decanter at mine. When I shook my head, he continued:

'This is all leading up to something I said to you the other night at the party when there wasnae time to explain.'

I cast my mind back: 'Was it something to do with Maggie McPhee?'

'Aye, that's right. I think ye might explain all her strange ways in terms o' a lesion in one o' her temporal lobes. In the war I had a lot to do with patients with temporal lobe damage. It does queer things to people. I once made a bit o' a study of temporal lobe epilepsy with a colleague; we wrote a paper in *The Lancet* about it ... I still have that, ye might like to see it?'

Dutifully I muttered that I would be very interested indeed and Hamish handed me an old journal that he had obviously put by him with the intent of giving it to me.

'I shall be glad to have your opinion on that. Take it awa' wi' ye and browse it over when ye have time. Anyway to get back to Maggie an' her so-called prophecies, my view is that they are all manifestations of some form of temporal lobe seizures.'

'I suppose it's just possible,' I commented doubtfully.

'I'm convinced o' it. People wi' that ailment frequently suffer the feeling that they have been there before, *déjà-vu* they call it, and have strange experiences while in a fit-like state. They don't usually convulse, but become disoriented and distant, sometimes anxious and they have strange mental experiences, such as visions. That could account for what Maggie calls her second sight. I don't think there's any other logical explanation for it.'

Once again Hamish sipped his whisky and relit his pipe, adding another match to the ashtray.

'I don't know if ye ever saw a really good film called *A Matter of Life and Death*?'

I shook my head.

'It came out not long after the war; I mind David Niven played in it. It was about a pilot in a Lancaster bomber, which was on fire. He had to jump and his parachute was burnt. He should hae died but he fell in the sea, suffering brain damage which left him wi' a temporal lobe defect. He kept having strange hallucinations, always preceded by a smell of fried onions. As ye ken, strange smells are a feature o' temporal lobe epilepsy.' He puffed on his pipe, deep in reminiscence. 'Aye, it was a brilliant film, they don't seem to make them like that any more. It was a good example o' the illness. It makes me wonder if Maggie gets any strange olfactory aura before she makes her pronouncements.'

Hamish lapsed into silence and stared into the fire and I took the opportunity to glance at my watch.

'Och, I meant to tell ye, I had a letter from that Icelandic friend o' yours. You know, the one who came to the party and hailed you as a war hero. Now where the hell did I put it? Ah, here it is under the decanter. Ye best tak a look at it.'

Dear Dr Robertson, (I read, noticing that the letter was dated six weeks before)

I am writing to you as the senior partner in Laigersay because I do not want to cause embarrassment to Rob Chalmers to whom I owe a very great debt. I would particularly like to donate a piece of equipment to the new surgery at Laigersay as a gesture of gratitude for Dr Chalmers saving my life. My business in Reykjavík has done extraordinarily well these last two years and I was thinking of a piece of equipment to the value of between £5,000 and £10,000. I would be most grateful for suggestions and look forward to hearing from you.

Yours sincerely,

Thorfinn Theodorsson.

'Hamish,' I asked, 'how long have you had this?'

'Not long: just a day or two. I misplaced it and forgot it. What d'ye think we should do aboot it?'

'Well the first thing might be to write back and thank the man before he changes his mind. This really is an extraordinarily generous offer. We need to think carefully, but my first reaction would be to update our x-ray capabilities. It would be an enormous advantage if we could do simple diagnostic radiology. And just think how it would save sending patients with fractures to the mainland. You know, in view of this news, I think I'll accept your offer of another dram.'

'That's the most sensible thing ye've said tonight, ye're no doin' justice to this whisky I chose for ye. It's a twelve-year-old Bowmore, I thought ye might like it,' he said. 'Come on, I need to fill your glass. Ye're celebrating!'

'What are we celebrating?'

He stared at me. 'Jings, I clean forgot to tell ye! I've told the practice legal man to rewrite our partnership agreement to give ye parity in the New Year.'

I looked at Hamish in amazement. This meant a fifty percent rise in income, and I was not due to increase my share of the practice from a third to a half for another five years.

'Now, will ye take a refill?' asked my partner.

'Certainly, I'll drink to that with the greatest pleasure.'

We managed to finish the whisky between us; when I left, there were at least thirty spent matches in the ashtray. Fiona forgave me for waking her with the news, delivered in what she said was a gale of Islay whisky.

CHAPTER 12

A New View of Hamish

Delighted at the windfall from Thorfinn, we started enquiries about new x-ray equipment. I was also quite overwhelmed by Hamish's generosity, as I had certainly not expected him to advance my parity in the practice. It meant we might at last be able to do something about the castle. At least there would no longer be tears over grocery bills, as had been known during our first years in the practice.

Hamish often surprised me. Usually he was a taciturn, monosyllabic individual who gave the impression he barely tolerated me as his junior partner, but at other times, as now, he could be extremely generous. A nagging doubt then made me wonder just how much greater a share of the practice work would be coming my way with the sudden advancement to parity.

It was with mixed feelings the night after my promotion that I opened the journal he had thrust at me. Clearly he believed that it would provide an explanation of Maggie MacPhee and her predictions. It was my night off duty and Fiona was giving a talk to the local Women's Rural Institute. I settled before the fire with Cuhlan at my feet, and examined the copy of the *Lancet*. As I flicked through the pages looking for my partner's paper, two old cuttings fell out. I picked them up and carefully unfolded the yellowing newsprint. One, with PROOF stamped on it, was obviously a draft page of an old directory which he was supposed to have checked and returned. The relevant part read:–

> Robertson, Hamish. MC, MB BS, DTM & H, DRCOG, Born 1918 Glasgow son of Merchant Navy Captain. Educated Fettes. Qualified Glasgow 1937. House Physician (neurology) Glasgow Royal Infirmary 1937–8. General Practice Principal 1938–9 Kilmarnock. RAMC 1939–47.

I folded it up again, returned it between the pages of the *Lancet* and looked at the second. It was dated February 1937, and headed:–

TRAGIC ACCIDENT KILLS HONEYMOON WIFE

> Trudi Robertson, 22, was killed in an avalanche while skiing with her husband on honeymoon last week. Dr Robertson said 'I heard the avalanche and turned to look at Trudi who was skiing just behind me. She had simply disappeared.' The couple were married in Scotland five days before. Mrs Robertson's body was later found several hundred feet below where her husband had last seen her.

I got up and stirred the fire, throwing more logs on it, and the great wolfhound thumped his tail appreciatively on the hearth. How like Hamish to let me know as if by accident about the tragedy in his past. Such a loss in the midst of the happiness of honeymoon must have been a terrible blow. Staring into the fire stroking the shaggy coat of the enormous dog, I imagined how it must have felt—turning, expecting to see the happy laughing face of the girl on skis ... to be confronted with emptiness. I found myself thinking of the time I tried to resuscitate my own lovely Fiona when she appeared to have drowned.

Poor Hamish, the old cutting went a long way to explaining his crusty personality. Trying to take my mind off this, I glanced at his paper. It concerned a number of cases of diseases of the temporal lobe of the brain. Two were of rapidly growing tumours that produced bizarre symptoms. The patients, a man and woman in their early thirties, both had temporal lobe epilepsy characterized by premonitory aura. One smelt burning before becoming disorientated, the other heard a bell tolling. In both cases the tumour developed rapidly and the patients died. A third case was in a young man who had suffered a head injury in a motor-cycle accident. He had curious episodes, during which people said he became 'absent' and started speaking oddly. Twice he described a scene in great detail, once of a tea party at which there were several people seated round a table. On the other occasion he talked of a rugby match at which a friend broke his leg. Both predictions came true within days—the people he described found themselves at tea together, and his friend broke a leg, not in a rugby match but falling from a tree. After surgery to evacuate a temporal subdural haematoma, he made a complete recovery, with no more clairvoyance. Hamish's last case was a Scottish travelling woman much in demand at fairgrounds for fortune telling. She specialized in studying tea-leaves and had an uncanny degree of accuracy in her predictions and in recognizing episodes from the past. A few lines in Hamish's paper caught my eye:

> She correctly informed a young widower of the circumstances of his wife's accidental death, which happened

abroad. As a result of this the widower made a study of her other predictions and found that the number of positive outcomes was greater than chance. Further research was prevented by the woman's accidental death by drowning. A post mortem, ordered by the Procurator Fiscal, revealed a large meningioma compressing her left temporal lobe.

By asking me to read this article of some years ago, it seemed to me Hamish was arguing his case for Maggie having a brain tumour. His argument was feasible, but I was not convinced. In any case, I could see no way of putting it to test, back then, other than by post mortem.

Then Fiona got back, excited after her talk to the WRI. She was full of her evening and complained of having had to eat too many home-baked sweet cakes. I ambled out to the kitchen and poured us each a dram while Fiona sat with Cuhlan before the fire.

'What have you been doing?' she asked.

'I've had a fascinating evening looking at Hamish's writing. I learnt a lot about him. Did you know he'd been married?'

'Hamish? Surely not, he's the archetypal bachelor. I wouldn't have thought any woman would have him!'

'Well, if my reading of an old news cutting is right, his wife died on their honeymoon in a skiing accident. Here's the article—see what you think.'

Fiona read the snippet of newsprint. 'Poor old Hamish. I suppose it fits: that sort of loss might well have made him the taciturn old so-and-so that he is, but are you *sure* it is him? Tell you what, the one person who might know is old Tet. If I get a chance, I'll ask him'

'He's the soul of loyal discretion. I doubt if he'd tell you, even if he did know.' I flicked through the paper in the *Lancet* again and explained to Fiona that Hamish had given it to me to support his contention that Maggie McPhee had a lesion in one of the temporal lobes of her brain.

'What do you think?' she asked.

'About Maggie? Well, I suppose it's possible, but it doesn't seem very likely.'

'Could she survive so long with a tumour?'

'Possibly, if it were a very slow growing benign tumour, but I think Hamish is hung up on the need for some organic brain lesion. After all there are many records of second sight and they can't all be caused by temporal lobe disease.'

'Are there really so many records of second sight?'

'Yes, many, but how well substantiated I don't know. I was so intrigued by Maggie's prediction that I was going to become laird that I took the trouble to read the subject up. There was the Brahan Seer, for example, a chap called *Coinneach Odhar*, though whether he was fact or fiction is debated. He was said to have foretold the railways and the making of the Caledonian Canal and even aeroplanes way back hundreds of years ago.'

'He sounds a bit like Leonardo da Vinci; after all, he predicted aeroplanes. Now I think about it, wasn't there also a woman in Perthshire?'

'That was the Lady of Lawers. She lived on the shore of Loch Tay. It's said that only one of her pronouncements has yet to come to pass. Among other things she foretold the fall of the Campbell dynasty at Breadalbane when "the last Campbell would leave on a grey pony leaving nothing behind" as, indeed, he did. Another prediction was "There will be a mill on every stream and a plough in every field." That came true with the improvement of agriculture, especially the cultivation of linseed for linen. But it all came to an end when the glens were cleared for sheep. The Lady of Lawers predicted that too—she said the jawbone of a sheep would clear the land of people.'

'But do you *believe* in second sight?'

'I don't know: there are more things in heaven and earth than is dreamt of in our philosophy... For the most part people with the so-called gift predicted death or disaster, but some foretold pleasanter things, such as betrothals... When you think about it, death is the only really predictable thing and you don't need special powers to predict that. I suppose you might say *I* have second sight, for I'm continually asked to predict the outcome of illness. In medicine that's called prognosis and a mighty chancy thing it is too, as any doctor will tell you.'

'Well, I'm going to go on recording Maggie's pronouncements,' said Fiona, fondling Cuhlan's shaggy head. 'We'll see if we can't inject some sense into all this.'

CHAPTER 13

Bikes and Cup Marks

Just before Christmas I made a deliberately unannounced call on old Frazer at Allt Beag Farm. Frazer was out on the hill seeing to his sheep and his wife greeted me with: 'You'll be wanting to see Ali's faither. Poor old man, he's no doing very well, and keeps falling. My hubby has tied him to a chair—he's feart he'll have a bad fall.'

She showed me into an unheated room with upright chairs around a central table. Old Frazer was tied to one of these chairs with a length of tarred rope. One strand of the rope had ridden up, presumably because of the old man's struggles, and was looped loosely about his neck. He was making a guttural noise of complaint.

'That's terribly dangerous,' I began. 'He might slip further down and hang himself.'

'I see that, doctor, but he was all right a wee while ago, and what are we to do? For if we don't secure him, he keeps falling. Ali says he'll no be held responsible for an accident.' From her tone I felt that Mrs Frazer was as unhappy as I was at how her husband treated his father. I untied the old man and helped him to stand, as he fumbled at his fly-buttons.

'Do you need the lavatory?' I asked.

He nodded urgently, and I helped him out of the room following his daughter-in-law as she indicated the loo. I held the old man as he emptied his bladder. From the time it took it was obvious that he must have been waiting ages, and he was obviously more comfortable as a result. I led him back to a more suitable chair.

'You know, if he's restless it means he's uncomfortable and probably needs the lavatory. It would be far better to help him there than to tie him up...'

'I ken that fine, Doctor, but Ali's often oot an' I canna manage him mysel'. Can ye no tak him back to the hospital?'

I explained that the hospital was full and that there was no likelihood of a bed in the near future. 'We have to keep the beds for people who really need them. Mr Frazer is up and about and only needs a little assistance to look after himself. I really cannot deprive some other old person with a greater disability by giving him a bed.'

'I see,' she said, 'I'll tell ma man.'

As I left the farm I glanced at the dead cat. 'Funny,' I said to myself, 'I could have sworn that cat was ginger.'

One advantage of a considerable rise in our income was a bit more for the family at Christmas. For the most part we led a pretty frugal life, saving what we could for renovation of Castle Chalmers. The first thing I did was to buy bicycles for the boys. We went to elaborate lengths to hide them and make finding them on Christmas day something of a treasure hunt. Fiona was not sure the boys would manage the clues, but I pointed out that now they were six they were reading simple words well. If I drew pictures as well I thought they would cope.

'But I'll be there to help, just in case they can't and get upset,' she insisted.

In the room we used as the castle's sitting room there was a great hearth where a fire smouldered, partially reducing the pervasive chill. Cuhlan was always to be found stretched out in front of it, except when hunger or other necessity dragged him away.

Fiona and I had decided some Christmases before that this was obviously Santa's portal of entry. We kept up the fiction by marking the hearth each year with a large sooty footprint. One Christmas Jamie contemplated this and asked: 'Why is there no soot on the carpet by the hearth?'

I improvised quickly: 'That's where "Cooly" was lying.'

This seemed to satisfy the questioner but every Christmas after that, Cuhlan suffered the indignity of being sprinkled with a little soot to keep the fiction alive.

As in most houses where there are small children, there was little sleep after five o'clock on Christmas morning. The stockings stuffed with little gifts, sweets and fruit amused the boys briefly, and then we heard them tripping downstairs to see if 'he' had been. Fiona and I followed them down. They were kneeling by the fire caressing the much loved dog, who was bigger than either of them. They had noticed that the traditional mince pie and glass of ginger wine left for Father Christmas had been consumed, and were spelling out the words on the placard I had left on the hearth beside what had become known as the footy sootprint.

Hamie was the better reader and was picking out the letters one by one: 'L-O-O-K I-N,' he began but Jamie, seeing my drawing of a room with guns in it, cut in with, 'The gunroom,' and disappeared with Hamie in hot pursuit.

We followed to find the boys standing in the middle of the gunroom looking round. We could see they were puzzled, but then Jamie looked up and saw another notice hanging from one tine of a stag's antlers on the wall.

'There, up there,' he shouted and, dragging a chair across the floor, climbed up and pulled the message down. Together they pored over it.

'It says "look in" again,' said Hamie.

'Yes and the picture looks like the kitchen,' added Jamie, 'and there's an arrow pointing to the corner.'

Hamie was spelling again: 'D-U-S-T-B-I-N, that's a funny place!' but his brother had already gone. From where we stood near the gunroom door we could see into the kitchen. They were getting the hang of the hunt and soon found the next clue on top of the bin. Hamie spelled it out. 'A-R-M-O-U-R, what's that?' Look at the picture, silly, it's the knight in the great hall.' Again Jamie led the way.

In the great hall was the huge suit of armour I had walked into in the middle of the night on my first visit. The awful clang it made still lingered in my memory. Now the twins were searching it for a message.

'There it is,' said Hamie. 'It's stuck on his breastplate.' Jamie brought another chair and climbed up. 'I can't see what the picture is,' he announced, while Hamie, beside himself with excitement, jumped up and down and said, 'Gie it me an' I'll read what it says!'

Reluctantly Jamie handed the message to his brother.

'Look in the loo,' Hamie laughed.

Re-examining the drawing, Jamie said, 'Oh, that's what it is,' but this time Hamie was ahead of him.

On the cistern in the downstairs lavatory was another clue. 'Look in the P-O-R-C-H,' read Hamie.

This time we were there before the two boys, breathless with excitement, skidded across the ancient flagstones to the lobby by the main entrance to the castle. We watched them find their bicycles there.

After that the rest of Christmas was anticlimax. Fiona and I were kept busy teaching them to ride. They had stabilisers and that helped, but we still had to run behind them assuring them that we were holding on tight.

We had decided they ought to go solo simultaneously. When it seemed they were quite steady and confident I shouted, 'Now!' and Fiona and I let go together. The bicycles wobbled but the riders continued across the yard outside the castle. Both were riding unaided and, more importantly, neither was first. Fiona and I cheered.

On Boxing Day the stabilisers were removed and from then on the boys were rarely off their bikes.

After Christmas every bit of spare time was spent on bikes. Fiona still had the bicycle she had used as an undergraduate, and I managed to find a second-hand one in Port Chalmers. Being used to travelling by car for so long, I became very stiff, even though the twins' range was relatively short. After a day or two my legs ached less, and I began to enjoy seeing the island more slowly and from a different vantage point. I soon got tired of staying near the castle, and hit on the idea of putting the bikes in the trailer that Erchie towed behind his Land Rover when working the estate. This allowed us to explore different parts of the island. Just before New Year we wrapped up warmly and set out for a picnic. Late December may seem a strange time for a picnic, but the Laigersay winter days, cushioned from extreme weather by the Gulf Stream, were often bright with sun if not exactly warm. With the bikes in the trailer we drove down to the southern end of the island around the lower slopes of Ranneach Bheag. We parked the car near the croft worked by Campbell and Isobel Patterson and unloaded the bikes.

Fiona nodded towards the croft. 'How are they doing there?' she asked, 'I was at school with Isobel, and she'll take her man's illness very hard.'

'I don't know much about them—he is one of Hamish's patients. He had a below-knee amputation for a melanoma. I know Hamish is worried about recurrence, but as far as I know all is going well at present.'

At that moment Campbell appeared on crutches from the steading behind the house and waved. Calling to the boys to wait we turned our bikes and rode up to him.

'Morning,' he greeted us. 'An' what's the laird an' his lady doing so far frae home on a braw December day?'

'Would you believe it,' answered Fiona, 'we are off for a picnic by the stones. It's good to see you, Campbell. I was sorry to hear about your leg.'

'Och well, frae what I hear, I'm better wi' it off. I'm managing to get about and do a bit work on the croft. Will ye no come in for a cup o' tea? I know Isobel would be glad to see ye, and wee Donald would love to show off his new presents to your lads.'

Fiona called the twins over and we went inside. Isobel busied herself making tea and cutting slices of Christmas cake. Hamie, Jamie and wee Donald were much of an age and were soon swapping news about what Father

Christmas had brought them. Fiona was in the kitchen talking to Isobel and remembering their schooldays. I asked Campbell how he was managing on the croft.

'There's no denying it hasnae made running the place any easier having sic a hirple. But I manage if I go at it slowly, an' it gets better every day. It's just a question o' practice, an' Isobel an' even wee Donald help a lot.'

Listening to Campbell I wondered just how much he knew about his disease. According to Hamish the original tumour had been under his toenail; a common site for a melanoma. Like most who developed such a lesion, he thought it was due to an injury and ignored it. That delay had certainly cost him his leg and, despite successful surgery, might well cost his life as well.

Isobel came bustling in with tea and soon the boys were sitting by the fire tucking into cake. But we did not stay long, as I knew the work of the croft was waiting and that now he was so slow Campbell would not want to waste time. As we left Fiona promised to look in again. 'I'm sorry we haven't seen each other for so long,' she said, 'and I enjoyed reminiscing about school. I'll look in again after Hogmanay.'

Mounting our bikes we rode slowly down the bumpy track. 'Will he be all right?' asked Fiona.

'Difficult to say. Sometimes they do well but usually the tumour comes back, sometimes many years later. It's a nasty cancer and it's a pity he waited so long before he told Hamish about it. He may be lucky—we must just hope, and wait and see.'

The great ancient stones at Ardreannach fascinated me, though I had only an imperfect knowledge of their archaeology.

'What are they for, Daddy?' asked the twins.

Realising that such a question required an answer, I did my best.

'Nobody really knows, but they must have been set here a very long time ago, probably in prehistoric times. The people who built this circle didn't have anything but their hands and a few levers and logs as rollers, yet they shifted these huge rocks. It must have been very important to them.'

'That big one looks like a witch,' said Jamie.

'That's what they are,' rejoined Hamie, 'They are all old witches turned to stone by a wizard.' With that the twins raced round the circle of menhirs leaving Fiona laughing at my introduction to archaeology.

Fiona led me into the centre of the circle and pointed to where another stone lay on its side.

'Some say this is where they made human sacrifices,' she said, 'but that's all hooey. I can't believe there was anything so gruesome in such a beautiful place. Do you see how they chose this magical place from where you can see way over west where the sun sets by America. We know now that the Vikings reached America long before Columbus sailed the ocean blue. Who knows? Perhaps even the people who erected these stones floated their primitive boats there too.'

'Oh my darling Fiona, I can't believe that!'

'Why not? The stones don't belong here geologically. The nearest source of this rock is on the mainland. People who could get huge boulders across the sea and up here might easily have crossed the Atlantic.'

'What makes you think they were brought here by people?' I asked. 'To me it seems much more likely that they were carried here accidentally by glaciers.'

'That's possible, of course,' she agreed. 'But it doesn't tie up with the natural occurrence of this type of rock and the north-east to south-west flow of the glaciers.' With that she called the boys over for their picnic.

'We'll have it on this flat rock,' she said. 'But boys, I want you to see something here. What do think these marks are?'

Fiona pointed to a series of shallow cups, which seemed to have been carved into the rock. I had not noticed these and at first I thought they were the marks of accidental damage. Then I saw that one of the cups had concentric rings surrounding it. That could not be accidental. Someone had carved these marks on the stone.

My thoughts were interrupted by Hamie. 'We make marks like that for our wee ba's!'

I looked at Fiona with raised eyebrows, and accepted a mug of hot broth to wash down baps filled with cold turkey.

'Marbles,' she explained, laughing. 'Something like that has been suggested before. There are many theories concerning these cup and ring marks: they may have religious significance, they may, as Hamie says, be for some sort of game. I don't suppose we'll ever know for sure.'

'Och no,' said Jamie, tracing the shape of the ring with his finger, 'it's just where a snake has coiled on the stone and left his mark there. They often do that in the sun.'

We all laughed at Jamie's explanation. 'That's a new one!' said Fiona, and we packed away the chilly picnic and remounted to cycle back to the car and trailer.

CHAPTER 14

A Game of Scrabble

The next time I was at Cold Comfort Farm was just after Easter in response to a call from young Frazer. This time Ali himself greeted me at the door, if such a word covered his terse remark: 'It's the old man, he's taken a blatter and cut his heid open. I thought I'd best call ye oot... In case anything happened like...'

'What's a blatter?' I asked suspiciously.

'Och, it's just a fall, but he's got a gullie gaw.'

Once again I found the old man roped to a chair. His face and shoulders were covered in blood, through which baleful eyes glared at me. Scalp wounds such as this 'gullie gaw' always bleed copiously. Though there was a dramatic amount of blood, the injury was not too bad after I had cleaned him up. Ali muttered something about being busy and left me with the patient. I injected local anaesthetic and sutured the laceration. To my surprise the old man smiled at me and, taking my hand in his one good one, he shook it as if expressing thanks.

I sat beside Norrie Frazer and, unsure how much he understood, explained how sorry I was about his situation, and reiterated the impossibility of taking him back into the cottage hospital. 'There just isn't a bed,' I added. The old man again took my hand and then pointed to a table in the corner of the room. To my surprise he seemed to indicate a pile of boxed games. When I picked up Monopoly he growled a guttural and incomprehensible noise and shook his head. The next box was Scrabble, and to this he nodded. I brought the box to the table by his chair. Again he nodded and I opened the box, revealing the familiar letter tiles of the game. His face puckered in his frustration at trying to speak, then with his good hand, he started trying to turn the letters. Realising he was trying to communicate with me, I quickly turned the tiles face up. He gave his twisted smile and touched a W.

'You want that one?' I asked, and was greeted by a vaguely affirmative grunt.

I separated the tile from the others and he studied the remainder for a moment, then touched the letter I. By now I was getting the hang and placed the tile after W. Again he looked at the letters and chose the letter L. I placed it after the I, so the message read WIL. I began to speculate: wild, wilful, William, wilt...? Clearly it was none of these, because the next letter was G, followed by E and T. I began to doubt if this was anything more than chance, when suddenly the old man launched into a flurry of activity and letters followed apace: M-C-F-A-D-E-N.

Norrie sat back with an interrogative look on his stroke-distorted face.

'WILGETMCFADEN,' I read uncomprehendingly. Then I remembered that the Writer to the Signet in Port Chalmers was called McFadden. I looked again at the letters. And suddenly the message gelled. 'WILL, GET

MCFADDEN.' Nodding, I picked out another L and a D and spelled out my interpretation, and as I repeated the message verbally I could sense relief from old Norrie.

I selected two more tiles and wrote, 'OK.'

I was just returning the game to its box when Ali Frazer returned.

'He's never had you at the Scrabble, doctor?' he asked. 'That was aye a favourite game o' his; I'm surprised he can still do it. Perhaps I'll gie him a game some evening.'

I was not surprised to see the old man vehemently shake his head.

Since I was now well behind time, I then had to get on to complete my round of visits. As I drove, I mused about brain function. Though it may seem surprising that old Frazer, so incapacitated by his stroke, could spell out his message to me, I knew that some parts of a severely damaged brain continued to function. I remembered an old doctor telling me about his own father.

They had been medical missionaries in China, where both spoke Cantonese, but had returned home when the father reached the age of seventy. The son had gone on working and had a part-time post at my medical school, where he told me the story. One day the father had a cataclysmic stroke that changed him from complete normality to a vegetable. He was admitted to hospital, where the son visited his bedside. The younger doctor was first distressed, then angry at the time he felt he was wasting by his father's bed, and later he felt guilty at his anger. With these emotions churning inside him he became intensely bored sitting by his unconscious father. To relieve his boredom he started speaking in Cantonese. To his amazement he had an immediate reply, and the old doctor was able to answer his questions. However the recovery was short lived and the patient died soon after.

Ever since hearing that story, I have always urged people to speak to their apparently unconscious sick relatives. Even if the patients showed no sign of perception, I knew that it eased the emotional strain on their relatives.

That evening, when surgery was over, I telephoned Mr McFadden at his home and told him about old man Frazer. The solicitor knew him well and commented that he had been sorry to hear of my patient's illness. I explained about the situation at the farm and how old Frazer had spelled out his request to see his solicitor.

McFadden listened without comment, and then said, 'I understand. Norrie Frazer is an old friend of mine. I'll just look up to the farm in a day or two and see if I can help. It sounds as though I'll have to play Scrabble too.'

I never saw Norrie Frazer in life again, because before my next fortnightly visit the old man had a devastating second stroke and died. There was nothing unexpected about the death and I was quite prepared to sign the death certificate. I could not help noticing that there was no grief on the part of the old man's son at his father's death.

That same evening when I got home after a seemingly never-ending surgery, Fiona greeted me at the door.

'You'd better look at this,' she said, waving a newspaper.

Taking the previous day's paper, I glanced where she was pointing at a headline: MURDER AT HOME FOR MENTALLY SUBNORMAL. Datelined Dumfries, it told of the abduction of a young woman from Pat Tomlinson's home. I scanned the piece, but it merely said that a patient from the home had disappeared two days before and that her mutilated and raped body had been found in woods a few miles from the residential home.

'Maantie?' I asked.

Fiona shrugged her shoulders. 'I don't know. Perhaps you should phone.'

I dialled the number that Pat Tomlinson had left with me. The phone was answered by an angry female voice: 'If that's the press again, you can just bugger off!'

'I can understand how you feel, Pat, but this is Robert Chalmers from Laigersay. We saw the paper. Is it Maantie?'

'Oh hallo, sorry to be so brusque, but the phone never stops and the pressmen are a right pain. No, it wasn't

Maantie—it was one of her friends, called Joey Bruce. The whole thing's horrible. I just can't imagine the mentality of a man who'd do that. I had to identify her ... I can't tell you how dreadful it was. The man must be sick.'

'Any idea who did it?'

'None at all. The police are questioning everyone in the area, particularly a camp of tinkers, but nobody knows anything. I shan't sleep easy until the beast is caught.'

'When did it happen?'

'The weather has been gorgeous, and a couple of days ago Joey went out to gather bluebells with her friend Maantie. They seem to have separated, because Maantie came back alone, very distressed. We searched everywhere —Maantie took us to the beech wood where she and Joey had been picking flowers. That evening I notified the police. She was found by a man walking his dog the next morning.'

'Poor you.'

'Oh to hell with that, I'm all right. I just wish I'd kept a closer eye on them. The trouble is we do try to treat them as normal as much as possible. You don't expect this sort of thing in such a safe corner of rural Scotland.'

During that unusually warm spring of 1974, Laigersay was as peaceful as I remember it. Even world affairs had taken a turn for the better after the nail-biting period of the Yom Kippur war in the Middle East. With Erchie running the estate, I felt free to concentrate on my medicine and improve the medical care in the island. The new surgery was far more efficient and, under the care of the ancillary staff—nurse, dispenser, receptionist and secretary—it ran like clockwork, except when Hamish threw spanners in the works.

By this time Jeanie Brown, the receptionist, was living with Gordon, her husband, in the flat above the surgery. One night they heard someone force a window in rooms below them. Gordon armed himself with a poker and tiptoed downstairs to surprise the intruder. He saw a man shining a torch and opening the locked dangerous drugs cupboard. Gordon was about to strike him with his upraised poker when he recognised Old Squarebottle.

'What the hell did you break in for? I could have brained you!' exclaimed Gordon.

'Dinna fash yersel, mon, I forgot ma keys didn't I? I needed some morphine for a patient wi' a heart attack but I've aye known the windae which could be forced open.'

Alison Goodbody, the practice nurse and midwife, was a great asset because she could sort out the urgency of the many and varied requests for help. One problem of dealing with a large and scattered area was finding the doctor on his rounds when there was an emergency. Long before car radios, Alison boasted she could find me anywhere in the island within fifteen minutes. She kept a duplicate list of my visiting schedule, and could guess my order of visiting. All patients on the phone were listed in a log, and she could usually track me down. There could be problems if I was between calls or had strolled down to a beach or on to the moor to look for birds, so she had lights installed in houses at strategic points about the island whose flashing could be widely seen, to request me to phone the surgery. Some houses she equipped with rockets provided by the coastguard, which were visible over most of the island, but these were only used in dire emergency. On one occasion, when I had slipped out to a hill loch behind the hospital to catch a few brown trout for supper, she summoned me by firing a twelve-bore shotgun from the roof of the surgery. Such drastic methods were seldom required, but the system of signalling was a great reassurance to the surgery staff and also to all those who depended on us.

The dispenser was Pat Cunningham, a lady of large proportions who devised our repeat dispensing scheme. Even as late as 1973 many of our medicines were either made up by mixing various tinctures and powders, or prepared by diluting ready-made concentrated galenicals —non-synthetic remedies—supplied in half-gallon

Winchesters by our pharmaceutical wholesaler on the mainland, and dispensing them in eight-ounce bottles.

Pat was in charge of these but also ordered and dispensed tablets and capsules, counting them out by hand. It was all rather laborious and, prior to the arrival of Pat, either the doctor himself or Jennie, the general factotum who ran the old surgery, had performed this routine task, which often took several hours a day. Pat saved us a lot of time, which could then be spent on the sick. Every medicine leaving the surgery was entered in the dispensary log with the patient's name, address and the date. This meant that anyone requiring a repeat of regular medication, say heart tablets, could identify the required drug by his or her name and the date of the last supply.

To start with, Rachel Swainson, our secretary, had difficulties. Island born, she was an excellent typist who had known most of the patients all her life. However it took her a long time to get to grips with medical terminology and we had a number of howlers. Hamish dictated to her straight and allowed her to sign his letters 'pp'. Once he referred an over-stressed patient to a dermatologist about his *pruritus ani* or, more prosaically, his itchy bottom. The man was doing a correspondence course for a scientific qualification. Hamish dictated: 'The patient's symptoms became worse when producing scientific theses.' Rachel misheard and typed 'scientific faeces'. The dermatologist's reply was that in his experience there was all too much of that!

But soon Rachel, and the others, got to grips with initial difficulties, and they made life very much easier, and released time which could be either devoted to patients or used to shorten the doctor's working day.

Fiona kept her promise to Isobel Patterson and frequently looked in to see her, more often than not taking a cake, or sometimes, if Erchie had been successful on the loch, a salmon. Sometimes she stayed for half a day and helped about the croft. When she came back with accounts of how the family was coping, she showed great insight into how people lived under the shadow of malignancy. One evening sitting in the kitchen after visiting the Pattersons, she told me: 'Isobel is under no illusions; her own mother died of breast cancer and she seems to be certain that it is only a question of when, not if, Campbell's tumour recurs.'

Rather tactlessly I congratulated her on her understanding of the problems facing the Pattersons.

After a moment's silence she burst out: 'Sometimes I think you and Hamish don't appreciate the contribution I can make to your work. You forget I was born here, grew up here, and went to school in Port Chalmers. I know many of your patients far better than you do, and Hamish too, for that matter. I am the continuity of this island from the long line of lairds of Laigersay and I, too, have had my troubles, with the loss of my parents and my beloved brother.'

I opened my mouth to make soothing noises, but Fiona was not finished.

'Let me tell you about Isobel and Campbell. I was close to them at school and I watched their courtship and heard the confidences from the virginal lassie that was Isobel. I even had a bit of a thing about Campbell. He was the son of our dominie, who had great ideas for him to go to university and become a teacher himself. But Campbell wanted to stay in Laigersay and work his own land. Now he's probably going to die. The poor man is devoted to wee Donald, his son, and devastated at leaving him. Hamish is marvellous, just "looking in when he's passing", not making a big thing of it. He's at his best in these situations. But I know more about Isobel and Campbell than even Hamish knows...'

For a moment she drew breath and then added: 'And another thing while I'm at it. I think you are confused about Hamish. I know him better, or at least for much longer, than you do. I asked Tet, but he didn't know if Hamish was ever married. He looked after me when I was a kid, through the measles and the chicken pox; then he looked after my mother's high blood pressure and cared for dad when she died. I can tell you, he's a marvellous man.'

With that my sensible, intensely down-to-earth and practical wife burst into tears and ran from the kitchen, leaving me with much to think about.

CHAPTER 15

Family Planning

Work in the practice kept me pretty busy that spring, and I really did not have time to brood on events in Dumfriesshire where Maantie was. I did not see anything of Nutty Jakes, and was slightly surprised when he failed to keep one of his routine monthly appointments. One excitement was the installation of the new radiology unit. I spent a day with the technician who installed it and found it so easy to use that I was able to teach Alison to take simple long-bone x-rays. After a bit of practice, she was managing chest x-rays as well. This saved time and lowered our aircraft costs: it halved the number of patients we had to send to the mainland. I had difficulty in reading some of the plates, so to be safe I sent them all to the mainland hospital to be checked by the consultant radiologist there. I was able to write to Thorfinn to tell him how extremely valuable his gift had been. He was delighted and promised to return to Laigersay one day to see for himself.

I was called to Allt Beag Farm again a few months after old Norrie Frazer's funeral. This time my patient was Norrie's spinster sister, who had come to the farm from Stornoway. She had rather vague intestinal symptoms but I could not find anything seriously amiss. I promised a bottle of symptom-relieving medicine, and asked if she were visiting.

'No,' she said, 'I own the farm now. Just before he died my brother altered his will, leaving the farm to me. Mind you, I don't expect to have it for very long, after all I am eighty-four! After me, it reverts to young Alistair again.'

'Really?' was all I let myself say. 'Well, I don't think there is anything seriously the matter with you. See how you get on with the medicine I'll send up with Postie, and if you are not feeling all right again in a few days, let me know.'

A few days later I had another call to the farm. Miss Frazer was worse and had increasing upper abdominal pain associated with diarrhoea. There was nothing to find on examination and, assuming the old lady had a viral gastro-enteritis, I prescribed a kaolin mixture. Two days later I was back: Miss Frazer was worse, and was vomiting. More seriously she seemed confused and told me she kept having nightmares. 'They are all about Ali,' she told me. 'In my dreams he is always brewing great vats of poison and keeps bringing me drinks and I'm sure there's something wrong with them.' The old lady laughed. 'I expect it's just because of the home-made wines he's always making in the steading.'

I listened to the old lady's rambling complaint, and a nasty picture began to form in my mind. 'What do you mean? Something wrong with the drinks?' I asked'

'Och, nothing special, he just puts too much sugar in my tea. I can't taste anything but sweetness.'

Increasingly uneasy, I promised to look in again the following day. The circumstances were enough to make anyone feel suspicious: the disinherited son was bound to be angry at his aunt owning 'his' farm. And now the old lady's ramblings about her tea being tampered with. Was it possible that this was a case of attempted murder?

Then, just as I was leaving, Miss Frazer announced that she had sent for her niece, daughter of another brother from Stornoway, to come and look after her for, as she put it, there was precious little kindness at Allt Beag Farm. 'My favourite niece, Augustina, will look after me all right,' added the old lady.

Back in the surgery I phoned Dr Francis Noble, a friend who was a consultant physician on the mainland, and discussed the case with him. He suggested that he come over to Laigersay at the weekend and take a look at the old lady, and was delighted at my offer of a bit of fishing on Loch Bradan. I phoned Erchie to check the fishing diary, because I knew Stanley Johnson often took the boat out, but Erchie said it was not booked, so I could take Francis out for a chance at spring grilse.

Francis came with me to the farm and spent an hour meticulously questioning and examining Miss Frazer. At the end he told me, 'I can't find anything specific, but I'm sure she's dying. If she had been ingesting poison all this time I am sure we'd spot it. But you could send blood and urine to the lab and ask for evidence of heavy metal poisoning. You know, Rob, I don't think you'll find anything; you've been reading too many detective stories!'

Taking his advice, I sent the specimens to the toxicologist on the mainland. All were returned normal.

On my next visit to the farm, I met Augustina Frazer, a completely down-to-earth 'Stornowegian' in her thirties. She was pleased to talk to me, because she hated Allt Beag farm. 'I have been here several times over the years,' she said. 'Old Uncle Norrie was a lovely man but Ali is a different sort altogether. I think he's got it in for Auntie because his faither changed his will only a wee whilie afore he died. Perhaps I shouldna say it, doctor, but I canna abide Ali. Did ye ever hear what he does wi' the cats?'

My mind went back to the corpse on the midden.

'He hates cats,' continued Augustina, 'an' he used to turn several out o' the steadings into the yard where they couldna escape and then chase them wi' his hay cutter. He seemed to think it a sport. He's naething but a sadist.'

Augustina heaved a heartfelt sigh and continued, 'But I'm here noo, and I'll see Auntie comes to no harm.'

I decided to confront Ali. It is a serious business to suggest that murder is being planned, and my evidence was slight and entirely circumstantial. I explained to him that I was unable to diagnose his aunt and that Dr Noble from the mainland had been equally baffled. However we both agreed that she was dying. I pointed out that when the doctor was unable to satisfy himself about the cause of a patient's death he was bound by law to refer the matter to the Procurator Fiscal. That, I said, was what I intended to do.

Ali seemed quite unperturbed by this: 'That's all right doctor, ye maun dae whatever ye hae to dae,' was all he said, but from that moment the old lady started to recover—a fact that did nothing to allay my suspicion.

Much of my work in the practice concerned family planning. Hamish held very strong views about the contraceptive pill, which had made its appearance in early 1961. He was adamant that 'mucking around with a young woman's physiology' was dangerous. In some ways he was right about the early oral contraceptives, which, with their high dosage of oestrogens, sometimes caused blood clotting problems. Though I was less conservative than Hamish, I shared his doubts to some extent and advised my patients that this method of birth control should be avoided where other methods were available. This meant learning as much as possible about alternative methods of contraception.

On a refresher course in the 1960s I heard about intra-uterine contraception. This was nothing new, for it was over fifty years since German doctors had invented devices which prevented conception when inserted within the uterus. For various reasons these fell into disrepute, only to be reintroduced in America in the 1950s, after pioneering research in Japan. The refresher-course lecturer said that the history of the method was much older, and stemmed from Arabian veterinary practice. Apparently female camels, providing they were not pregnant, could tolerate water deprivation better than males. If one had to make a long desert journey one chose a female camel, but it was vital to ensure that she did not become pregnant. Since biblical times this had been done by putting a pebble into the camel's uterus (the mind boggles as to how).

Back in the island, I discussed this with Hamish. He liked the story about the camel but, entirely predictably, did not want any part of this method. He did concede that a foreign body in the uterus was theoretically less harmful than chemical interference with a woman's menstrual cycle. I telephoned a friendly gynaecologist on the mainland, who agreed to teach me to fit what were popularly known as 'coils'. The task is not difficult but, because there is good deal of very intimate manipulation, we needed a chaperone. Alison, the practice nurse, was keen to help because she, like many of the island ladies, was none too keen on oral contraception. Soon we had a flourishing trade in coils, and before long I was publishing results of the first hundred cases of fitting intra-uterine contraceptive devices in general practice. Because this was relatively new, and few doctors were offering this service at the time, I was getting referrals from all over western Scotland. This not only provided a popular service for many a Scottish lassie but also earned a nice little extra income for the practice ... as well as for several guesthouses where the visiting ladies stayed.

So busy was I with catering for the family planning needs of the island and elsewhere that on one occasion, while having lunch by myself in the Charmer Inn, I spontaneously burst out laughing. There were nine men in the bar, farmers and fishermen, and they were all my patients. They asked me what the joke was. But I simply could not share it with them, since it was the sudden realisation that I had fitted each and every man's wife with a coil! Such are the intimacies of rural general practice.

Of course there were many other methods of avoiding pregnancy. Perhaps the oldest was *coitus interruptus* which was so widely practised throughout Scotland that it was called, with broad Scottish humour, 'getting off at Haymarket' (if you take the train from Glasgow to Edinburgh, Haymarket Station arrives a bare minute before Waverley, Edinburgh's main station). Rhythm methods were not popular except with Catholic folk, who had little other choice. The condom, vulgarly known as the French letter by Britons and as the *capot anglais* by the French, was widely used but never popular. Foreign bodies such as caps and pessaries, and even half lemons, were used as barrier methods when placed in the vagina. The lemons were probably effective because of the acidity of the juice. Of these barriers the most novel were hollow balls with bells inside. One wag claimed that these were the origin of the phrase 'listen, darling, they're playing our tune!'

But still there were people for whom nothing would do. Increasingly men who had had enough of bairns, wet nappies and worn-out wives came asking for vasectomy, or the 'snip' as it was called. This is a minor operation, quite within the capability of a well-equipped general practitioner's surgery, particularly where the doctor is surgically inclined. Once again I went to the mainland to learn the technique and soon we had another thriving business. The procedure was not complete until semen analysis proved the absence of spermatozoa. So there was a succession of embarrassed young men bringing in their specimens to the surgery for analysis. It was important to keep these specimens warm and when she received them, Pat Cunningham, our well-endowed dispenser, would say 'Don't worry I'll keep it warm for you'. With that she would tuck the small tube in the cleavage between her ample breasts and smile angelically at the thoughtful young man as he left the reception desk.

Miss Frazer's improvement only lasted a week or two before I was again called to the farm. The old lady still had abdominal symptoms but without anything on which I could base a diagnosis. However Augustina was by now so convinced that Ali was out to poison her aunt, that one day she took me aside and told me there had been another strange death at the farm many years before. This had occurred before Dr Robertson had come to the island. The doctor then in the practice had referred the case to the Procurator Fiscal. There had been, she told me, a post mortem, but nothing had ever come of it.

Trying to remain as calm as possible, I promised to see if I could find out anything about this previous suspicious death. I had to visit the mainland the following day, and

I took the opportunity of calling in to see my friend and colleague who did all the local forensic autopsies.

Dr Barlow was a kindly man despite having to spend much of his time dealing with some of the nastier aspects of human behaviour and some distinctly unpleasant human remains. He listened to my tale with a smile that suggested that he was humouring me. Then he reached into his archives and found a file for the year in question. For a moment he turned pages and then he said: 'Ah, here we are, George Frazer of Allt Beag Farm, Laigersay, back in May 1952.' For a moment he studied his records and then closed the file.

'Go to the police,' he said. 'Twenty-odd years ago I was unable to establish the cause of death, and I made a note to treat any other death at that farm with extreme suspicion. I have no doubt that the police should be informed.'

At that time I was quite ignorant of how one might go about reporting a suspected case of homicide. Feeling that I ought to carry out my colleague's instruction at once, I went to the local police station there and said to the constable on duty that I had a problem to report.

The constable was busy and asked me to wait with several others sitting on a bench. In turn they were called up to report a lost dog and a possibly stolen bicycle. Eventually it was my turn and I said confidentially that I had come to report a suspected homicide.

'Oh aye,' remarked the constable. 'We don't get many o' those hereabouts!' Particulars were taken and my dramatic pronouncement was duly logged. I was thanked for my trouble and was told that the police would be in touch if they wanted any further information.

Feeling an utter fool, I returned to the island vowing to myself that I would never again report serious crime to the police if that were all the notice that was taken. Of course I had misjudged the law, for a few days later I found a detective inspector and his sergeant exploring the farm and asking questions. Ali Frazer's attitude to me was distinctly chilly and I wished I had never started this hare on such tenuous suspicion. But following this police interest, my patient's health again started to improve.

Police activity at Cold Comfort Farm stopped after a day or two, and I had a phone call from the mainland saying that no further action was being taken, but that when the old lady died they wished to be informed. Then, just as she appeared to be over her illness, she suddenly died. I informed the police, who removed the body and a great deal of evidence from the farm, and an inquest was set for the following week. Called to give evidence, I dreaded my appearance before the Procurator Fiscal, but he was charming and merely opened the inquest before adjourning it pending results of the police investigations.

Three weeks later, the inquest on Miss Frazer was reconvened. The Procurator Fiscal returned a verdict of death from natural causes because, as I heard later, all tests had been normal. In court, Ali Frazer's hostility towards me was palpable. I was humbled and felt that not only had I made a fool of myself but I had made false accusation against my neighbour. I vowed never to do the same thing again.

A week later I had an early morning telephone call from Pat Tomlinson, beside herself with anxiety. Maantie had disappeared as well and it was feared that the killer had struck again. The police were mounting a search of the area, dragging lochs and beating their way through woodlands. Pat had rung me in the hope that we might have heard something. I too was horrified that perhaps the trusting Maantie might have suffered the same fate as her friend. I could offer no help, but promised to speak to Charlie Kerr.

As I replaced the receiver I said to Fiona, in bed beside me, 'Maantie's missing, they're combing the woods for her. That was Pat Tomlinson. She wondered, as Maantie made so many friends here, if we had heard anything.'

'How could we have? How could the girl be in touch with anyone here?'

'Absolutely, but even so I said I'd ask Charlie Kerr.'

Of course Charlie knew nothing, but he was as upset as we all were at Maantie's disappearance.

As if that were not enough bad news, Hamish told me he had found signs of recurrence of Campbell Patterson's tumour. When I told Fiona she was upset but not surprised. 'I was down there a week ago, and thought Campbell wasn't looking well. Poor Isobel. I'll go and see her again.'

CHAPTER 16

Terror and the 'Ornithologist'

That summer marked the arrival of our first medical student. Had I known what effect it was to have on the island I would probably have taken the matter much more seriously. Just as winter was finally departing from the island a friend from my student days, now teaching at the Birmingham Medical School, had phoned me. He had a student who wanted to see something of rural general practice for his elective—could I help? It transpired that Birmingham students were allowed two weeks away from their studies at medical school to follow elective courses, which they designed themselves, but which had to be approved by their teachers. My friend said that the student, Terence Goldsworthy, was very bright but, as he put it, 'untidy and very Brummie'. I thought it might be interesting and with little thought agreed to accept the lad.

As Terence's arrival drew near, I began to worry about what I had taken on. I was busy enough in the practice and Hamish's contribution to our ever-increasing workload was erratic. However my real concern lay not with the increased demand on my time but on my self-doubt as to whether I had anything to teach. My friend wanted a line from me at the end of the student's attachment to say how he had got on: I wondered what sort of report the student might make on me! Having a keen, enquiring mind dogging one's every footstep can induce paranoia, and after the Frazer affair at Cold Comfort Farm I had had more than enough of that.

However I reflected that if the young man had been brought up in Birmingham, Laigersay would be a breath of fresh air to him. Perhaps he just wanted a break in a remote place. We could certainly cater for that: Laigersay in summer is the nearest thing to heaven and that year the weather was exceptional and much better than any I had experienced since I came to the island.

The first sign of spring had started in February when, true to form, the first oystercatchers appeared in the meadows round Castle Chalmers. Erchie greeted me on St Valentine's Day saying, 'The oysties are back, they aye come in the middle o' February, snow, rain or shine.'

St Valentine was a great lover of birds and his day, the 14th of February, marks the beginning of the avian mating season, and so has become a day to be celebrated by human lovers as well. In the shrubbery round the castle, the first blackbirds and song thrushes were soon nesting, as the full joyous breeding season burst on the island in an orchestration of song.

Snowdrops and aconites gave way to a mass of golden daffodils nodding their heads in the garden. Helen Chalmers, Fiona's mother, whom I never met, had been a great gardener and had filled the castle policies with bulbs so that spring was coloured by a million blooms— narcissi, tulips, hyacinths and fritillaries. Later, as the beech trees were putting on their magical green vernal foliage, the bluebells painted an azure carpet at their feet. Erchie always corrected me when I called them bluebells.

'No,' he averred, 'yon's hyacinths, the bluebells o' Scotland dinna floor till later.'

Spring progressed to summer, and when the student was due to arrive, I thought I should go down to Port

Chalmers to meet him off the Friday evening ferry. I had not the slightest idea what he would look like and so I had to eye up each young male as he disembarked.

Angus Andersen was returning from some professional conference on the mainland and was one of the first to walk down the gangway.

'Hallo, Rob,' he greeted me. 'Here to meet me?'

'No, Angus, I'm picking up a medical student who's supposed to be working in the practice for a few weeks.'

'There were a lot of young folk on board, mostly holiday-makers, I expect. And there was Lachlan Mackie, the new silversmith chap, from Lutheran. One young man with pimples and a guitar was singing with him all the way from the mainland. They played and sang quite well together.'

'Does that sound like a medical student?'

'Well, I think you are about to find out. That's him next to the harbourmaster, and now he's coming this way.'

An unkempt, pale young man with severe acne, a rucksack and a guitar approached me. ''Scuse me,' he said in a broad Birmingham accent, 'are you Dr Chalmers?'

'Yes, and you must be Mr Goldsworthy?'

'That's right—I'm Terror!'

Angus pulled a face of mock alarm. 'Thanks for meeting me, Rob, but I think I'll slip away quietly.' With that he picked up his valise and marched off through the thinning crowd towards the Port Chalmers esplanade.

Looking at the student, I thought that it was no bad name for such an untidy, even rather smelly, individual. I noticed whisky on his breath and wondered just what kind of guest had been landed on us for a fortnight.

'Terror?' I echoed to the newcomer, hoping that my unfavourable first impression was not too obvious.

'That's what me Dad used to call me, sir, when I was little, and it kinda stuck. Dad used to get fair disgoosted wi' me at toimes. But I reelly loiked 'im. I was just gootted when he died last year. Everyone calls me Terror now though it should, by rights, be Terence.'

I shuddered inwardly at the heavy accent from this very 'Brummie' townie, and I asked myself how he would be accepted by the ultra-conservative island patients.

'Well, I hope you don't live up to your name here. Laigersay is a pretty peaceful place.'

'I can see that, and I had a lovely sail over. Made friends with Lachlan, a great guy who could be me grandad 'cept he's wearing hippy gear. Says he's here to work on jewellery an' things. I told 'im that was what me dad did—in Brum's jewellery quarter. We sang all the way over. If there are people like Lachlan here, I'll like it.'

If he'd crossed the Minch with Lachlan that probably accounted for the whisky, but I seriously wondered what this rather unprepossessing young man was going to be like as a house guest. Without more ado I led him to the Land Rover and drove to the castle.

He was full of questions and it soon became apparent that he had hardly been out of Birmingham in his life. He stared round at what must have seemed as strange as a lunar landscape. He had never seen mountains, or moors or the tumbling gin-clear waters of the burns. Questions poured from him in a torrent of Brummagem speech, and I was hard put to it to answer one before the next burst out.

In the time it took to drive to Castle Chalmers he had learnt about the oystercatchers nesting by the roadside, the buzzards overhead (he thought them eagles) and the massed purple of the northern marsh orchids on the banks. It was an entirely new world to this twenty-year-old city-dweller and his enthusiasm compensated for his uncouth exterior. I wondered what Fiona would make of him.

It was not long before I found out. She was working in the garden when we arrived and came to greet us with a bunch of lily of the valley in her hand.

'This,' I announced, 'is Terence Goldsworthy—Terror, to his friends; it's nearly the first time he's ever left Birmingham and he never stops asking questions!'

'Welcome to Castle Chalmers, Terror!' she said.

But for once the lad was silent. He looked at Fiona and then up at the ancient crumbling turrets and machicolation of the castle. Then he burst out laughing.

'I'm in a dream,' he managed at last and the accent seemed a little less palpable, 'a dream with a beautiful princess in a magic castle in a magnificent island and on a perfect evening. I didn't know such wonderful places existed outside fairy stories.'

So Terror arrived in the healing island.

I showed him to a small room in one of the towers that Fiona had decided was best for him. In view of the guitar I was rather glad she had placed him well away, for I was no fan of pop music. He asked if he could have a shower and a change as he had sat up in the train overnight from Birmingham.

While he was cleaning up I joined Fiona in the kitchen where she was preparing supper. 'Ah bet 'e takes the buzz down the Perzshaw road,' I said, mimicking his heavy Brummie accent.

'You mustn't tease him, Rob,' she said charitably. 'He's a bit rough but there's a nice boy in there somewhere and our task is to find it.'

A moment later there was a clang from the hall. 'God! he's walked into the suit of armour, that's just what I did the first time I ever came here.'

As I spoke, a slightly tidier Terror came into the kitchen, his face red in between the spots.

'Sorry,' he said, 'I was looking at the pictures and not where I was going. I crashed into a knight in the hall. You must show me round—I need to try to understand that all this is real... the portraits, the ancient weapons and the great dog who came and put his paws on my shoulders and licked my face....'

'*Cuhlan did that?*' I questioned. 'He only does that sort of thing to his closest friends. If the wolfhound likes you, Terror, you've scored a hit. He's a very strange animal is our Cuhlan. But supper's nearly ready, would you like a drink?'

'Strewth, I could murder a beer.'

'You're in luck, we have some very special ale brewed in the island to a secret recipe by one of my patients. Mhairi has retired now, but her daughter carries on the tradition at the Charmer Inn.' As I spoke, I poured the dark amber liquor into a tankard. 'Try that.'

Terror sipped, 'Ah,' he said, 'I ain't dreaming after all; I really am in heaven; that beer's nectar.'

At supper we had a chance to find out more about our young guest. As he relaxed his accent became less strident. As he had already told me, he had been born in Birmingham, the only child of a worker in the city's jewellery quarter, and had lost his mother at an early age. Although from a fairly humble background, by sheer drive and personality he had made his way first to grammar school and thence to the university. He had competed for a bursary to finance this elective and, having won enough money to travel, decided he would like to visit a remote island. He said he wanted to see as much and do as much as possible while he was in the island. 'I need to know all about what happens here, the people, their work, their play, their music, what they eat, how they worship God and, of course, how you look after them and keep them fit to do all these things.'

'That's a slightly tall order for two weeks...' Fiona began.

'Don't worry, Mrs Chalmers, I'll do it. I can't tell you how excited I am to be here and I'll wring every last drop of juice out of my stay, you see if I don't.' Then abruptly he yawned. 'But I was up all last night on the train, so if I may I'm going to turn in so I can be up early in the morning to make a start. What time's breakfast?'

The following morning I was down early but there was no sign of Terror. I set about my usual routine of a meeting with Erchie Thomson.

'I saw yon pluky laddie who's here to be made into a doctor,' said Erchie, when I went into the estate office. 'It was afore six. He tellt me he was here to learn all aboot Laigersay an' was there a bicycle he could borrow? He was awa in no time saying he'd be back for his breakfast. He's gey keen, I doot he'll wear ye all oot!'

Terror was not back for another hour, hungry for bacon and eggs and full of his exploration. He had cycled as far as Lutheran on my old bone-shaker, had a coffee with Lachlan Mackie, the recently-arrived silversmith, had met a blind man swimming with his dog and had a dip with them, and could hardly draw breath while he scoffed his breakfast and recounted his morning adventures.

Then he asked me if I minded if he explored Laigersay and spoke to some of the islanders. 'I want to spend the weekend getting the feel of the place before I see how you work,' he explained.

To tell the truth I was a bit relieved, for I was not sure if I could get any work done with this youngster at my heels. He reminded me of a labrador puppy, always demanding another stick to fetch. So after breakfast I went later than usual to my Saturday morning surgery and left the student to terrorise the island.

It was getting dark when Terror came back to the castle. It struck me that Tigger might have been a more appropriate name for the lad because, like Pooh Bear's friend, he was overfull of bounce. I guessed that the twins would like him. They had been away at their friends the Nicholsons the night before, and had yet to meet him. Now they mobbed him as he wheeled my old bicycle into the shed behind the castle.

'Hello Terror,' they called to him as one, then: 'I'm Hamie,' and, 'I'm Jamie.

'Ah, the terrible twins, I've heard all about you two from Mr Farquharson on Assilag. I've been fishing with him today. Look what he gave me for your father.' And, digging into my saddlebag, Terror waved a large lobster at the twins. 'There's haddock, too,' he added.

'So you've met Alex, have you?' I asked. 'Come along and have a drink and tell me about your day.'

Terror and the twins came into the sitting room where Cuhlan was sleeping in his usual place before the fire. He lifted his head briefly and thumped the carpet twice with his tail. Cuhlan was always a welcoming host, but never exaggeratedly so. He preferred sleeping to company. I busied myself at the bar and Fiona came in to join us.

'Tell us what you've been up to, Terror,' she said, obviously infected with the student's ebullience.

'I have had a wonderful day. I went all along the east coast road to the south of the island, hoping I could get round to Lutheran that way, but I'd left the map behind and found there was no road, so I came back and cut across the middle of the island by a big lake...

'That's Loch Bradan,' I interjected. 'That's our best salmon water...'

Terror nodded. 'Then I went back down to Lutheran—Lachlan told me I could cross the causeway there at low tide, so I did that and met a super old chap called Alex Farquharson who was setting out in his boat, so I asked if I could go with him an' we lifted his lobster pots an' there was this huge lobster—he gave it me to bring home to you an' lots of prawns. Then he took me fishing an' we caught masses of haddock an' something he called lythe—do you know I've never bin fishin' before, or even out in a boat, come to that, I've only seen the sea twice before in my life, so it's bin a marvellous day.' Only then did he pause for breath with a gasp and the twins were smitten with admiration that anyone could speak so quickly and with such enthusiasm.

They clamoured to tell their new friend about their own fishing with old Alex, and the three young males, who seemed to Fiona and me to be much of an age, though Terror was in fact fifteen or sixteen years older than the twins, were soon competing with their stories.

Fiona went off to see about supper saying that as she had waited to see when Terror got back before cooking we might as well eat Alex's haddies while they were fresh.

Terror turned to me and said: 'I asked Mr Farquharson about the odd name for his boat and he told me to ask you about it.'

I laughed 'I don't think "Ornithologist" is any odder than Terror as a name. But in fact Alex named the boat after a shared hero, a Scottish naturalist called Alexander Wilson...'

'Never 'eard of 'im, who was 'e?'

'He was a Paisley man, born in 1766, son of a former smuggler and illicit distiller who had turned to weaving. He tried weaving, but the monotony of the looms irked him and he preferred to read poetry. Soon he was writing himself, but his verse was often libellous. He was clapped into the tolbooth—sorry, that's the gaol—and his poetry was burnt by the hangman. Let out in 1794, he sailed to America with nothing but a flute, a fowling piece and a few shillings.'

'Gosh! that must have bin quite an adventure!'

'In the New World he was so fascinated by the birds that he vowed to paint all of them. He spent six years walking throughout eastern America and discovered many birds new to science, some of which now bear his name.'

'I sometimes think all the exploration's bin done, there's none left for my generation. It must have been great to launch out like that!' Terror's eyes shone with excitement. 'In a way,' he added, 'that's why I wanted to come to a Scottish island. My friends thought I was mad!'

'Anyway, Wilson made many friends, including the two great American explorers who opened up the West— Meriwether Lewis and William Clark—and he named birds after them. He also met Thomas Jefferson at the White House. In 1810, he explored the Ohio River in a small boat that he had named the "Ornithologist".'

'Ah,' said Terror, I wondered when you'd come to that.'

'He called at Louisville on the Ohio. There he showed his paintings to a storekeeper, who was also an amateur bird painter. This was Audubon, who was inspired by Wilson and became the greatest name among bird artists.'

'Wow!'

'Anyway Wilson, nearly dying of fever, completed his 3,000-mile journey to New Orleans, discovering more previously unknown birds. He completed the eight volumes of *American Ornithology* just before his death from dysentery aged forty-seven. The man has always been a hero of mine.'

'I'm not surprised. It must be wonderful spending one's life doing something like that—making a triumph from nothing!'

For a moment I eyed the student, guessing that he was thinking about his own future. Despite his outward appearance, I found I was warming to the boy.

'Well,' I continued, 'when Alex lost his boat saving my wife and I from drowning, he got a new boat. The previous laird, my father-in-law, contributed to it. Mr Farquharson named it the "Ornithologist" partly as a tribute to my own interest, but also because Alex also admires Wilson. I love the "Ornithologist" and often fish with old Alex, a remarkably indomitable old man. You are lucky to have got to know him so soon.'

The haddock was delicious, served with a light cheese sauce and leeks from the garden. Afterwards Terror asked if he might play his guitar. Associating this instrument with modern pop music played at a painful level of decibels I was not too sure about this, but cautiously agreed. In a moment I was again surprised at this outwardly unprepossessing youngster. He played superbly and my favourite piece of classical guitar music slipped easily from the lad's fingers. When he finished, he laughed softly.

'I bet you thought I would play the Beatles ... I can do that too but, though I am no Segovia, I thought you might prefer Villa Lobos.'

Though Pat Tomlinson had promised to let me know as soon as there was any news of Maantie, I had heard nothing for a week or two. Then suddenly, the Saturday after Terror arrived in the island, a senior police officer from the mainland rang and said he was in Laigersay. Could he fix an appointment to see me at the surgery? He said something about fishing, and I assumed that like so many others he wanted to come and try out Loch Bradan.

I thought no more about this until, at the end of a morning surgery, Jeannie Brown, my receptionist, rang through to say Detective Inspector MacIntosh and a sergeant were in the waiting room. As soon as the inspector came through the door I could see that it was not fishing that had brought him to the island. Inspector MacIntosh was a big officious man who came straight to the point. I was glad he was not the same inspector who had been in charge of the case at Cold Comfort Farm.

'Thank you for seeing us, Doctor. I am investigating the murder of Joey Bruce from Nith View Community Home, near Friar's Carse in Dumfriesshire. I understand you treated a friend of hers called Mandy McTavish when a party from the home were camping here last year.'

'That is so. Maantie—she can hardly speak, you know, and that is how she says her name—fractured her ankle badly. She went to the mainland for surgery and then convalesced here at our cottage hospital. I heard she too had disappeared from Nith View. I sincerely hope you are not bringing more awful news?'

'Well, Maantie's still missing, and we haven't found the killer of her friend. We've failed in our searches for her, and we're now treating her disappearance as another murder.'

'Oh, God. Who'd do a thing like that?'

'This means,' continued the inspector, 'we are following up leads among any friends she may have made. I understand she has a distant relative here, a man named Charlie Kerr, and that she was also close to a man named Jakes Ormerod.'

'That's right—Nutty Jakes,' I said and immediately regretted it.

'Why do you call him that?' asked the sergeant with alacrity.

'Well, he's a bit odd; wanders round the island with placards predicting the end of the world.'

The inspector pulled a face. 'One of those, is he? I suppose he is not so nutty as to be a ... threat to society?'

'He is a patient of mine, inspector, I keep him under close supervision. I've known him for several years and there has never been anything, since I've known him, to suggest that degree of mental instability.'

'What about before you knew him?'

I was unhappy about this line of questioning. I certainly had no wish to shield anyone who was implicated in murder, but at the same time I wanted to protect my patient from anything which might exacerbate his problems. However I knew that several years before, Jakes had been committed to a mental hospital under a section of the Mental Health Act, diagnosed as suffering from paranoid schizophrenia.

The inspector sensed my unease, and asked, 'When did you last see him?'

Then I remembered that Nutty Jakes had missed an appointment, and began to feel even more uneasy. 'Hang on a moment,' I said. 'I'll just go and find out exactly.'

Leaving the two police, I hurried out to the reception area, and soon had Nutty's medical record in my hand. The last entry, two weeks before, read 'DNA'—shorthand for 'Did not attend'. Prior to that, Nutty had attended meticulously at four-weekly intervals against which were noted prescriptions for his Largactil tablets.

Back in my consulting room, the two policemen were conversing quietly. They stopped as I entered the room.

'When was it that the murder occurred?' I asked.

'The Bruce killing?'

I nodded and the inspector said, 'The last day of April.'

Looking at the notes in my hand, I felt a weight being lifted off my shoulders. 'Well I can tell you that Jakes cannot have done that. I can provide an alibi for him myself. That day, he was here in Laigersay and in the same chair you are sitting in right now, Inspector.'

The detective's expression did not change. 'Thank you,' he said. 'That's most helpful, but I would still like to talk to Mr Ormerod and also to Mr Kerr. Perhaps you could give me their addresses.'

I looked at the notes in my hand, and read out Jakes' address. Then I rang through to reception and asked

Jeannie to look out Charlie Kerr's notes and tell the inspector how to find his home.

'If there is anything else I can help you with, Inspector, I am always about the island somewhere and my staff can usually find me fairly quickly.' I wished the two policemen good morning and ushered them out.

CHAPTER 17

Squarebottle and Pimples

The following day Inspector MacIntosh again called to see me. He told me that he had been to see Charlie Kerr but had been almost totally bewildered by him.

'I could hardly understand a word,' he complained.

I smiled. 'That figures; at the best of times Charlie is pretty hard to talk to and I've no doubt that a visit from what he calls "the polis" would make him all the more incomprehensible. Did you find Jakes Ormerod?'

'No. His place was all shut up. It seems pretty primitive, little more than a shack. There seems to be no trace of him in the island. Could he have got to the mainland? There is no record of him being on the ferry.'

I thought for a moment. 'I believe he has a little sea-going kayak, but he'd never cross the Minch in that. There's the puffer, I suppose he could have hitched a lift on that.'

'What's the puffer?'

'She's a little collier that brings in heavy, dirty cargo like coal. She spends the summer pottering round the west coast coming and going as her skipper likes—as far south as Stranraer and away up as far north as Lochinver. I know Jakes is kind of friendly with Old Jock, the puffer's skipper.'

'Thanks. I'll follow that up. I'm pretty sure he isn't involved, but it's odd that he has disappeared. I suppose if he did go off in the puffer he could be anywhere.'

Terror spent that Sunday exploring the island. Rather than spend precious time on my old bicycle, I asked if he had a driving licence and, at his nod, suggested he took the estate pick-up, which we used as spare transport, to tour the island. I remembered how Hamish had lent me his car on my first visit to Laigersay and how much I had appreciated that.

By Monday morning, Terror had visited the main villages and met the Chalmers of Pitchroich. He commented what a stunner Thomasina was. Then he had a long chat with Angus Andersen, whom he had met briefly on the ferry. He also seemed to have talked with many farmers, fishermen, shopkeepers, and the cottage hospital nursing staff. He had run into Jennie Churches who, armed with a couple of plastic buckets, was striding out into Camus Coilleag. In his usual way he went over to her, introduced himself and asked to be shown how to gather cockles. And then he lunched with her off cockle omelettes, just as I had done when I first came to Laigersay. He was indefatigable and, from the feedback I was hearing, becoming popular, but then it was hard, once one was used to his acne, not to like his ingenuous enthusiasm.

I need not have worried about teaching him. He was a sponge, absorbing all that happened in the surgery. I had arranged for Jeannie, our receptionist, to warn patients as they arrived that I had a student observing in the practice, and if they did not want him at their consultation they had only to say so. All the time he was there, only two patients insisted on seeing me alone. In retrospect, I decided that in each case my relationship with those patients was strained; it suggested that they were not objecting to the presence of Terror but rather to me. That was a salutary lesson. In many ways teaching Terror was a learning experience for me; once a patient turned to him during a difficult consultation and said, 'Do you know, I've never been able to tell Dr Chalmers about this...' and then launched off into doubts about his sexual orientation. It seemed that some people could communicate with me best through a third party, which I had not realised before.

Most of the time Terror sat silently beside me, taking occasional notes but more often observing and listening intently. During gaps in the flow of patients, he would refer to his notes and ask questions. Once he commented, 'You seem to know everythin' about them, not just their illnesses but how they live and even what they think. I'd never realised how important that is in carin' for people.'

'Not only in caring: it's often vital in diagnosis too. When you're evaluating a symptom, you have to ask yourself, "What does *this* complaint signify in *this* person at *this* time?" You see, people vary in their tolerance of pain, worry or discomfort: some complain easily, while others bear horrible circumstances with unbelievable stoicism. A slight complaint in, say, a farmer at harvest time is much more serious than the same complaint at a quieter time of year. I don't consciously think all that; it's part of the subconscious understanding of every problem that patients present to me.'

'I can see that. Sometimes you are more friend, even confessor, than physician. I have never really understood that as being important before.'

'Of course the mutual trust between us enables me to do things which would not be permissible in others, such as the physical examination of women. And I can probe behind the outward façade which people show to the world, to the real man or woman behind. We're lucky, as doctors: we see the most intimate parts of other people's lives.'

As we drove round the island together, Terror came to understand the intensely personal relationship that exists between a country doctor and the people he cares for. He was perceptive. 'You know,' he observed, 'the science of medicine is fascinating, learning all about pathology and that, but the medicine you practice is intensely personal. I mean, it's about people. The science is important, of course, but much more intriguing is how humanity copes with disease. I have never thought of that before. It's like the natural history that you are so fond of here in the island; the ebb and flow of the tide, the migration of the birds and the seasonal change of plants. I see why you are such an ardent natural historian.'

I laughed. 'Yes, you're right. I was interested in wild life long before I was even thinking of medicine. Personally I think that is a natural progression.'

Each evening we sat together over a drink with Fiona and, when they were not too busy with their friends, the twins would join us and eat all the crisps. Remembering my wife's impassioned outburst that she knew the island and its folk better than Hamish or I did, I asked her to talk to Terror. Not that she needed encouragement. She told him all the history of Laigersay and every time Terror mentioned the name of a patient we had seen that day, she would recall her memories of the man or woman concerned.

One evening, not long after the student had arrived, Fiona mentioned that she had been to see Isobel and Campbell Patterson. 'I am afraid it's not good,' she said. 'Campbell is obviously ill again and he's lost a lot of weight. Isobel told me that Hamish had confirmed that the tumour has come back. He even warned her not to be too hopeful; apparently Campbell's liver is involved now.'

I nodded. 'I gathered that from what Hamish said.'

If I really enjoyed Terror, and loved seeing the routine of my daily work through his uncluttered eyes, Hamish was ambivalent. He referred to Terror as 'His Spottiness' or 'Pimples' and never had much to do with him. However he could not fail to hear the feedback in response to Terror's presence in the island. One day in the student's second week, Hamish announced that if I could spare young Spottiface for a day he had something to show him.

When I mentioned this to Terror he pulled a face. 'To tell the truth I'm a bit in awe of Dr Hamish,' he said. 'But I suppose I ought to spend a bit o' time with 'im, after all 'e's part of the Laigersay scene.'

So it was that Terror set out to spend a day with Squarebottle. I did not see him all day, and was surprised to find how much I missed his company, and his enthusiastic questioning of everything I did. He returned to the castle after six, and said he was dying for a beer.

'How did you get on?' I asked, pouring him an ale.

'Very interesting,' he said thoughtfully, 'he's quite different from you. Sorry if that sounds rude, but in fact I didn't realise how different two doctors could be, doing the same job in the same place.'

'You'd be surprised how often people say that.'

Terror went on: 'I was afraid of him to start with, especially as he kept asking me questions. We were in the car for over an hour driving down to near the Assilag causeway and he kept stopping to walk his dog. Whenever he wasn't asking me questions, he was talking to the dog about what he was seeing, as if she was human. But his questions were difficult. I'll need to think about what happened today before I can really explain it to you.'

Unusually the student went quiet. He gave me the impression he was struggling to control his emotions. Then he finished his beer and got up.

'Look, would you mind if I went out for a bit of a walk and a think?'

'Of course, do what you like. I know Hamish can be very thought-provoking!'

In fact it was some time before I really understood what had happened that day and then only when I had pieced together the information I collected in bits and pieces from Fiona, Hamish and Terror himself.

It appeared that the day had started simply enough, driving and walking on the moors. I remembered similar walks with Hamish when I was new to Laigersay. He used to like to talk about what he called the 'philosophy of medicine', often seeming to speak to his dog rather than to me. Terror described to me the conversation he had with Hamish:

'"What do ye ken aboot pain, laddie?" the Doctor asked me. I had to tell him not a lot, though I did not like it when I broke my leg.

'"Ever bin in love, lad?" he asked me and when I told him I thought so, he laughed and said if I only thought so I had not experienced the real thing. Then I found myself telling him about how heartbroken I was when my long-standing girl-friend broke it off with me.

'"An' did that hurt, lad?" he asked again and I told him, yes, very badly indeed.

'"Which would ye rather, break your heart again or yer leg?" and I knew that the pain of my leg, bad though it was, would be better than breaking my heart again.

'"Then ye've learnt something aboot pain, haven't ye?" he said.'

Terror paused then, before saying to me: 'I suppose speaking about the break-up with my girl-friend made it easier to talk to Dr Robertson. He seemed to know just how I'd felt; it was as if he'd had a similar experience himself. You know, I haven't been able to talk to anyone like that since Dad died.'

The lad walked over to the window and looked at the magnificent evening. Then, recovering himself, he went on: 'Anyway, after that we walked on the moor and he talked more about pain. I have never really thought much about it, but he said there were many sorts of pain. There was the pain of my broken leg, then there was the different psychological pain of a broken heart...'

This was one of my partner's favourite subjects and I could visualise the situation clearly. I had had the same tutorial from him myself in my first year in Laigersay. Hamish had told me that, in addition to physical and psychological pain, there was social pain: what happened when one was completely deprived of human company. He stressed the importance of understanding precisely what people mean when they say they hurt.

Then I asked Terror if Hamish had told him about a man he knew who had been 'sent to Coventry', when nobody would speak to him. After a few weeks, the man was crazy with his suffering. When I saw the student nod, I asked if Hamish then spoke of spiritual pain, distinguishing religion from spirituality because, as he said, everyone was spiritual, but nowadays fewer and fewer were religious. When Terror nodded, I explained that Hamish had told me of a dying Roman Catholic priest who was furious with God, who, after he had served Him all his life, had cursed him with cancer, making him lose his faith. That man's pain was unendurable, until fortunately another priest found a way of helping him.

Then there was a clue to Terror's pent-up emotion, he looked quite distressed: 'That's what happened to my dad just before he died,' he said, and I could see the boy's eyes fill with tears.

Apparently it was then that Siller, the old labrador, put up a covey of grouse, and man and youth watched them as they flew, protesting, over the heather. Hamish called the dog off and they went back to his car. Terror said he would have been glad of a bit of respite, for Hamish's questions came so close to his own unresolved bereavement and guilt; but in the car Hamish would not let it alone.

'"So how would you try and help a man like that?" he asked me,' said Terror, 'and, without waiting for an answer, Dr Hamish explained that when you see someone in anguish you have to analyse the cause in physical, psychological, social, and spiritual terms. Until you have done that you cannot give them ease. Opiates are all very well but they could not help you with your broken heart or that priest who had lost his way to his God.'

As Terror paused again, I remembered something Fiona had told me that afternoon.

'Tell me,' I asked, 'did Hamish take you to an isolated croft near Ardranneach Point, down by Ranneach Bay?'

'How did you know?' the boy replied, 'I had not been there before. It is particularly wild and beautiful and there's a great big standing stone...'

I nodded, for I knew it well.

'Then Dr Hamish said that this was what he had wanted to show me. The crofter was a young man dying of a melanoma. Hamish explained that though the disease had not caused any physical pain, the young man suffered intense anguish because he was leaving his wife and adored only son. He told me that we think of the living as being bereaved by death, but those that are dying also suffer bereavement, for they also lose their loved ones.'

Now Fiona had visited the croft shortly after Hamish and Terror left, and Isobel told her what happened: 'Dr Hamish introduced young Mr Goldsworthy to me and when he asked how Campbell was, I told him "Very distressed, for he's desperate aboot wee Donald."'

Fiona told me that when Hamish had asked if Campbell was in pain, Isobel had said, 'God forgive me, I almost wish he was, for he is so strong it might be easier for him to bear physical pain than the agony of his loss o' the wean; and he is fair eating his heart out. Wee Donald is fine, but of course he's too young at six to understand what's happening.'

When Hamish asked, 'May we go in and see Campbell?' she said, 'O' course, he'll be right glad to see ye, his face aye lights up when ye come.'

She led them into the bedroom and Hamish again introduced Terror. I could imagine the scene for I had seen Campbell myself, not long before, when he appeared comparatively well, but painfully thin. As his wife said, his face always brightened when he saw visitors.

Terror was worried that he might be intruding, but immediately Campbell turned to him and said he was glad to see him and asked if he realised that he was with the most marvellous doctor. 'Like a lot o' his patients,' the dying man continued, 'I used to be feart o' Dr Hamish, but that was afore I kent him weel. He's kind an' wise an' that's what's aye needed in a man o' his calling. But I'm glad he's brought ye here, for when he said you were here in Laigersay to learn doctoring I tellt him I had a message for ye. Ye see most doctors get cancer all wrong. It's no' the disease itsel' that's so bad, but it's the fear o' it that maks a man dread. Once ye come to terms wi' the fear, nearly everything's bearable.'

'Then,' said Terror, 'Dr Hamish drew up a chair and reversed it so as to sit astride looking over its back. He signalled to me to do the same and as I sat down, it occurred to me that standing over a recumbent patient, as we always do on hospital rounds, puts the patient at a disadvantage, makes him inferior to the doctor ... like talking down to someone from horseback. Dr Hamish, by sitting, put his eyes on the same level as Campbell's, making them equals.

'Then the doctor started speaking. To my surprise he told Campbell I came from the English Midlands and had lost my parents. He said I was enjoying Laigersay and that it seemed the island was enjoying me. He told Campbell I was exploring the island and had come under its spell. The sick man smiled and agreed that it was the most perfect place in the world. Then he took me by the hand, and held it for a moment before asking if I had children. I shook my head.

'"You should do something aboot that," he said. "My wee boy is a great boon."

'Shortly after that we left and Dr Hamish thanked me for coming. "I didna want to tell ye afore," he said, "but Campbell had heard aboot ye and asked me to bring you to see him. Ye probably did more to help him than ye ken. Remember what he said aboot the fear o' cancer being worse than cancer. If more doctors kent that, the disease might be better understood both by the profession and the disease's sufferers."

'Then, when we left the croft, he said there was something else he wanted to show me. We drove down to the huge standing stone at the point. The doctor told me about the people who built the ancient burial chamber beneath it and explained about their lifestyle. He told me that a mound at the site was almost entirely made of discarded shells from their food.

'"Just imagine," he said to me, "for centuries they lived here, hunting and gathering, loving and dying." He went to the monolith and put his arms round it. "Just imagine," he said again, "when they hadna onything better to do they put up this muckle great stone. What a labour yon must hae bin. It must hae bin gey important to them. Like what Campbell wantit tae say to you."

'Then Dr Hamish sat beside the standing stone, lit his pipe and traced the incised ring at the base of the stone with his finger. The old labrador sat beside him.

'"Look at that view," Dr Hamish said, "Isn't it just the finest thing ye ever saw? D'ye see how the water oot to the west is calm and all silver in the light. Siller an' me, we often sit here together, don't we girl?" And the dog, knowing she was being spoken to, thumped her tail on the stone.'

Terror paused in his account of his day with my partner:

'Then he drove me to the Charmer Inn and gave me a very late lunch and brought me home. What a thought-provoking and emotional day. It's one I'll never forget. I think I learned more about being human today than anything they've taught me at Birmingham. They speak of anything like that as "soft soap" and not real medicine.'

But that was not the end of the day. As we were finishing supper the phone rang. Fiona answered it and came back with a long face. 'It's Douglas White,' she said, 'he wants to talk to you about Hamish. Apparently his old labrador, Siller, was taken ill suddenly this evening and Douglas has had to put her down. He says Hamish is devastated.'

I went to the phone and heard the voice of the vet.

'Rob, I'm worried about Hamish. His old bitch started fitting early this evening and he brought her in. There was nothing I could do, and I had to put her to sleep. Hamish was beside himself. You'd never credit that the dour old stick could be so upset. He insisted on holding Siller while I gave her the injection. When it was over he sat down and wept into the dead dog's coat. There was a full waiting room, but I got him out the back way. He said he could drive, but I'm worried about him...'

'Poor old Hamish. He was absolutely devoted to that dog; all the more so since his other lab, Florin, died. I'll slip round and see him.'

Returning to the table, I explained what I was doing. To my surprise Terror asked quietly, 'Can I come too?'

I hesitated and then said, 'OK, if you want to,' and together we went out to my Land Rover.

Hamish's house was in darkness and the car was not there. We had a system of leaving messages for each other when we needed to discuss a patient, so I put a note on the pad by his front door asking him to ring me when he got home. 'I don't think there's anything else we can do just now,' I said to Terror, and we returned to Castle Chalmers.

Hamish did not phone and by midnight we were getting anxious, but there still seemed nothing to be done, so unhappily we all turned in. Despite my anxiety about my partner I was confident of the resilience of the man and, once my head hit the pillow, I slept soundly.

Next morning there was still no news of Hamish. Fiona was down getting breakfast when she called up to me 'Have you seen Cuhlan this morning?'

'No, isn't he in his bed?'

'No, I can't find him anywhere. Erchie hasn't seen him either. Wait a minute, Erchie's saying something...'

There was a pause then Fiona added: 'Erchie says the pickup's gone from the yard.'

By this time I was down in my dressing gown. 'If the pickup's gone, that must be Terror, but surely he wouldn't take Cuhlan as well?'

As we were staring at each other in puzzlement the phone rang. To my great relief it was Hamish. He sounded drunk. 'I think ye'd best come an' get yer dog an' while ye're aboot it ye may as weel collect Spottiface. I doot he's no very weel.' And the phone went dead.

All was revealed when I dressed hurriedly and drove to my partner's house, to be greeted by a very subdued

Cuhlan. Hamish was sitting in his usual chair obviously very drunk. Terror was lying on the sofa breathing stertorously. He, too, was far gone with drink, almost unconscious.

'What the hell's going on?' I demanded.

'Not now,' said Hamish. 'I'll tell ye later. Right now I think ye should get that young man to his bed an' I'm awa to my ain.' My partner swayed to his feet and made for the stair. Somehow I managed to half carry, half drag Terror to the Land Rover. A downcast Cuhlan climbed guiltily into the vehicle behind us.

At the Castle, Fiona and Erchie helped me to lay Terror on a couch in the estate office. Ensuring that he was in the recovery position in case he vomited we drew the curtains and left him to sleep it off.

'The lad's had a right skinfu',' announced Erchie rather admiringly. Shaking my head in disbelief at the goings on of a very senior and very junior member of my profession, I went to work. Fiona promised to keep an eye on Terror, and to feed him strong coffee when he showed signs of life.

That evening I heard what had happened. After we had all gone to bed Terror could not sleep and suddenly had an idea where Hamish might be. He stole downstairs without disturbing the household and was on his way to the yard where the pickup was parked when Cuhlan nudged him from behind. The wolfhound was obviously pleased to see him and seemed to relish the idea of an outing. The huge dog leapt into the pickup and together man and dog drove south towards Lutheran.

Terror had remembered the way Dr Hamish had talked to his dog only a few hours before, and with that came the certainty that he knew where Hamish was.

Terror found him sitting motionless beside the standing stone staring out over the burial chamber towards Ranneach Bay. Now by the light of a gibbous moon the calm sea was even more silvered than it had been earlier. Hamish sat motionless, staring at the sea, and his face was wet. Cuhlan ambled up to him and nuzzled the man. In reflex, Hamish's hand came to the dog's head and stroked the shaggy ears. Cuhlan sat beside him and Terror sat too.

The older man stirred. 'Thanks for coming,' he said, 'and thanks for bringing Cuhlan too, that was a good thought.' Then there was a long pause and he spoke again: 'I've just remembered what Axel Munthe said about this sort o' thing: "It is not *a* dog we love but *the* dog".'

There was another long pause and then Hamish spoke again to the dog and the boy: 'Come on you two, we need a drink. Leave the pickup where it is, we can get that in the morning, get in my car an' come back home wi' me.'

'And that,' explained Terror later, 'was how I spent the rest of the night getting blind drunk with Hamish!'

Later, when it came to reporting on Terror and his elective to my friend at Birmingham Medical School, I omitted any reference to his drinking spree with my senior partner. Apart from that notable omission I gave him a full and first-class report. We were all sorry to see the boy go ... but he gave us his oath he would be back.

CHAPTER 18

The Present

Not long after Terror's visit came to an end, a new worry began, like a cloud no bigger than a man's hand on the horizon, to obtrude on my peaceful existence in Laigersay. August 1st was Fiona's birthday and I was in a great quandary about what to do about it. Obviously it had to be something important and of great and appropriate significance. But I have never been good at choosing presents let alone for an occasion as important as my wife's thirtieth birthday. I knew she dreaded departure from her youthful twenties and wanted to find something that would both express my love and ease the pain.

One morning Erchie found me sitting in the estate office he had created in one of the castle's smaller rooms. He must have seen I was abstracted, as I was staring into space racking my brains about the problem.

'Och, it canna be that bad!' he interrupted my thoughts. 'Whit way d'ye no tell yer uncle Erchie what grieves ye so?' he continued in mock humour.

'It's my wife, Erchie.'

'Aye, I jaloused it might be; they're queer cattle an' a source o' woe. That's why I've aye avoided the snare.'

'No you misunderstand, it's her birthday and rather an important one. I don't know what to give her.'

'Jings! I'd never hae kenned the lass was forty!'

'God, Erchie! Never let her hear you say that ... not even in ten years' time. She'd have a fit... I want to give her something special, but have no idea where to look.'

'When's the day?'

'First of August—there's time yet.'

'Ah'm nae so sure. I ken fine what I'd dae, but what I hae in mind taks a wee whilie.'

'Come on, spit it out, man, what is it?'

'Well if it was me, I'd hae a word wi' Lachy Mackie. But I doot ye may be ower late. Lachy's an awfu' slow worker an' awfu' dear forbye.'

'I don't know much about his work. Is he good?'

'Probably the best in Scotland. I hear tell he makes his gewgaws for Balmoral. Why not go an' see him? He'll want to talk aboot it before he comes up wi' a plan. Ye'd be best to ring first though, he likes notice o' visitors.'

Taking my factor's advice, the following day I stopped on my round by appointment at Lachlan Mackie's workshop in Lutheran. I had heard a good deal about him but did not know him. I found him sitting in his untidy workshop cluttered with instruments of his trade; burins and hammers of all sizes and shapes and a great steel contraption with lots of handles and levers which I took to be a press. Lachy was sitting and peering through two pairs of spectacles at a large silver bowl on which he was drawing in black ink. He looked up as I tapped on the open door.

'Ah, me dear, come in, come in. I take it I'm in the presence o' the laird himself?'

The man stood up, and I found myself looking at a tall, cadaverously thin scarecrow. He must have been six foot four, possibly more if he stood straight but years of sitting at a workbench seemed to have given him a permanent stoop making him resemble an elongated question mark. He had a flowing beard and long hair gathered in a bun at his nape. I guessed they had once been a flaming red but were now faded and shot with grey. He looked about sixty. There were flecks of silver sparkling in his whiskers. But it was his dress that was the most startling. Faded old corduroys were fastened loosely with a broad leather belt clasped by a large silver buckle. His torso was enveloped in a multicoloured jumper of indeterminate age and so darned and re-darned with differing wools that it was a kaleidoscope of hues. Lachlan Mackie, with shoulder-length hair and a straggly beard, looked like something from Grimm's Fairy Tales. I didn't altogether like what I saw, but reminded myself how Terror had taken to him.

'So what can I do for the Laird o' Laigersay?' he asked without any further greeting.

'Well I was, sort of, looking for a special birthday present for my wife...' I began hesitantly.

'Ah yes! That will be the aptly named Fiona Chalmers. A very beautiful lady; I've seen her once or twice about the island. What had you in mind?'

'To be honest, I haven't the slightest idea. That's why I've come. My factor suggested you.'

'Oh aye, Erchie Thomson. A great guy, we do a bit of rather unofficial fishing together sometimes. Do you want a little look? You might get ideas.'

With that the strange man unlocked a large safe and took out several trays. Suddenly I was transported to an Aladdin's cave. There were bowls and beakers, rings and necklaces, bracelets and bangles. He brought out more and more boxes and trays. Some pieces were huge silver dishes and goblets, some tiny pendants. Most were in silver embellished with superb engraving; many were in gold or silver ornamented with gold. and a few were platinum. Yet others showed precious and semi-precious gemstones set in either gold or silver. I was reminded of naval days when I had visited a lapidary in the Persian Gulf and bought the jewels that, much later, had been made into Fiona's engagement ring.

Bemused by the quantity and quality of the man's artistry, I examined one piece after another. Somewhere a telephone rang; the silversmith apologised and left me alone with what must have been a fortune in precious metals and stones. He did not seem very security conscious.

A few minutes later he was back. 'Sorry about that,' he said. 'It was a client from Argentina asking how I was getting on with a commission he gave me last year. It's a big job and has taken time, but it's nearly done now.' He picked up a locket nearly three inches by two. 'This is the piece. It's a fine bit of jade set in filigree gold with a silver back.' He opened the locket to show the interior. 'He's a big cattleman who lives in Buenos Aires. He lost his wife and wants a frame to hold a miniature he's had painted of her. The painter kept changing the dimensions. Now, do you see anything here that gives you ideas?'

I was a bit daunted for, much as I wanted something special, this work looked very costly. 'It's all very beautiful,' I said, 'but I fear it may be rather more than I can afford to pay.'

'It needn't be,' he said, 'some of the smaller silver pieces you can pick up for a fiver. But sit ye down for a moment and let me find out about you and your lady. I know she was the daughter of the former laird, from whom you inherited and, as I say, I know her to be very beautiful.' He paused, smiling at me. 'Yes. Just thinking about her makes me feel that whatever I make for her must be a fine piece, and very definitely Scottish, or better still Celtic. If you like, I could make a drawing?'

I felt I was being sucked into a vortex. I remembered the leaking roof of the castle and wondered if I were being very foolish ... but the man's work was truly magnificent. 'Would that be very expensive?' I ventured.

'Well, it could work out at whatever you wanted to pay. If you give me a sum—say £20 or £200—I could cut the cloth to suit the cost. I won't rob you, you know, and I like to make beautiful things for lovely people, especially when they are local. I tell you what, let me think for a bit, make a rough sketch or two and we can have another chat?'

There seemed no harm in that. I could always restrain him if the piece became too costly, and so I agreed, and we made an appointment for the following week. As I rose to go, he stopped me and said: 'On another subject, I believe you know an unusual lady called Maggie McPhee?'

'Of course,' I said. 'She is probably the most bizarre person I have ever met.' As I said this, I could not help thinking to myself that Mr Lachlan Mackie was running her a close second.

'It's just that Erchie Thomson told me I should meet her. He said she and I would get on well, and I'm told she has the gift of second sight, which has always fascinated me. I understand she is in some sort of old folk's home in Port Chalmers and that you are her doctor. Would it be all right if I wrote to her and asked her if we could meet?'

'Maggie is blind and deaf, she's not easy to communicate with,' I warned him. 'But she likes meeting new people, especially a talented craftsman such as yourself. If you like I will mention it to her. I am due to see her in a day or two.'

'Yes, I would be grateful. From what Erchie tells me, she is a fascinating person.'

When I saw Maggie a few days afterwards, she was at first nonplussed about meeting Lachlan Mackie. But when I mentioned his extraordinary many-coloured jumper with its multiple darns, she looked interested. 'I recently had a puzzling dream about a man in Joseph's Coat. Perhaps this Mr Mackie may have something to do wi' it. It'll do no harm to see him, an' I get few enough visitors nowadays.'

I told her about Fiona's birthday, that Lachlan had talked me into letting him design something for the occasion, and that I was worried that perhaps I would be spending more than I could afford on something Fiona wouldn't like. When Maggie asked what the piece would be like I could only be vague: 'He said it ought to be Scottish or Celtic, and that he liked making things for beautiful people.'

'He sounds all right,' she said. 'I think you should spend as much as ye dare, for I ken that one day money will be of no concern to you.'

'That's all very well to say,' I laughed, 'but you don't have the upkeep of a castle to keep you awake at night.'

'Aye,' Maggie repeated, 'spend as much as ye dare.'

When, a week later, I returned to the studio, Lachy was wearing the same clothes and was sitting as before at his bench. The only difference was that he was adjusting the fitting of a large boulder opal in a huge gold ring.

Shuffling around among pieces of gold and silver in various stages of development, Lachy found an old envelope with a drawing on its back. 'I've been busy,' he added, 'but I made a sketch the other day. It's only rough yet, but I have a good idea how it will look.'

He passed the envelope over, letting me see the Indian-ink drawing. It may have been an early draft, but already the shape was clear, complete with intricate Celtic intertwining curves and lines. 'I think it should be in silver: about two inches long by three-quarters. What I'm not sure about yet is whether it will be a brooch or a pendant. What do you think?'

'Gosh, I don't know, could we keep the options open?'

'No problem.' Lachy got up and shuffled over to the safe from which he drew a tray lined in black velvet. 'There are some bits and pieces here, to give you an idea. When did you say the birthday is?'

'August 1st, just before the opening of the grouse season. The estate will be busy then.'

Malcolm nodded. 'That's Lammas or Loaf-day, about ten weeks away; I should be able to manage that OK. I'm glad you approve of the rough sketch. The finished piece will look much better. Leave it with me and I'll be in touch when I've something to show you. I don't think the lady will be disappointed. Now I expect you want to get on with your round—by the way, did you fix anything with Maggie McPhee?'

I explained that Maggie wanted to meet him and that the best time to visit would be early one afternoon. Then, feeling that I was dismissed, I left to complete my visits.

A month later I had heard nothing from the silversmith and, growing increasingly anxious, I gave him a ring. Lachy answered the phone and, on hearing my voice said, 'Hello, me dear.' Other than that he seemed to have forgotten all about my commission! Eventually he seemed to recall it, and said, 'Oh yes, I remember now, the sketch is hereabouts somewhere. Don't worry, it'll be in time. As they say in the theatrical world, "Don't ring me I'll ring you!"'

With that extremely slender reassurance I heard him hang up. I called on Maggie McPhee again and she told me Lachy had been to see her. 'Did he mention the work he was doing for me?' I asked.

'I cannae mind,' she replied. 'But I am sure anything he does will be well done, and done on time.'

By the third week in July, I was getting desperate. Then, out of the blue I got a message from Maggie. Could I possibly look round for a dram after evening surgery, as she had something personal she wanted to discuss. This was the first time the old lady had formally invited me, and I was filled with curiosity, for any summons from Maggie McPhee was likely to be surprising. I readily accepted.

As soon as surgery was over, about 7.30, I jumped in the car and went to *Cuil an Darach*, the residential home where the old lady now lived. A member of the staff answered my ring and told that Maggie was expecting me and I was to go straight up. To my surprise I found she had another guest. Lachy Mackie was sprawling in a chair several sizes too small for him. He held a glass and beamed from ear to ear.

Maggie always suited her demeanour to the occasion and was now in hostess mode. 'I expect you'll take a dram, Dr Chalmers?' she asked. 'I am afraid it's Hobson's choice, but I seem to remember you like the Islay malts. This is quite an old Bowmore, old enough to have mellowed to a really delicious and not too peaty flavour. My father liked this one.'

Maggie is always a surprise—it had not occurred to me that she might be something of a connoisseur of whisky. I thanked her and greeted Lachy, wondering what he was doing there. Then I sniffed and sipped my drink and let its mellow smoothness flow around my tongue. The seaweedy flavour of the Islay malts was subdued and mellowed in this marvellous whisky, which must have been very old and probably very costly. I had never tasted a whisky like it, and I guessed this had something to do with the satisfied look on the lapidary's face.

'My! This is magnificent, Maggie. For goodness sake, how old is it?' In my enthusiasm I had forgotten how I communicated with this blind and deaf old woman. Slipping my stethoscope from my pocket I placed the earpieces in her ears and bellowed again, 'Maggie, the whisky is magnificent! How old is it?'

The old lady beamed. 'I still have a few bottles my grandfather laid away. He paid nearly five shillings a bottle for it, in days when that was more than a weekly wage for most folk. I wanted something special for this evening—and I owe you an apology. You see, Lachy and I have been a little devious. But the time has come to let you into the secret. Show him, Lachy.'

The lapidary stood up, and fumbled in a pocket to find a small black box. Passing it to me, he said: 'Maggie told me a whole lot of stories, and as a result I designed this little number. I hope you like it, for it is unique.'

I was suddenly rather overawed, and gingerly took the box. The catch sprang at my touch, and there, lying on its bed of black velvet, was a magnificent brooch... or was it a pendant?

Lachy explained, 'We never did decide between brooch or pendant, so I have left the choice to the wearer. What's your first impression?'

'It's quite magnificent!' I said but, even as I spoke, I wondered if I could afford such a beautiful piece of jewellery. 'My first impression is that it combines simplicity with extreme sophistication.' Carefully I removed the piece from its box and held it in the light. I held it first as a brooch by the pin on its back and turning it saw the intricacy of the engraving on its surface—the Celtic intertwined pattern, produced by the art of a consummate engraver. The light, caught by the incised pattern in the surface of the silver, shone and sparkled like diamond. On the back were engraved Pictish symbols that I had come to know as the comb and mirror. A ring attached at one end would allow the long axis of the piece to hang vertically; the pin on the back would cant the brooch at any angle the wearer wished.

Finally, knowing I had to have this piece whatever it cost, I said, 'It is quite lovely, I am sure she will adore it. It's such a splendid sinuous shape... I can only call it "banana-form".'

Lachy smiled, 'I'm glad you chose that word. Now pass it to my friend and co-conspirator, Maggie. Of course she has seen it before, but put it into her hands, for her sensitive Braille-reading fingertips will tell us more about that half-ounce or so of silver than any human eyes could.'

Maggie took the silver in her hand and gently caressed it, much as I remembered her caressing my face on the first occasion that we had met. She had said then it was to find out about me. Now she was reminding herself of Lachlan Mackie's work.

'Lachy came to me because he wanted to know as much as possible about the laird and his lady.'

'That's why I asked you to set up a meeting for me wi' Maggie,' cut in Lachy.

'So I told him how you came to the island, about how we first met and I told him that I knew right away you would be laird. But back then it seemed almost impossible. You were set on working in London, and we already had a perfectly good successor to old Admiral Chalmers. But I knew that you would meet Fiona and from then on your life would change. When her brother Murdoch died you nearly lost your bonnie new wife. Grief and suspicion poisoned her love for you, but I knew that through the near death of you both in the tides of Assilag Bay her love for you would return. For it has long been told that you and Fiona will restore the greatness that was once attached to the lairdship of Laigersay.'

The old woman paused and sipped her whisky. 'Aye, my grandfather was a wise man when he invested in this *uisge beatha*; it is nectar.' She savoured the liquor. 'You must be patient with an old woman. I have much to say. Lachy came to see me several times; we got to know each other. He told me he wanted to do something Celtic and I pointed out that your wife's birthday fell on *Lughnasadh*, the ancient Celtic harvest festival on the day of the Sun-God Lugh. Later, in the Christian calendar, this festival was renamed Lammas.'

Again Lachlan interrupted. 'I was so glad to talk wi' Maggie. I thought I knew my mythology but I'm ignorant beside her.'

'The equinoxes and solstices,' the old woman continued, 'were important in Druidic religion and great temples were raised to mark these major changes in the seasons. The most important was Yule, the winter solstice, when pagans celebrated the return of the sun. In Ireland there is the Great Cairn of New Grange and there's another similar one in Orkney at Maes Howe where the sun's rays at Yule penetrate to the heart of the ancient building.'

Again Maggie took a sip from her glass.

'Lachy has created this piece of silver with a design based on the great stone at the entrance to New Grange. He has taken a little stylistic liberty with it as befits a great artist. For the stone at New Grange is straight, whereas Lachy's is slightly curved—you called it banana-form. There is good reason for that, as you will see.

'The intertwined endless chain of lines is typical of Celtic mythology: it represents the endlessness of time in which all that will ever happen in the future has already been and will come again. You see, foretelling the future is simple for those who know enough about the past.'

Pointing to his creation Lachlan explained: 'The curvature of the piece represents the moon in all her fickle feminine changeability; when worn as a pendant it represents the curvature of the erect phallus, while horizontally it is the broad, child-bearing hips of womanhood and the concave side represents...'

'What my grandfather used to call the *pudendum muliebre*,' interjected Maggie prudishly. 'Thus the piece becomes a symbol of fertility and fecundity.'

'It might be prudent not to tell Fiona that!' I commented.

Lachlan grinned at me and added: 'But the real mystery comes in the inscription...'

'Inscription?' I echoed, 'I saw no writing.'

'That's because you did not know where to look. Take it back and look again.'

'I re-examined the brooch. Ah! Here's a small mark...'

'No,' said Lachy, 'that's the assay mark. That has to be there by law, and the squiggle beside it is my signature. I always sign pieces I'm proud of. Look along the edge.'

I stared at the side of the flat piece of silver. 'I can only see some dots and scratches.'

'That's right, that's the inscription.'

'But they're just meaningless marks.'

'No,' said Maggie, 'that is Ogham script. Lachy, have you got your drawing of the inscription? It's a good deal bigger; that might make it easier for the laird to read.'

'Aye, it's here.' Lachy passed me a scrap of paper on which was written a series of symbols. It looked like this:—

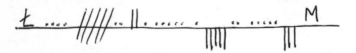

'The crossed L and the M are simply Lachy's own mark and of course the date is included in the assay mark. The rest is Ogham,' explained Maggie.

'I have heard of that but I know very little about it. Can you tell me what it means?' I asked.

'It is a form of script from way, way back in time. It was Celtic and used by the Druids, who were not only priests but were the most educated men in their society. It has about twenty symbols, and was used on the edge of a stone, or sometimes a tree branch.' Maggie took the silver symbol back and continued: 'The edge of the silver is represented by the line in Lachy's sketch. That is called the stave. Ogham letters are mostly written above the stave but some come below it and others cross it. Look just here at the top.' She traced the marks with her finger. 'After the first four dots there are five diagonal lines which wrap around the edge of the silver, that is, they cross the stave. These lines are the consonants, and the dots are vowels. The language was Celtic in the old days, but it's easy to write English words in Ogham so long as you only need the twenty Ogham letters.'

Maggie traced the inscription round the edge of the brooch with the nail of her index finger. 'It reads: E – R – O – D – A – I – A – N – O – I – F.'

Lachy burst out laughing. 'Maggie read it anticlockwise, but Ogham, like most other writing, should be read from left to right. Try it the other way round.'

CHAPTER 19

The Macnab

That summer the news was full of international troubles, which cast a shadow over the idyllic nature of the Hebridean summer. India detonated a nuclear bomb, making the smouldering Middle East seem to me yet more dangerous. Nearer home there were bomb blasts in Dublin, and at Westminster the running sore that was Ireland seemed impossible to heal. Some of these headlines made me wonder what humanity was coming to and what the future held for my two boys.

As so often, when I felt depressed like this I went fishing. Casting over trout soothes me as nothing else. In boyhood, fishing provided respite from the bullying at my school. In my early 'bent-pin' days, angling had always been with bait of some sort. Father shared my hobby and had some unconventional ways of acquiring bait. Just after World War Two a hot summer caused a plague of wasps. That led to my father, a recently demobbed Home Guard officer, developing a short-lived dual interest in wasps and explosives. In those permissive days it was possible to buy black gunpowder at any gunsmith's shop. A peculiarity of this explosive is that when mixed with water, to a clay-like consistency, it burns slowly with a shower of sparks, like a Roman candle. Father used to sprinkle large quantities of flowers of sulphur on a finger-sized piece of this gunpowder clay and wrap it in newspaper. That gave us a charge with which to deal with wasps' nests. The ignited firework was thrust into the hole in the ground leading to the nest, which was sealed with a turf. The resulting gasses dazed the insects. After a decent interval we dug madly at the nest, before its denizens awoke in a rage, and were rewarded with papery cakes filled with beautiful grubs we could use as bait. They were a great temptation to the roach and perch of my boyhood angling. Then authority stopped the unlicensed sale of gunpowder and an interesting phase of my life was closed... but the excitement of those Guy Fawkesian forays for bait lives on in memory.

One summer, years later, I took a fishing holiday and spent two weeks in the Outer Hebrides. There I learnt to combine fishing with another lifelong interest: ornithology. These two interests came together when I learned to tie fishing flies. I have to confess that I have never been an expert fly-tier, but there are enough foolish trout for me to have had the pleasure of filling the freezer with the aid of self-tied flies. Today I would be a better fisherman if my attention was not distracted from rising fish by a passing osprey or hen harrier. I would be a more proficient ornithologist if I could stop watching rising fish in an effort to find a logical explanation for the behaviour of trout.

Fishermen and others keen on field sports have competed since Victorian times, when Prince Albert popularized the pursuit of game in the Highlands. One challenge from the past is said to have originated in the exploits of one John Macnab, who was an archetypal Highland daredevil of a gentleman-poacher of the Edwardian era. John Buchan used him as the mythical central character of the classic novel of the same name set after the First World War. In his novel, published in 1925, Buchan tells of three bored society gentlemen, an ex-attorney general, a banker and a cabinet minister who set themselves the challenge of poaching a deer and a salmon (grouse did not feature in the original challenge, but were added later) from neighbouring estates, having warned the owners of their intention and the time and place where the acts would be carried out. In the event of success £50 would be paid to a charity appointed by the estate owner, but failure would be a forfeit of £100, paid by the three 'poachers', all of whom operated under the *nom-de-guerre* John Macnab. Though the substance of the challenge was very different from today's Macnab, the triple feat of catching a salmon, stalking a stag and bagging a brace of grouse, all in a single day, has now become a popular challenge amongst sportsmen, especially Americans, and contributes handsomely to the income of several estates.

One day out of the blue Stanley Johnson telephoned and said he'd had a brilliant idea. 'What about repeating the Macnab here in Laigersay?' he asked. 'It could do wonders for the letting of sporting rights on your estate. The Americans love that sort of thing. Why don't you and I have a go at it, we could make it a competition.'

Rather unenthusiastically I conceded its publicity potential. However I pointed out to Johnson that I no longer shot and had sold my shotgun some years before. There, I thought, the matter was left, but Stanley was a persistent fellow and he must have got on to Erchie in his capacity as my estate factor, for he accosted me a few days after Johnson's phone call. 'Ye ken Mr Johnson o' Tom Bacadh has the notion o' the Macnab?' he enquired. 'It could be a good way o' attracting revenue to the estate, especially if we could draw the Yankees in.'

'Oh, Erchie, I'm not very keen, besides you know I don't shoot myself.'

'I jalouse that needna be a problem,' the big man said. 'Ye see, there's always been the tradition in the Highlands o' the laird's champion. It dates way back to the auld days when sometimes an aged laird wasnae up to fighting. If you accepted Tom Bacadh's challenge ye could name me champion in yer stead, an' I'd be proud to serve ye.'

I was unconvinced but promised to think about it. After all, the man paid a good rent for Tom Bacadh. I got as far as searching out John Buchan's novel in the library at Castle Chalmers. Soon I was engrossed in it, and the more I read the more the idea appealed. Although I would be happy to have a go at the salmon, I would shoot neither grouse nor stag. I phoned Stanley and told him of my change of mind, and my terms. He was delighted, and was quite happy for Erchie to act as my champion for the grouse and stag, but stipulated that I should at least be with Erchie when he was shooting.

Erchie was delighted at the prospect of being my ghillie for the salmon, and having me as his for the stag and grouse. He grinned at me, and put a question: 'Have ye no heard aboot the *Royal* Macnab?' he asked.

'No, what's that?'

'It's a new variant on the standard Macnab, some Yankee fellow invented it. When ye have your three trophies ye have to have at least one o' them for supper and then bed the cook who made the dish!'

'For God's sake don't tell Johnson that!' I protested.

'Och ye'd be bound tae win, sor, for I doot Mr Johnson's no got it in him; and just consider who your cook is!'

I was not sure I liked this reference to my wife and changed the subject abruptly: 'So, when is this contest to take place, Erchie?' I asked.

'I reckon as soon after the grouse open as we can make it. We've got a shoot fixed for the 12th o' August itself but any time the following week would do.'

So it was arranged that Friday 18th August should be written into our diaries. It seemed far away at the time, and the approach of Fiona's birthday rather took my mind off the Macnab. I need not have worried about the gift. Lachlan Mackie and Maggie McPhee were absolutely right: Fiona was enchanted by it, especially the inscription when once she had learned to read it.

However, as early August passed, I concentrated on the challenge. I did not want to be shown up by my tenant, whom I had sometimes found to be a devious and not entirely likeable man. The main problem exercising Erchie and me was the order in which we should take our fences and just where to pick for our target areas for each trophy. In discussions with Tom Bacadh a complex system of scoring was decided, based on the nature of the capture and the time it was made. After all, if we both completed the Macnab we still had to decide who had won. Erchie and Johnson's new keeper between them drew up a scale of points.

The time of bagging each trophy was to be logged— the first would score two points and the second only one. Similarly, the heavier salmon would get two points, the smaller would be worth a single point; and those taken on a fly would score two to a single point for a fish caught spinning. When it came to grouse, the two keepers had a long discussion and it was decided that young birds, which were better for eating, should score two, and older birds one, with a bonus of an extra two for a brace shot with a consecutive right and left barrel. It was agreed that reports would be phoned throughout the day to Angus

Andersen, who was appointed umpire. This would permit independent logging of the time each bag was made.

It all seemed very complicated, but I realised that interest ran high when I heard that in the bar of the Charmer Inn bets were being laid, and that the unofficial bookmaker of Port Chalmers had opened a book on the results.

Erchie—and, I suspected, the Tom Bacadh keeper—spent several days on the hill observing the red deer, and anxiously watched the weather. Drought would make the river unfishably low, and he had already decided that the Allt Bradan was the venue for me to have the best chance of a big fish on a fly. There would be nothing to stop me trying a spinner in Loch Bradan later, but the loch fish tended to be smaller. If we were to win, we needed the best salmon we could get. The grouse were fairly plentiful and he believed they would present the least problem and should be left to last, allowing more time for the stag and the salmon which were likely to be the more difficult.

The bag they took disappointed the party that had taken the shooting for the 'glorious twelfth' that year, for it was a wet and dreich day and something of a wash-out. Normally Erchie would have been depressed by such weather, but this year he was exultant.

'Yon rain will raise the river just nicely. You'll get a good fush right eneuch,' he predicted. But then when rain fell solidly for the next three days he grew gloomy: 'Och, it's just terrible, the spate'll be too high and the river too coloured, I doot ye'll have to try the loch after all.'

Then miraculously the rain stopped and the sun came out and everything steamed. 'That'll do for river,' Erchie gloomed, 'but just think what the midges'll be like on the hill. They'll all hae tackits in their boots.'

At last the day dawned, and both parties left their respective castles at precisely nine o'clock. I had wanted to start earlier but Johnson said 9am was early enough for gentlemen. Only poachers, he said, took game before breakfast. The day was splendid, under an azure dome with only a zephyr of wind. Erchie glanced judiciously at the sky.

'I'd like more breeze,' he said, 'and it's no in the best quarter. It'll no be easy getting near the beasts but I think the high corries aboon Ranneach Bheag'll suit us best. Let's go there first. Then, when we've got the stag, we can retrace oor steps to the Allt Bradan for the fush.'

So we sped south through Port Chalmers to turn west across the island past Tom Bacadh.

'How's the competition?' I wondered aloud as we neared our rival's home.

A moment later Erchie pointed to two figures walking with a dog near the northern end of Loch Bradan, 'They're goin' for the grouse first,' he said. 'That's Mr Johnson's springer spaniel quartering the heather for him.'

As he spoke we saw the distant flash and seconds later heard a double report. But the walkers moved steadily on.

'That's guid,' said Erchie. 'He's no got a right an' left onywye. I think he missed wi' his second barrel. That bodes weel, but mind I'll hae to do better than that.'

We hurried on, for by starting close to Tom Bacadh the opposition had got ahead of us, but we had the whole day before us. As we crossed the bridge at the estuary of the Allt Bradan we both glanced at the river.

'It looks grand!' I exclaimed.

'Aye, its just aboot right,' agreed Erchie. 'Ye should do weel. But it's the beasts up the hill I'm worried aboot.'

We parked at the end of the road near the little jetty at Ranneach Bay. Shouldering his rifle Erchie led a terrific pace along the west bank of the little burn that came tumbling down from Ranneach Bheag.

'There's nae beasts doon low, so we can make a guid pace till we reach the shoulder before the first corrie below the western ridge. The wind's got a guid deal o' east in it so we should be able to stalk upwind under the summit o' Ranneach Bheag. There's been a stag wi' a braw heid on 'im there all this last week.'

I nodded to my factor, keeping my breath to match his furious pace. As we neared the ridge, Erchie slowed to a standstill and swept the hillside with his spyglass. I preferred binoculars, and I too searched. I knew he did not want to see deer here. Suspicious hinds would soon spot us and betray our presence to the stags, which we hoped were in dead ground in the corrie beyond the ridge.

'It's clear,' pronounced Erchie after a careful scrutiny of the hill ahead of us. 'Now we maun ca' canny. If we show oorsels at the ridge, we can kiss goodbye to the beasts in the corrie, for they'll be awa' tae Ranneach Mhor in a jiffy. It's crawlin' frae noo on.'

Erchie slid down on to hands and knees and led the way through heather that was still damp from the rain earlier in the week. Soon my stout tweeds were dripping with water, adding to the inner damp of sweat from our fast climb. We crawled a hundred yards and Erchie again stopped to sweep the hill with his glass. His prediction that the midges would be bad was fulfilled, and I thought that every winged insect in Scotland had descended on me. I removed a spider-like tick from my jacket, for I did not want that eating me as well.

But my factor was beckoning me on, and again we crawled fifty yards to the shelter of a large rock on the ridge that hid us from the corrie below. Cautiously we peered round the rock, with the freshening breeze blowing into our faces. Several hinds were feeding quietly a few hundred yards below. They were unconcerned, and so we were undetected. Further over to our left I could see a group of stags.

Erchie whispered, 'Yon's the beast at the far left. He looks like a twelve pointer, a fine head, he's the fella we want. But it's a hard stalk. We'll need tae go back doon and move gey quietly roond to oor left. D'ye see yon white rock ower to the left o' that bonnie patch o' purple heather? That's where we need to be; if he doesnae move, he'll be in range frae there.'

With his plan made, Erchie slid back below the ridge and gesturing to me to be silent and to keep down, he led the way leftwards well below the skyline. It took half an hour over very rough terrain with knee-high rank heather, and it was exhausting. At last we could see the whitish rock jutting into the skyline above us.

'Noo for our last crawl,' said Erchie. 'Wi' a bit o' luck he'll still be whaur we last saw him. Noo, be verra quiet and dinna show yersel.'

I followed the big man's sturdy buttocks as he inched to the rock above us. Erchie signalled to me to go right of the rock and he wriggled to its left. The stag was there, fifty yards ahead of us. Erchie slipped off his safety catch and slowly slid the rifle forwards. He seemed ages perfecting his aim, and when the report came I jumped.

Ahead of us, the hillside was alive with startled deer racing away to the far side of the corrie. The stag stood so motionless I thought it was a miss. Then slowly he crumpled and fell—with Erchie's bullet in his heart. I noted the time: it was 12.27.

The relative inactivity of our long slow crawl ended as my factor launched himself into the corrie and ran to the dead beast.

'We maun gralloch him as soon as we can for we still have the fush and the birds to get,' he shouted, as he raced down the hill to the dead stag. The disembowelling was soon accomplished, for Erchie had much experience with his knife.

'That's done all right,' he said. 'Noo we'll take a couple o' bearings to locate the carcase accurately, and we'll send young Thomas the underkeeper up wi' a garron to bring the beast doon the hill. Come on noo, we're way ahint o' time, but I doot yon Johnson'll no hae sae fine a beast.'

Erchie set off again and I followed as fast as I could, several breathless yards behind him, marvelling at the man's fitness. He had no right to be so fast on the hill, considering his enormous thirst for whisky. I caught up with him in the phone kiosk near where we had parked the car.

'Mr Andersen?' he was asking. 'Erchie Thomson here. We've had oor first kill at 12.27. It's a royal stag in the corrie on the east side o' Ranneach Bheag.'

He listened and then pulled a face. 'Aye, we'll have tae pu' oor socks up but it'll no be long afore I call ye back.'

Turning to me he said, 'Johnson has his grouse and he reported catching a grilse on a spinner in Loch Bradan twenty minutes ago. He's awa' after his stag noo.'

We jumped in the Land Rover, Erchie reversed in a scream of tyres on gravel and we sped on our way to the Allt Bradan. This was to be my contribution to the competition. I assembled the rod in seconds, and soon my 'General Practitioner' fly was curling out over the river in a Spey cast. Erchie perched himself on the bank behind me, watching.

'Try ower under the far bank, sor. There's a muckle great fush lying there—I can see him wi' my glass.'

When I cast again, the fly dropped just short of the far side where the current eddied and had undercut the bank.

I thought I saw movement, and Erchie said, 'He came to look at the fly; try him again.'

The second time my cast touched the water a couple of feet further upstream.

'He's moved again,' shouted an excited Erchie. But the fish had taken; I saw line inching out and the spool of the reel turned half a circle. Holding my nerve I counted to three and then I lifted the rod tip. All hell broke loose. The fish turned towards the sea and made a huge rush, tearing line out furiously. He ran out of the lie where I had hooked him down to the pool beneath the road bridge. There he settled into a sulk and I had to pump the line carefully to make him move again. Then he shot upstream and leapt from the water, leaving me gasping. This was the largest salmon I had ever seen in the Allt Bradan, or anywhere in the island for that matter.

Erchie was shouting encouragement behind me: 'Losh, it's a muckle great fush. Ca' canny noo, an' dinna go for anither swim. I dinna want tae have tae break mair ribs!'

Even as I played the salmon, I could not but laugh. After half an hour the fish tired. As the fish turned on its side and came to the bank he slipped the big landing net under it and administered the last rites with the club known as a 'priest'. That meant we were two down and only the grouse to get.

'Mon! that's as guid a fush as I've seen frae this wee river,' said Erchie. 'It'll be fifteen pund if it's an ounce. Johnson'll be hard pressed to beat that. Look, it's fresh oot the sea, see the lice on it.' He shook me powerfully by the hand, showing me his great strength and reminding me of the damage he had done to my chest years before.

'Noo,' he said, 'it's the back o' three. We'd best go north to Milton o' Bacadh: there's plenty o' birds there an' I doot it'll no tak ower long tae finish the job. We can stop at Lutheran postoffis to phone the minister.'

Smiling at his way of saying Post Office as one word, I jumped into the car with the fish at my feet. This time when we stopped to phone, it was I who spoke to Angus. I told him about my fish and he congratulated me. 'Johnson may be ahead on time,' he said, 'but it sounds as if you have the bigger fish, and on a fly too. He's away up the north side o' Ranneach Mhor above Pitchroich for his stag just now, and I've not heard anything from him for an hour or two.'

When I relayed this to Erchie, he looked at the sky. The wind had changed and dark clouds were coming in from the southwest. 'If he's on the north side o' the big Ranneach he'll have trouble wi' this wind. Wi' a bit o' luck we'll beat him yet. Come on, let's get those grouse.'

This time we returned to the moors we kept for our own guests. Unlike Johnson's keeper, we had not brought a dog. Erchie preferred walking the birds up himself, his eyesight was such that he never missed where a bird fell.

We got out of the car and were immediately heartened by the 'Go, go, go back' call of a cock grouse. We struck out a few yards apart walking through heather, which was short and not so exhausting to struggle through as it had been on Ranneach Bheag. But the midges were every bit as bad, and I cursed and rubbed my forehead and ears at the onslaught. Erchie, alert with his gun at the ready, seemed blissfully unaware of the biting horde.

A covey of grouse exploded at our feet. Erchie had two with the first barrel and swinging round got another with his left. Picking up the birds, I saw that the two outermost primary wing feathers were pointed and not worn as they would be in aging birds: these were young grouse. That completed the Macnab and, it seemed, with a goodly score. We hurried back to the car and returned to Feadag Mhor village where the telephone box united us again with Angus Andersen just as my watch showed a quarter past five.

'Done it!' I shouted down the phone. 'We had three grouse with two shots.'

'Well done!' came the reply, 'but I the others have just beaten you. They are just down off Ranneach Mhor and they killed their stag at 4.35.'

The chagrin I felt at this defeat amazed me. I had not been keen on this challenge, but once engaged on it the excitement carried me forward and, despite my reservations about shooting game, I had thoroughly enjoyed the day.

When we got home, we all met for a dram and counted our points. Johnson had two old grouse, not with a right and left, but he got them before we did scoring two points. He had had a grilse of 5lbs on a Devon minnow, which he got first, scoring another three. His stag was after ours and was only a ten-pointer, earning him only one other point. He had a total of six points.

We had three for our stag as it was a better beast and shot first. We got three for the larger salmon, a splendid fish taken on a fly. The grouse were young and were shot with a right and left, earning another two and making three points for the birds. We had a total of nine points altogether.

Stanley Johnson quoted the Dodo from *Alice in Wonderland*: 'All have won and all shall have prizes.'

Fiona gave us all a marvellous dinner. The venison would need to hang for a while, but the fresh salmon and the grouse served with my favourite rowan jelly were excellent. We were all exhausted, and as we bade the guests goodnight I noticed Erchie was grinning.

It was not until he joined me in the estate office for our morning meeting that the reason for his mirth became clear.

'I hope after all the exertions o' the day,' he said 'you werena too tired to make it the Royal Macnab!'

CHAPTER 20

A Series of Emergencies

After the excitement of the Macnab, the rest of the summer passed peacefully enough. The colours of early autumn were magnificent and the island basked in long days of late summery sunshine. Fiona and I were still concerned by world news, but the autumn was so superb I was able to keep from brooding about all the troubles which afflicted the planet. During this Indian summer the good weather brought a large number of late visitors to the island. By chance when doing visits in Port Chalmers, I ran into Vivian Pickering, a consultant physician friend of mine from Inverness, who had come over from the mainland on the ferry and was staying with his wife at a hotel in the town. He was doing some fishing and I promised to take him for a day on Loch Bradan when I could get off from the practice.

The spate of late tourists coupled with early autumn respiratory infections increased my workload. As usual there was more than enough to do, but I enjoyed my work in the peace of the island.

Late on a September evening after a relatively quiet period in the practice two calls came almost together just as my wife was putting supper on the table. A strained male voice said, 'Doctor, can you come at once. It's my wife ... I think she may be pregnant ... she's just fainted in the loo. She's come round now but she has severe tummy pain and can't move.' Fearing an ectopic pregnancy, I jotted the address down, said that I was on my way and replaced the receiver. The phone immediately rang again. Sounding at once fussy and unconcerned, a mother said: 'I wonder, doctor, if you happen to be in Port Chalmers this evening—could you take a look at my Andrew? He's seventeen and he's been helping with the harvesting and he's got a spot on his lip. I am afraid he's been picking at it. He's running a temperature and now he's got a funny eye...'

I cut her short because I wanted to see the pregnant woman quickly, but I promised to look in after the first call. Dashing from the house I shouted to my wife, 'I've got a ruptured ectopic and a cavernous sinus thrombosis, so I may be some time,' and with that I fled. Doctors' wives get very used to such things; I cannot count how many meals have been ruined that way.

Arriving at the first house I was met by the young woman herself, full of apologies for her husband's panic. 'I'm a bit overdue, that's all, and when I did start, I fainted and then I had a bad tummy ache.' The bleeding preceded pain, examination was entirely normal and I concluded that the shared panic of doctor and husband was, after all, quite unnecessary. But ectopic pregnancy from implantation of an embryo in the fallopian tube causes internal bleeding which may be catastrophic and needs urgent surgery. It was just as well to have made sure.

I pottered on to my second call enjoying the beautiful tangential early autumnal evening light, which threw all the folds of the hills into a succession of shadows each more blue than the one before. I did not hurry, because I did not really believe there to be any emergency. My facetious suggestion of the dangerous but extremely rare condition of a cavernous sinus thrombosis was, as Erchie would have said, 'juist a bit o' nonsense'.

But in fact Andrew, the teenage son of the local garage proprietor, was clearly very ill. His mother, hurrying me into his bedroom, was not so calm now: 'I've just had another look at him,' she said. 'He looks awful.'

Indeed he did, and it only took a single glance to see that, after all, my jesting comment to Fiona had been spot on. Cavernous sinus thrombosis used to be invariably fatal before the days of antibiotics, and even today is a seriously life-threatening condition, arising when infection from around the upper lip is carried via the facial veins to the great venous sinuses inside the skull that drain the brain. The cavernous sinus lies behind the orbit and may become infected from septic lesions such as carbuncles around the lips. This is a dangerous place for infection and the risk of spreading it is greatly increased by picking.

The boy lay with his back and neck extended; almost as though he was supported on his head and his heels. The golden crusts of impetigo were obvious on the left side of his upper lip where he had scratched an injury from the cornfields. His left eye was protruding grossly, and he had a marked squint from paralysis of the nerves to the muscles that moved his eye. He felt very hot, but I did not waste time taking a temperature. With his mother's help, I carried him to my car. We drove the mile to the cottage hospital and got the boy straight to the ward. While the nurses were getting him to bed I rang the hotel in Port Chalmers where I knew the visiting consultant, Dr Pickering, was staying. By good luck he was in, and just finishing dinner.

'Sorry to bother you, Vivian, when you're on holiday, but I really need your help. I've got a seventeen-year-old lad with a cavernous sinus thrombosis. He's desperately ill and I think you are probably the only person who can save his life.'

At once Vivian Pickering was supportive. 'Where are you?' he asked and when I explained how to find the cottage hospital he said: 'I am coming straight away.' He put the phone down and came, much quicker than I had myself.

Within minutes of Andrew's admission I carried out a lumbar puncture and soon the cerebro-spinal fluid from the intrathecal space in his lumbar spine (that is, the space surrounding the spinal cord in the lower part of his back) was dripping into a culture tube. I could see it was slightly turbid in contrast to its normal gin-clear state. Vivian arrived as the CSF was dripping into the specimen bottle. He took one look at Andrew's face and grunted.

'There's no doubt about your diagnosis,' he said, 'smart of you to recognise it, it's not a common condition. While you've got that needle in there we'd better get some penicillin into him intrathecally. Give him ten thousand units of penicillin through your needle as a start. Any more than that may make him convulse. Then give large doses intramuscularly, say five million units every four hours. It would be as well to give Chloromycetin as well: the boy's very ill indeed. He'll be lucky to survive.'

I was extremely grateful to have the reassurance of a consultant by my side and Andrew was lucky that the specialist happened to be in the island when he was taken so ill. With the antibiotics and the speed with which we treated him the boy made a complete recovery, but was very fortunate to do so. I have never seen cavernous sinus thrombosis before or since, but I shall not jest about it again.

On a lighter side, Morag Farquharson came to see me with her wee boy Geordie who had tonsillitis again. She looked worried and when I asked what was making her so concerned, she told me she had received a final demand from the electricity board. 'They say we haena paid oor bills,' she said, 'but we've never had any. The post has been gey erratic lately, but the electric are threatening to cut us off.'

'Well, you can't pay bills you've never had,' I said. 'By the way, did you ever get Geordie's appointment with the ENT specialist on the mainland?'

'No, to tell the truth, I thocht ye'd forgotten all about it.'

I turned out Geordie's medical record envelope with some apprehension.

'I have to admit I do sometimes forget things but, see, here's the carbon copy of my letter to the specialist.' Suddenly wee Geordie, who had been very quiet, burst into floods of tears. It took some time to quieten him down. Then he confessed: 'I didna want ma tonsils oot and every morning I met Postie and destroyed any letter that could hae come frae the hospital.'

I told Morag I thought Geordie had a brilliant future. 'He'll probably get to be a cabinet minister,' I added.

'Aye, or end up in Barlinnie,' said his mother. 'Just wait till I tell the electric.' Fortunately officialdom was as amused as I was, and the outstanding bill was soon settled.

Police enquiries continued all that September but it seemed that they were no nearer solving the murder of

Joey Bruce or the disappearance of Maantie. What with Fiona's birthday and the Macnab, I had had little time to follow what was happening. As far as I was aware, the police had not traced Nutty Jakes either. By now he must have long since run out of his medication and I felt anxious about him. It was time for me to call on Charlie Kerr at his home, close to the little jetty at Ranneach Bay, with its fine view over to Sgarbh an Sgumain.

The old man was in his vegetable patch, where immaculate rows of plants were strictly dressed by the right, in military precision. There seemed to be a large quantity of them, but I understood he sold them to local customers. Two or three busy hives of bees buzzed under the burden of the last of the heather harvest. And an old dog fox woke from a doze in the sun, eyed me suspiciously, and slunk away to hide in a woodpile.

Charlie greeted me: 'Walcome *Dhoctair mhòr*. 'Tis canty tae see ye, aye douce an' couthie is't. Whit way can I be helplie?'

By now I was beginning to understand Charlie's peculiar speech and I translated in my mind: 'Welcome great doctor it is cheerful to see you, yes pleasant and agreeable. How may I help you?'

'Well, Charlie, I was wondering if you had seen Nutty Jakes. He's not been to see me for some time, and I'm worried that he's out of his tablets. If he doesn't take them, I am afraid he may get ill again.'

'I haena seen Jakes sin long afore Bartleday. I dinna ken whaur he stays noo.'

Erchie had mentioned Bartleday as St Bartholomew's day, the 24th of August, now about five weeks past. I studied the old man as he hoed a row of leeks. I had a feeling he was trying to avoid my eye and that he was keeping something from me. That would not be hard for Charlie, given the complexity of his language. This time I sensed the barrier was more than linguistic: he was hiding something.

Our conversation took its tortuous way without shedding any light on what could have happened to

Nutty Jakes. But I decided to make a few enquiries about Charlie, though I had little hope of finding out much.

A few days later, a call to one of Charlie's few neighbours took me south to the tiny hamlet where he lived. My patient was the son of a holidaymaker at a let cottage a bare hundred yards from Charlie's home. The medical problem was soon dealt with, and I asked the boy's mother if she had met Charlie Kerr.

'Oh yes,' she said, 'we have got to know him a bit; you see we have been coming here for a fortnight each summer for a year or two. He sells the most marvellous vegetables and often brings gifts of mackerel and haddock. He's very kind, I just wish I could understand what he says to me!'

'Does he do a lot of fishing?' I asked at random.

'Oh yes he keeps a little blue boat, the "Blue Belle", with an outboard down by the jetty. He's out in the bay most days when he's not working somewhere on land. He's busy from dawn to dusk.'

As I drove home up the hill above Ranneach Bay I stopped the car and got out for a stretch. The view looking down into the bay was superb, with the bulk of one of Laigersay's three volcanoes making up the mass of the island of Sgarbh an Sgumain. To the southwest lay the skerries, made aeons ago where the ancient lava flow had plunged, hissing steam, into the sea. Further round still, the southern tip of the mysterious island of Mulcaire was visible. Shading my eyes against the bright sun, which had turned towards the west, I could see a small blue boat moving slowly between the skerries and Sgarbh an Sgumain. That, I guessed, was Charlie Kerr out fishing.

Each time my rounds took me to the south of Laigersay I watched for Charlie's boat. I noticed that he seemed to favour the shore of Mulcaire for his fishing; the easily recognisable 'Blue Belle' was never far from the island.

Later that autumn there was a breakthrough on the Joey Bruce case. The papers announced that an arrest had been made following an almost identical murder in Sutherland.

Though the papers were necessarily vague, the suspect appeared to have a history of violence and mental instability. No name was mentioned, but the man charged with murder was clearly not Nutty Jakes. But the mystery of the whereabouts of both my patient and Maantie remained.

Increasingly I suspected that the clue to Nutty Jakes' whereabouts lay with Charlie Kerr. I had a breakthrough one day when visiting another tourist family in the same holiday let near Charlie's cottage. They were visiting Laigersay for the first time, and when I asked said they knew nothing of their neighbour Charlie. However, as I left their cottage I spotted a column of black smoke moving slowly westwards through the deep channel between Laigersay and Sgarbh an Sgumain. That dirty smoke could only mean one thing: the return of the puffer.

I drove to the little jetty, noticing that the 'Blue Belle' was once again away from her mooring. I scanned the bay but this time could not see Charlie's little boat. The puffer crept slowly to the jetty, reminding me of Para Handy's 'Vital Spark'. I hailed her skipper, old Jock Dewar, whose pipe reeked almost as badly as his funnel. I knew him slightly as he had consulted me once or twice over chest problems almost certainly related to the dreadful shag he consumed in huge quantity.

'Hallo, Doctor,' came the reply. 'Come aboard for a cuppa.'

Jock made the puffer fast and came to offer me a hand onto his grimy deck. 'I'm chust in wi' a load o' coals for Charlie an' his freends. I'll no be long, for I've to be in Tobermory the nicht. How are ye keeping, Doc?'

'I wanted to have a chat with you, Jock. Did you know the police have been trying to find you?'

Old Jock handed me a steaming mug of hideously strong tea sweetened with condensed milk.

'Aye I ken fine. I heard tell they was speirin' aboot ma freend Jakes who sometimes crews for me. Ach, they didna find me, an' I led them a right dance up an' doon the coast. When ye know the islands as I do, it's easy to gie them the slip. Anyway frae what I hear young Jakes is no so interestin' to the polis the noo, for they've got their man. I doot they'll no be interested in me neither.'

'Did you know anything about Jakes.'

'Aye, did I no take him an' his wee bit scooter through Crinan to Lochranza? An' frae there over to Ardrossan to drop Jakes an' his wee bike on the mainland. I didna stay long because a mate told me the polis were speirin' for me so I was soon awa tae Bute then ower to Campbeltown. I spent most o' the summer dodging atween Gigha, Jura, Colonsay an' Luing. Aye, I had fun layin' false trails for the polis. It's been a braw summer.' Jock laughed loudly, displaying teeth blackened by strong tea and his foul shag.

'What happened to Jakes?'

'Och, I dinna ken. I haena set eyes on him since I dropped him an' his girl freend here at this very jetty at the back o' May.'

'Girl friend?' I echoed.

'Aye a bit o' a simple lass wi' a muckle great heid.'

There was no doubting who *that* was. 'You mean Jakes and his girl have been hiding here in Laigersay?'

'Och, I dinna ken aboot that, all I know was the pair o' them met up wi' Charlie Kerr when I sailed. Goad only kens whit happened after that.'

I gulped as much of Jock's tea as I could stomach, thanked him and soon excused myself because of more visits I had to make. I left the puffer with my mind awhirl, irritated that Charlie was away and I could not question him. As I drove to the vantage point on the hill above the cluster of white cottages round the Ranneach Bay jetty, I could see old Jock offloading his coal bags. As I watched he heaved his last bag on shore, cast off and returned to his wheelhouse. The puffer belched smoke and turned south to round Mulcaire and Solan on her way to Tobermory.

Then I saw 'Blue Belle' picking her way through the skerries back to her mooring. She detoured briefly, for a shouted conversation between Charlie and the puffer's skipper, and then resumed her course back to the jetty. By the time I had driven back down the hill Charlie was standing looking at his new consignment of winter fuel.

'Good morning Charlie,' I greeted him. 'I'd like some words with you.'

'Aye, Doctor Laird, I've been thinking ye might,' he replied in the clearest phrase I had ever heard him say. 'Come up to my cottage and I'll tell ye all ye want to know.'

So saying, he led the way to his garden gate. He paused looking at the late autumn vegetable plot. 'Aye, it's been a bountiful season, the tatties have done better than I ever remember. Just as well too, wi' extra mouths to feed.'

I was amazed at the change in the man: gone were his convoluted Scotticisms and he spoke with hardly a trace of the thick accent he normally affected. 'I can see ye're puzzled,' he said. 'But I can speak as clearly as any man when I choose. It's just that if folk canna understand what I say it helps preserve my privacy and I kinda like it that way.'

He led his way into the cottage and I gasped in astonishment. The room we entered was a miniature library stacked high with books. As I glanced round I saw favourite classics of my own: Gilbert White's famous *Natural History*, Bewick's *History of British Birds*. Then there were works by other famous writers of the past: I spotted Pennant's *A Tour in Scotland and Voyage to the Hebrides 1772* and Martin Martin's, *A Late Voyage to St Kilda*. And then, filling two whole shelves, there were the complete volumes of Sir John Sinclair's Old Statistical Account. Other shelves held ancient books on Scottish history, many of them in Gaelic.

Charlie was watching me, a faint smile at the corners of his old, thin lips. 'I do not let many folk in here,' he explained, 'just one or two foreign scholars who come to see me about history or birds. As I said, I like to keep my privacy but I always welcome educated people like yourself, especially when, as now, I need your help.'

I turned to him. 'My help? I need yours. Do you know where Jakes Ormerod is?'

'Yes, and it is for him and Maantie I need your help.'

'They're together? Don't you know half the Scottish police are looking for them?'

'I know that too. It has been difficult hiding them. Maantie is with child and now that Jakes has had the suspicion of the murder of her friend lifted from him, I feel it is time for her to have medical care.'

'So I suppose Jakes is the father?'

'That tends to happen with married folk.'

'Married?'

'Yes. I married them myself in this very room.'

'What on earth do you mean *you* married them? What right do you have to marry people?'

'The ancient power of the *seanachaidh*. In times past in Scotland marriage by the process of handfasting could be performed by several lay folk such as clan leaders, *seanachaidhean*, or even by blacksmiths—as happens at Gretna. Jakes and Maantie were married the day they arrived back in Laigersay. Old Jock Dewar, who brought them here in the puffer, was witness but I swore him to secrecy. They completed their marriage by jumping the besom. That is not essential, but they wanted to do it.'

I stared at the old man, completely astonished. 'Is the marriage legal?' I blurted out.

'Technically it has to be registered with the Registrar General, but that's a formality. Some day I'll explain it to you, but just now I want to take you to see Maantie. She seems in good health, but I'd be glad if you'd check her.'

'Where is she?' I asked, glancing at my watch and thinking of the rest of my day's work.

'Right here, in the next room.'

'And Jakes?'

'No, we decided it was best for him to stay in hiding until the police have their conviction.'

With that Charlie led me into another room simply furnished as a bedroom. The room was dimly lit by a small window, and at first I could see little. But I heard a laugh. As my eyes adjusted to the dim light, I could see Maantie lying in the bed, clad in a nightgown.

I held out my hand to her. She laughed again and, as she had done before she clasped my hand to her heart. Then with another laugh she slid my hand over her belly and said, 'Babby inside.'

Clearly her ability to communicate had improved.

'Well done, congratulations,' I mouthed at her and she laughed again.

I turned to Charlie. 'I'll need my bag from the car and some more light, then I can have a look at her and see that all is going well.'

When I got back from my car Charlie had a paraffin lamp going, shedding a bright light in the little room. Maantie was seraphic. She was looking better than I had ever seen her, and had lost her institutional pallor. She was now deeply tanned, as if she had spent the summer in the open air. The real change was in her expression; instead of the helpless waif-like look she had before, she seemed fulfilled and proud of her incipient maternity.

To my surprise she handed me a little bottle saying, 'Jacks said you'd want.'

I took her urine sample and showed her what I was doing as I tested the contents of her bottle. Then I put my thumb up to show success, and again she laughed. As this was my first examination during her pregnancy I listened to her chest and heart, finding no abnormality other than the easily palpable catheter, which drained excess fluid from her head to her peritoneal cavity.

'God bless the Spitz-Holter valve,' I muttered to myself before looking at her abdomen. I noticed Maantie had lost a good deal of weight since I last examined her; indeed she seemed to have quite an attractive figure. Her blood pressure was normal and I could feel the fundus of her uterus and estimate her pregnancy at about sixteen weeks. Then I pondered for a moment, at some time I should have to carry out a vaginal examination to assess the capacity of her pelvis. Explaining seemed too difficult and I decided to postpone it until I had a nurse with me. I again made my thumbs-up sign to her, and was rewarded with another chuckle.

I saw Charlie and explained that I should want to see Maantie in the surgery fairly soon. I needed to be able to assess whether this woman, who was quite old for a first pregnancy, would be capable of a normal delivery or whether I should refer her to a consultant obstetric unit on the mainland. But at any rate, for the time being she was splendidly normal.

'That's a great relief,' he said. 'I don't understand these womany things and I was getting worried about her. I'll get on to the surgery and make a time for her when the tide's right.'

I glanced at him and, realising he had made a slip, he added with a deprecating smile and relapsing into his old way of speaking: 'I dinna want to miss the fushing.'

As I motored up the hill on my way back to Port Chalmers I reflected on what I had heard. The idea of a union between a paranoid schizophrenic and a congenital idiot hardly seemed a recipe for marital success but, to judge by Maantie's present state, it seemed to have transformed her. I wondered what Jakes would be like.

CHAPTER 21

Cuhlan and Fand

After Hamish lost Siller, he was more dour, silent and downcast than I had ever known him. The acute phase of his bereavement was mercifully short, largely due to the support of Terror, who, in his last few days in Laigersay had become very close to my sad senior partner. After Terror had returned to Birmingham, Hamish shut himself away. He continued working, but spoke only when he had to and he rarely smiled. By early autumn I could stand it no longer and suggested he took a holiday for, to be frank, I was depressed enough myself by news from around the world and needed a break from my unhappy partner. At last Hamish agreed to visit friends on the mainland.

Soon after Hamish left on the late ferry for the mainland, I had one of the strangest experiences of my life, and one that made me rethink the whole question of second sight. I had finished evening surgery and was alone in the building after the staff and patients had all left. I had put out most of the lights and was writing notes beside my desk lamp, when I heard someone enter the building. The door silently opened and in came a young man I had never seen before. He was wearing a white mackintosh, which in the dim light from the lamp on my desk gave him an odd ghostly appearance. He sat in the patient's chair on the other side of my desk, studying me silently. Then, without the slightest warning, he drew a knife and lunged at me across the tabletop. I was terrified and with my hands under the heavy desk, I turned it on to him to throw him off balance ... and at that moment I woke to find myself in bed. I had dreamt it all. When I stopped shaking, I explained my nightmare to myself in terms of too much cheese for supper, and eventually went off to sleep again.

The very next evening I had finished surgery and was writing notes. Someone entered the building and, in the instant, my terror of the night before returned. I saw the door open slowly and there, as I knew he would be, stood the man in the white mackintosh. Without a word he sat in front of me, and my hands grasped the desk ready to turn it against him in self-defence.

But then he started to speak and I did not need to listen long to realise that he was suffering an acute schizophrenic illness. This, alarming though it was, was not so frightening as my dream. I was trained to cope with psychosis and my grip on the table relaxed. Though the situation was still alarming, at least I understood something of schizophrenia, whereas I had very little knowledge of, or real belief in, second sight.

This boy of about twenty was very disturbed indeed, hearing voices urging him to kill someone with his knife. I felt certain he should be in hospital to protect both him and society. But I was alone in the surgery and could not see how to arrange this. It would mean getting the air ambulance out and I was only too well aware how the pilots felt about flying the severely mentally disturbed. Eventually I took a risk, led him to my car and drove him to his home where I could talk with his family.

His father was also unknown to me; he was defensive and aggressively refused my suggestion of immediate admission. I considered signing a committal order on his son but as the patient seemed a little less confused I dropped the idea, and agreed with his father that I would treat him at home, at least for the time being. I gave the boy a powerful sedative injection and went home feeling inadequate, foolish and very worried. Next morning I saw him early: he was much better and father was jubilant that he had proved me wrong. I said I would see him again the following day and went about my day's routine.

At midnight that night I was just getting into bed when the phone rang. It was our local policeman.

'Doctor,' he asked, 'do you know... ?' and he named my disturbed patient.

'Yes,' I replied, 'I did know him, and you are ringing to tell me he has just killed himself...'

There was a gasp from the other end of the line. 'How could you know that? It's only just happened.'

But I was right. The boy had thrown himself under a car in the main street of Port Chalmers. He died instantly.

This sequence of events disturbed me more than I can say. I felt overwhelming guilt in that I had failed my patient. If I had not taken the easy way and had stood up to the boy's father and insisted on admitting him to a place of safety he would still be alive. And I was astonished at my precognitive dream. Was there after all something in the belief that sometimes the future could be 'seen' in advance. Why, I wondered, did such strange things always seem to happen when Hamish was away from the island? Not for the first time, I missed the wise and reassuring presence of the dour older doctor.

But Hamish was not due back for nearly two weeks, and in his absence I had to run the practice single-handed. Work is always the best anodyne and I was so busy that I had little time to dwell on the death of the young schizophrenic. I decided eventually that rather than an example of second sight, a more logical explanation was that I had experienced a subliminal observation of the lad. Just as once before I had picked up clues to the problem of Luigi's brucellosis without being aware of it, so I felt I must have seen something that had triggered my prophetic dream. I tried to think what might have been the clue. Perhaps I had seen the boy about in Port Chalmers—certainly the white mackintosh was very noticeable. Then schizophrenia is often associated with odd posturing movements; could I have perceived this subliminally and so have been forewarned of the possibility of mental illness? Or was it I myself, fearful about the terrifying state of the world, who was quietly going mad?

The problem was unresolved when Hamish phoned to say he was coming back. It was only after I put the phone down that I realised he had said, '*We're* coming back on tomorrow evening's ferry.' In retrospect I thought he sounded his old self, even happy. Just what, I wondered, had the old boy been up to on his holiday?

When I told Fiona about it she stared at me in disbelief. 'You don't suppose... ?' she began.

'No, I can't believe the old misogynist would get himself a woman. It's just not believable. But I tell you what, we'll meet the ferry and see who it is.'

So the next evening we watched the arrival of the ferry with mounting curiosity. Fiona, incurable romantic that she was, had the conviction that Hamish had secretly married while he was away. After all he did keep making short trips to the mainland, ostensibly on 'refresher' courses, though he never told anyone anything about these alleged courses or, for that matter, how he was refreshed. Then he always seemed so pleased with himself when he came back, and nobody would ever accuse Hamish of not being a full-blooded man...

Soon he was waving to us from the deck of the ferry. As soon as the little ship berthed Hamish walked on to the gangplank with a sprightly step. Beside him ambled an Irish wolfhound.

'How do you like her?' he greeted us. 'Friends said I needed another dog. I could not face having another lab so I followed your example and bought this bitch.'

Fiona was on her knees beside the dog and her eyes were level with the hound's. 'Hamish, she's lovely, just wait till Cuhlan sees her! What's her name?'

'Not sure. I've got ideas, but I dinna want to rush it. I only got her a couple o' days ago. She's a pup, aboot a year old, very aristocratic wi' a pedigree a mile long. I think I'll come to like her, but she's so different from the labradors I am used to. She seems wise and detached, while Florin and Siller were so emotional and loving.'

Fiona laughed and glancing at me said: 'That was quite a surprise, Hamish ... not what we expected at all!'

I was glad he did not ask us what we *had* expected.

My partner was a different man. He was engrossed with the new dog, teaching her and talking to her all the time. He took her on his rounds, stopping to walk her over the moors. Once I saw his car parked by the road in the far south of the island and guessed he was walking her by the standing stone and burial chamber where he used to go with Siller. It was more apparent than ever just how isolated he had been after the death of the old dog, and I was glad to see how her successor was helping him. I remembered him telling Terror that 'it was not *a* dog we loved but *the* dog.'

One day he had business on the mainland and asked me if I would look after the new dog for the day. I was glad to do so and took her home to Castle Chalmers. This was the first time she met Cuhlan and their meeting was remarkable. At first the two huge dogs studied each other rather suspiciously, their gaunt shaggy faces mirroring each other. Then a change came over the serious young bitch, and all at once she became a skittish teenager. Spreading her forepaws low along the ground she lunged at the surprised Cuhlan, who was unused to such a forward, flirtatious approach. He contemplated her seriously as if not sure how he should cope with such frivolity. She responded by suddenly galloping in circles round the forecourt of the castle. For a moment an astonished Cuhlan watched her manic circling. Then suddenly he shed a dozen years and joined the bitch in her dance of joy. Cuhlan, it seemed, deigned to approve.

It so happened that that day I made my routine visit to Maggie McPhee in her home in Port Chalmers. Both the wolfhounds went with me, almost filling the car. Their exuberance had subsided and Cuhlan at any rate had resumed his normal gravitas. I took them with me into Maggie's tiny sitting room. Cuhlan immediately sat at the old woman's side, and lowered his great head on to her knee.

'*Ach Chuhlan a chill mo chridhe,*' she greeted him in Gaelic, and as the bitch copied him by putting her head on the old woman's other knee, she added, '*Fhand, is tu m'annsachd.*'

'What did you say to them?' I asked .

'Och, I just called Cuhlan my dearest dear, and then I said to Fand as if from Cuhlan, "Thou art my beloved."'

'Fand? Why do you call her Fand? Hamish hasn't yet decided on her name.'

'Is there no end tae your ignorance, ye that are both doctor and laird? Fand was the mistress o' Cúchulainn. Do ye ken naething aboot the legends o' your adopted land?'

Sadly I shook my head. 'Sorry, Maggie, you'll have to teach me. I am afraid I know nothing about Cúchulainn except that he was some ancient Celtic hero.'

The old woman bent low over the heads of the two great hounds that sat by her with their heads in her lap. She fondled their ears and spoke again to them in the old tongue. They seemed to understand and sat motionless, their sighted eyes fixed on Maggie's sightless ones.

'It's a gey long tale o' long, long ago,' she began. 'Way, way back when all the world was young and folk held to a different faith. Then there was a god o' the sun, his name was Lugh and he was all-powerful. Lugh fell in love with Deirdre, the wife o' King Conchobar. Thae gods all used to lead complicated love lives back then. It's said Cúchulainn was sired o' Deirdre by the sun god Lugh. One tale says that Lugh changed into a mayfly and entered Deirdre's body after falling in her wine.

'The boy wasnae called Cúchulainn at first. As a lad he was named Sétanta, and even as a child he was immensely strong. When he was about seven, King Conchobar took him on a visit to a banquet given by Culann, the blacksmith o' the heroes, who made their weapons. Culann was a terrible man and he kept an even more terrible hound. Sétanta didnae want to go to the banquet and stayed outside playin' wi a ball. Culann, not realising the boy was outside, loosed his dog, who ran at Sétanta to kill him. But the boy threw his ball into the hound's maw so hard it choked him, then seized the massive dog by its hinner legs and beat his brains oot on a rock. Culann was furious with Sétanta and the boy apologised and promised to replace the hound. Until he did so he would fulfil the position of guard dog himself. That was how he got the nickname of Cú Chulainn, Culann's hound, by which he has been known ever since.'

Maggie paused in her story, stroking the dogs' ears as they sat motionless beside her as if listening to her recount the ancient myth.

'O' course,' she went on, 'Cúchulainn came to epitomise the Celtic hero. He fought many battles against terrible odds. There were many women in his life, one was an Amazon o' a woman called Aoife, who's supposed to have taught Cúchulainn some o' his war skills after he'd defeated her in battle. Cúchulainn and Aoife became lovers and, unknown to him, she bore him a son called Connlai who grew up to be as great a warrior as his father. Cúchulainn and Connlai met in single combat but didn't know each other until after Cúchulainn had slain his only son.

'Cúchulainn was wed to Emer but he forsook her for Fand, the wife of Manannan Mac Lir, the sea god an' king o' the Isle o' Man. It's my belief that o' all the women in his life it was Fand that Cúchulainn loved best.'

Again the old woman paused. 'Just look,' she said, who couldn't. 'See how these two great dogs hae taken to each other. Whatever Old Squarebottle says aboot her name, it just has to be Fand. And, ye just mark my words, they will found the great line o' the hounds o' Laigersay.'

'Maggie,' I began cautiously, 'there's something else I wanted to ask you. I was talking to a man the other day who called himself what sounded like a "sennachy". I may not have the word quite right, but can you tell me what it means?'

'If ye were here in the island that would be Charlie Kerr. He's the only *seanachaidh* we hae in Laigersay and even Charlie doesna like to confess it.'

'But what does it mean?' I asked again.

'In the old days every community had its *seanachaidh*. He was really the local storyteller, someone skilled in history and law. He was probably the most important person in the community, after the clan chief.'

'Could he marry people?'

'Aye an' often did. That would be by handclasping, ye ken. Indeed my own parents were wed that way. It's the way they still marry folks at Gretna, but there it's done ower a studdie or anvil in a smiddy by a bruntie.'

'A bruntie?'

'Aye, ye would call him a blacksmith.' Maggie paused obviously thinking back over her long life. 'I would like to have been a *seanachaidh* myself, but it's no open to a woman. Mind, I think I'd hae made a guid one.'

'Can you explain about handclasping?'

'Handclasping is very old, for centuries it was the main way of blessing the relationship between a man and a woman. It is non-religious; neither pagan, Christian nor beholden to any other religion; it is just humanistic. Aye, the clan chief, the *seanachaidh* or even the village blacksmith could perform the rite. It was done by placing a cloth called a *ban* over the wrists o' the betrothed. It wasna tied, ye ken.'

'What did the *seanachaidh* do?'

'Well, the couple would be holding hands, and the celebrant would lay the *ban* across their wrists symbolically binding them together.' Maggie stopped and chuckled softly. 'They didna tie the *ban* till a year later. That gave the couple the right to change their minds if things didna work oot. I sometimes think that widna be sic a bad thing today, the way the young folk carry on. If all went well the couple would visit the *seanachaidh* again after a year to reaffirm their bond, then the *ban* would be formally tied.'

I told her the story of Jakes and Maantie.

She listened, nodding occasionally without comment, then reminded me: 'I told you he was only mad when the wind's nor-east; Jakes aye knew his hawks and handsaws.'

She had quoted Polonius to me eighteen months before, on the night of the ceilidh for the new surgery.

It was just after this that Charlie Kerr brought Maantie to the surgery, late one evening to avoid curious eyes, for her assessment. I was somewhat dreading this. Of course I have carried out intimate genital examinations on a huge number of women, and the procedure was quite routine. But that was when I could explain to the patient what I was going to do and the reasons for it. I discussed the problem with Alison Goodbody, the practice nurse and midwife, who was sure that so long as she was there holding Maantie's hand there would be no problem.

'You know, Maantie trusts you implicitly. I am sure she'll no think ye're up to houghmagandy!'

I was not sure that this was reassurance but in the event there was no problem at all. Maantie was patient, co-operative and unfazed. I was relieved to find she had a capacious pelvis, which augured for an easy birth.

Alison and I discussed where to send her for the birth. I was for sending her to a specialist unit on the mainland.

'How d'ye think she'll manage with not a soul she kens?' asked Alison. 'Listen, with the helicopter standing by you could get her to the obstetric unit if she did suddenly need a Caesarean section. Maantie is simple but she's very human. She will want her baby here with her husband and friends looking on. I bet ye she has an easy labour, she's just like some o' the beasts o' the field.'

'OK, let's book her provisionally for delivery in the cottage hospital. But I must say I'm not altogether happy; after all she must be nearly forty now, a very elderly primip.'

('Primip' is short for primipera, which is what we doctors used to call a woman who was pregnant for the first time.)

Maantie reappeared from the examination room, beaming as usual. I called Charlie in and explained to him what we had decided. 'But,' I added, 'if there is any hint of difficulty I shan't hesitate to send her to the mainland.'

'I am sure that she would prefer to be here with you,' he said. 'She loves the cottage hospital and she'll want her husband by her. Which reminds me, Jakes asked me to invite you to visit them. He said any time would suit him and that you should fix a time wi' me.'

I was immediately curious, and we decided that I should meet Charlie by the jetty in Ranneach Bay the following weekend and that he would take me.

'Bye the bye,' continued Charlie, 'the couple are now officially married. Yon pompous offeecial took a deal o' convincing but I had taken the precaution of knowing just where to tell him to look in his law books. 'Twas wi' ill grace he signed his wee bit form, but sign it he did, and stamped it forbye!'

The following Saturday afternoon I drove to Ranneach Bay and found Charlie polishing brass on the 'Blue Belle'. He greeted me, sat me in the stern of the little boat and immediately cast off. We bounced south through the bay and turned westwards, Charlie picking his way delicately through the skerries towards the northern point of Mulcaire. As we approached the island, I could see the old farmstead on a small cliff above the headland. There were two people there waving from the cliff-top and soon I could identify them as Nutty Jakes and Maantie.

Suddenly all my anxiety about the sinister secret of Mulcaire flooded over me and I remembered Stanley Johnson's dire warnings. In the past I had suspected that the island was contaminated with anthrax spores but, once another explanation for the source of Adrian Porteus's fatal infection had been traced, I had pretty much lost interest in the Mulcaire mystery. Now I was suddenly aware that an unspecified danger still existed.

Charlie brought the 'Blue Belle' round under the headland and I saw there was a cave which now, approaching low tide, was navigable. Charlie steered the boat under the arch of the cave and we both had to duck as the 'Blue Belle' entered under the low roof. Inside the cave the roof was higher and there was a landing stage carved into the rock of the cave wall.

'McTavish made this back in the 1930s,' said Charlie. 'It was his secret boathouse, entirely sealed off at high tide.'

He jumped ashore; made the 'Blue Belle' fast and walked up the dry shingle floor of the cave in the dim greenish light reflected into the cave from the sea outside.

'When McTavish was here, the cave linked up wi' the cellar o' the hoose. After the war the sodgers came and bricked up the cellar. They didna make a verra guid job o' it. The walls were all broken down and Jakes and I built them up again. There was a lot of old junk lying aboot here, but we tidied it all away.'

He shone a torch and I could see the steps leading upwards; I heard a clatter of footsteps and suddenly Nutty Jakes was with us carrying a lighted Tilley lamp. With a broad grin and outstretched hand he ran towards me.

'Welcome to my new home, Doctor,' he said, pumping my hand. 'I can't think of anyone I'd sooner have as our first visitor. Ye know I thought ye might have found me out that time you came to Mulcaire. You surprised me that day, and I thought ye must ha' seen me.'

Suddenly I remembered the shadow I had seen on the day when a protesting Alex Farquharson had brought me to the little island.

'Come upstairs, Maantie is dying to welcome you too. You see,' continued Jakes as he led me through the cave, 'I often came over to Mulcaire in my kayak. I always wanted to live here, and even then I was working on repairing the house. Be careful here, I haven't finished clearing away all the Army's walls. They'd blocked this section of the cave and I had to open up the way to the secret jetty so Charlie could come to us.'

I followed Jakes up the steps, which seemed to have been hewn out of the native rock, and soon we were in what appeared to be the cellar of the old farmhouse.

'This was the basement o' the house where Maantie grew up before the war. She wanted to come here. Now Doctor, you take the lamp and go up the stair in front of you.'

The bright light illuminated a rough stone stairway closed at the top with an ancient wooden door. The door opened easily to reveal Maantie with almost as big a grin as Jakes. She spread her arms wide and hugged me.

'Walcum Mulcar,' she said. 'Walcum ar home.'

Jakes and Charlie were soon with us and my former patient was explaining: 'Maantie's old home was in a poor state when we got here but it's been a good summer and we've worked hard. We got the roof sealed and now we're quite comfy and ready for the winter.'

'Aye, they've both worked hard,' added Charlie.

'We couldn't have done it without you, Charlie.' Jakes turned to me. 'He was over in his boat several times a week bringing tools and timber, to say nothing of grub.'

'What did you do for water?'

'That was easy. Maantie remembered the old well, and I soon got that cleared and working. We always boiled it to be safe. As for food we got a lot from the sea. I remembered what I read about St Kilda and we have eaten a lot of puffins and fulmar. They're not bad, just a bit fishy. Then this island is overrun with rabbits. Maantie doesn't like me killing them, but they make a good stew. And then there's masses o' shellfish.'

'I was a wee bit worrit aboot the scurvy,' said Charlie, 'so I brought fresh vegetables from my garden, that an' a sack o' tatties and a bag o' oatmeal.'

'You see, we've been living like Alexander Selkirk and Friday!'

I raised an eyebrow questioningly and Jakes said, 'Oh, you call him Robinson Crusoe but I used to live in Fife, where he was born, and I know his real name was Selkirk.'

I marvelled at the obvious good health of the former schizophrenic. I looked round the room and could see that they had made the place habitable. Their simple furniture was built largely of driftwood and the room was decorated by the combings of the beach. Fishing floats and shells adorned the table, made of an upturned fish box raised on rocks. The table had a simple cloth spread over it where mugs of steaming tea were ready to welcome guests. The two beaming newlyweds gestured to us to sit and Maantie disappeared for a moment, to return with a dish of scones. She laid them on the table with butter and blackberry jam.

'Maantie mak,' she said.

Jakes added: 'Not the butter; we don't have a cow yet but we hope to get one soon. Maantie cooks on a Primus stove, or the old range. She uses the range at night so nobody can see the smoke.'

I turned to look at this strange, almost decerebrate, woman, realising that there was so much more to her than met the eye.

Tea was surprisingly good and I enjoyed the scones whilst marvelling at the changes in my host and hostess.

'Jakes,' I said, 'I have been worried about you; what about your medication?'

The young man looked embarrassed. 'Well, Doctor, I've a confession to make. I knew what store you set on those pills of yours. I used to collect them regular as clockwork.'

'Yes and they kept you well. That was why I was worried you did not have them.'

'Well no, it's not quite like that doctor. Ye see I never took them. I've got thousands o' them all safely stowed away at my old home. You can have them back if ye like.'

'You mean... ' I began, but my voice trailed away as I realised that the no longer so nutty Jakes had been fooling me all along. 'What about those scissors in your gullet that used to worry you so much?'

'Doctor, I havena had trouble with them for years, not since I was in hospital in fact. Och, it suited me fine that everyone thought I was mad. That's how I got my money on your certificates. I saved a good deal over the years and now I've got Maantie an' a baby on the way, I'm taking on crofting here on Mulcaire an' we'll soon be self-sufficient.'

Shortly after that, Charlie looked at his watch. 'We'll need to be away,' he said, 'the cave will be impassable in ten minutes' time, and we need to be across the bay afore the rip starts.'

So saying, he led me back through the cellar into the cave. Then, recalling the pomposity of Stanley Johnson, I remembered he had gone south for a week and laughed aloud to think how all this would surprise and no doubt annoy him. There was no time to pursue these thoughts for Charlie was urging me into his boat.

CHAPTER 22

Winter Festivals

Christmas brought the usual flurry of cards. One came from Terror. He was full of apology for being a bad correspondent and compensated with quite a long note. Work kept him busy but he remembered Laigersay and longed to come back. 'I don't get teaching here like you and Dr Hamish gave me. I expect it's grey and chilly in the island right now but I often think of you, Mrs Chalmers and Cuhlan before a great roaring fire and wish I was there. Hope you have a Happy Christmas love Terror.'

There was a PS: 'They gave me prizes in Surgery and Medicine so that bodes well for Finals. PPS my spots are much better after using the pills you told me to take.'

Fiona and I chuckled over the card as we shivered in the Castle Chalmers draughts.

'It sounds as if he's doing well,' commented Fiona.

'Maybe too well; if he's winning prizes like that he's probably one of their high-flyers. There will be a lot of pressure on him to specialise after he qualifies. It would be a pity: that lad has the makings of a first-rate GP. I felt once or twice when he was here he was the sort of chap I'd like as a partner.'

'I'm glad his spots are better. I must remember to tell Thomasina Chalmers. She told me when he was here that he'd be all right if it wasn't for his complexion.'

'Fiona, you're incorrigible, and don't waste your time matchmaking. With academic results like those I doubt we'll see "yon spottiface" again.'

Perhaps the time I like least in Laigersay is the depth of winter. In that northern latitude in December it is rarely light before nine in the morning, and by half past three the dim light of the short day is already going. Though it was true that the island was at its most beautiful on bright sunny days of cold frost, when the summits were salted with a dusting of snow, I was always thankful when the winter solstice was past.

Hamish had strong views on Christmas, as on most things. He claimed, not without justification, that it was a pagan festival and had nothing to do with Christianity. All the mythology about Christ's birth was, he argued, without historical basis and the early Christian church had simply adopted the ancient feast of Yule that celebrated the rebirth of the seasons with the return of the sun. As people had not liked giving up their established beliefs and because it is easier to adapt old circumstances to new rather than do away with them altogether, early Christians had grafted the legend of Christ's birth on to the ancient tradition of Yule. So the custom had lingered on in what Hamish called 'the tinsel and tawdry' of Christmas. This was a view quite widely held among some Christian sects, especially in the Western Isles. Hamish was quite entitled to his ideas, which in any case suited me fine. He was always on duty at Christmas, when, as a family man I wanted to be free. (In fairness, I took the weight at Hogmanay.)

'Ye can keep yer Christmas, an' its frippery,' Hamish would say. 'Me, I canna understand why so many folk near bankrupt theirsels buying presents they canna afford for people they dinna like who don't want them anyway.'

'Ebenezer Scrooge,' I told Fiona, 'is alive and well and living in Laigersay!'

That Christmas was white and Fiona and I spent much of the holiday playing with the twins in the unusual snowfall. High up in the corries of the Three Witches the snow was firm and smooth and we were able to introduce the boys to the joys of skiing. We had thought of giving them skis for Christmas but winter conditions were so unreliable in Laigersay it had not seemed worth it. We gave them roller skates instead, which were singularly useless with six inches of snow. However Fiona remembered that as a child she and her brother had spent hours on skis. A search of the castle attics revealed not only their old equipment but a sledge as well. For the twins, these were more of a success than the costly, gimmicky 'must haves' of that year's Christmas season. We were out high on the moors all day and came home with burning skins and ravenous hunger. I had vetoed turkey, which I find the dreariest of eating. Instead we had delicious island food; smoked salmon and tender young grouse, which had survived since August in the freezer and were perfection. Boxing Day was again spent on skis and the sledge, and by the evening the exhausted, happy twins were getting quite proficient. Then the snow thawed and at last the roller skates came into their own.

That winter I had started to be worried about the approach of Maantie's confinement. True, everything throughout the pregnancy had been completely normal. But the woman, now thirty-nine, was what was then called an 'elderly primipera'. Having a first baby at such an advanced age was recognised as a hazardous business.

Late on the evening of 16th February, the phone rang and I heard that Maantie was in labour. I anticipated a long first stage and decided to go and check her before getting some sleep in readiness for whatever might happen.

Alison met me at the hospital. 'Maantie had a show this afternoon and started contractions early this evening.'

'How is she?'

'Blissful and seraphic. I don't think I've ever seen anyone in the first stage so completely unconcerned. You'd think she'd had a dozen! She's already about two fingers dilated.'

It was true. Maantie greeted me with a great smile and said, 'Maantie's bab cumin.' She squeezed my hand. A brief examination confirmed that the baby's head was well down into the pelvis and that its heart rate was normal and steady.

'You're doing fine,' I told her. 'Is Jakes here?'

Maantie nodded and held her breath for a moment. My hand was still on her swollen belly and I could feel the uterus contract. A moment later she breathed again and said, 'Jacks wants see.'

I nodded, wondering to myself whether the delivery would be normal enough to let him watch. Then I left her and spoke to Jakes, reassuring him that everything was going well. Alison was happy with her patient but told me she might need me later, and suggested I got some sleep. 'She'll be some time yet,' she added.

It seemed only minutes before the phone rang.

'She's fully dilated and starting to push.'

'All well?' I asked as I jumped out of bed.

'Aye, she's doing fine, not a whimper from her, and she's even been dozing between contractions.'

'Good, I'm on my way,' I said, pulling sweater and trousers over my pyjamas.

At the hospital I went straight to the labour ward. Alison was bending over Maantie whose knees were folded back on to her huge belly. Her hands were tucked behind her knees pulling them to her. She was red in the face with effort. The contraction passed and the knees came down.

'The foetal heart's fine,' Alison reassured me.

At the head of the bed, a slightly pale Jakes took Maantie's hand as she released her knees.

'Well done, Maantie!' I mouthed at her. 'You're doing famously.'

'Maantie's babby near,' she said. And then, as another contraction came and she drew her knees up again. Jakes moved from the head of the bed to watch as the perineum stretched and the vulva gaped.

'There, you can see the head,' said Alison, pointing.

A thin trickle of bloody liquor oozed, and the head disappeared again with the passing of the contraction.

Everyone was applauding. 'Not long now!' Alison said and Jakes translated this with a hand signal to his wife.

Maantie laughed and said again, 'Maantie's babby near.'

There was another contraction. The perineum bulged hugely as the head crowned. A spurt of blood marked the tearing of the vulva and the purple, vernix-coated head was born.

Alison ran her gloved fingers round the baby's neck. 'No cord,' she said, and in a moment the uterus contracted again and the child slipped easily into the midwife's hands

'Maantie, you have a little girl,' said Alison, as she clamped and cut the cord. And she handed the bloody, greasy little scrap of humanity to her mother.

God knows how many babies I have seen arrive. It is always a wonderful, inspiring moment. But never have I found tears suddenly spurting into my eyes as the mother took her child to her breast and sang to her, just as she sang to the selkies. The first sound that baby ever heard was the song of the seals.

Alison was busy. The placenta delivered with the next contraction and, as my sole contribution to the procedure,

I injected ergometrine. The uterus at once contracted with only a slight blood loss.

Alison inspected carefully. 'I thought there might have been quite a tear,' she said, 'but it's only a nick; she doesn't even need a stitch.' She turned to me and said, 'As it turned out, you might just as well have stayed in bed! But I'm glad you were here for all that. Gosh, just look at this,' the midwife continued, 'I dinna think that did much good!' She showed me the intact placenta and amnionic membranes. There, embedded in the afterbirth, was Maantie's IUCD.

I turned away, for I did not want the midwife to see how moved I was and said: 'I'd forgotten all about that, but now I remember Pat Tomlinson did tell me a coil had been fitted.' Then I added 'You know I would not have missed that for the world.'

'Me neither,' said the new father.

Then Maantie spoke quite clearly: 'She's Caitriona,' she said and I recalled that that had been her mother's name.

CHAPTER 23

An Unusual Sea Sickness

The phone on my desk shrilled, interrupting Aggie Henderson in full flow. Perhaps appropriately, she was informing me in graphic detail of the pain she experienced behind the ears when passing water. The jangling phone was a welcome relief.

I heard Jeannie's voice: 'It's the coastguard, Doctor. He says it's urgent.'

'Put him on.' After a click, I heard a familiar drawl.

'Morning, Rob, Wullie Stewart here. The place has gone mad the day in this storm. There's a tanker in trouble off

Port Chalmers, Peter's taken the chopper oot to her; she's fu' o' crude an' we dinna need that in the bay. Mountain Rescue have reported some silly bugger fallen on Ranneach Mhor, and noo I've got a signal from an American yacht that's crossed the pond in this storm and all the crew are ill. They are somewhere oot in Assilag Bay. I haena' a man to spare and both lifeboats are awa' to the tanker. I managed to raise Alex Farquharson. He wasnae at home but I got him on the "Ornithologist". Onyways Alex says he thinks he can see their boat. He says if ye can get doon there he'll get ye oot to her. But ye maun hurry, the tide's coming and the causeway'll no be clear more than forty minutes or so.'

'OK, Wullie, I'll be on my way, but can you tell me anything about the sick people?'

'Och not much, their signal was gey weak. The skipper said they werena seeing properly, had very dry mouths and were vomiting. He sounded frightened; ye dinna expect that in folk that can sail across the Atlantic.'

'Thanks Wullie. Tell Alex I'm on my way and I'll meet him where he keeps the "Ornithologist".'

'OK, roger an' oot.'

I apologised briefly to Aggie, who said, 'I'll just come again same time next week.' As the old soul shuffled out I grabbed my emergency bag and, stuffing it into a rucksack, ran to the office, shouting to Jeannie, 'I'm away to Assilag. There's a transatlantic yacht in some sort of trouble. Please reschedule the surgery.'

Jeannie nodded and thrust a flask into my hand. 'I brewed some coffee as soon as I heard it was Wullie, he always spells trouble. Take it with you.'

As I turned the car out across the western road to Feadag, I wondered what on earth could cause such a sudden illness in the whole crew of a boat that had been at sea some time. Some sort of infection came to mind, but it was hard to see what could affect all of them at the same time so long after contact with other people. I began to think of the ways toxic substances could be released in a yacht. As I raced southwards towards Lutheran, it occurred to me that accidental release of carbon monoxide from an engine or a faulty cooker might be the cause.

I raced down the rough road to where Alex kept the 'Ornithologist'. There was no sign of Alex but I soon found him crouched over his radio in the boat's cabin.

'Aye, so there ye are, Doctor. I am chust trying to raise "Silver Darling" again. Yon's the yacht's name; she's from Nova Scotia.' Alex was signalling rapidly in morse.

'I made contact with her a while back. She's chust off the south point o' Assilag and sailing into the bay. But they are in big trouble. The skipper said he thocht his mate might be near deid. They can only chust manage the boat in this wind and there's chust an hour an' a hauf till the rip starts. Och, I'm chust wasting time here; they'll no answer ma call. We'll cast off and go and meet her an' see what's what.'

Alex went to his engine controls. 'Cast off astern, Doctor, and we'll investigate.'

The 'Ornithologist' turned into the wind and bounced fast over the waves under the thrust of her powerful outboard. As the spray lashed into my face I wondered what I might find when we reached the 'Silver Darling'.

After twenty minutes buffeting, Alex shouted, 'There she is,' and, sure enough, the graceful shape of an ocean-going yacht was visible through scudding rain. She seemed to be deserted, and then I saw a man stagger across her deck and wave to us.

Alex manoeuvred the 'Ornithologist' close astern of her and the man threw us a line. I caught it and made fast and managed to grasp a ladder and scramble aboard.

'If you're a doctor, I sure am glad to see you!' the man greeted me in a strong New England accent. 'We're all very sick, but you'd best see Joe first: I don't think he's gonna make it.' And he led me below. A large man was lying on a bunk apparently unconscious. But when I stood beside him he gazed vaguely at me and I realised he could hardly see me because of widely dilated pupils.

'You are all right now,' I reassured him with more faith than I felt. 'We'll soon get you fixed up.'

The man tried to speak, but his mouth was so dry that speech was impossible. There was fresh vomit by the bunk. I turned to look at the other man, whom I took to be the skipper, and noticed that he was staggering and seemed unable to control his limbs. Whatever it was, this illness had produced a marked central nervous dysfunction. Two other men and a woman were also turned in on their bunks. One man had a squint.

'Does he always look like that?' I demanded.

'No way, that's come on in the last few hours,' replied the only member of the crew still on his feet.

'Can you tell me what happened?'

'Not really. We were fine day before yesterday but we hit this gale. It was hairy and the boat was all over the place and we were kept so busy we could hardly stop for chow. Betsy there'—he nodded at the woman—'managed to get a scratch meal together from cans. We haven't eaten anything since. First it was too rough, then none of us wanted to eat. I was on watch so I was last to eat, perhaps that's why I'm still on my feet.'

'That last meal—anything unusual about it?' I asked.

The woman roused herself on one arm and stared unseeingly at me. She appeared disorientated, but when she spoke her thinking was clear enough: the illness did not seem to affect mentation.

'Why no,' she said, 'I just opened some cans, that's all I could do with the sea running as it was.'

'Cans? You mean tins?'

'Sure, they were canned meat and some string beans ... we been eating them all the way across ... the beans I canned myself ... they came from my backyard.'

I began to be filled with an appalling fear. 'Home canned string beans?' I repeated. 'Can you remember anything odd about them?'

'No ... wait, one of the cans farted when I opened it.'

'*Farted?*'

'Yeah, sort of fizzed and let out gas, but the beans looked okay and tasted fine.'

'You all ate them?'

She nodded, and, with a feeling of gloom, I asked the man I took to be skipper: 'Can I use your radio?'

He showed me into a tiny radio cabin and soon I was in touch with the coastguard. Wullie Stewart's reassuring, calm and familiar voice crackled over the airwaves,

'Wullie, we have problems. We have five very, very sick people. I am pretty sure they have botulism. That's B – O – T – U – L – I – S – M. It's very serious, probably life-threatening. They need antitoxin as soon as possible. I don't know where you get that—Glasgow probably. Get on to Hamish Robertson, he'll know what to do. We have very little time. The likelihood is that they will all die.'

'OK Doc, I hear you. Can you tell me where you are?'

'Not sure exactly, but we're well into Assilag Bay. Alex is aboard somewhere. I know he's anxious about the rip.'

'Aye, that'll be right.' There was a pause, then the coastguard added: 'Tell ye what, I'll get on to Hamish and get back to ye when he knows what's happened. You talk to Alex and find out about the seaworthiness o' the vessel, your position and what he suggests. I'll be in touch again in a few minutes. Over an' oot.'

I raced back on deck. Alex had been busy while I had been with my patients. The 'Ornithologist' was bobbing astern with her painter affixed to the yacht's taffrail. Alex was at the wheel and the 'Silver Darling' was making speed northwards along the coast of Assilag.

'How are yer patients?' he asked as I approached him.

'If my provisional diagnosis is right, they are very sick indeed. I think they've got botulism.'

'Never heard o' that! What is it?'

'It's a very rare form of food poisoning, and the most serious, with a sixty to a hundred percent mortality. Our only hope is to get antitoxin to them as soon as possible.'

'And how do ye do that?'

'I've spoken to Wullie Stewart, he's getting on to Hamish to organise the antitoxin ... trouble is, it's so rare I don't know if, or where, we can get it. Meanwhile

Wullie wants to know just where we are, and about the seaworthiness of this yacht.'

'That's no problem, she's a beauty. My immediate concern is the rip. We must be about thirty minutes from high tide and we need to get into safe water as soon as possible—or that bottle thing ye were on aboot will no be a problem after all, for the rip'll droon us a'. Is Wullie going to call us back?'

'Yes.'

'OK, here's what to say to him.' Alex peered over his left shoulder at the coast of Assilag. 'We're off Signal Rock the noo, and making about eight knots in this wind, with luck we'll make it. Now they'll no be able to reach Assilag wi' ambulances, and the helicopter's no big enough for five souls ... and I doot ye'll want to go wi' 'em?'

I nodded.

'So here's what we'll dae: I'll sail "Silver Darling" over the causeway ... there should be enough water at high tide ... and I'll take ye all roond to Lutheran. Tell them to get the stuff ye need to the jetty at Lutheran and have the ambulances standing by to get them up to the airport. Wullie'll get an emergency flight fixed for them an' they'll be in the District Hospital in no time.'

A moment later I was back in touch with Wullie, who told me Hamish had used all the weight of his considerable personality to galvanise officialdom in Glasgow and that five hundred thousand units of botulinus antitoxin was already on its way to the airport *en route* for Laigersay. When I told Wullie our position, he harrumphed and said, 'I could wish you further north: ye're gey vulnerable to the rip there. And did ye say Alex was taking an ocean-going yacht ower the Assilag causeway? That's awfu' risky, even for Alex! Both my lifeboats are tied up wi' the tanker. But I have got the chopper back, that's one good thing. I'll just need tae get on to the minister to ask for *special* help for ye. Guid luck an' keep in touch. Over an' oot.'

There was nothing I could do to help Alex, so I went back to my patients. The fittest man, who was, as I had suspected, the skipper, had turned in now. That was good, for by now he was hardly able to stand. He wanted to know what was going on, and it was clear that despite the damage to their nervous systems all the poisoning victims were alert of mind. As I rechecked the five sick people, I reassured him that his vessel was in the charge of one of the most experienced inshore seaman of the islands. I thought it best not to tell him of Alex's plan to sail 'The Silver Darling' over the causeway. Trying to sound casual, I asked: 'What's the draft of this boat?'

'Eight feet, why do you ask?'

'Oh, Alex at the helm asked me to find out in case he wants to go close inshore, but that's OK.'

The man they called Joe was severely dehydrated, so I busied myself setting up a saline drip. With fluids running into his arm he seemed a little better, but I knew he would almost certainly die unless he got antitoxin soon.

Returning on deck, I found Alex sailing north as hard as he could go and singing hymns. 'Och,' he said conversationally, 'I've discussed the matter wi' God and it looks as though we shall beat the rip. Forbye crossing the causeway will be interestin'.'

I told him the draft of the 'Silver Darling' and he grunted again: 'Aye, it'll be verra interestin' indeed! I aim to get there exactly at high tide, to have as much water as possible under her keel. It's chancy, mind, but there'll be a very high tide the day, an' wi' this wind we should chust manage. That's the only way we can save their lives.'

By now the tide was reaching the full and with it came the force of the rip. My earlier experience of the tidal race that occurred off Assilag had been exhilarating to the point of terror and disaster. This time the rip acted in our favour. By the time we felt its force under the keel of the 'Silver Darling' we were well to the north of its main thrust, which would have carried us down towards the skerries between Tuilleag and Mulcaire. Instead, this time the swelling mass of water drove us north into the upper part of Assilag Bay, where the sea was strangely calm. Alex turned 'Silver Darling' towards the shore, keeping a close eye on his watch and on the tops of the causeway marker poles, just visible above water level.

'We hae chust a few minutes to high tide,' said Alex and we're in luck, for it's unco high the day. Count the poles from the Laigersay end, they're easier to see there. We maun pass over between the eleventh and twelfth pole, that's the deepest part o' the causeway an' there's chust room for this muckle great sailboat to squeeze atween them. We need every inch with the big draft the "Silver Darling" has.'

Alex eyed his watch: 'It's 12.43 precisely; that's high tide today.' He swung the wheel over and the yacht responded immediately, turning to pass between poles 11 and 12. There was a judder and a horrible scraping noise; the 'Silver Darling' hesitated, trembled and then sailed on. We were through, with the marker poles brushing her beam on either side.

Alex beamed: 'By chings it was only chust! But chust is enough, and we must thank the Good Lord who guided us between Scylla and Charybdis.'

Once through the causeway, it was only a short half-hour sail up the coast to Lutheran Bay. As we turned into the shelter of the bay I could see a throng of people out looking for us. Among them the stooping figure of Lachlan Mackie was clearly visible. The orange coastguard helicopter came into sight, hovered and landed by Lutheran jetty. Picking up a pair of binoculars, I could see Hamish running from the chopper. He was carrying a parcel. It looked as though the precious antitoxin had arrived. In the background I could see the two Laigersay ambulances. In no time Lachy Mackie was catching our line and tying us up at Lutheran Jetty. Hamish jumped aboard with his parcel.

'That was a fancy diagnosis, laddie—I hope ye're right. I gave it to the public health people in Port Glasgow hot and strong, and if ye're wrong my stock'll no be very high.'

The antitoxin was soon injected and, among the general jubilation, even Hamish congratulated me while Alex, the real hero of the day, slipped quietly away to give his thanks to God.

Later, serology and the analysis of what was left of the last meal the crew had taken revealed conclusive proof of the presence of *Clostridium botulinus* and its terribly potent neurotoxic poison. At the hospital they had a tough time with Joe and, though at times we thought we might lose him, in the end all of the crew of the 'Silver Darling' survived.

CHAPTER 24

Holiday in Assilag

After the excitement of the rescue of the 'Silver Darling', peace once again descended on Laigersay. With the twins growing fast, that spring was a joyous time for the family. The estate and the practice gave me less time than I would wish to spend with the Fiona and the boys. Every morning I was busy before breakfast in the office with Erchie and then I hurried away after a brief snack to do morning surgery. Sometimes I had a sandwich lunch in the car, but once or twice a week I got home to share a meal with the family. The afternoon surgeries were usually for women, either family planning or ante-natal clinics. I enjoyed these, because I could spend time chatting and getting to know the young mothers of the island. It was often a social rather than a medical time when, as parents together, doctor and patients could exchange news of their families.

On one occasion, an elderly male interloper disturbed my antenatal clinic. I found him sitting in the waiting room nonchalantly reading a book.

'I'm sorry,' I said to him, 'this is my antenatal clinic, perhaps you would like to book an appointment for the general surgery this evening.'

He glanced up from his book. 'So sorry, doctor but I had a wee accident wi' m' mower. I wonder if you have a bandage or somethin'. You see I keep pushin' the bone back but as fast as I do it keeps poppin' oot.'

It was only then that I saw the mangle of bone and blood that had been his toes and it was my turn to apologise. The patient had driven from near Lutheran with this awful trauma. The injury was not as bad as it looked but it took time to clean away the soil and grass mowings, realign the toes, and sow up and splint the foot. He was in the cottage hospital for a month.

This incident was typical of the hardiness of so many of the islanders. It also underlined a problem of general practice that, try as one would it was impossible to order one's work, for the unexpected was always turning up to disrupt carefully planned schedules. Sometimes I would get back from a call in Assilag, only to find that I had to return to the same part of the island. This made my annual mileage phenomenal, but I loved it. The people were hardy, trusting and appreciative and I never tired of the beauty of Laigersay.

The only thing I resented was the paucity of time to share with the family. Hamish was utterly unpredictable, especially about the so-called duty rota. This unreliability grew noticeably worse after he gave me parity in the practice. But occasionally he would say I was looking tired and should take a week's holiday. That happened in the May shortly after the botulism adventure.

Fiona was delighted and said we must get away from Castle Chalmers. 'If we stay here,' she said, 'you'll just be at the beck and call of the patients and the estate. The cottage on Assilag is empty. Let's go there; it will be like old times.'

So we escaped to the estate's tiny cottage near Alex Farquharson where we had spent our honeymoon. The week was idyllic, with nonstop sunshine. The twins, released from school, were ecstatic and together we lazed on the beach constructing castles and canals, burying each other in the sand, collecting shells or just throwing sticks for Cuhlan to retrieve from the sea.

One day Fiona found some little pieces of agate and serpentine and started teaching the boys about gemstones. Soon two new interests filled the twins' waking days. For Jamie it was bird-nesting; for Hamie it was the rocks that made up the fabric of the island. Jamie was the first to indulge his fixation. Walking along the beach he found a nest. He came running to me and led me back to his find, which he had marked by placing a piece of sea-bleached driftwood nearby.

'Look, Daddy,' he said excitedly. 'I nearly walked on it an' it's so hard to see I thought I might not find it again to show you. That's why that old stick is there to show me where to look. Isn't it lovely? But what sort is it?'

I bent down to examine the nest, which was nothing but a shallow scrape among the shingle lined with tiny stones. There were three grey-buff eggs lightly speckled with black and so like the surrounding gravel as to be almost invisible.

'It belongs to a ringed plover,' I told him, 'and there is the parent bird watching us anxiously over there by the sea margin. You did very well to spot that, it's so hard to see. That's how the bird manages to have her family right out here in the open. She relies on invisibility for safety. It's called camouflage.'

I called Hamie to see the nest. He admired it, but was more interested in a stone he had picked up on the beach. 'Let's move away,' I said. 'We're upsetting the ringed plover; she's afraid we'll steal her eggs.'

From then on, rocks and eggs dominated our holiday. We explored the cliffs near the northern end of the causeway to Assilag. There, though the questions came thick and fast, the stench from the serried ranks of breeding birds above us on the cliffs was enough to send a protesting Fiona back to the cottage to make lunch.

Hamie pointed up to the cliffs. 'How did they get made?' he asked, using his favourite geological question. I sat on a ridge of basalt and squinted up at the cliffs where fulmar wheeled and auks sat shoulder to shoulder.

'Once upon a time the three witches, that's Ranneach Mhor, Ranneach Bheag and Sgarbh an Sgumain, were all active volcanoes. They breathed fire from their summits and every now and then they erupted, throwing up huge quantities of molten magma...'

'What's magma?' interjected Jamie.

'Molten rock, silly,' replied his brother. 'Rock's just like candle wax, if you make it hot enough it melts and runs like wax on a candle.'

'That's right,' I continued, 'but it has to be ever so hot.'

'Daddy,' asked Hamie, 'when wax runs from the candle it suddenly hardens and forms funny shapes.' He looked doubtfully at the basalt cliff above us. 'Is that what happened with the cliff? It looks as though the rock ran down to the edge of the sea and then suddenly hardened to make the cliff.'

I looked at the boy, enjoying hearing him think aloud. 'Well done, Hamie, that is just the sort of thing that happened. Can you imagine when all that molten rock hit the sea? What a noise and explosion of steam there must have been! And then you can see how the rock formed those weird shapes as it suddenly cooled, to leave the jagged skerries that are so dangerous to shipping.'

'Daddy,' asked Jamie, tiring of geology, 'it looks as if all the birds of one kind choose different places to nest on the cliffs. There are puffins at the top, then those are guillemots up there all close together. Then the razorbills are together lower down and bottom of all are the black guillemots.'

'Well done, Jamie, the different auks all choose slightly different places to breed. There are so few suitable sites that they all crowd together where the cliff suits them. Look at the guillemots, they are so tightly crammed together and mostly facing the cliff while they hatch their eggs...'

'Must be awfy boring staring at the cliff all the time!' commented Hamie.

'There is an interesting thing about their eggs,' I continued. 'Most birds eggs are oval and roll, but many seabird eggs are pointed; when the wind rolls them they move in circles and don't fall off the edge. That's particularly so of the guillemots. The razorbills nest in crevices lower down the cliff and their eggs are less prone to be blown off and they are not so conical.'

'Daddy, how do they know to make their eggs pointy?'

'I don't think they do. What probably came about is that that just happened to a few eggs by accident. But because those eggs were less likely to fall and get broken, so more birds that produced pointy eggs survived, and now after hundreds of years all the guillemot eggs are pointed and do not blow off the ledges.'

'And the black guillemots at the bottom?' asked Jamie.

'We are lucky to have them here in Laigersay. They generally breed in the north, specially Shetland. They are conspicuous with their white wing patches and red feet. Your mother says they wear red wellies.'

'Red wellies!' laughed Hamie, but Jamie said: 'That's good, they do look like big red boots. What's for lunch?'

So we walked back across the causeway, more than ready for fish from Alex's early morning catch, and chips from the tattie patch in his planticru.

CHAPTER 25

The Green-Eyed Monster

Fiona was as busy as I was during that summer. With the growing popularity of Scottish holidays, especially in out-of-the way places like Laigersay, prosperity came with every ferry. The airport seemed busier too. Each year brought more tourists and Fiona was increasingly in demand as a guide or as a lecturer on the island's history and wildlife. In early summer she teamed up with Alex Farquharson to run excursions round Ranneach Bay for visitors who never tired of watching puffins and seals. Sometimes there were other marine species to spot: basking sharks or cetaceans such as porpoises, dolphins and occasional minke whales.

Alex also found himself earning 'baccy money' with fishing trips from Assilag. His own fishing was so profitable that he had built a small smokehouse where he smoked haddock, which were even more delectable than the famous Arbroath Smokies of the east coast. He also smoked the abundant mussels from the rocks below the cliffs, and supplied these delicious shellfish to Tet's increasingly popular restaurant in Port Chalmers. The smokery proved so successful that Erchie worked with Alex to provide both hot-smoked, and the more traditional cold-smoked, salmon to delight the taste buds of the visitors. So Laigersay flourished by relieving increasing numbers of tourists of their money.

The marvellous summer started to draw to a close. The days were shorter and already there was a chill in the evening air. The swallows were gathering like crotchets on the staves of the telephone wires. They chattered briskly together as if discussing the best route to North Africa. Although it is the most beautiful time in Laigersay, it is tinged with a purple of regret at the coming of winter, which matches the late heather on the hills.

Early one September morning I arrived for morning surgery to find Jeannie in a tizz.

'That awful man's here. He hasnae got an appointment, but says he maun see you urgently.'

'What awful man?' I asked. 'Whoever he is, I'm sure we can fit him in.'

'It's that Ali Frazer frae Allt Beag Farm.'

'That's unusual, I've never known him come to see me in the surgery. Let him wait a bit, I'll see the folk with appointments and fit him when I can.'

'All right, Doctor, but I shouldnae be ower long. He's got a bottle o' whusky wi' him and he's started in on it.'

'At this hour in the morning? Oh well, I'll see what I can do.' I glanced into the waiting room, and saw the man sitting by himself nursing his bottle. He was even more unkempt than usual, as though he had slept in his clothes, and with a couple of day's stubble on his chin.

Fortunately surgery was quiet, and only about a third of the bottle had gone when I called Frazer into my room. The smell of unwashed clothes was not strong enough to mask the alcohol on his breath. But despite his appearance he was calm and moved soberly.

I greeted him and asked what I could do for him.

'Doctor, ye ken I don't come here often, but I'm desperate an' need help. Though God knows what you or anyone else can do. Ye see it's my wife...'

'What's the problem?'

Frazer paused and stared me in the eye. 'She's a harlot, she shags around.'

I remembered the little timid mouse of the woman I had glimpsed at the farm and the few words I had exchanged with her on the phone, and waited to see what else Fraser would say.

'She's been like it for years, Doc, but it's worse lately. I caught her at it i' the hay oot in the byre. That time she was wi' the young lad who helps a bit on the farm. I sent him packing soon enough. Then she sent for an electrician to fix something in her kitchen, an' she had him on the kitchen table. Even Postie's no bin in the hoose a wee minute but she's had his trousers off. I tell ye, man, she's at it wi' everyone. She's just like a callin' cat with the toms. Can ye no do something for that sort o' problem? I don't know, 'ormones or something?'

The man in front of me laid his whisky bottle on my desk, and burst into tears. There was no doubting but that he was in turmoil. I don't think I have ever heard a tale like that. Trying to be objective about this man, whom I disliked intensely, I wondered if his accusation could possibly be true. Admittedly I had never met a nymphomaniac outside the stories we all heard as students, but the woman I remembered seemed totally inconsistent with nymphomania. On the other hand, if it *were* true, perhaps this was the explanation for the man's unpleasant reputation. With a wife like that any man might behave badly.

I was in a quandary and after listening to more of Ali's tales of his wife's infidelity, I seized on the opportunity Frazer had provided by asking about hormone therapy.

'Listen, Mr Frazer, it might be possible to modify your wife's behaviour with medication, but before that I'll need to see her. I suggest I come up to the farm tomorrow and by that time I will have had time to think about the problem and perhaps take advice from a specialist.'

The man seemed satisfied that at least something was being done, and in his usual ungracious manner left the surgery, to finish his bottle on a bench outside.

When the last patient of the morning had gone, Jeannie brought coffee.

'How did ye get on wi' Frazer?' she asked.

'Well, I agree with you that he's quite horrible, but it does sounds as if he may have big problems at home.'

'Frae what I hear, I doot it's no him but his puir wife that has the problems,' she commented. 'Anyway there's the list o' visits for the day, an if ye're no wantin' me just noo I want to slip to the Co-op for some messages. I'll be back before ye've finished wi' coffee and the post.'

Telephoning the psychiatric hospital on the mainland, I asked to be put through to Dr Sylvia Mathieson. Sylvia was a woman of great knowledge and experience who specialised in the mental problems of scattered communities. Scots men and women are, for the most part, down-to-earth, hard-working, God-fearing folk. But, when they do go off the rails, especially with alcohol, they can present some of the gravest emergencies of mental illness. I just hoped I was not dealing with one of these.

'Hallo Rob, sorry to keep you, they had some difficulty finding me in the hospital. It's nice to hear you, but I suspect this isna just a social call.'

'I am afraid not, Sylvia.' And I described Ali Frazer and the startling problem he had laid before me.

'This is morbid jealousy,' she said after hearing me out. 'Some people call it the Othello complex, and it's always a real bugger to deal with. I have had two or three of them. Sometimes, of course, there is substance to the accusation and the lady in question just simply can't satisfy her appetite. Usually there's no truth in it at all, and the man is deluded into believing his wife's infidelity, often producing the most telling circumstantial evidence. It can turn nasty. I have had two cases of homicide following cases of Othello complex, and a double suicide. How have you left things?'

'Well, Frazer himself raised the question of medication for her and I seized that as an excuse to visit the farm tomorrow, ostensibly to see Mrs Frazer.'

'That's good. I suggest you follow them up tomorrow, and then have another word with me after you've seen them. If necessary, we'll have to section him. Does that sound OK?'

'Yes, that's what I hoped you'd say.'

'Fine, give Fiona my love and I'll hear from you.'

Already I felt better after having discussed the case with an expert, and as soon as Jeannie was back with her messages, I set out on my routine of house calls. Work was light that morning and I was home early for lunch. When I told Fiona about the Frazers, she listened in astonishment. 'Why is it called the Othello complex?'

'If you remember your Shakespeare, the play is about jealousy. Iago, the arch-villain, persuades Othello that his beautiful and much loved wife is unfaithful to him. Though the accusation is groundless, the distraught Othello smothers Desdemona in her bed and later commits suicide. A similar story unfortunately is sometimes re-enacted in real life, hence the name.'

'Well, I simply can't believe that of Catriona Frazer. All right, I haven't seen her for years, but she was an absolute mouse at school, and I can't believe that if she were such a nympho the whole island would not be talking about it. I heard that lad had got the sack at Allt Beag Farm, and that he was fed up about it. He spends a lot of time in the bar and I can't believe, if he really had had Catriona Frazer, that the whole island wouldn't know about it. I think it's plain that Frazer's lying. What a bastard the man is!'

I was surprised at my usually charitable wife's outburst. 'Whatever the truth, it's going to be very awkward to deal with tomorrow. There's nothing I can do about it till then, so I must try to stop worrying about it.'

Just after lunch the phone rang and I answered it to hear the familiar voice of Wullie Stewart, the coastguard. 'Glad I found you, Doctor. Seems we got a problem in Assilag Bay. Jock Fordyce has just been on the radio to say he's seen two distress rockets go up north-east o' Solan Light. The keeper at Sgarbh an Sgumain light saw them too; he said they were to the west o' him. I've scrambled the chopper; I think you'd better go too. I'll get Peter May to collect you at the castle; he can put down just outside the gates. Can you be there in five minutes?'

'Sure, I'm on my way. Let us know anything that comes in.'

'Right you are. Bye.'

Shouting to Fiona that there was some sort of emergency in Assilag Bay, I ran to the car and got my bags. As I got to the castle gates I could hear the chopper flying low from Port Chalmers. It hovered and touched down on the road. Bending low I ran to its door which Peter May held open for me.

'Glad of your company, Doc,' he greeted me. 'I'm on my own the day.'

'What's on, do you know?'

'Absolutely nothing 'cept a distress signal in Assilag Bay ... could be anything; that's why the boss said to pick you up.'

We took off and turned south, leaving Loch Bradan to starboard and as always I enjoyed viewing my property from the air. I heard later that the unusual sight of distress flares had caused a flurry of activity... Charlie Kerr, busy lifting tatties in his garden, threw down his fork and jumped on his bicycle, pedalling hard to the jetty and the 'Blue Belle'. Alex Farquharson dropped the creels he was mending and strode to the 'Ornithologist'. Meanwhile one of Stanley Johnson's keepers was phoning his boss. Even an unknown admiral at the Holy Loch was having his lunch disturbed.

By now the helicopter was over the estuary of the Allt Bradan and I could see the pool where I had hooked the big salmon for the John MacNab. The bay beneath us looked calm and featureless. Near Assilag I could see a small boat making its way into the bay.

Pointing, I shouted to Peter May, 'I bet that's Alex, he'll be on the radio to Wullie in no time.' Peter nodded and as he did so the radio crackled into life.

'Port Chalmers Coastguard calling helicopter, do ye hear me?'

Peter pressed a button on his headset: 'Copter to Coastguard, loud and clear.'

'I have a report from Alex Farquharson. He's out in the bay in "Ornithologist" but there's nothing to see. Same report from Solan Light. Wait, something's coming in from Sgarbh an Sgumain. I'll get back to ye. Over an' out.'

Peter shrugged his shoulders. 'I'll just carry on over the bay; keep your eyes skinned.'

'They are, but it would help if we knew what we're looking for.'

The radio crackled again 'Coastguard to chopper. Sgarbh an Sgumain report smoke north-north-west of them; it may be near Tuilleag. Go and have a look. Over.'

'Roger and out.'

The chopper veered as we turned a few points west. Below, the sea of Assilag Bay was as calm as I had ever seen it. Ahead the bulk of Tuilleag came into view and I could see its one farm at its northwest corner. I had been there a year before to a tractor accident in which a boy had been badly injured. I could see someone waving. Peter saw it too, for he turned towards the farm. I could not see any smoke. The waving continued and children came out of the farmhouse and they too were waving.

'I do wish people wouldn't wave at helicopters,' grumbled Peter. 'You never know if it's an emergency or not. I think it's the latter but we'd better go and see. Hell! Tuilleag farm's got a phone, but I suppose it might not be working.' He again pressed the button on his headset: 'Copter to Coastguard. Am over Tuilleag Farm—there's lots o' people waving. Can you raise them on the phone? Over.'

'Coastguard to copter. Wait. I will try.'

Peter continued circling and I could see that Alex had altered course and was halfway across the bay to Tuilleag.

'Coastgauard to copter. Tuilleag very excited to see you but they have no problem. Sgarbh an Sgumain report more smoke. It could be from Mulcaire. I have just had a very pompous Mr Johnson on the line saying nobody must land on Mulcaire. I told him where to go and he got angry so I cut him off. Does that suggest anything?'

I nodded furiously and shouted, 'It's Mulcaire.'

'Copter to Coastguard; we're on our way.'

The aircraft lifted sharply and as it did so the northern tip of Mulcaire came into vision behind the bulk of Tuilleag. Now I too could see smoke. I began to fear for Jakes, Maantie and wee Caitriona.

Peter took the machine higher and as we flew due south, more of Mulcaire came into view. The smoke was thicker now: it looked as though it was coming from where Maantie had her home. Then I saw someone waving. Immediately, even at long distance, this was a different sort of wave. It had urgency, desperation even, quite unlike the social wave of the folk at Tuilleag Farm.

Peter was speaking again: 'Copter to Coastguard. I think we have the problem. A fire on Mulcaire. I can see someone waving. We'll be there in a couple o' minutes. Over.'

'Coastguard to copter, this is Janice. I've taken over from Wullie, who seems to be in trouble with the Navy. They are giving strict orders that you are not, repeat *not*, to land on Mulcaire...'

I snatched the radio connection out of its socket. 'Don't acknowledge, Peter. If there are lives at risk down there we must land. Go on in and I'll take responsibility. Who's Janice, by the way?'

'The boss's wife. What's going on?'

'I don't know. There may be something dangerous on Mulcaire, as far as I can make out. Officialdom gets hot under the collar about it, but those people have been living there for months. The first thing to do is to go and get them out and away from whatever it is.'

'Okay, but you'll have to explain when we get back. Look, there are two people there now.'

'Thank God for that! I can see Maantie and she's got her baby. Look at the house, it's an inferno.'

Peter landed on a flat stretch of turf. I jumped out and ran to Maantie, who was stumbling towards me.

'Maantie burned,' she said showing a horribly injured arm, 'but Caitriona OK.'

Jakes was unhurt, and he took the baby as I helped Maantie into the helicopter. Peter had us airborne at once and we took off over the skerries towards Ranneach Bay. Far below I could see a little blue boat heading for Mulcaire. I guessed Charlie was going to the rescue.

Suddenly there was a flash and a rumble and the little aircraft lurched so violently that Maantie screamed. While Peter got his machine under control, we all turned to see a great plume of black smoke where Maantie's house had been.

'What was that?' exclaimed Peter. 'I'm glad that didn't happen when we were down there! I'm making for home now. Can I put the radio back on?'

I nodded, busy examining Maantie's burnt arm.

Jakes, staring at where his home had been, murmured, 'I told her not to make chips on the Primus.'

'Copter to coastguard, do you hear me? We had trouble with radio transmission but I think it's OK now. Over'

'Coastguard here,' came the reassuring voice of Wullie Stewart. 'Sorry I had to hand over to my wife. There's all hell let loose here. Where are you?'

Peter winked at me. 'Wullie, we've just rescued three souls from a fire at Mulcaire. And we're coming home. The doctor is looking after a patient with burns. By the way Mulcaire seems to have blown up.' Without his usual 'over' Peter again winked at me and pulled the connection from its socket. 'I think our journey home may be more peaceful without radio contact,' he said.

I was glad to be busy putting a temporary dressing on Maantie's arm while I wondered what sort of hornet's nest I would find awaiting me in Port Chalmers.

Peter dropped us at the cottage hospital. Jakes was in shock but apparently uninjured. Maantie had mostly first-degree burns of most of her right forearm, with an area of second-degree burns where the fat from her chip pan had adhered. She was also in shock and a great deal of pain. I gave her morphine and re-dressed the burns, and admitted all three to the hospital. There was nothing wrong with Catriona that a change and a bottle would not put right.

When I was finished, sister told me that the coastguard and another man were waiting to see me.

'I was rather expecting them. It may have been a good thing to let them cool their heels for a bit.'

Rolling down my sleeves I walked out to the waiting room to face the music. Stanley Johnson was smoking his pipe right under a 'No Smoking' notice. He looked as though he might bite through the pipe stem.

'What can I do for you gentlemen?' I asked insouciantly.

'What the devil do you mean by landing on Mulcaire against my repeated orders?' Johnson demanded.

'Saving lives, I believe. All of my patients are safely here. The woman has bad burns, but they should heal.'

'You're all bloody lucky to be alive!'

'Yes, it was a big bang. May I point out to you that we have a lot of volatile liquids in this hospital; their vapour too is explosive. Hence the notice behind your head.'

Stanley turned, and then stuffed his pipe into a pocket. Turning to Wullie Stewart, I added, 'We lost radio contact with you at one point. Since we could not raise you, I took command and told Peter May to go in and pick up the survivors of the fire. Just as well we did too. There was a huge explosion seconds after we took off.'

Wullie grinned at me. 'Och, I doot there'll be a few questions to answer. The Admiral doon at the Holy Loch seemed a wee bitty upset. But it seems as though we've got awa pretty lightly.' He grinned at me. I knew that later on he too would be putting a lot of those awkward questions, but for the time being he was on my side. Wullie turned to Stanley. 'By chings, Mr Johnson, sir, there's smoke pouring oot yer chacket pocket.'

I went home to put my feet up and tell Fiona about my adventure over a dram before supper. Wullie was right, there were a lot of unanswered questions, but only time might unravel them.

And the day's events were not over.

That evening we had just finished supper when the phone rang. I answered it and could not at first hear anything. Then I was aware of a whispered voice.

'Speak up, I can't hear you,' I said.

The voice grew a little louder and I heard: 'This is Catriona Frazer from Allt Beag farm. I need help. I think my husband is going to kill me.'

'All right, Mrs Frazer. I can hear you now and I'm leaving for the farm immediately. Try and keep well away from him. I'm on my way.'

Turning to Fiona I said: 'That was Mrs Frazer, she says her husband is threatening to kill her. Get on to Hamish and tell him I may need his help and phone the police.'

As I ran to the car, Fiona ran after me. 'Rob, do be careful,' she said, threw her arms round me and kissed me.

'Don't waste time,' I said. 'Get on to Hamish and the police.'

Scaring sheep in the dark, I sped over the moor. At Feadag Beag I turned on to the potholed track to the farm, bouncing heavily on the uneven surface. I had no idea what I would find at the farm, but suspected the worst.

The farm was dark as I turned into the yard. Grabbing my torch I made towards the back door. I caught a sound from a steading on my left and went to investigate. It sounded as though something was dripping from the upper floor. I tripped at the lintel of the steading doorway and fell, dropping my torch. My fingers touched wetness on the floor, and there was something dripping on my hands. I gathered the torch and shone it upwards. A rough timber stairway led to a hayloft on the upper storey of the steading. I mounted the stair and must have let out a cry of horror. The naked body of Catriona Frazer lay at the top of the stair. The whole of her lower abdomen was a great blackening hole, from which blood still poured, dripping through the floorboards to the level below.

A sound behind me made me turn and step down from the stairway. Suddenly a bright light from a single bulb suspended from the ceiling dazzled me. As my vision cleared I found I was staring into the twin muzzles of a sawn-off shotgun. Ali Frazer was standing immediately under the light.

Suddenly, as if smelling honey, I remembered the voice of Alex Farquharson when he told me about his encounter with the bear. I seemed to hear him saying, 'If ever things look really bad, stay quite still and ask for God's help.'

I froze, keeping every muscle still. It was a terrible effort: I was petrified and wanted to run, but my best hope was to stay quite still and keep him talking.

'Hallo, Mr Frazer,' I said, as calmly as I could.

'Ah! it's the doctor. I expect you've come to have a bit too, just like everyone else. Well you're too late me boyo, the whore is dead. There was a man here when I got home tonight ... some hiker off the hill. I saw him running frae the hoose and I knew she'd been at it again. I found her in the bath. She aye goes there after she's had a man, to wash awa the signs o' her fornication. I told her then I'd kill her. When I went to get ma gun she ran oot here, stark naked, just as she was. I couldna find her at first then I saw she'd hidden in the hay loft ... that was aye her love-nest. When I set foot on the steps, she was standing above me ... she got a dose o' buckshot right up her.'

The man gave a savage laugh, with one hand keeping the shotgun trained on my face. I could see his finger shaking on the trigger. With the other hand he lifted a half-drained bottle of whisky to his mouth and took a great swig.

'You know, Doctor, I've been looking forward to meeting you like this. You made things difficult for me when Auntie took over the farm.' He paused, taking another gulp of spirit from the bottle.

'What happened with your aunt?' I asked as steadily as I could manage, trying not to look into the twin barrels only a foot from my face.

'Huh! I fixed her with yon organo-phosphorous insecticide; she was only a bloody louse anyway. Those new pesticides are hard to detect. I was worried when you turned the police on to me, but they never found the poison. Now it's payback time, Doctor. One barrel for you, one for me.'

Frazer took another hefty gulp from the bottle and threw the empty over his shoulder to smash on the stone floor behind him. He took the gun in both hands and I saw his finger tighten on the trigger.

There was a sudden violent movement, a flash, a bang, darkness, my face was warm and wet. I tasted blood in my mouth, and then I fell.

CHAPTER 26

Epilogue

Later Hamish was to tell me what happened.

He had heard the shot as he raced over the pot-holed track to Allt Beag Farm. He could only have been a few minutes behind me, and was aware of the flashing blue light of the police car following him. He heard the shot and accelerated, fearing he would break all his springs in the ruts. The farm was in total darkness. Hamish left his car beside mine with the headlights beaming through the open door of the steading. Seizing the powerful torch he always carried in his car he ran to the door.

'Eh laddie!' he told me afterwards, 'I canna describe how awful it was. I've seen horrors in plenty in the war, but this fair beat a'. There was blood everywhere and a bit o' Frazer's skull was stuck in the ceiling beside the light fitting. The bulb had been shattered. Frazer had fallen forwards on top o' you. His heart was still beating when I arrived, pouring blood oot the empty eggshell o' his heid on to your chest and face. I thought ye were deid too, ye were sic a mess. The polis came. They ordered me not to touch anything. But I noticed your hand move and, whatever the polis said, I tore Frazer's body off you and saw ye were still alive. Ye were in sic a state I couldna credit it. Then ye sat up and asked, "Where am I?" just as if naething had happened.

'Man, I couldna believe it. So I had a look at ye, and cleaned ye up a bit. The only injury I could find was a wee bit graze on the back o' yer heid, where ye'd hit the stone floor. That must a knocked ye oot for wee whilie.

'The polis was fair mad at me for moving the body, but I tellt them the first concern was for you, and they saw that. Once we found you were OK, we had a guid look round. Man, I think ye were saved by this.' He showed me the broken shard of a square whisky bottle. 'Yon Fraser was so drunk he had forgotten to reload after he killed his wife. He must have pulled the trigger on the barrel he'd already fired and then blown his ain heid awa wi' the second.'

Then, to my surprise after all that carnage, Hamish burst out laughing, 'I mind another time when another shotgun killing was prevented by yin o' these,' and again he hefted the square end of a well-known bottle of whisky.

As I came to groggily, my partner told the police they could get on with their job because he was taking me to the cottage hospital. 'All ye need, laddie, is a good shower and clean clothes. I'm no letting Fiona see you looking like ye are.'

Putting me in his car, Hamish drove to the cottage hospital and marched me in, telling the duty night sister to get out of the way or she'd have the fright of her life. In the bathroom mirror I saw what he meant. Startled white eyes stared back at me from out the gory mess that covered my face and upper chest. I started peeling my clothes off. Hamish was back as I was climbing into the shower.

'Here, laddie, this is the medicine you need.' He thrust a tumbler of neat whisky into my hand. 'I'll take all your clothes; the polis may want them, an' I've phoned Fiona just to say ye've had a wee bit o' a mishap an' ye need a change o' clothes.'

For once my phlegmatic senior partner seemed to be really enjoying himself and was fussing round me like an old hen about a chick.

It was only later, safe in bed in my wife's arms, that reality struck me and I began to shake uncontrollably. Fortunately Fiona knew how to cure that.

It was not only me that needed tidying up. There were a few more loose ends. Hamish protected me by announcing that I was suffering fom shock and was not to be disturbed by the coming and goings of several senior naval officers. Slowly it transpired that after the wartime crash on Mulcaire there was a large amount of highly toxic and dangerously unstable explosive material found at the crash site. Just what the toxic materials were was never specified. But there are few substances that could have wiped out the McTavishes (who were not near the crash but no doubt went to investigate it) as well as the seal population. It was never said, and never denied, but that it was some prototype nerve gas like Sarin seemed generally understood. The explosive formed part of the delivery mechanism of the poison. A violent electrical storm and a lightning strike caused the aircraft to crash, which must have released some of the gas.

The island had immediately been declared off limits and a decontamination squad did its best to make safe a number of intact cylinders of gas. It was decided that, as a matter of secrecy as well as safety, the material should be left on the island, bricked up in the cellars of the old house and Mulcaire declared a forbidden area like Gruinard island nearer the mainland. In time the poison gas degraded and was probably no longer a risk, but there was no way of knowing this. The explosive did not degrade, however, but became even more unstable—and lay in wait for Maantie's accident with her chip pan.

Maantie's arm healed well. In time the Ministry of Defence let me have my island back, and gave me compensation for the loss of the farmhouse and steadings. We rebuilt it, and Jakes and Maantie went back to farm Inch Mulcaire and to sing to the returned seals.

Also by Robin Hull
from Steve Savage Publishers

The Healing Island

When Rob Chalmers arrives on the remote Scottish island of Laigersay, he means to stay just a few days—a big interview is coming up in London, one which could open the door to his surgical career.

But Laigersay, its inhabitants and its wildlife exert a peculiar charm on visitors, and before long he is seriously considering becoming the local GP and staying for good.

But all is not as it seems on the 'healing island'—as well as finding love and fulfilment, Rob is soon to be confronted with mortal danger.

Set in the 1960s, Robin Hull's *The Healing Island* combines rural medicine, unexpected romance and high adventure.

'The author's wide knowledge of Scottish birds is put to good use, and his many years as a GP ensure authenticity as he skilfully blends humour, action and romance.'

—*The Scots Magazine*

ISBN 978-1-904246-10-7

Paperback. RRP £7.99.